The
POISON TREE

The
POISON TREE

Erin Kelly

Pamela Dorman Books

Viking

VIKING
Published by the Penguin Group
Penguin Group (USA) Inc., 375 Hudson Street, New York, New York 10014, U.S.A.
Penguin Group (Canada), 90 Eglinton Avenue East, Suite 700, Toronto, Ontario,
Canada M4P 2Y3 (a division of Pearson Penguin Canada Inc.)
Penguin Books Ltd, 80 Strand, London WC2R 0RL, England
Penguin Ireland, 25 St. Stephen's Green, Dublin 2, Ireland (a division of Penguin Books Ltd)
Penguin Books Australia Ltd, 250 Camberwell Road, Camberwell, Victoria 3124, Australia
(a division of Pearson Australia Group Pty Ltd)
Penguin Books India Pvt Ltd, 11 Community Centre, Panchsheel Park,
New Delhi – 110 017, India
Penguin Group (NZ), 67 Apollo Drive, Rosedale, North Shore 0632, New Zealand
(a division of Pearson New Zealand Ltd)
Penguin Books (South Africa) (Pty) Ltd, 24 Sturdee Avenue, Rosebank, Johannesburg 2196,
South Africa

Penguin Books Ltd, Registered Offices: 80 Strand, London WC2R 0RL, England

First American edition
Published in 2011 by Viking Penguin, a member of Penguin Group (USA) Inc.

10 9 8 7 6 5 4 3 2 1

A Pamela Dorman Book / Viking

Excerpt from "The River Road" from *The Drowned Book* by Sean O'Brien. Published by Pica-
dor, an imprint of Pan Macmillan, 2007. Reprinted by permission of TriplePA on behalf of the
author.

PUBLISHER'S NOTE: This is a work of fiction. Names, characters, places, and incidents either are
the product of the author's imagination or are used fictitiously, and any resemblance to actual
persons, living or dead, business establishments, events, or locales is entirely coincidental.

LIBRARY OF CONGRESS CATALOGING IN PUBLICATION DATA
Kelly, Erin, 1976–
    The poison tree : a novel / Erin Kelly.
        p. cm.
    ISBN 978-0-670-02240-3
    1. College students—Fiction.   2. Brothers and sisters—Fiction.   3. Family secrets—Fiction.
4. Murder—Fiction.   5. London (England)—Fiction.   6. Psychological fiction.   I. Title.
    PR6111.E498P65 2011
    823'.92—dc22   2010024260

Printed in the United States of America
Designed by Nancy Resnick

This book is dedicated to the father of my child

The way we'd go on summer nights
In the times we were children
And thought we were lovers.

—Sean O'Brien, "The River Road"

The
POISON TREE

Prologue

I LET THE TELEPHONE fall from my hand. Panic first cripples and then revives me. My fingertips tingle as they feel their way around the coffee table, scrabbling first for my car keys and then for my cell phone. I seem to have eight limbs as I try to get dressed in the dark, pulling on my coat and a pair of oversize sheepskin boots that I usually wear as slippers. At the threshold I hesitate for a second, then rush back to my desk and fumble in the drawer for my passport and a credit card that I keep for emergencies. I pull the door behind me in silence, although blood roars and rushes in my ears. With shaking hands I double-lock it: whether to keep someone in or to keep someone out, I can't know yet.

Outside, I tiptoe, but there is a crack and a squelch as I flatten a snail beneath my sole, and when I tread in a puddle by the gate, cold water seeps through the soft suede and licks unpleasantly at my bare toes.

In the dark interior of the car I turn the key in the ignition and wince as the air blows icy cold, dispersing the fluffy clouds of my breath. My hands are so cold they feel wet; I am relieved to find a pair of woolen gloves bundled in my left pocket. Before putting them on, I use my cell phone to cover the last caller's tracks. I call the house phone, wait for the click of connection, and hang up before it has a chance to ring. The windshield is opaque with frost and I do not have time to wait for the heaters to defog the glass. I wipe a porthole in the passenger window and squint back into the dark recess of the bedroom window. If he had heard me, the light would be on by now. He would be silhouetted at the window, mouthing my name. Would that stop me? Would anything?

The car is pointed directly at the front of the house. If I turn the headlights on, they will shine into the window, so with no beams to guide me and only a smeared handprint of visibility through the windows, I pull out into the road. Only when I have guessed my way to the end of our lane do I switch on the full beam. The countryside is frosted and stark. Naked hedgerows cast eerie shapes in front of me and the high banks of the narrow road throw up shadows that take human form. The dead, the missing, and the missed surround me now, passive spirits who have become active ghosts. I am afraid to glance behind. They pursue me as I drive aggressively, suicidally, mounting the grass verge when I take a blind bend much too fast. The seatbelt digs into the flesh between my breasts as I make an emergency stop to avoid hitting the truck that suddenly looms in front of me. It's a filthy vehicle of indeterminate color, tools loose in the back, moving so slowly that the driver must be drunk. I have no option but to slow to a crawl behind him.

I ought to use this enforced pause for rational thought. But there is nothing rational about this situation. I am driving alone in pajamas and wet, clammy boots on a country lane in the middle of the night. Nobody knows where I am or why. I had only been thinking of the others, but for the first time it strikes me that my own safety might be compromised if I continue.

A glance at my speedometer tells me that we are traveling at twelve miles an hour. I toot and flash, but by the cold blue glow in his cab I see that he is making a phone call. I map the road ahead in my mind. I have driven it so often that I know every pothole, kink, and curve. I take a deep breath, crunch the gears, and plunge blindly into the passing place I calculate is just to my right. The driver of a black car coming in the opposite direction has had the same idea and we skim each other as we pass, with a sickening screech of metal on metal. I accelerate. Let him chase me if he wants to make something of it. My left-hand mirror is wrenched from its casing and falls to dangle lifelessly at the side from a lone wire, like a severed limb attached to its body by a single vein. The retreating driver sounds his horn angrily, the Doppler effect making it drop a forlorn semitone as it continues in the direction of my house. The truck is between us and it is too late to turn and see if the driver was alone or carrying a passenger, if it was a regular car or a taxi.

I pick up my crazy pace. Only a speed camera, predicted by a luminous sign, persuades my foot to the brake. On the borders of the town the scrubby roadside edges give way to narrow pavements and trees thin out to accommodate houses, a pub, a gas station. Lampposts appear, imitation Victorian globes like a parade of tiny moons, and I realize with a corresponding lucidity that this is it. The event I have been expecting and dreading for a third of my life is finally here.

It suddenly feels very hot inside the car. My hands are sweating inside my gloves, my eyes are dry, and my tongue is stuck to the roof of my mouth. I have given up so much and done so many terrible things already for the sake of my family that I can only keep going. I do not know what is going to happen to us. I am frightened, but I feel strong. I have the strength of a woman who has everything to lose.

I

TRY TO SEE the city through his eyes. It has been only ten years, but London has changed. Will he notice the subtle developments of the last decade? Does he register the lack of telephone boxes or the proliferation of Polish grocers? What about the plugged-in pedestrians with white wires connecting their ears to their pockets? The red circles on the road that welcome us into and usher us out of the congestion zone? I'm dying to know what he is thinking. His eyes, though, are fixed on the sycamore pods and leaves stuck under the windshield wipers. Running commentary has never been his style, but this silence is unnerving.

Alice is talking enough for the three of us, a high-pitched stream of consciousness that spills from the backseat. She has made this journey from southeast London to our home on the Suffolk coast four times a year, every year of her life. She loves traveling home through town, preferring to inch through dirty streets rather than cruise around the highway, even though it adds hours onto our journey. I always save this route for a special treat, when her behavior throughout our visit has been particularly good, or when she and Rex have found saying good-bye harder than usual. Sometimes I drive through town when I need to think, knowing that Alice's nose will remain pressed against the glass as the car crawls from suburb to inner city to suburb again, that the questions she asks will be about what that man is selling or what that building is, rather than another discussion about why Daddy has to live so far away.

But this afternoon's detour isn't at Alice's request. As we creep along Holloway Road, her favorite part of the journey, her focus is inside the car. She does not seem to mind her demotion from the front seat to the back. She ignores the Caribbean barbershop she loves to wave at and the metallic, space-age university building we saw being built, panel by shiny blue panel. We even pass the grimy cell phone store that holds such a strange fascination for her without the usual argument about when she will be old enough for her own telephone. We stop at a red light and with a click and a giggle she slides out of her seatbelt and squeezes between the driver and passenger seats. Her twiggy fingers weave in and out of Rex's hair, tugging it, massaging his scalp, shampooing it and revealing silver threads around his ears and temples. She shoots out rapid-fire questions one after the other without waiting for answers.

"Will you take me to school when I go back next week? Will you drive Mum's car or are we going to have two? Lara's mum and dad have a car each but she *still* walks to school. Don't you think—oh my God, you can come swimming now! What's your best stroke? Mine's front crawl. Will you take me swimming?"

"I'll do whatever you want," says Rex, and Alice kisses the top of his head. Her knees fold forward and nudge the gearshift while an elbow knocks against my head as I try to negotiate the Archway traffic circle. I shout at her when I had sworn I wouldn't, not today. She shrugs off my scolding. The car swings to the left as I take the exit for the Great North Road. Rex crosses his legs, folds his arms, and shifts in his seat. He knows where I'm going. Perhaps he was expecting it. Perhaps, like me, he needs this one last visit to the past before we can build our future.

Archway Road is unusually clear, and the three of us cruise underneath the bridge in the long, low autumn dazzle. The neighborhood has been gentrified in the decade since we lived here. We pass a designer baby boutique where a thrift store used to be. The liquor store that would sell us two bottles of nasty wine for five pounds, even at three in the morning, has now been upgraded to a wine merchant, and even the old pubs and restaurants look cleaner and brighter than I remember them: more plate glass, fewer metal shutters. But Archway still has some way to go, I think, as I swerve to avoid chunks of glass exploded from a bus stop window and scattered across the street like ice cubes.

Neither of us has been here for over a decade but I can still drive this street, anticipate those lights, make these gear changes, on autopilot. I could do it with my eyes shut. For a reckless second, I'm tempted to try, to close my eyes and lock the wheel on a right curve. But I make the double turn into Queenswood Lane wide-eyed and unblinking. The noise of the city falls away as we enter the secret sliver of wildwood, where the ancient trees muffle the sirens and the screeches of the street and the half-hidden houses occupy a dark green private universe, cushioned by money as much as by trunk and bough and leaf. I drive carefully between the expensive cars, their side-view mirrors tucked into their bodies in case someone unfamiliar with the road drives too quickly and knocks into one. But I am more familiar with this lane than any other road, including the one I grew up on and the one I live on now. It's the setting for most of my memories and all of my nightmares. I know every old brick wall, every bump in the road, every lamppost. The 1860s apartment block with its Italianate walled garden still sits alongside that glass-and-concrete bubble, someone's vision of the future from the 1960s that would never make it past the conservation society today. Stern Victorian town houses tower over a pastel-colored fairy-tale mansion. Their windows glower down at us.

I deliberately don't look toward the last house, the place where everything happened, before the street surrenders to the trees. I focus on the road as the leafy tunnel swallows this car for the first time and park with the house behind me, telling Alice that Mummy and Daddy need to stretch their legs. She tumbles out of the car and skips into the trees, her tracksuit a flash of pink through half-undressed branches. The little red lights in the heels of her sneakers wink at us like tiny eyes.

"Don't go too far!" I call. We watch as she drags her feet through the fallen leaves, tracing letters with her toes, staining the hem of her trousers with flakes of wet bark and leaf mold. She doesn't know it, but she's playing yards away from the spot where she was conceived. Rex speaks first.

"It's got to be done, I suppose." He circles the car to open my door. I get out and point the key at the car, and it locks with a *pow-pow* noise. Rex raises an eyebrow. "Very swish," he says, taking the key from me and examining it as though it contains an entire album of high-energy dance tracks. I close my eyes to make the turn, and when I open them, there it is. Exactly where we left it, I think—although where could it have gone? The four-story town house surrounded not by cars and concrete but by lime and plane and birch and oak; half stucco, half gray brick, it really belongs on the end of a terrace in Islington or Hackney. Its incongruity is one of the things that always made its presence on the edge of the forest so magical. It has changed, of course. It looks naked, cleaner and more metropolitan than ever now that someone has pulled down the dark green ivy that covered all of the side wall and half the front one and found its way in through the windows in the summertime. The creamy stucco gleams, not a single peel or crack in the paint. It looks *innocent*. But then, so do I.

The flaked black paint on the front door has been replaced by flawless turquoise gloss, and the golden lion door knocker gleams. The steep front steps—formerly a death trap of long-dead herbs tufting out of broken terra-cotta pots, lone roller skates, empty wine bottles, and never-to-be-read free local newspapers—have also been restored, and instead the door is flanked by two perfectly symmetrical bay trees with twisted stems in aluminum pots. Six recycling boxes are stacked neatly and discreetly behind a magnolia tree in the front garden. Instead of the nonworking bell pull which no one ever bothered with, there are six buzzers. The first time I ever came here, I spent ten minutes looking for just such a row of doorbells bearing different names. It didn't occur to me that people my age could live in the whole of this building rather than occupy an apartment within it. I don't need to get any closer to know how the place has changed on the inside. Without peering through the white-shuttered windows, I know exactly how the interiors of these apartments will look: coir or sisal carpeting, because the battered floorboards were beyond restoration even for the most dedicated property developer. The black and white hall will have been renovated, an original feature that will have added value to the house price. It was in terrible condition when we lived there, and afterward, there was that terrible stain.

There will be magnolia walls with flat-screen television sets flush against them, stainless steel kitchens, each boxy white bedroom with its own frosted-glass bathroom. It had been sold, but not until a long time after the police and the press had gone. The redevelopment had begun as soon as the yellow incident tape had been taken down and the cameras and reporters had moved on. Only then did the real estate agents begin to throng the house. I had often imagined the swarm of suits trampling polystyrene and paper coffee cups discarded by reporters, looking beyond the building's grisly history, seeing only the rare opportunity to sell a sensitively converted character property in a highly desirable location, situated seconds from the Tube and on the edge of the historic Queen's Wood.

The violent physical reaction I was half-expecting—a swoon, or a full faint, or even vomiting—doesn't come. Rex too is calm, indecipherable, and it's he who has the most, and the most gruesome, memories of this place. It was his home for twenty-four years and mine for only one summer. Alice breaks the reverie, dropping five feet from a tree I hadn't noticed her climb, bored now, asking Rex for a can of Coke because she knows I'll say no. I shrug and let him decide. Tonight, we'll sit down and establish some ground rules for dealing with Alice before she becomes hopelessly, irretrievably spoiled. But today, I'll let Rex play the indulgent father. One day won't hurt.

She gets her drink, but not from the newsstand near Highgate Tube; I bet it's still owned by the same family. They might not recognize me, but of course they would remember Rex. They would have sold enough newspapers with him on the front page. Instead, we drive up Muswell Hill Road and I let Rex and Alice jump out and into a more anonymous convenience store. Did I ever go there? The fruits and vegetables piled up in front of the shop, their dull skins patiently absorbing the fumes from my exhaust, do nothing to jog my memory. Rex and Alice are in there for a while, and it's not until she emerges, red-faced and holding out her hand, that I realize I haven't given him any money.

Before we've even reached the North Circular Road that links Rex's old part of London to his new home, Alice has slipped out of her seatbelt again and is lying across the seat, kicking at the air, singing to herself and spilling sticky cola all over her clothes and the car seat. Ten years fall away and I remember another journey on this road. It was the day Rex's credit card arrived, and we celebrated by driving to the supermarket to stock up on all the food and drink we could cram into my little Fiat. Rex sat beside me losing a wrestling match with the sunroof, while Biba took up the whole of the backseat, so Guy can't have been with us. She dangled a cigarette out of the left-hand window, her feet poking out of the right-hand one in a desperate attempt to cool down. I can feel the gummy heat of that summer now. I remember the prickle of my heat rash and the way the sweat from my body made my cheap purple T-shirt bleed dye onto my skin like an all-over bruise. I remember the way perspiration gave Rex a permanent kiss-curl in the middle of his forehead, like Superman. I can still see the crisscross sunburn lines on Biba's back. A pink leg comes between me and the rearview mirror.

"Put your seatbelt on, Alice," I say. She walks her feet up onto the ceiling, printing a thin layer of leaf mold in the shape of her shoes across the pale gray ceiling. She's testing me and I fail. "I said, put your fucking seatbelt on, Alice!" Or did I say something else? Rex looks at me in horror while Alice, more interested in the unfolding drama than offended by my swearing, is suddenly silent and upright.

"*What* did you call her?" he says in a whisper, and at the same time Alice asks, "Who's Biba?"

2

MY MOTHER STILL HAS the letter. It is dated January 1993 and tells the reader that I have been awarded a scholarship to study modern languages at Queen Charlotte's College. It is stuck to the mirror in my parents' hallway, the letterhead bleached by light and time but the main body text still decipherable. When I had opened it and we had all read it three or four times, she pasted it to the mirror for safekeeping, accidentally using my father's extra-strength wood glue, and the bond was permanent. My mother went mad, not because the mirror was ruined but because she had denied herself the opportunity to brandish the letter at bus stops and bank counters and street corners. She was all set to ask the college for another copy just for this purpose until my father talked her out of it, even though he was as proud as she that the first person from our family ever to enter higher education should do so at such a prestigious university. I noticed that in the months that followed we had more visitors than usual, and my mother would serve them cups of tea in the entrance hallway, a strong picture light trained on the gummed glass.

If my mother was a whirlwind of enthusiasm, then I was the calm at the eye of the storm, watching the celebrations and preparations with the detachment that was my way back then. For I had a guilty secret—or what felt like one at the time, before I knew what guilt and secrecy really felt like. The thing that I did not have the heart to tell anyone, not my parents or my teachers, was that where they saw burning ambition there was only inertia. The four languages I had mastered by my sixteenth birthday had come effortlessly, and when I was praised for my dedication and clutch of precocious A levels I felt like a fraud. The ability to wrap my tongue around alien sounds, to master the clicks, lisps, and rolls of foreign languages, was something I'd always been able to do. As a child, I could mimic the accents in the soap operas my parents watched, perfecting Liverpudlian and Mancunian and London accents. When I was ten, we went abroad for the first time, to Madeira: I came home almost fluent in Portuguese, and my secret was out—I could pick up new languages as easily as the other children at my school copied radio jingles and cartoon catchphrases. After basic instruction in the grammar and syntax, it was usually a case of plowing through a novel or two with a dictionary by my side, or watching a couple of foreign films with the subtitles on, and it was in. It's a science, not an art. It's something I can do, it's not who I am. Before I met Biba, it was the defining thing in my life, and had I not met her, I expect that it still would be.

The name of the college conjures images of Regency buildings, a Nash terrace housing oaky libraries and elegantly striped seminar rooms, or at least it did to me when I submitted my application form. It couldn't have been less like that. The main campus on the north side of Marylebone Road was a cobalt-blue, sixties-built tower block, double-glazed to keep the traffic noise at bay. The windowless corridors were painted the sickly pea-green of military hospital bedclothes, and the flecked gray vinyl floors reflected the neon strip lighting on the ceiling. It was a horrible combination, able to steal the color from the cheeks of the youngest and rosiest students, but once I got over my initial disappointment at not being able to waft through quads in crinoline, I grew to appreciate the place. It had a neutrality about it that's important when you're studying several different languages.

The student halls, however, lacked not just romance but also safety and privacy. I was allocated a grimy shared studio in Crick-lewood that had the twin disadvantages of being too far out of the center of town to be cool and not far out enough to be comfort-able. Emma, my roommate, was a friendly, horsey type from Sur-rey with a warm laugh and immaculate vowels and was clearly even more terrified of our new neighborhood than I was; her pressed pastel clothes marked her out as a moving target on the strip-lit grays and blacks of Broadway. In our introductory lecture we met Claire and Sarah, two other students in the same position. Friend-ship was instant, inevitable, necessary.

"I can't bear it," Sarah told us as we waited for the bus on Edg-ware Road, arms aching with the weight of textbooks in stretched Blackwell's shopping bags. "I'm going to ask my father to buy somewhere. He'll rent it to us for less than we pay here. Are you in?" I thought she was joking, but by October the four of us were ensconced in a house share in Brentford, a West London hinter-land with no Tube station. But the house was clean and airy, and the street was safe. It was not the student life I had been expecting: we never burned incense or stole a traffic cone or slept until noon. But it was different enough from my old life to feel like progress.

They all had nineteen years to my seventeen, having taken a year off, and seemed worldly and sophisticated to me. Their world was one of tennis clubs, aerobics classes, theaters, and restaurants. What their friendship lacked in bohemian adventure it made up for in shared experience, a revelation to me after the loneliness of school. We did everything together, including travel. Queen Charlotte's had a unique reciprocal network of exchange programs with similarly eccentric language departments all over Europe, and the course involved frequent and intensive trips abroad. I always felt so sorry for the exchange students who came from the great and ancient universities and found themselves housed in the misleadingly named International House, a dingy little tenement just under the overpass on Edgware Road. But we made the sys-tem work to our advantage, pooling our travel grants so that we could afford to hire a car rather than pay four individual fares and rent apartments rather than stay in hostels. By the end of the four-year course, there was barely a museum or art gallery in western Europe we hadn't visited. We ate together, cooking, shopping, and washing dishes by strict turns. Every eight weeks, a hairdresser came to the house and gave us all the same haircut. And we dated together, too, all hooking up with members of the QCC rugby team at their Christmas 1994 ball, a glorified disco held on the HMS *Belfast*. Simon, a fullback who owned his own tuxedo, asked me to dance. By the time I found out that grace and coordination on the rugby pitch and dance floor did not necessarily translate into the bedroom, the relationship was already established, and besides, I liked and admired him. He read all the newspapers from cover to cover every weekend. He always called when he said he would. He taught me how to marinate a steak and choose the right wine to drink with it. He was the first person I ever heard use the phrase "New Labour."

My parents had worried that student life would send me "off the rails." In fact, I had given them the opposite cause for concern: my father once accused me of being middle-aged at twenty. I put this down to insecurity on his part: it must have been hard, I thought, for him to see me growing away from the world I was born into and assimilating into a different class with new and intimidating rules and values. I was happy to have friends and to belong and to progress. As I neared the end of my course, the only uncertainty was whether I would continue to study or take an internship in an embassy somewhere. This I had decided to leave to fate, intending to take the first opportunity that presented itself. I held my life loosely in my hands, unaware that I was about to relinquish my grip. In the space of a week, apathy suddenly gave way to a passion I had not begun to guess I was capable of.

I transferred the file from hand to hand. It was a hefty sheaf of paper, perfectly squared off and fastened with a steel clip. The pages contained twenty thousand words of thesis comparing self-conscious theater in Italian and German, an undertaking as humorless as it sounds. The compulsory literature module was the only component of my degree that didn't come easily to me, but after I had submitted my dissertation my degree was all but over. Only a handful of exams remained, and exams were the easy part (although I knew from past experience it was a good idea to keep this theory to myself).

I let the file drop into my tutor's in-tray, where it landed with a gratifying thud. Outside, the sun was shining. I had been in the library for so long I had forgotten what a blue sky looked like. I rolled up my sleeves as far as they would go and felt the sun on my skin for the first time that year.

They were waiting for me at home. Claire, Sarah, and Emma were perched in a row, two pairs of feet in slippers and one in socks, resting on the edge of a pale cream sofa that had cost more than my travel grant for the whole year. They had been watching a film but had paused it when they heard my key in the lock. Julia Roberts's wide laugh, struck through with a white flickering scratch of videotape, hovered on screen. Sarah held the remote control in her hand and was twisting it around and around. A tyrannical control over the television and video was her only abuse of the power she gained from her father's ownership of the house.

Claire glanced meaningfully at my feet, and I dashed back to the hall and kicked off my shoes. A piece of chewing gum was stuck to the sole of my right shoe. In a tiny, pathetic, and deeply satisfying act of rebellion, I deliberately transferred it to the carpet.

"And why are you three sitting here like the three wise monkeys?" I said when I came back. I slapped my forehead. "It wasn't my turn to cook tonight, was it?" Even as I spoke I knew that wasn't the case. We had played tennis last night, which meant today was Sarah's turn. Three heads shook, matching glossy bobs swinging like shiny hoods.

"Simon's here," said Claire. "He's in your room." That was unexpected. Simon and I never saw each other on a Thursday. The girls didn't meet my quizzical gaze but stared at their laps instead. "You'd better go up."

He was leafing through the only book in my room that he would have deemed masculine enough to warrant picking up: a biography of John Lennon that my dad had left here when he'd last visited. When he saw me he tossed it away so quickly that I knew he couldn't have been reading it properly.

"Hello, Karen," he said. We didn't kiss. "How are you?"

"I'm fine," I said, swinging down on the bed and hoisting his legs up over my lap. I had intended to squeeze his toes but had second thoughts when I saw that his socks were damp with sweat. "This is a surprise."

"I might as well get straight to the point," he interrupted, speaking like the management consultant I believe he subsequently became. I had heard him use this voice over the telephone and when ordering (for both of us) in restaurants, but never to me before. He took his legs off mine, and I felt the dull buzz of pins and needles.

"We've been together for a couple of years now." There was no disputing this fact. "And we'll be graduating soon." He left another pause, so I nodded. "And I think it's time for a fresh start all around as we both enter our adult lives. Our professional lives."

The titles of the books on my shelf zoomed in and out of focus. I knew what was coming next, and felt only the linguist's scholarly interest in how he would phrase it.

"I think that we shouldn't see each other anymore. With immediate effect." He waited for me to fill the silence that followed. I thought back twenty-four hours to the uncomfortable sex we'd had on his creaking bed in Fulham, my mind absently tracing the outlines of European countries in the textured whorls of his ceiling while he grunted his way through his short repertoire. I reflected on two years of interminable Sundays spent watching rugby matches in the pub and felt a mad little flutter of relief that I would never, ever have to go to a sports bar again.

"That's fine by me," I realized.

"Really?"

"Yep. I think it's for the best, too. I take it the girls know."

Simon nodded. "I said I wanted a serious talk and they . . . I thought they should . . . just in case you . . ."

The three of them probably still had their film on freeze-frame, waiting anxiously for my wails of grief, or perhaps they were looking up, expecting Simon's body to break through the ceiling in a cloud of plaster and rubble and for my tearstained, heartbroken face to appear in the ragged hole above. I didn't care to imagine the conversation in which my boyfriend had told my friends that he was planning to dump me, so I blocked it from my mind. I could do that with things I didn't want to think about, like snapping shut a book.

"Don't you want to know why?" he asked. I had a pretty good idea, and it took the shape of his mother, hair like a curly helmet, finger like a jabbing spear. "Not the right sort of girl . . . Fine while you're at university, but you've got to start thinking about the rest of your life now, Simon . . . Things that don't matter when you're young become important when you're in the real world . . . I know she's clever, but the novelty of that will wear off. She'll want to work, you know . . . And those parents of hers, with that accent . . ."

"Not really," I said. Simon looked angry. I realized he'd rehearsed a speech that would let me down gently, and I relished depriving him of the opportunity to deliver it.

"I think you'd better go," I said, getting to my feet. The numbness had worn off my legs now and a sense of lightness suffused my body. "Tell the girls I'm going to stay up here for a bit."

I smoothed out the indentation his legs had left on my duvet cover. A thick, black hair from his head was on my pillow. I pinched it between thumb and forefinger and dropped it in the wastebasket next to my bed. I reshelved the John Lennon book and scanned my room for any other evidence of him. There was only a framed photograph that I couldn't be bothered to take down from the wall. The low voice he could never quite manage to suppress into a whisper resonated through the crack under the door as he spoke to my friends. Since when did they become his confidantes, I wondered?

I sat on my bed and waited for the tears to come, but I could coax only a few drops from my eyes, even when I looked in the mirror and tried my hardest to feel sorry for myself. My reflection gave an infectious smile. Instead of grief or anger I felt only a sense of reprieve and freedom.

That night, I could not sleep. I was more wide awake than I knew it was possible to be, alive with potential, sharp and bright. I thought only of the things I could do, unfettered by a relationship. Crop my hair. Blow my savings on a ticket to China and learn Mandarin. Get a job in a nightclub. It was time for my second reinvention. I had the sense that I had effectively been sleepwalking my way through my four years at the university, and I had only one summer left in which to redress the balance.

That's the thing about sleepwalking. You can walk, eat, hold conversations, and even drive cars in perfect safety. The danger comes from waking up too quickly.

3

I SOMETIMES WONDER IF, that day, I was like one of those chicks that hatches and thinks the first creature it sees is its mother—would I have taken up with anyone who offered the hand of friendship? Perhaps. But I doubt I would have fallen so hard. I met her in the afternoon, and by the evening, everything had changed. She was in the same building as me all morning, only a few rooms and floors away, but I didn't feel a crackle of electricity or notice a surge in energy. The only difference in atmosphere in Queen Charlotte's College was the constricting silence that coiled around us more and more tightly as our finals drew nearer.

I was thinking about this the day I met her, and deciding that I would do my PhD somewhere beautiful and ancient. The next place I studied would have wooden doors and crooked staircases, and my rooms would have leaded, ill-fitting windows. I failed to let the grim realization that this might mean some degree of independent effort, perhaps even exertion on my behalf, compromise my enjoyment of this picturesque daydream. I shouldered my way through set after set of heavy green fire doors, heading for the elevator.

The landing was empty except for a girl writing a notice on the department board. I mean, she was literally writing it on the pin-pricked cork with a fat red marker. She had her back to me and I watched her form the letters in silence. There was a careless grace about the way she moved.

WANTED: NATIVE GERMAN SPEAKER FOR TRANSLATION AND ACCENT
TUTORING

She paused to consider the next line. This gave me more time
to consider *her*. It was the summer when the Spice Girls were inescapable; most of the university's female students had declared a
fashion allegiance to one or other of the singers, decking themselves out like clowns or children or girls who worked at a perfume counter. The girl before me appeared to be dressed like all
five of them at once. She wore purple crushed-velvet flares, sneakers with a platform sole that elevated her to just beyond my height,
and a shiny, tiny England football T-shirt that looked older than
she was, with a hole in the armpit. She also carried a brand-new
Gucci handbag of padded leather with gold chains for straps.

I CAN PAY YOU—CONTACT ME—THANK YOU!!! BIBA XXX

Biba. I rolled her name around inside my head and willed her to
turn around. She slipped her red pen into her bag and would have
walked out of my life forever if shock at her audacity hadn't made
me half gasp and half laugh. The vandal turned to face me with a
sardonic, overcasual, "What?"

The deep gurgle of her laughter made an instant conspirator of
me. She smiled, glassy brown eyes sparkling from beneath heavy
round lids fringed with thick, stiff lashes. I'd seen eyes like those
before, on a doll when I was a little girl.

"Are you going to tell on me for defacing university property?"
she asked in a tone that made it clear she trusted me not to.

"No," I said, "I was going to point out that if you don't leave a
number, nobody will know how to contact you."

"Fucking . . ." she said. Again, my laughter mirrored hers. "I'm
always forgetting things like that." She spoke like a BBC announcer
from the fifties. If voices really can be clear as bells, hers was: the
small, silver kind you use to summon servants, not the heavy iron
church sort. She rummaged in the bag again for the red pen. Tis-
sues puckered with old chewing gum bobbed above its surface like
white horses on the sea.

"Maybe I can help out," I offered, before she had a chance to remove the cap. "My German is fluent."

"You don't *look* German," she said, which surprised me: many people in northern Europe took me for a native before I began to speak, and sometimes afterward too.

"I'm not," I said. "What do you need translated?"

"I'm an actress," she said, as though I should have known. "I'm doing a play about a woman who's a nightclub singer in Germany. Well, she's working as one—she's actually got amnesia, she's really Italian—why am I telling you this? The point is they've just decided they want me to sing a song in fucking German for the opening."

"*Come tu mi vuoi. As You Desire Me,*" I said. "Pirandello."

"You know it?" The accompanying smile split her tight little jaw in two.

"I studied it in Italian lit last year." I didn't tell her I'd hated it.

"I thought you studied German," she said.

"I do all sorts."

"Then you're perfect. Don't you see? This is fate that I found you. It can't be a coincidence, can it? You can help me, can't you?" The gear change from humor to intensity was alarming, and instinctively I took a step back as she took my elbows in her hands and gently shook my crossed arms up and down in a bizarre pumping movement. I was also, however, flattered by her attention and, with a middle-class sycophancy I despised in myself as soon as I acknowledged it, rather mesmerized by her voice. "Fantastic. What about now?" I thought of the surly teenager I was due to coach in French at five. The thought of the smell of socks and sweat and spunk that hung around him was certainly a disincentive. He was always late, even to his own bedroom. It wouldn't kill him to wait for me for a few minutes.

"We can make a start now, yes," I said.

"I'm Biba Capel," she said. I liked the way she pronounced her last name: to rhyme with *apple*.

"Karen Clarke," I said, holding out my hand. Hers was tiny in mine.

"Karen," she said, and for the first time I loved the way my name sounded on another person's lips. "Do you mind if we take the stairs? I can't bear elevators. It's one of my things." She kicked the double doors open with one bulky shoe and let them swing back into my face. Before following her I quickly unpinned and retacked a notice advertising an end-of-term ball to cover the space where she had written. Loops of red ink were still visible on either side of the poster, but you'd have to be looking for them. I joined her on the landing, where she was craning her neck to see the top of Madame Tussauds and rolling a cigarette with the fingers of one hand. She licked the gummed edge of the paper. "The only problem is that I don't actually have any money, as such," she said. "Will you still help me?" Biba ran down the flight of stairs, flat feet thudding on every other step, shedding flecks of tobacco behind her as I floated down the staircase in her wake.

Our spontaneous tutorial took place in Charlie's, the student bar tucked away in the basement of the college. This was a novelty in itself. Only a few days beyond my seventeenth birthday when I came up to QCC, I'd been issued a union card that instructed bar staff that it was not legal to serve me alcohol. I don't think anyone would have asked me for ID but the thought of challenge or rejection was enough to keep me away for the first year, and after that, not going into the bar had become a habit.

It was dark inside with navy velour seats lining the walls and matching stools screwed to the floor. Trying to find somewhere to sit that didn't ooze stuffing or wasn't damp with spilled beer was a challenge but Biba rose to it, staking a place at an unwiped table near the bar.

"Can you buy a bottle of red, darling? A Merlot if they've got it," she said, and I wondered how someone whose voice and bag suggested an expensive education and a credit card could be too poor to afford student bar prices. "It's so much cheaper than by the glass, and we won't have to keep going to the bar." Red wine had always given me headaches but I ordered it then, and because Biba and Rex drank little else, I trained myself to like it that summer. I have never had a sip of it since, though. For me, the bouquet of rich red wine is now indivisible from another smell, metallic and warm and meaty all at once, one that summons up a slideshow of frozen images in my mind like a series of photographs in a police incident room.

She unfolded a concertina of sheet music before me. I skimmed it: I didn't know the song, and the lines and dots of the music were indecipherable to me, but the lyrics were simple enough.

"The first thing you need to know is what you're singing, so I'll translate it for you," I said, digging out a pencil from my bag and writing the English equivalent under the words.

"D'you want a cigarette while you work?" Biba asked, sloshing wine into the two glasses.

"I don't smoke, thanks."

"You're so *lucky*," she said wistfully. She scooted closer so that she could read the words over my shoulder. She slung an arm around me so that our cheeks were pressed together and mouthed the words as my pencil formed them. Personal space was clearly an alien concept to her. That, coupled with her eccentric clothes and complete lack of self-consciousness, meant that by now I was pretty sure I was dealing with a mad person; fascinating and disarmingly different from everything I was used to. If I closed my eyes, the image of her was indelibly printed on the inside of my eyelids. She smelled of shampoo and cigarettes and something else I couldn't pin down. I couldn't remember ever being this close to someone who smelled so human and so female.

"For a start, what's that funny letter there?" she said, pointing to an *Eszett*.

"It's like a double *s*," I said. "And you're blocking my light." I flicked my ballpoint backward and rapped her on the nose. She moved even closer in.

"Are you always this bossy?" she said.

"When I'm teaching, yes. Then what I'll do is write it down phonetically for you so you know exactly *how* to say it. German's hard to learn, but it's not that tricky to pronounce. There's nothing in here you won't be able to say with a bit of practice."

She read aloud from my phonetic version. I was surprised by her confidence and the way she was able to bury her own strident English enunciation. I've noticed that often people with strong accents struggle to reshape their palates to adapt to foreign languages, but she stuck her tongue to the roof of her mouth to pronounce the harsh *sch* sounds without me having to tell her to.

"How am I doing?" she said, after a couple of read-throughs.

"Really well. You need to work on your long and short *u*'s—there's no real English differentiation that's an equivalent—but really, that's just practice." I made her pout her way through some umlauts.

"Thank you so, so much." She folded the document back into her bag, then asked the question everyone always does. "So if you're not German, how come you can speak like that?"

"It just comes easily to me," I said. I hated explaining what my mother called "my gift" and my father called his pension plan. Biba jumped to the usual conclusion.

"I understand," she said. "It's innate, you can either do it or you can't. Like acting. It's a vocation."

"Not really," I confessed. "It's just the way my brain works."

"Like a language computer," she said, closer now. "An automatic translator. Like that fish in that book that can translate things? What's it called?"

"The Babel fish," I said. She'd hit on my father's nickname for me.

"The Babel fish, exactly! My brother's got that book. It tends to attract nerds, doesn't it?"

"I wouldn't know," I ventured, trying Biba's boldness on for size and finding the fit comfortable. "I'm not a nerd, I'm a genius."

"Can you draw a perfect circle freehand?"

"What? I don't think so, no."

"You should try. That's supposed to be a sign you're a genius," she said. "Leonardo da Vinci could. I tried and tried when I was a kid, but I can't. I was so disappointed when I realized I wasn't one. It would suit me, wouldn't it? Still, you seem quite normal for a genius. You've got social skills." She looked me up and down. I was nursing my wineglass with both hands because I didn't know what else to do with them. Her eyes lingered on my interlocked fingers in a way that told me she could translate body language as easily as I could flit between dialects. "I mean, they're pretty basic, but that's nothing we can't work on." Even her insults had a flare of charm.

"We'll call it a skill swap, then," I said, and she laughed with me. I uncurled my left hand from around the glass and, as an experiment, let it rest on the table where it didn't flap like a caught fish but stayed still. With a covert glance she signaled her approval at this development.

"You're so lucky, not having a vocation," she said, apropos of nothing. She peered wistfully out of the window so that I turned my own eyes to follow her gaze, but I saw only the lower half of a row of garbage cans. "You see, I have to act, whether acting wants me or not. It's not like a job you can take or leave." This kind of intense, passionate conversation might have been de rigueur among the drama students but it was new to me and I found her lack of restraint embarrassing. Attractive and compelling, too, but chiefly embarrassing. Biba shifted back into her own seat and I noticed how thin she was. Her legs crossed at the thigh, not the knee, and her belly didn't pop out when she leaned forward but folded inward, like a piece of thin cardboard. "Fucking . . ." She used this word when she was thinking of what to say next, like the French *alors*. "Fucking acting's more than a vocation. It's a coping mechanism," she explained, waving her cigarette so near to my eyes that they began to water. I wondered what she had had to cope with. "I don't understand why you *don't* want to act. Because whatever happens to you, however awful it is, or even wonderful experiences, you can get through it by thinking, hold on to this, remember what it felt like, I can use that one day. You can't be a truly brilliant actor if you've had no life. That's why I want to do everything; try everything, meet everyone, *taste* everyone. Don't you see? Because the more reserves I have to draw on the more I can do as an actress. In fact . . ." self-awareness seemed to strike, and she put on a pompous, gravelly voice, "one owes it to one's craft to live an extraordinary and sensational life." I laughed, relieved that she'd broken her own tension, and saw my opportunity to change the subject. I had to pull this conversation down from the sky if I was going to contribute to it.

"So was your mum a Biba girl in the sixties? Is that where you got your name?"

"I wish." Biba grimaced. "It's actually *Bathsheba*. Isn't it vile?"

"I think it's lovely," I said. "Four consonants all in a row. That's unusual."

"Really? No one's ever picked up on that before. Perhaps you're right about being a genius after all. When I was a baby, Bathsheba was too much of a mouthful for my brother—he's only three years older than me and all he could manage was 'Biba,' thank God. I couldn't return the favor, though, he's fucked: his name's Rex and what can you do with that? You can't shorten it, and his middle name's Caspian so he can't resort to that, either. But that's seventies parents for you, isn't it? A whole generation of us lumbered with these awful hippie names."

"Tell me about it," I said, thinking of the Deans, Scotts, and Tracys from my class at school.

"What about you?" she said.

"There's not much to tell," I said, because before I met her, there wasn't. My questions for her backed up behind my lips like bottlenecked traffic. Where did you learn to talk like that? Is Rex an actor? What does your mother do, and is she beautiful like you?

Most of all, how can I make you my friend? I allowed myself a private cringe: my modifications to my speaking voice had been successful, but my inner monologue still had a Midlands twang. I noticed with dismay that Biba's glass of wine was down to the dregs: I was still on my second and the bottle was empty.

"That's all the money gone," I said.

"Where are you going now?" she asked.

"To the Tube, I suppose."

"Excellent! So am I. Which one?"

I loved the Regent's Park Tube station. It wasn't the nearest one to college, but the detour I made to get there was worth it. It had never been modernized like some of the central London stops; the dark green tiles that clad its subway and ticket hall had been restored rather than replaced, making you feel like you were in a museum. Even the steel ticket barriers couldn't detract from the loveliness of it. I fed my Travelcard through the slot, surprised as always by the swiftness with which it emerged and this time newly astonished by the way a pair of hips propelled me through the barrier. I loped clumsily through and Biba tumbled after me, on my ticket. "Keep walking," she whispered. She swung her bag and smiled sweetly at the back of the attendant who was explaining to a rucksack-laden tourist how to work the ticket machine.

We stood between the two platforms. Down here the color scheme was what my mother would call coffee and cream, the Bakerloo brown and ivory tiles giving the impression of a sepia photograph. I liked to think that the tiles were pale yellow not because they were manufactured in that color but that they were still stained yellow with nicotine from Londoners sheltering from the Blitz.

"Where do you go from here?" I asked.

"Highgate," she replied. I pulled up the map of the Underground that I carried around with me in my head. She would need to go all the way down to Embankment and then double back along the Northern Line.

"This isn't the most straightforward way to get to Highgate."

"I needed you to get me into the system. I told you, I haven't got any money. And besides, it helps me to spend a few more minutes with you. It's been ages since I met a new interesting person." She squeezed my arm. For the seven or eight minutes the train took to reach Embankment station, I tried to think of an excuse to see her again. My curiosity about her was urgent, but I needed to express it casually if I wanted to avoid sounding like a lovestruck thirteen-year-old asking his crush to the cinema.

I braced myself for an awkward good-bye as we faced each other in a tunnel between the Northern and Bakerloo lines. The walls were white and shiny with abstract stripes of primary-colored pigment in them. I never understood why. Surely the tourists who thronged that part of the Underground wanted something more traditional and quaint, or was that just me? Did that make me a tourist? A warm dusty wind blustered through the tunnel. Strands of Biba's hair blew into my face and whipped at my eyes with their blunt edges. I blinked and held my hand to my eyes rather than step back from her.

"What are you doing on Saturday?" she asked. "Because Rex and I are having a party. Well, I'm having a party, so Rex hasn't got much say in it."

"You live with your family?"

"Oh, it's just me and Rex. We're orphans." A new set of questions formed a disorderly line on my tongue. "My twenty-first," she continued, "so it's going to be huge. Heinously large. Queenswood Lane, N6. Can you remember that? I haven't got anything to write it down. There isn't a better party in London this weekend, so don't pretend you've got something better to do."

Queenswood Lane, N6. I committed it to memory. Panic was unfamiliar to me but I felt it then as a series of obstacles presented themselves. What would I wear? How would I get home?

"Bring fabulous people," she instructed. The panic must have shown on my face. My roommates . . . oh Christ. I could already see the antipathy between them, crackling like static on nylon sheets.

Her next words were spoken with unexpected gentleness. "Don't worry. You don't have to bring anyone at all. Just promise me you'll be there." In the glow of her understanding, I felt as though I were being read and interpreted for the first time, unfolded and examined like a map left in a drawer for so long that its creases and pleats come permanently to describe their own topography. It was at once unsettling and reassuring.

"I promise," I said.

I have spent a lot of time since then, at least an hour a day, wondering where the cutoff point was in the chain of events that led me to where we all are—or aren't—today. My life, had it continued along its predicted trajectory, would have been unrecognizable. No Alice. No Rex. But if I'm honest with myself, my fate, and hers, and the fate of the others, was sealed the second I first saw her.

4

I WENT TO THE party on my own. I know that there are some people who can do this sort of thing as a matter of course, who love to work their way around a whole house full of potential new friends without the encumbrance of a date to introduce or fetch drinks for or apologize for. All I can say is I don't know how they do it. I had never been to anything alone that wasn't to do with the university—whether it be a new course or introductory drinks for foreign students in a new country. Even the thought of turning up at the party alone made my bowels loosen and my hands shake with a new and delicious kind of fear.

I looked up Queenswood Lane, N6 in my A–Z. The tatty atlas wanted to fall open two-thirds of the way through at the pages that displayed the southwest London suburbs and I had to break the spine in a second place to smooth out the Highgate pages. I think I was hoping that seeing the location depicted in yellow and green with solid black outlines would make it easier for me to travel there. And it did. It gave my amorphous, directionless obsession with Biba form and shape and line and number. The pink blocks indicating buildings were as cluttered and disarranged as anywhere in central London, but the page was dominated by two green blobs, Highgate Wood and Queen's Wood. I squinted to read the name of the road that divided the two woods like a spine bisecting a pair of lungs—Muswell Hill Road. The relevant offshoot of this road, Queenswood Lane, was tucked away next to the station. It was so slender that the lettering spilled out of the yellow stripe and into the green. I stared at the page where she lived (as I was beginning to think of it) and tried to transcend the limitations of block color and bulky font by imagining the neighborhood. I envisaged an area rather like Brentford or Kew, but with fewer shiny cars and dusty houseplants on every window-sill. I had never been to Highgate but remembered Sarah's father deciding not to house us in that part of North London, despite its proximity to the college, because it was full of "scruffy lefties and lesbians." It wasn't clear whether he made a distinction between the two.

Obsession made an eideteker of me and for the first time images, not words, sank effortlessly and permanently into my memory. I had the lines and blocks of page 32 memorized by Saturday evening but took my A–Z with me anyway as a kind of talisman, occasionally tapping my cotton shoulder bag to check that it was still there, reassuringly soft and solid. The bag also contained a bottle of sparkling wine that had been too cold to touch when I took it from the fridge but was rapidly, and unpleasantly, absorbing the warmth from my body and the train carriage. An unforecasted searingly hot day heralded the annual exposure of pasty flesh, or, in my case, time to show off the tan I had caught running in the park at lunchtime. I wore Doc Marten boots to hide my sock line and a green tie-dyed sundress picked up in a flea market in Spain, which I had never worn because Simon had hated it. The reflection I saw on the concave glass showed a nervous girl fidgeting with the bag on her lap, so I closed my eyes and rested my head against the clammy, clear plastic carriage divider, opening them only when we stopped at stations. I grew more nervous the closer we crept to Highgate.

Each Underground station has its own peculiar smell. If Regent's Park is tile and soot, then Highgate smells like the elevator lubricant that I had only smelled before in Italy. I don't know why: probably something to do with the escalators, some of the tallest I'd seen. A lung-hammeringly steep concrete hill pulled me out of the station and up toward Queenswood Lane. Seeing the road sign declaring my destination in black and white, the N6 a little red footnote in the right-hand corner, sent a fresh wave of anticipation and terror through me. I rested against the fence for a few seconds to let the sweat on my brow evaporate. My hair, washed only a couple of hours ago, was already plastered to my head. I turned my head upside down and massaged it at the roots, despairing at the stringy blond curtain that fell into my face.

Before me, the wooded street shimmered in the early evening heat: the houses were fuzzy and the trees smudged like an Impressionist painting. That I did not have the house number didn't matter: I gravitated toward the beat and the screams and the laughter. The house itself was set aside from the other buildings on the lane by a distance of ten feet or so and an untended scrub of shrubs and litter. Tall and thin and tatty, it stood like a sulky, scruffy teenager not wanting to associate with the other houses. Up close, it seemed to give off even more heat, like a giant kiln. I wondered how many bodies were radiating warmth inside. Most windows showed two or three figures talking, dancing, smoking, or doing all three at once. It was a huge building, far too big for two people to live in. I wondered if it had been their family home and, if so, whether death had shattered or dissolved that family. Had her parents died together or separately? Either scenario was both desperately tragic and massively intriguing.

Sucking beads of sweat from my upper lip, I found an old rope bell pull and tugged it. When nobody came to let me in, I gave the door a gentle push. It swung wide open. Inside, the air itself was different: hotter, muggier, infused with smoke and bodies and incense. It felt like when you walk off a plane into a far-off place with a different climate and take your first step into the new atmosphere. No matter how much you've planned or packed, it's not until the humid air fills your lungs or the icy wind stings your cheeks that you realize you really are in another country now.

5

I KNOW THAT THE most significant thing about that party is that I saw killer and victim together for the first time. But I'm afraid when I think about it I don't see it as a dark and portentous meeting of doomed souls. I just remember the best night of my life. It was the tipping point between innocence and experience: the perfect window of pleasure after which everything began to descend into chaos, so subtly at first that I didn't realize it was happening, and then at such a breakneck speed that events were beyond the control of any one person.

The entrance hall, a vast space floored with black and white diamond-shaped tiles, took up most of the ground floor of the building. They were more like garden tiles than interior ones. Concrete was visible where some were missing. Many were crackled across the surface and the glaze had worn off so that they were no longer shiny but dull and porous. Existing stains looked permanent and new ones would be indelible.

The hall was dominated by a huge staircase, lit by a string of paper lanterns wound around and around the banister. I picked my way through the half-light, glad that it was too dark to make eye contact with the people who sat cross-legged on the floor. I tried to stride purposefully through the house and was grateful that no one was watching me, as I had to keep turning back on myself. The place was an impractical warren of corridors that twisted and turned, dipped down and then rose again, often without reaching any destination save for a window or a cupboard. No two rooms on any given floor were on the same level. There was no uniformity of design to guide me through the labyrinth: carpets changed pattern midpassage and a hodgepodge of different wall coverings represented every decorative fad from the last century, from dusty plaster to flock wallpaper to bubbling Anaglypta. I found one airing cupboard and two bathrooms, the second with a man asleep in the bath, vomit splattering his white T-shirt. Three years of cozy evenings spent watching medical dramas on television triggered a reflex action and I found myself shaking him awake. He was very good-looking, I noticed, as I held him by the shoulders and tried to pull his body upright.

"I need to clear your airway," I said to him. "Please. Wake up. You could choke on your own vomit." Bloodshot eyes struggled to focus on me, then closed with relief when he understood the reason for my concern.

"Oh, it's okay, love," he said, "it's not my puke." My efforts to look nonchalant as I closed the door behind me were wasted: he was asleep, or unconscious again, within seconds.

A tiny box room next door stood empty apart from an ancient treadmill and a drum kit. The skin of the bass drum visibly reverberated, keeping time with the music that thudded through the bricks of the house. On the first floor I found the kitchen, a pantry really, far too small for such a big house. Patches of black mold speckled the pale blue plasterwork and the fridge was plugged into a broken socket, green and red wires spilling from the wall. The sink and counter heaved with a flotsam of plastic cups and half-empty bottles. I poured a glass of my sparkling wine into a plastic cup, downed it in one, and felt my nerves begin to melt. A girl with white-blond, cropped hair pulled a bottle of screw-top wine out of the humming fridge and pressed her lips to its neck. I decided to abandon my plastic cup and take the bottle on a further tour of the house. I just hoped no one would ask for a swig from it: I hated sharing that kind of thing.

Half an hour later, no closer to finding Biba and not apparently visible to the other guests, I sequestered myself in an alcove, nursing the remains of my bottle. The small flight of stairs opposite me was even more dangerous than the last; candles in jam jars were placed on the outside edge of each step, the flames perilously near to the rims. Just one kick from a drunken toe, I thought, watching the guttering glow, and we all go up in smoke. I appointed myself keeper of the flames. If I contributed nothing else to this party I would make sure that no one died on this particular staircase. I tried to convince myself that it was enough to be at a party like this and watch, even if you didn't quite join in or even say hello to the hosts. But I failed either to convince myself that I was right or to get up and introduce myself to people. By eleven, I was beating myself up for being so pathetic while simultaneously trying to recall the time of the last train home when my rescuer, the birthday girl herself, appeared from an unseen door and extended her arms down toward me.

"Darling!" she breathed, catching my hands and pulling me up out of my harbor. She wore a long white dress and those awful chunky sneakers again. She looked like a bride who had run away from her own wedding. "You've been hiding from me!" she chided, tucking a strand of hair behind my ear. "Come upstairs and meet everyone." When she turned around, I saw that her costume actually was a wedding dress: the dirty train trailed perilously near to the flickering flames, and like a dutiful bridesmaid I gathered the grubby satin in my arms, out of fire's way. Her vertebrae protruded like a string of pearls suspended between her shoulder blades. "Happy birthday," I said to her back.

The room that we entered, through the one door I had not tried, spanned the entire length and breadth of the house. At the front, the high windows overlooking the road were pinned with pink, orange, and purple drapes. They were saris, Biba later told me, bought from a thrift store for next to nothing just for the party. They would stay there for as long as I did and bathe the house in sunset colors every morning.

At the opposite end of the room were two huge sets of French windows that gave onto a stone veranda. Behind the terrace a constellation of fairy lights winked in a tree but gave out no real light. It was impossible to tell where the garden ended and the woods began. Framed by the open windows, a boy about my own age was frowning over a pair of turntables. Speakers as tall as a ten-year-old child flanked him, one balanced precariously on a Greek urn. His right hand clamped a pair of headphones to his ear while the other glided over the vinyl, as smooth and dexterous as a potter at his wheel. His still, intense concentration was at odds with the wordless music that pulsed from the speakers: I didn't know what it was called, but it was chaotically urgent. Simon, who was dismissive of any tune that didn't have a verse/chorus/verse/chorus structure, would have said that it wasn't "real music." This in itself was an incentive to try to understand it.

The room was strewn with bodies: some dancing, some sitting, others standing around and chatting. I identified one or two faces from college, but their blank stares didn't reciprocate that recognition. A fat woman with curly hair who lay in shadow on a fraying, sagging sofa in the middle of the room was the only one to return my smile. Biba pulled me down onto a duvet cover thrown between two chairs. Its centerpiece was a makeshift ashtray that might have started the evening as a bowl of hummus.

"This is Karen," she announced to the other members of the strange picnic. "That's Chris on the turntables," she said, waving at the DJ, who nodded back. She introduced me to Rachael, the girl I'd seen in the kitchen, and a handful of other people; drama students, whose names I instantly forgot. Nearest to me were Tris and Jo, a couple in matching tie-dyed trousers and with matching blond dreadlocks wound into rope turbans on their heads.

"Good to meet you," said Jo. Her brown, ringed hand stroked my cheek in greeting. It was dry and calloused. "Want some mushrooms?" She unfolded a foil square that lay in her lap, exposing a brown pat of slimy-looking fungi against the silver. "They're

Mexican," she said, widening her eyes conspiratorially. I didn't know what that meant, but declined by gesturing to my bottle. I held my hand out to Tris. "Fuck that, give me a hug," he said, and wrapped me in an embrace that was more headlock than hug. Jo dangled a brown sliver of mushroom above her mouth and gulped it down like a baby bird guzzling its first worm. Tris released me and opened his mouth obediently as Jo fed him a mushroom. Then he forgot our new friendship and with closed eyes began to pat at an imagined pair of bongos a few inches above his lap.

Biba unclenched a fist to reveal a little white pill in her palm. "Have an E!" She giggled. "They're free, from Guy!" She gestured to a figure in the shadows, the hollows of his face briefly illuminated by the flame of a Zippo, and popped the pill into my open mouth, pressing a finger to my lips to silence any protest as well as to make sure I swallowed the drug. I didn't have time to consider who Guy was or why he had gifted me an ecstasy tablet: it began to melt on my tongue before I could discreetly spit it out. I needed to think, and quickly. My lack of experience with drugs was less a prudish moral stand and more a case of never having been offered any. Even the drug dealers who hung around my school gates had taken one look at me and decided I wasn't worth pushing to. There had once been some marijuana going around a party at Simon's house, and I had taken a few inexpert drags when he wasn't looking. It hadn't done anything for me except to make me breathless the next day and cost me my tennis match.

I was still well informed enough to know that ecstasy and wine didn't mix, and I had had a lot of wine. While my mind was playing squash with my options, my mouth decided for me: the pill dissolved bitterly on my tongue and I swallowed to make the taste go away. I leaned back into the side of the sofa, went back to my position as observer, and waited for something to happen.

I watched Biba dancing, hoping her behavior would give me clues as to what to expect. A pale woman in a long white dress ought to look like a ghost, but in the blur of figures Biba was luminous, more real than anyone had ever been. I watched her winding between the bodies as I waited for something to happen.

Half an hour. Nothing. An hour: nothing, and I had a dead leg from sitting cross-legged. I stood up to revive it and suddenly felt like a broken elevator was traveling at breakneck speed down through the floors of my body. My legs were made of springs and the floor beneath my feet was made of sand. I reached to steady myself on the sofa and staggered. There was a tug on the hem of my skirt and Jo was looking up at me. "Are you all right?" I shook my head. "First pill?" I nodded. She and Tris exchanged an indulgent glance, like new parents cooing over their baby's first steps. "Come with me." I followed her out onto the terrace and dry-retched over the balcony. The next body part to leave the building was my jaw, which began chattering uncontrollably and, I was sure, unflatteringly. Jo fumbled for a pocket in her voluminous trousers and eventually came up with a stick of chewing gum, which she unwrapped for me. It was the fruity kind, not the minty sort. I felt better once it was in my mouth.

"This will stop you pulling funny faces. If you need any more just come and find me. The trick is to dance it out. Okay?" Biba emerged from behind a speaker. I felt a surge of love and confidence and knew that everything was going to be all right.

"Why aren't you dancing with me?" What a good question. Why wasn't I? It was suddenly and abundantly clear to me that my whole life had been leading up to the moment where I danced with her. I was wildly amused by the realization that all my life I had used my legs for walking and running and playing sports, when all along they had been designed for marching on the spot to a series of screeches and bleeps. We plunged back into the party. There were around fifteen people left dancing and I was able to make eye contact with every single one: none of my smiles was rejected. I had become not only visible but the nucleus of the party. The music began to make sense to me: the low notes grew deeper and louder while the screeching high-pitched scratch that passed for a melody seared off into bat-audible territory. Bass and treble seemed to be having a tug-of-war and I was in the middle, being pulled apart. I didn't know if I wanted to be put back together again. The focus of my panic changed from what to do with this rush to a sudden and gripping fear that this feeling would outlast the party. If the music stopped while I was still ready to dance, then what would I do? How would I live? I was still pacing and twirling when Biba took my hand again and pulled me out of the living room and into the kitchen. "Time for you to chill out, dancing girl," she said. "Have some water."

"I don't have to go home, do I?"

She shook her head and smiled. "Are you getting rushes? This should make them amazing."

She whipped my body around and began to knead the flesh of my shoulders, which yielded to her bony, inexpert fingers. But the feel of skin—her skin—on mine compensated for the imprecision of her touch. I closed my eyes and prepared for my body to dissolve under her hands, only for the massage to come to an abrupt end.

"Oh, bloody hell." She sighed. The man who stood before us, arms folded, had to be Rex. The face was her own, re-sexed. Straight, thick, unplucked eyebrows framed the same brown eyes. (I thought with a sympathetic wince of the effort her grooming routine must involve.) The small teeth and tight jawline were the same, as was the pointed nose, but the long neck was interrupted by an Adam's apple that dipped and rose. Without the glow and spirit that made her face beautiful, his was top-heavy and beaky. He ran his fingers through his hair: it formed a quiff and retained its shape.

"Just checking you're okay," he said to her, holding her by the chin. "How much have you had? Your eyes are like *pins*." How could he tell how big or small her pupils were? Last time I had looked into her eyes, the black-brown irises merged with the pupils, surrounded by unbroken whites. Perhaps it was different if you had the same eyes, if you were used to looking at them in a mirror.

"Just half a pill, Rex, don't *fuss*," she said, her voice echoing his own rising intonation. "Do you want one? Guy's got loads."

"Who the bloody hell is Guy?" he snapped, and then, "No, thanks. Someone's got to stay vaguely compos mentis." Biba kissed him full on the lips and smoothed his hair. It bounced up again almost immediately.

"This is Rex, the best brother in the world," she said to me. "And this is my new best friend, Karen," said Biba. "She is a linguistic genius, and she has taken a whole ecstasy tablet, and she is very much enjoying herself, so you're not to tell her off or nag her at all."

"Wouldn't dream of it," said Rex. "But you two take care. Have you got enough water? Remember only to drink if you're dancing. Okay then."

The intense rush died down to be replaced by muzzy feelings of benevolence. The girl called Rachael, so intimidating a couple of hours ago, now numbered among my new friends. She offered me not a joint or wine but a sip of the tea she was drinking from a chipped mug.

"Biba and her brother are very alike, aren't they?" I said.

"Ridiculously so," agreed Rachael. "They almost give truth to those bizarre plots in Shakespearean comedies, don't they? It's such a pity Rex can't act. They'd be a shoo-in for *Twelfth Night*."

"He's not a drama student, then?"

She barked a cynical laugh. "Rex? He's not an *anything*."

A new and irregular beat came not from the amps but from the front door. A male voice was raised in anger. Edging away from the dance floor, I crouched on the landing and peered through the banisters. The candles had long ago blown out.

"What's wrong with you people?" The voice cracked as the man strained to make himself heard above the noise. "My wife is *pregnant*!" He wore a T-shirt and sweatpants, probably pulled on moments before. I saw only the top of his head and wondered if he knew about the incipient bald patch at the crown, or if it was still a secret his wife kept from him.

"This is the worst one yet!" His voice rose to a screech. "I've written it down in my noise diary, and I'm calling the police if you don't turn it off *right now.*"

"We'll wind it up, Mr. Wheeler." Rex's voice was gentle. "I'm sorry if we kept you awake. It's Biba's twenty-first, so we're in quite high spirits."

His composure exacerbated the other man's hysteria and he began to repeat himself. "It's four o'clock in the bloody morning! My wife is pregnant!"

There were no antisocial behavior orders then, but I think that this is when Wheeler began to research their 1997 equivalent. The next time we saw him he had memorized the relevant council bylaws and was able to quote them to us.

I raced ahead of Rex back into the heart of the party; he had a word with Chris at the turntables, pointing at his watch and raising his palms to say, I'm sorry but what can you do? Everything was over so suddenly. Chris said he knew a club in King's Cross that they could probably get into for free and would let them dance until at least 9 a.m. He left his turntables and records where they stood as most of the remaining guests, including the girl called Rachael and the boy called Guy, followed him down the stairs and out of the front door like children tagging behind the Pied Piper. Biba didn't seem to mind the sudden exodus of her friends, settling into an earnest, whispered conversation with the fat woman on the sofa. I felt a throb of jealousy and joined Rex on the terrace.

"It's beautiful here," I said to fill the silence. "How long have you lived here?"

"Forever," he said. "It's the only home I've ever known. My grandparents lived here. And my mum." This last was said in a tone that didn't invite further inquiry. He was smoking a cigarette or a joint, to keep his hands busy rather than for the hit, I thought. The prop didn't suit him: he had an edgy, nervy quality, like a librarian a whisper away from a nervous breakdown. A pair of glasses, constantly slipping from the bridge of his nose and pushed back up by a middle finger, would have been a more suitable nervous tic.

The first light of the day had started to lift the color of the wood from dark gray to green and draw a line between treetops and sky. It went on for miles, only a few roofs and the odd church spire breaking the rural illusion.

"Daybreak," he said, looking out at it. "I've always thought it was funny that dawn should be called daybreak. This is when the day is made: it's the beginning. It's the best part: you've got all the potential of the day to come, and you haven't wasted it yet. When it gets dark, *that* should be daybreak. When the day is broken. When it turns into nighttime, that's when it all starts to go wrong."

"I don't know," I said. "I'd be quite happy if tonight never, ever ended." The look he gave me made me uncomfortable. You'll see, it seemed to say. Biba had told me he was twenty-four, only four years older than I was, so why was he acting like a concerned parent?

By six, there was only a handful of people left in the room. I stretched out on a blanket, conversations drifting over my head as sleep pressed down on me.

When I awoke dry-mouthed at ten, someone had covered me with a patchwork quilt that stank of stale smoke. The smell of the room, of sweat and bodies and cigarettes, made me retch. I hadn't noticed it last night. Now, it was an assault on my senses. I had company under the blanket: Biba, the sleeping bride. Her mouth lolled open and a zephyr of rank breath traveled under my nostrils. The tinny sound of a cheap stereo and the odd thud were audible through the ceiling. I imagined Tris, still wide awake and playing his air drums, and was glad I'd declined the mushrooms. I took back what I'd said to Rex earlier: now that the night was over, I wanted to be home, and clean, and if not asleep then at least between my own sheets. Nobody was awake to hear my good-bye.

I had always rather envied those girls you saw in last night's clothes, wondering what their stories were, but now I was one of them—I was the one with the story and I wanted to tell it. I wanted to shake awake the dozing man with the Tesco shopping bag opposite me and ask him if he had ever had a night like mine. I made do with replaying the events in my mind: the sounds, the sensations. The only people I didn't want to tell were my housemates. They would disapprove and would never understand. I would not have understood myself had I not been there. I was relieved to find a note on the kitchen table telling me that they were playing tennis all day. They were with Simon and his new girlfriend, although I didn't work that out until later.

Even when I was showered, minty and lying between the clean sheets of my bed, I couldn't sleep. I turned on my clock radio and heard the opening bars of a hit from a few summers before that still wouldn't go away. As a baritone voice intoned the refrain "I've never met a girl like you before," no lyrics had ever rung so true. My last thought before I drifted off was that I had finally met the person that all the love songs were about. And it was a girl—a weird, wild girl living in a filthy house with a creepy brother. And there didn't seem to be anything I could do about it. Oh, fuck.

6

OUR COTTAGE IS CALLED an artisan's dwelling, which is real estate agent–speak for tiny and shabby. Its size reflects the kind of mortgage that freelance translators, even good ones, can get. The stone fireplace and thick little leaded windows are supposed to compensate for the lack of space, but I didn't realize how small it was until now. It went from cozy to tiny the minute Rex stepped inside. I had forgotten how tall he is. For the last ten years I've only seen him sitting down, and then in a hall fifteen feet high. He has already hit his head twice on the low doorway that divides the front room from the kitchen. I don't need to remind him to stoop, though. His posture has changed: he now holds himself constantly on the verge of a cower. Even when he is in a different room he fills the house up. His shuffling footfall is heavier than Alice's and tells me where he is when he's upstairs. The Capiz chandelier on the living room ceiling shakes when he treads, the shells making a brittle tinkling sound that is mildly distracting to me now, a sure sign that in a couple of weeks it will drive me mad.

While I've got the living room to myself, I switch on the television and flick straight to the twenty-four-hour news channel. I half expect to see footage of him leaving the prison, followed by stills from ten-year-old newspapers with those awful photographs to remind us of the victims. I know I'm being stupid. Worse people than Rex are released from prison and it doesn't make the news; I don't think I've ever seen footage of anyone outside a prison gate except in dramas. But the blown-up snapshot that fills the screen is not Rex's. The grainy image is not of anyone I have ever known but of a little girl, a three-year-old, who has been missing from home for two days. This, I have come to understand, is the kind of story that will bury all others. A rich-kid killer from ten years ago can't compete with a missing child. It's not "sexy" enough, isn't that what the media say? It's a grotesque shorthand for the kind of news stories that people can't get enough of. The phrase disgusts me but not as much as I disgust myself. I'm unable to suppress a horrible hope that the little girl stays missing for a few more days, just long enough for Rex's release to be old news. Isn't that an evil thing to wish for, when we have already done enough? I turn over to the white noise and rainbow blur of a music channel.

Turning out the light so that no one outside can see me, I check the recessed scrub of grass and gravel opposite our terrace that is the unofficial parking lot for everyone who lives here. I'm half expecting to see a man with a camera, but there is nothing out of the ordinary save for a battered maroon Range Rover that I've never seen before and a white Nissan Micra. Are either of those the kinds of cars that journalists would drive? As I watch, Dave, my next-door-but-one neighbor, jogs out of his front door and lets himself into the unlocked Range Rover. It must be new, or at least new to Dave. He revs the engine two or three times before pulling out. A churn of mud frills out from his fender and splatters the white paint job of the smaller car. The Range Rover's tail-lights illuminate a figure in the driver's seat of the Micra; man or woman, it's impossible to tell. Dave tears noisily down the lane and the smaller car, perhaps afraid of being seen by me, quickly follows in his slipstream. I draw the curtains and am glad that nobody witnessed this ridiculous exhibition of paranoia. I turn the light back on—a side lamp, this time—and bring my attention to the telephone.

They must know he is free. There has been a phone call once every two years or so. Sometimes they are print journalists, sometimes they are TV researchers. They are always female, young and well spoken in a confident, blond sort of way. There was a spate of calls at the five-year anniversary and then another when Roger Capel received his OBE. I can't stop them rerunning old stories about Rex, but so far I have succeeded in keeping Alice and myself out of the news.

Usually, the journalists are easy to fob off with a lie: I tell them that I have the same name as a girl who knew the Capels, that I get these calls every year or so, but I can't help them. I got the idea when I was translating an interview with a Spanish actress who said that when her fans accosted her, she claimed that she was often mistaken for herself, or that she was a professional look-alike. I even wish them luck chasing their stories. Only one of them, a TV researcher named Alison Larch, was persistent enough to visit me at the house. I knew that she was bad news from the way she knocked on the door: five loud and rapid bangs that made me spill the tea I was carrying. I'd been right about the blond thing, but naive about my deflective techniques. She was working, she said, on a film about "rich kids who went off the rails."

"I know you knew them," she said, although she didn't say how. "I'm going to make this film with or without you: you might as well be onboard." I called her bluff, and her investigations must have come to nothing, because when the documentary aired six months later, there was no mention of the Queenswood murders. It was after that that I persuaded Rex to change his last name to mine: it is Alice's last name, after all. I didn't tell him about Alison Larch. I wonder if she is the one who keeps calling and then hanging up. The journalists who have called in the past have been businesslike and overintimate, wheedling and threatening, but they have never been silent. Perhaps this is a new technique, designed to break me. It is very nearly working. If the police had been half as industrious as Alison Larch, our story could have had a very different ending.

The phone trills, breaking into my thoughts, and even though it is under my hand I fumble to pick it up, fingers groping blindly for the answer button before Alice or Rex can reach the handset in the bedroom. It's my mother, wanting to know how today went and when will be a good time to visit. I can hear her loading the dishwasher as she speaks and then the whir of the machine fades as she marches her new digital telephone into the living room and sinks into the sofa next to my father. By the time we have finished arranging dates, it is dark.

"She's asleep," says Rex, sliding onto the sofa beside me, long legs doubling up to avoid the coffee table. It's only seven o'clock, which means she'll be up again at ten and then awake until midnight, which means that getting her up tomorrow will be a battle of wills I'm not sure I have the strength for.

"Ah," I say. "It's way before her bedtime. We should have talked about her routine before you came home. It's really important not to disrupt it. We should go and wake her up."

"She's had a long day." Rex sighs. "She'll sleep." Frustration balls in my throat and I want to shout at him not to be so stupid. He doesn't know the first thing about Alice's sleeping patterns. She's nine, not six. I draw breath to tell him off but then remember that he isn't six either. He's thirty-four. He puts his head in his hands, parting his hair to reveal those shoots of gray hidden around his ears. I take in the delta of veins that bulge on the back of his hand: they are new, too. Tenderness and guilt engulf me.

"I'm sorry. It's okay. We'll leave her," I tell him. There is nothing I can say that will make him better but there is something I can do. I open my arms and he collapses into them. A sleeping spring of desire bubbles up and spills over, as sudden and inevitable as tears, and I'm not sure who is healing whom.

7

THE WEEK UNTIL I saw her again was a long, hot one that dragged its feet like one of my students on the way to an after-school tutorial. The heat wave that had swaggered into the city on Biba's birthday had settled in for the summer. The sun sucked the river near Brentford into the sky so that the air hung hot and humid and dirty. Running was impossible anywhere but in the middle of the park or in the air-conditioned gym at the tennis club—a place I wanted to avoid in case I saw Simon. The atmosphere at home was hushed and heavy as Claire, Emma, and Sarah crammed for our looming finals. I watched them poring over dictionaries trying to force in words they didn't already know and wondered why they bothered. At this stage, either you could do it or you couldn't. Even when the girls weren't studying, there was a tension in the house. Their breezy hellos when I entered a room suggested sudden ends to conversations, hastily ground out like illicit cigarettes. They had always had more in common with one another than with me, but this feeling that I was on the outside of a circle was a new and unwelcome one.

I spent my days at the library, not because I needed to study but to get out of the house and increase my chances of bumping into Biba again. I even took the stairs everywhere, remembering her aversion to elevators. Queen Charlotte's library was a square block that squatted next to the humanities building. Stuffy even in midwinter, it now developed a tropical microclimate all its own. The huge picture windows in the languages section could be opened only a couple of inches, reportedly to prevent student suicides at this time of year. The slow ceiling fans did little to relieve the heat but plenty to displace the dust that rose and spun in the slats of sunshine that bleached the spaces between bookshelves. I blamed my lack of concentration on the heat making my skin damp and parching my mouth and eyes, but it wasn't the need for fresh air that drove me to the drama department two or three times a day. I visited Biba's mailbox more often than my own but every day another envelope or flyer was wedged into the little wooden hollow. That we had shared the same building for three years without bumping into each other didn't lessen my disappointment when she wasn't there.

I spent the weekend in Brentford tutoring teenagers and torturing myself with visions of Biba sitting impatiently in the languages department waiting for me. On Monday my worst fears were confirmed: her mailbox had been emptied but no note had been shoved into mine.

If she wouldn't come to me, I would find her. I walked the mile from college along Euston Road to Warren Street, hoping that fresh air and exercise would clear my head. I was wrong on both counts: the air was thick and gray with sun-baked traffic fumes, and the walk made me sweat so that the smog stuck to my skin. I submerged myself in the Tube and sweltered my way up to Highgate.

The early evening music of Queenswood Lane was soothing and cooling after my journey. Domestic noises accompanied the rustle of leaves. The chink of silverware and the tinkle of ice cubes, a strain of classical music wafting through a high oriel window all sounded like the carefully orchestrated background noise you hear in a radio play when the director wants to convey upper-middle-class affluence at rest. As I retraced last week's footsteps up the stone staircase, I felt the echo of last week's nerves. But this was different. Then, I was nervous because Biba's world had been an unknown quantity. Now, I was apprehensive because I knew how much I wanted to be part of it.

The front door stood slightly ajar, which made me hesitate more than if it had been closed. A muffled "Come in" sounded from somewhere in the building's foundations before I had a chance to knock; I pushed the door open and made sure I closed it at the exact same angle. "Down here!" sang a female voice that wasn't Biba's. I followed it, and the hiss and crackle of a radio, down a narrow set of sagging steps into a huge and shabby basement kitchen as vast and busy as the little galley upstairs was tiny and bare—although they were equally grubby. Children's drawings were tacked onto grimy whitewashed walls and appliances and utensils cluttered every available work surface. In the middle, like a dais, was a battered table that might once have been pine or larch but was now colorless. The woman I thought of as the fat girl from the party sat at its head, her fingers in a mixing bowl. She was older than I, closer to thirty than to twenty, and she smiled as though she had been expecting me.

"Nina Vitor," she said, holding out a floury hand to me. When I shook it, the bangles on her wrist jangled like gypsy bells. "You must be Karen. We didn't meet properly at the party but I'd have recognized you anyway from Rex's description."

Irritation that he had been talking about me wrestled with disappointment that his sister hadn't.

She gestured to a chair. "Sit down. Have a drink. I've made far too much coffee to drink on my own, and I could do with some *adult* company," she said, rolling her eyes and her *r*'s. The lilt in her voice confirmed the Portuguese origin her name suggested. She was mixed race, although I couldn't say which races were in that mix. She was all swoops and curves: her honey-colored hair was like a tangle of question marks, her short, wavy eyebrows like two tildes. Rolls of fat oozed over the top of the purple sarong she wore and the nut-brown skin of her hips and breasts was slivered with pale fawn stretch marks, but a pair of cheekbones that her excess flesh couldn't disguise made her beautiful. I slid onto a bench that ran the length of the table, hoping I hadn't been staring at her. Nina's smile suddenly expanded.

"Oh, my babies," she cried. I thought she was talking about Biba and Rex until two small children, urchin-filthy, toddled into the kitchen. The little boy licked his hand and smoothed down his curls.

"I'm four and a half," he announced.

"This is Inigo," said Nina, ruffling his hair so that his curls were loosened. She scooped the girl up onto a generous hip. "And this is Gaia." The little girl picked her nose and ignored me.

"She's not four yet," said Inigo, and then, "What are you doing in my house?"

"I didn't think it *was* your house," I said before I could stop myself, but I hadn't offended Nina.

"We've got the whole of the basement," she said, only partially enlightening me. "There's a couple of bedrooms back there that are sort of tucked under the garden steps. Didn't you notice the other night?" I twisted my spine to see that the back wall of the kitchen was made up of long, tall shutters that reached from floor to ceiling. One of these wooden panels had evidently swung open to let the children in.

"I didn't make it this far down," I replied, but she was distracted. Gaia tugged on her mother's earring, a piece of jewelry as complex and beautiful as a coil of human DNA. Beads of yellow and green amber like fat raindrops were suspended in silver corkscrews. I fingered the silver coffee bean on a filigree chain around my neck, a gift from Simon, and wished I wasn't wearing earrings that matched.

"How long have you lived here?" I asked, sipping my coffee. It was hot and bitter, not like English coffee at all, and I knew it would keep me awake for hours.

"About a year and a half. No, two years, I met Biba in summer ninety-five," she remembered. "And I started going out with Rex on Carnival weekend."

"Rex?" I said, picturing the brittle, shambling figure I'd last seen slurping tea and staring forlornly into the new day. Then I looked at Nina, sexuality as abundant as her flesh. It was easier to believe that she'd eaten him than been his lover. "Rex?" I said again. "*Really?*" Gaia slid off her mother's lap and waddled up the stairs. I tried to find a polite way to phrase the obvious question. "So why did . . . I can't imagine . . . what did . . . how did you two meet?" I asked.

"You don't need to be polite, I know we're an odd couple." Nina cringed cheerfully. "I needed somewhere to live. We were living on this barge in Camden and it was just so . . . filthy. I knew that once we were sleeping together he'd feel obliged to house us." The revelation was harder to swallow than Nina's coffee. "You think I'm cynical, I can tell. It's different when you've got kids. I've had sex with worse people for sanctuary," she said, leaving me to wonder who else she had shared that generous body with, and in what circumstances. She refilled her cup and I placed my hand over my own even though it was nearly empty. "He's a sweet boy, it was lovely while it lasted, but you know what it's like. The irony is, Rex is someone's idea of a perfect fuck. But not mine. I need it a little bit more *Latin*, know what I mean?"

"Er, um," I said, having no idea what Latin sex might be like, and wondering if I should be troubled by the lack of it in my own life. Gaia came through the door in a forward roll and offered me a little round pill with a dollar sign etched in its chalky surface. Nina snatched the ecstasy tablet away from the toddler, who started to howl.

"Although when things like this happen, I'm glad I won't be here much longer," she said.

"You're leaving?" I said. "Why? This is the loveliest place I've ever been to. If I lived here, I'd stay here forever."

"You say that, but it's not always easy actually living here," said

Nina, picking lumps of dough out of the barbed-wire bracelet that circled her plump wrist. "I've already got two kids. I don't need to become a substitute mother for two more who are old enough to look after themselves."

I saw my opportunity.

"When did their parents . . . leave?" I asked, hoping the euphemism would make the question sound casual.

"Christ, all that happened long before I met them," said Nina. "It's a tragedy. I sometimes wonder how they stay here after all that. They didn't have much choice, I suppose."

"Oh?" I raised an eyebrow.

"It's no wonder they're the way they are." She drew her children closer to her, her focus returning to her own family, and the conversation was steered out of my control again. "Like I said, I owe my own babies a future. I'm going to educate the children. Not school them. There's a difference. I mean really educate them, take them traveling. Inigo's school age now, but I want to save him from all that." Nina launched into a brief rant about the toxicity of formal education before detailing her plans to teach the children herself by taking them on a tour of their various genetic heritages. It comprised most of the countries touching the Mediterranean Sea, due to Nina's Algerian and Portuguese parentage and no small doubt about Inigo's paternity. I was only half-listening as she told me how easy it was to "live off the radar" as she put it. Later, I would wish I had paid more attention.

"If you work cash in hand, and you don't claim benefits, no one bothers with you. And I'm a jewelry designer." She grinned and twirled her earring with a silver-adorned hand. "It's the ideal trade for someone living on the run. You just pack up your jewels and you go." I thought about my own life and its lengthy paper trail. My education had been measured out in consent forms, grant applications, exam board papers, and scholarship documents. That it was possible to survive, let alone thrive, outside the state system, was a revelation. I was shocked and thrilled in equal measure. If I hadn't seen Nina do it so carelessly and confidently, would I have had the courage to do what I did later? What she told me over a cup of coffee influenced the way I reacted when everything had happened. She taught me how easy it is to disappear. How easy it is to hide a child from the world.

&

We dance a clumsy excuse-me around the bed, unsure who has claim to which side of it. Rex and I used to sleep on different sides depending on whose room we were in: he would always want to sleep next to the wall. In this room, both sides are exposed. We always slept naked—it was too hot that summer to do otherwise—and now he is staring at the folded nightclothes I have handed him.

"Gone off me already?" he says, eyebrows disappearing under a wing of hair. The reverse is true. The weight he has put on has softened his jaw and covered his Adam's apple and brought his arresting good looks down to a more manageable level. His hair is accidentally fashionable. Back then, it was de rigueur for men his age to wear their hair either very short or floppy and parted in the middle, and Rex always looked out of place. Now men spend money on products that tease their hair into the mess of peaks and quiffs that he always struggled to control.

"It's not me," I say. "It's Alice. She comes in in the night . . . I did tell you."

Alice has slept with me almost every night since she was old enough to toddle from her room to mine. I tuck her into her own bed each evening but I never wake up alone, even when we're on holiday, or at my mother's. At around four o'clock every morning, the corner of the duvet is tugged and a little voice says, "Can I dig in?" and she curls around me. I don't even notice her do it anymore.

"Oh," he says. "You did tell me. I'd forgotten. Yeah, that might be a bit weird."

Rex knows that ten-year-olds don't climb into bed with naked fathers. The years when she might have surprised him in the shower or late at night are long gone: a pocket of innocence that Rex lost out on along with diaper changes and her first steps. All families have their own codes about this sort of thing, unwritten rules about where you can and can't be naked, that silently and organically establish themselves over the years. We, on the other hand, have been thrust into devising new codes and rules for every situation that is new to us.

He shakes out the starched pajama bottoms in a multicolored skinny pinstripe and the crisp white T-shirt with matching trim. He regards them blankly and I know that I wasted my time and money on the designer label.

"There'll be lots of little things like this, won't there?" he says, sliding into the right-hand side of the bed. "Faux pas. Things I don't know. Stuff I get wrong."

"Only for a little while," I try to reassure him.

I change into the blue camisole and shorts that have replaced my usual flannel pajamas: a self-conscious compromise. It's ten o'clock, and still no noise from the bedroom next door. Maybe Alice will sleep through the night after all. Rex catches me looking at the clock.

"I was right about bedtime, though," he says, his voice a caricature of smugness.

"You were lucky."

"She's happy to have me back, I think. Isn't she?"

I lie on my front, my chin resting on his chest. He sighs so deeply I sink another inch into the bed.

"She's elated. We both are."

A car passing the road outside swishes a beam through the bedroom curtains, a brief illusion of searchlights that sweep over the bed where we lie. The car's low purr fades into the night. The only noises left are the soft sound of his breathing and the odd rustle from outside the window. Last time I lay with him, the night before it happened, it was like this, only then we had the white noise of the A1 fleshing out the skeleton of silence.

"Shall we tell her?" he says suddenly.

We both know that the question is rhetorical. It is when, not if. We have to tell her, and soon. The story she knows is not too far from the truth—that there was a fight and a panic and two people died, and although Daddy isn't a bad man, he had to go to prison to say sorry. To her credit, she never struggled with accepting the concept of a good person living in prison, and has never questioned Rex's character. She is young enough now not to ask questions. I sometimes think I have deliberately kept her young for this reason. But next year she will be ten, she will soon leave the tiny village school where she has been cosseted for so long and be thrust into a huge comprehensive where I can't protect her. Ours is the kind of secret that gathers power the longer it is kept.

"You know we have to."

"But not just yet," he says. "Can we have a little honeymoon period first? Time to settle in?"

How long does he need? How much time do we have? What if tomorrow is the day my mystery phone caller decides to play his or her hand? I am still protecting Rex from the calls, feigning frustration when yet another "call center" interrupts a meal or a television program. We are living by a stopwatch, but only I know it.

"Another week or two won't hurt," I concede. "But we must tell her."

"What? Everything?"

"Christ, I don't know." I pull away from Rex and prop myself up on my elbows. "I've had ten years to think about it and still I don't know. Edited highlights?"

"You know her better than I do," he says nervously. "What parts is she old enough to understand?"

Now it's my turn to sigh.

"I'm not sure it works like that. I still don't feel old enough to understand it sometimes, and I was there."

"Please don't say that." His voice rises and his face assumes a familiar expression, one I used to hate. Panic and neediness etch themselves into the crease between his eyebrows. "You have to understand. Who else will? No one else was there. If you don't understand, then what did I do it all for? What have the last ten years been about?"

"Hey, I'm sorry. I didn't mean it like that. Come here." I flip onto my back and he curls around me like a baby. His breathing slows to a light snore but I stay wide awake.

Rex thinks that the talk we must one day have with Alice is the last hurdle he needs to leap before he can relax and resume his life. He thinks it's the last loose end we need to tie up. Of course, he is wrong. There is another, greater secret that only I keep. The real question is not shall we tell her, but should I tell him?

8

BIBA DIDN'T COME IN through the front door but emerged from the back garden as the children had. I wondered if she'd been lurking in the underground rooms all this time, but the bag under her arm and the lick of perspiration on her forehead suggested otherwise. I tried not to make my delight too obvious.

"Karen! I'm glad you're here," she said, as though I had kept an appointment. She kissed me hello on the lips, opened the fridge door, and then shut it again without really looking at its contents. "Help yourself to whatever. *Mi casa, su casa* . . . that's Spanish, that is," she said with a wink in her voice before eyeing the pastry that Nina was working on. "What are you making? How many are we for dinner tonight? Me, you, Rex, Karen, the kids . . ." She flicked a finger up with each name so that her hand was splayed like a fan stripped of its lace or paper. "Are Tris and Jo around?" Nina nodded.

My eyes were dragged to the pavement outside by the sight and sound of a pair of scuffed brogues shuffling up the outside steps. I'd met him just once, but I knew that walk, feet barely breaking contact with the ground, could only belong to Rex. He shambled about overhead for a bit before creaking his way downstairs. He appeared in the doorway in a light gray shirt and faded denims, corner shop bags the color of cornflowers slicing into his palms.

"What have I said about the front door?" he said to the whole room. "It was swinging wide open when I got home. Anyone could walk in."

"Anyone did," said Biba, nodding at me.

"Hello, Karen," said Rex, putting the shopping bags on the one clear patch on the counter and flexing his hands. "Nice to see you again."

He crossed the kitchen and started cleaning up after Nina, heaping mismatched dishes and silverware into a white sink big enough to bathe a toddler in and old and battered enough to be fashionable again. Occasionally he plucked a glittering mineral from the suds and consigned it to the box containing Nina's jewelry-making apparatus.

Biba foraged in the bags, opening a round wrap of goat cheese and eating it straight from the packet, and Rex reached over and smacked her on the wrist as though she were one of Nina's children. She smirked and began to load the fridge with the wine, milk, olives, and butter he'd bought. She had a white crumb of cheese on the middle of her bottom lip. I watched her fiddle with the ancient Pye radio, a black brick with a perforated wooden fascia, flecked with paint from some decades-old redecoration. The aerial had long ago ceased to extend fully. She chased through all the stations, finally achieving a fugitive and fizzing reception of Radio One. The evening's soundtrack taken care of, she picked a lemon from the fruit bowl and threw it across the room over my head. I followed its arc with my eyes. Tris, emerging through the doorway, caught it in his fist. "Two for a fiver!" said Jo, presenting a pair of cheap-looking screw-top bottles of Merlot to Nina, who was evidently in charge of drink as well as food. "It's gonna taste like piss, but it'll get you where you want to be. Carrie, isn't it? Nice to see you again."

"Karen," I said, but she was already facing Rex.

"The front door was open again, by the way," she told him.

"You've really got to get it fixed." Rex put his head, heavy with the weight of this domestic chore, in his sudsy hands.

Tris stood in the middle of the room like a displaced tree, solid and sun-gnarled, and the children used him as a climbing frame. He grinned as a sandal slapped his left temple and hauled Inigo up above his head before depositing the little boy on the table. In the sober light of the early evening, the couple was less alike than I had thought: Jo's features were more delicate than his and her skin was a uniform pale gold. The strands of her hair that weren't bound and matted into dreadlocks were fine and blond. Tris was ruddy, his tan not a tan at all but rather thousands of joined-up freckles, and his hair was reddish and curly at the roots. It was their clothes and mannerisms that were identical and made them such an extraordinary couple. They finished each other's sentences like twins and mirrored each other's gestures. They were always touching and kissing, as though breaking contact between hands or lips would sever some invisible oxygen supply, but there was nothing overt or embarrassing about this. You could sit with them and listen and watch for hours but never feel like a voyeur.

"So this is everyone," said Biba, looking around the table and lingering on me for longer than anyone else. "Our whole menagerie." Behind us, Nina held a wooden salad bowl out to Rex and he placed it in the center of the table without looking at her. The ex-lovers shared the same intimate, comfortable, utterly desireless body language as my parents. I peered into the hollow and discreetly removed a long, curly hair that had wrapped itself around a crescent of tomato.

"How did you and Tris come to live here?" I said to Jo, eager to piece together this funny little family.

"We met Biba in the woods," Jo answered me with a mouth full of bread. "It started with a row, actually. We're conservation volunteers, we help to clean all the crap out of the woods, help out with reforesting and things like that. We're very pro–zero trace—it's a movement among climbers, ramblers, mountaineers, people who are into wildlife—do you know what it is?"

Tris took up the thread.

"It means that you leave nothing behind you when you're in the natural environment, although we practice it in the built environment too." He leaned forward, a lock of hair springing free from the knot on top of his head and swaying alongside his face. "You can't leave any litter, obviously, but nothing else that might disrupt the biodiversity of a particular environment. Like, you can't even leave a seed from your apple core. And so when we came across Miss Capel leaving cigarette butts on the ground we had to give her a lecture . . ."

Biba groaned and hid behind her hands in a pantomime of shame.

". . . and the short story is that she felt so guilty, she asked us to come and live here," finished Jo.

The main dish was placed unceremoniously in the middle of the table, a rich spinach mix under layers of phyllo pastry. I could tell it was undercooked just from looking at it. "What's tonight's culinary delight?" asked Tris.

I answered for Nina. "It's spanakopita, it's Greek."

"Well done," said Nina, and then to the others, "She's a traveler, like me."

Jo made a face. "It's a bit raw."

"It's a bit salty," added Biba.

"Piss off," said Nina affectionately, to the delight of her children.

While the rest of us sat, Rex scurried about getting glasses for the wine. When my drink was poured, little bubbles of dishwashing liquid frothed at the rim, and when I turned the glass around to drink from the other side of the lip it had a chip in it. Gentle probing with the tip of my tongue judged that the chip had been worn smooth enough to drink from. My mother would have spotted this career-ending flaw in the glass while it was still a fissure invisible to most naked eyes and thrown it away. I tried not to hear her voice lecturing me about the bacteria that hide in cracks, and let my breadcrumbs join the powder that settled in the splits and crevices of the tabletop. There was still plenty of food to pick at long after dinner was over.

"We're off soon, though," said Jo to me. No one else looked up so I deduced that news of their impending departure had already been broken to the rest of the household. "Most of our lot have gone traveling for the summer, and me and Tris are going to work for a friend of his in Devon. A friend of ours has bought a small farm there, and he's setting up a kind of commune, like an experiment to see if we can live off the land. There's no real point in being in London in the summertime, is there? All that crap in the air. Smog. Fucks up your lungs." She punctuated this last sentence with a long drag on a hand-rolled cigarette. If Biba had done that, I thought, it would have been with a nod to the juxtaposition of actions and words, but the irony was lost on sincere, solemn Jo. "We're going to stay in a yurt," she carried on. "It's like a Turkish tent and they're basically as good as a house. There's going to be loads of us. You should come!"

I was taken aback by the invitation, although I didn't doubt its sincerity. I don't think that Jo had mistaken my reticence for assent, or that she recognized me as a particularly kindred spirit. She was just one of those rare people able to offer a genuine welcome to any stranger into wherever she happened to call home that month. I turned down the invitation with a silent smile that I tried to hold in place as I felt a pressing on the small of my back. Inigo had placed an oily green hand on my waist and left a lurid smeared handprint on my white tank top.

"Ummmm," pointed Gaia. "Look at the lady."

"It's fine," I said, jumping to the sink and rinsing it under the tap.

"I'll need to wash that in hot water to get the stains out." Rex clearly occupied the role of household washerwoman. "I can't do that while you're wearing it."

"Well, I can hardly sit here in my bra," I said. "Don't worry. I'll sort it when I get home."

But Biba had other ideas. "To the wardrobe!" she said, leaping up from the table, knocking over an empty glass. There was a collective groan.

"Good luck, Karen," said Jo, while Tris gave me a mock-solemn farewell salute. "Be careful not to go too far into it in case you end up in Narnia."

It was dark now, and when Biba flicked on the landing light a trio of moths woke suddenly and began to dance a suicidal tango around the swinging naked bulb. A wide scarlet runner was precariously held in place with stair-rods on most of the steps; Biba walked this red carpet with the poise of a Best Actress nominee on Oscar night.

The first floor had been the epicenter of the party. I glanced through the living room door and saw that either the postparty cleanup had been abandoned, or a new party had started: mottled wineglasses and beer cans overflowing with cigarette butts jostled for space on a coffee table. The crumbling sash windows that lit every landing were home to forlorn little window boxes containing shriveled and dusty herbs. "Do you know what all the rooms are called?" she asked me. "They all have their own names. This is the Velvet Room because all the furniture used to be velvet when we were little, although it's a bit bald and slimy now. The bit where you come in is the Black and White Hall, and where Nina and the kids sleep are the Kitchen Bedroom and the Garden Room." We stopped on the second floor where the carpet was blue with peach flowers. "That's Rex's room," said Biba, jabbing her thumb toward a closed door. "Up there"—I followed her eyes up a farther, smaller staircase with woodchip-papered walls that sloped up into the eaves of the house—"is where Tris and Jo live, in Attic

One. There's an Attic Two as well, but it's full of junk. And *this* is mine."

She shouldered the door opposite Rex's room and carved an arc of visible carpet in the mulch of multicolored clothes that blocked the threshold and covered the entire floor. It was less bedroom than wardrobe: the half-dressed mattress resting on a tatty bed frame against the far wall seemed to be an afterthought. The remaining space was filled with rails, drawers, cupboards full of clothes, clashing colors and fabrics tangled, writhing and competing for her attention. You could tell these costumes had been scavenged from flea markets, sales, friends, and thrift stores. A 1950s gas station assistant's uniform customized to make a minidress hung in the window, blocking the light. There were rows and piles of shoes, boots, and sneakers, in pairs but more frequently alone, none of which, I supposed, was molded to Biba's feet but described the footprints of their previous owners. She had disappeared behind an overflowing tallboy, pulling clothes out of its tiny drawers like a magician pulling scarves out of a hat.

"*Mi* wardrobe, *tu* wardrobe. What about this for you?" She proffered a floral printed tea dress in all the wrong shades of pink and brown. It was unironed and hailed from a time when clothes needed to be pressed, and it smelled musty and essential, like Biba herself. I turned my back on her while I changed, surprised and delighted to find that it fit me perfectly. In Biba's borrowed dress I felt more interesting and vital: like the dress, I felt elegantly rumpled, as though each imperfection had an interesting story behind it. I felt more like the kind of person who belonged in this house.

"You look lovely," she said. "I want to get changed now, too." She held up a backless green dress studded with rhinestones.

"Isn't that a bit dramatic just for wearing around the house?"

Biba tutted. "If I waited for a proper occasion to get dressed up I'd never wear half of these clothes. Put on the clothes and you make things happen to match them. It doesn't work the other way around." She hoisted her arms over her head the way a child does when taking off a sweater, crossing her arms at the wrists and stripping herself with one swift pull. She was naked beneath her sundress. For a second my eyes were rooted to the unexpected swell of her breasts and the scrub of dark hair between two bony hips. I turned my back to her and studied my part in the mirror. I could still see her naked, this time from behind, as she shook out the petticoat that hung inside the dress.

"I'm so glad you came to find me. I was dreading another night in this house with Rex mooning over the children."

"I think you're lucky," I said. "I've had more fun here in two nights than I have in three years at home."

"Now that was spoken like someone who lives with a boyfriend," she asked. "Do you?"

"I haven't got a boyfriend, just an ex," I said happily. "He dumped me last week after three years together."

"Oh, you poor darling. Did he break your heart?"

"Actually, no, he didn't, which was a bit of a blow to his ego."

Biba laughed. "I've never really had a boyfriend, you know," she said.

"What? How come?" I managed to bite back the obvious line about someone as beautiful as her and held my breath in anticipation of her reply.

"I've had lots of flings, but nothing you could really call a relationship. It just always fizzles out. I've always been massively in awe of anyone who can make a go of those things."

"Maybe you just haven't met the right man."

"Maybe," she agreed.

I turned slowly to find her dressed and standing by the window, where the pane of glass was half-obscured by a diaphanous peach evening gown, probably a corporate wife's best dinner party outfit from the summer we were both born. She slid her hand into the wide chiffon trumpet of its sleeve and her flesh melted into soft focus. "Come on," she said. "Let's get out of here." She shoved the window sash upward violently. Flakes of paint flew into the air and floated like snowflakes down to the clothes pooled at her feet. She sat on the second-floor ledge with her back to me and her hands resting on the sill, the blackness of the garden and the wood close enough for her to touch. Then she jumped and was gone.

"Biba!" I negotiated the hazardous floor in seconds, sticking my neck out of the window, needing and not wanting to look down. The top of her head was inches beneath my chin.

"Gotcha," she said. She stood on a balcony missing its railings that jutted out from the wall like a small stone diving board.

"For fuck's sake!" I said.

"I'm sorry, I never can resist that." She jumped down onto the terrace below, ridiculously sure-footed in flip-flops. "Careful. It's tricky the first time you do it."

I landed heavily and scrambled after her across the veranda and down the steel spiral staircase that led down into the garden. The space was half-lit by Biba's bedroom window, making the darker, denser plants bleed into the background. The only visible landmark was the arc of lavender bushes that divided the garden in two diagonally: even in the dark, they gave off a blue haze that I could see as well as smell.

I turned back to face the house and saw the basement level from the back. Another set of French windows gave onto a bedroom, which must have led in turn into the kitchen. So that was how everyone was getting in and out. Gaia sat in the open doorway.

Biba held out her arms for a kiss. "Will you be a good girl and tell Mummy that we've gone for a walk?" Gaia waddled off purposefully. "Quick, while she's not looking," said Biba, shoving me toward the fence. "I don't want her to know this is here. Fucking . . . can you imagine? If she goes through it Nina will *kill* me."

She lifted a curtain of ivy to reveal a two-plank gap in the fence that divided the garden from the wood, and we climbed into the most absolute darkness I have ever known in London. The lights of the house were extinguished and it took a few minutes' hard blinking before I could make out the branches and trunks. The forest floor remained unknowable to me but presented no obstacle to Biba. I stumbled blindly, trying to copy Biba's rapid and deft footfalls but tripping on roots and sliding on moss.

"Trust me," said Biba, giving me her hand. "Nobody knows this wood better than me and Rex. I've been running through it all my life. They never do anything to this wood, it's a nature reserve, so once you know the way to go it never changes."

Twigs cracked and branches sprang into my face as she pulled me at speed through the trees, down into the wood. She flicked her lighter on, but the orange flame that lit up her face in a ghoulish chiaroscuro only deepened the darkness that swirled around my feet like quicksand. I wanted to tell her I was frightened but settled for the more acceptable, "This is freaking me out."

"I'm sorry," she said, coming to a stop. "I can't remember the first time I came here, so I don't know what it's like for new people. Look, we're nearly on the path." I felt the ground become more even and the branches that poked their fingers into my eyes part and withdraw. A sharp tug on my wrist sent me wheeling around to my right and I blinked as though a switch had suddenly been thrown.

The clearing we were in was surrounded by upward-sloping woodland. Silver light shone down on a child's round wading pool, dry and empty apart from a few scuffed leaves. The turquoise paint in the base of the pool had faded and peeled but it made a mirror for the full moon, which hung directly above, a perfect circle the color of champagne, just for us.

"The heart of the wood," she announced, swaggering into the center of the circle and sinking to a cross-legged squat. She pulled a joint from behind her ear and ran it under her nose.

"It's lovely," I said. "It's like something from a storybook."

"Henry VIII used to hunt here," she said. "Well, not in the wading pool, obviously, although there is a rumor that Elizabeth I splashed about here as a toddler. This is part of the ancient wild-wood that used to cover the whole of England. It's technically the same wood as the New Forest. Just with a few hundred miles of buildings in between. There's only this and a couple of other forests left of it in London. This is the best one, though. And no one loves it more than I do."

She ignited her lighter again, this time to light her joint. The flame missed its target as her coordination faltered and a shower of sparks rained down in my direction. She was drunker than I was, and I was very drunk: her clear voice had grown cloudy, like glass that has been in a dishwasher too many times. I lay back next to her, my hot skin making grateful contact with the cool ground.

"The first show I was ever in was held down here," she said. "A school play. We did Hansel and Gretel. In the round. I was Gretel, obviously. You can imagine how excited I was, doing it in my back garden. I was so desperate for my mum and dad to get good seats that I made them sit on that bench there from noon. The play didn't start till two. And then when I went on . . . everything changed."

"What?" I said, picturing her parents spontaneously combusting, or a light aircraft crashing onto the bench.

"I found out that I was an actress," she said, as though she were telling me about the day the doctor told her she had cancer. My playful swat missed her by a hand span. "It'd be a great place to fuck, out here. I made a bet with Rex about it. I said first one to do it out here gets dinner at the restaurant of their choice."

"Who won?" I said.

"No one yet," she said, wrinkling her nose as if puzzled by this. She lit the joint, took a deep drag, and stretched out next to me. We lay back, moonbathing in silence. The heat of her body warmed the left-hand side of mine and when she passed me the joint our fingers touched. I coughed before I had even put it to my lips.

"If you're not used to it, just go easy."

"Who says I'm not used to it?" I said. "For all you know, I've got a long-term crack habit."

"You haven't, though, have you?" she said.

"No," I admitted. She held me in her gaze and suspended me in time. I broke eye contact and turned my attention to the ember between my fingers. I inhaled deeply, filling my lungs with smoke as rich and heavy as red wine. As I exhaled, the stars pricked into sharper focus and I let out a hoot of exhilaration that turned into irrepressible, infectious laughter; tears bunched Biba's eyelashes and she drew her knees up to her chest as she rocked with silent giggles. A swimming, stoned lust flooded my body. I wanted to crawl all over her. I wanted to be closer to her than her makeup. A pulse hammered between my legs and my heart no longer beat but vibrated. I rolled onto my side, a clumsy and intoxicated prelude to a kiss. A rush of vertigo paralyzed me, my center of gravity swung suddenly and violently forward, and I passed out facedown on the floor of the pool.

When I was shaken awake a couple of hours later, a cloud had covered the moon and Rex was standing over us with a flashlight and a look of disappointment. We followed his beam the long way home: a pebbled and even path that held few surprises and led directly to the sofa he had made up into a bed for me. As I surrendered to sleep for the second time that night I was already grateful, with a relief as overwhelming as sexual release, that my attempt to consummate this friendship had failed, although I couldn't tell if it was rejection or reciprocation I had had a lucky escape from.

It wasn't until years later that I realized it wasn't about sex. It was affection and confusion, the thrill of peer acceptance at last. It was a desire to communicate something that I couldn't express in any language. But how could I have known it then? I didn't know anything about desire. That was still to come; the night when Rex changed everything was still weeks away. He finished something that was started that night, when I lay with my best friend in an empty pool in the middle of history, puddled in moonlight and stupid with love.

9

IT'S A DRY AND sunny day, so I bike to the shops. Usually I pace myself on this route, not because it's particularly dangerous but because Alice is behind me and I try to lead by example. Today I freewheel down the shallow hill, legs sticking out on either side of the pedals, hair free of my helmet and combed out by the wind. The level Suffolk countryside has been stripped of leaves and the bare branches make it seem flatter and more endless than ever. This road stretches as far as the eye can see and the temptation is to keep pedaling over the horizon and never stop. I know people who did that. Nina did it all the time. Why shouldn't I? If I go, Rex and Alice will still have each other. I know I won't do it, not really. It's just a weird compulsion—the same crazy instinct that makes you want to leap off a cliff when you stand on its edge.

The road forks in front of me and muscle memory or duty or both of these things turns the handlebars left. This curve I take with my eyes closed, knowing the road well enough to take this little risk. When I open them on the other side of the bend I see the straggle of little red houses and street signs that mark the village boundary.

In the small supermarket I fill a basket with groceries and, as an afterthought, a bottle of sparkling wine. While we were apart I barely drank at all, and certainly never alone. Now, just a week after Rex came home, sharing a bottle of wine with him—white, of course—is as much a part of our nightly routine as it was the first summer we spent together. I know that he has missed it desperately. Not just the alcohol but the privilege and the freedom to decide for himself when his day is at an end and to drink in silence or companionship in a home of his own. I drink very differently now. Wine then was usually something I drank to chase pleasure, to incite adventure and then to prolong those moments when they happened. Now it's something I do to get me through the night. We never get through more than one bottle an evening, or at least we have not done so yet.

I meet Dawn Saunders at the deli counter. Dawn lives in one of the huge houses on Aldeburgh Road and is never knowingly underdressed. Although her husband runs one of the largest employment agencies in the southeast, she has not worked since the day she ceased to be his employee and became his wife. Today she's in white boot-cut trousers and a taupe wrap top that skims her tidy curves. Her daughter Sophie is in Alice's class at school, although they will separate next year when Dawn sends her child to the large private school farther up the coast and Alice goes to the local comprehensive. Dawn is an acquaintance but if anyone local asked me I suppose I would call her my friend. We air kiss once, right cheeks not quite touching, and she leans over and peers into my basket.

"Champagne, eh?" she says. It's Prosecco, but I don't correct her. Dawn's voice has the local rounded whine. Certainly her children do not sound like she does, the result of Saturday morning elocution lessons disguised as drama classes. I often wonder why, when she has spent so much of her husband's money on decorating her house and body, she hasn't tried to modify her own speech. In her situation, it would be the first thing I would tackle. "What's the celebration?"

I have remained deliberately enigmatic on the whereabouts of Alice's father. Some people believe I am a widow, while others believe that his identity is unknown. Telling Dawn about our change in circumstances is tantamount to sticking a notice to that effect on the community bulletin board that dominates the wall behind the cash registers.

"Alice's dad has come back to live with us." Her mouth circles and her eyes stand out, making her look like the trout on the slab behind her. "We've decided to give it another go," I say.

"That's fabulous, Karen," she says, and touches my forearm with a recently manicured hand. Three diamond rings, engagement, wedding, and eternity, weigh heavily on her ring finger. "It'll be so good for Alice to have a father around. We must throw a dinner party to welcome him to the community."

I think of the last dinner party Rex and I attended together, the impromptu supper cooked by Nina and attended by Biba, Tris, and Jo. Dawn's gathering will be formal and stilted, and the talk will be not of art and travel and love but of house prices and school fees and reality TV shows—until the subject of Rex's absence is subtly, tactfully broached. It is time, I suppose, that we came up with a story.

By the time I come home, it is apparent that dinner preparations have begun without me. Alice and Rex are elbows deep in a mixing bowl, a recipe book curling on the table before them. Flour clings to every surface in the kitchen and eggshells carpet the floor.

"What are you making?" I say.

"A quiche," says Rex. There is a smear of dough on his nose and his hair sticks straight up like egg white whipped into a peak. "It was supposed to be a surprise."

"Yeah, well, it was supposed to take twenty minutes," says Alice, her tone and her folded arms laying the blame entirely on her father. "We've been here for nearly an hour and it's still all lumpy. I can't make it all nice like you get it."

"It's under control," says Rex. "Come on, Alice. We can do this." His cuff is dangling into the mixture. Alice tuts and begins to roll it up for him. He pulls away, but not in time.

"What happened here?" she says, holding up his wrist and twisting it to expose the hairless white flesh on the inside of his forearm. The skin is puckered and pocked with scars. How did I fail to notice them last night?

"I got splashed with hot fat," he says, hastily rolling down his sleeve. "Occupational hazard of working in the prison kitchen."

"I thought you worked in the library," I say. He has pulled his cuff down to his knuckles.

"Oh, I only did the one shift," he replies, and looks away.

"You can totally tell," says Alice. "I'm not being rude, right, but I think I'll cook with Mum from now on."

I do not get another chance to examine his arm until he is asleep, his lanky form curled into a fetal position as though he is afraid to take up too much space. By the light of my bedside lamp it is obvious that the tiny craters of pink shiny skin are too circular, too regular to be the result of an accident. He stirs in his sleep as I pull up his T-shirt. There is another scar on his chest, three more on his back. The shape is familiar: I have seen something like it before. Suddenly I recall a drunken Biba grinding out a cigarette on the leather arm of a chair and drop Rex's arm so suddenly I am surprised he does not wake. Some of the burns are pale and faded while others are deep and red, suggesting that people used his flesh to extinguish their cigarettes more than once, that it was a regular occurrence over months or perhaps years. I feel the familiar, futile guilt at my failure to protect him while he was inside, and my resolve to defend him now that he is outside grows stronger. I curve my arm around his sleeping form.

"Oh, my poor baby," I whisper. "What did they do to you in there?"

***

Biba gripped the rim of the sink with her arms and swung her body up so that it was perched on the edge. "What do you want to do today?"

"I've got to head back." Emma had called a house meeting, and I wanted to cross London on the relatively clear midday roads. Biba turned the corners of her mouth down and swung her leg in front of her in a lazy kick aimed at no one in particular.

"Oh," she said. "I'll miss you."

"I'll leave my number," I said. "Call me whenever you want. Have you got a pen?" Biba scrabbled in the silverware drawer and produced a stub of black eyeliner. I dictated the number to her: she scribbled it on the wall next to the mounted telephone, doodling a star and the letter *K* next to the seven digits. It stayed there for the rest of the summer, smudged but legible. Rex has since told me that he used the minutes between my leaving the house and his arrest to wipe it from the wall.

"There. Even *I* can't lose it now. I'll walk you to the Tube."

There was nothing but twenty or so houses between Biba's front door and the entrance to Highgate Tube station, but she managed to steer me into a café before I even realized that I had made a detour. Somehow she had got me to cross Archway Road without my noticing. She ordered two coffees, which we drank from polystyrene cups, sitting gingerly on rickety aluminum chairs that wore a patina of North London smog. The café was placed directly opposite another café, the Woodman pub, a bus stop, and the Archway Road entrance to the Tube station, and afforded a perfect opportunity for people watching.

"See that couple across the road?" said Biba, pointing to a middle-aged man and woman at the bus stop. They were kissing passionately like teenagers. His hands were in her graying hair, and her bag lolled open at her feet. The public display of affection was at odds with the tasteful and muted autumn colors of their clothing. "How long do you think they've been together?"

"They're very new," I said. "That's not normal at their age."

"They're having an affair," she deduced.

"They're not having a very discreet one, snogging at the forty-three bus stop," I said.

"They're not local," she said authoritatively, as the couple made a hand-in-hand dash across three lanes of traffic and disappeared into another café a few doors down. "They only come up here because they don't know anyone in this neighborhood."

Some people say, "Oh, I can sit in a café for hours and watch the world go by," but they don't mean it: they've usually got a book on the go, or a paper on their lap, or these days, a cell phone in their hand. But Biba was like me: she could happily pass entire days people watching. I had never met anyone who shared my enthusiasm for the position of bystander before, although her capacity for imaginative conjecture impressed even me. Simon alone had noticed my voyeuristic tendencies and had remarked that if I had gone to a decent school as a child, someone would have pointed out to me that it was rude to stare, but that he supposed it was too late now. Claire, Emma, and Sarah had no need to people-watch: inseparable at all times, the other girls had never gone anywhere without one another and spent their time turning toward one another in a kind of never-ending triangle of reflected interest and affirmation. My parents had noticed my love of loitering in cafés but had identified it as a strange continental habit I had picked up, like bottled water. Of course, Biba and I had slightly different motivations. Mine were more by default than by design. If you are the kind of person other people tend not to notice, you naturally become a spectator. This tendency to voyeurism had been compounded by spending the last few years constantly showing up in new countries knowing nobody, hanging around at airports and in the strange corridors of foreign hostels and universities. Not only is it an excellent way to pass the time, it helps you grasp the idioms and gestures that make the difference between the schoolgirl linguist and the mother-tongue speaker.

Biba too observed with a view to imitation: her desire to be a better actress was not too far from the surface of anything she did, and passersby were potential case studies for future roles. I'd often catch her repeating phrases under her breath that "characters" had just uttered. She believed that any serious actress must also be a kind of anthropologist, but she was more of an anthrophile, with a genuine interest in other people that went beyond her desire to master voices and mannerisms. She was drawn not to those like herself, whose personalities were a full-frontal assault, but to those who slunk and skulked and made you work to guess their stories. I began to share her conviction that even the mousiest of passersby squirreled away colorful backstories, perhaps because her own past was a whirlpool of chaos and mystery.

By the time I finally pried myself away from the café and began my homeward journey, the unsupple muscles of my cheeks ached from hours of laughter. We had surmised about several other people, including the waitress from the café, three single men enjoying early pints in separate windows of the pub, a heavily pregnant woman carrying a pumpkin, and an elderly woman who, we decided, might have once been a nun but left the convent for a love affair that turned sour. To my delight, the couple from the bus stop appeared behind me on the descending escalator, bickering about whether it was quicker to get to London Bridge by Tube or bus. I gave up a silent prayer of thanks for my luck when they got on the same southbound train as me. They intrigued me: they kissed like illicit lovers but argued like an established couple. I sat opposite them, invisible, determined to solve the mystery of their relationship and save their story for Biba.

I let myself into an empty house that smelled of pine air freshener, a chemical tang as unlike a real pine forest as plastic is unlike wood. It was my turn to cook: the fridge was full of wine, two baskets of mushrooms, and a cellophane pillow of spinach. Two peeling shallots rolled together in the salad compartment, the only unpackaged food in the house. I checked the freezer: sure enough, there was an ice tray filled with frozen yellow blocks. Bottles of wine frequently went unfinished here, and Sarah, who could not bear waste and had done a cookery course before working as a chalet girl on her year abroad, would freeze them for use in the elaborate recipes she alone could be bothered to follow. I couldn't imagine this happening in Queenswood Lane. There, bottles would be drained or, if not, filled with cigarette butts or used as candlesticks while the inch of wine at the bottom clotted and turned to vinegar. I flexed the tray and four cubes shot out onto the counter, their crackled, bubbled, and uneven texture telling me that in their liquid lives they had been champagne. What kind of people save champagne for cooking, I wondered?

The gleaming tiled walls of the well-appointed kitchen seemed to lurch and squeeze in on me, giving me a sense of anger and claustrophobia. The checked-off cooking rotation sneered at me from the wall. This wasn't what a student kitchen was supposed to look like—pine units with a dark brown work surface and integrated appliances. I wasn't too far gone to recognize the surge of anger and panic the ice cubes triggered as entirely irrational, but this realization didn't diminish it. I now knew I should have spent the last few years toughening up my immune system in a sprawling, crawling kitchen like the one in Biba's basement. I was coming to the end of four years that were supposed to be about irresponsibility and squalor, and I had spent it living in the kind of house my parents still aspired to own.

When Sarah had first invited me to share this house, I had been so flattered and proud and excited. I soaked up the girls' stories about childhood holidays in their parents' *gîtes* in Provence. I was thrilled that finally I was living with people who actually came from somewhere: big houses in villages with greens rather than houses surrounded by houses surrounded by houses surrounded by a ring road. Now that I had met Biba, with her crumbling urban castle and her chaotic glamour, my housemates seemed unbearably generic. They didn't come from somewhere amazing at all. They just came from a different kind of nowhere from mine, one with more money and riding lessons. I was angry at myself for not realizing this sooner, and angry at them for not being Biba. I took my resentment out on the shallots, chopping them finer than any food processor. By the time the girls came home I was able to smile my usual hello to show that nothing had changed.

"The dirty stay-out is back!" said Emma, peering into my pan. "That looks gorgeous."

Claire, with a glance down at her concave stomach, said, "Don't add any Parmesan to mine, thanks, hon."

Sarah laid out four wineglasses.

"Might as well have a glass of vino with dinner tonight, to celebrate," she said.

I realized that they had taken their last exams today and immediately thought of the party I would have with the Capels when my own finals were out of the way.

"How did you get on?" I asked, adding risotto rice to the pan and stepping back from the buttery steam cloud that burst into my face.

"No idea," said Emma. "And there's no point worrying about it now. Besides, I'm more interested in hearing about your new man." She flicked me on the leg with a dishtowel and I shrugged away from her, turning my attention back toward the pan to hide my blush.

At dinner, I drank faster than everyone else. It was a good wine, creamy and light, and perfect with risotto, but I couldn't savor it. I had already got used to guzzling wine when I was around Biba, not just to keep up with her but also to stem the adrenaline that she injected into me. Now, drinking quickly dissolved a different kind of tension, that of boredom and resentment and that strange energy in the house that should have ended with the last exam. I regarded my old friends as though they were strangers and they looked at me with new eyes, too, so that I couldn't help but wonder if I looked as foolish and giddy to them as I felt. After the first glass I felt relaxed enough to break the silence around the table.

"So," I said, tipping back the glass a little too quickly and conscious of the trickle that ran down my chin. "Why do we need to have a house meeting? Is everything okay?" I addressed all three of them at once. Somehow I knew that it wasn't a meeting so much as an interview, with the three of them forming a panel who knew more about the outcome than I did.

"We were just wondering," said Sarah. "What are you going to do with your summer, Karen?"

As I didn't know their agenda, there was no point in answering other than honestly.

"Oh. I'm not sure. I won't be traveling this year, I don't think." (I can't leave her.) "I've got to stay near college for my results, then probably apply for funding for a doctorate. Um, get work experience? I haven't really decided."

"The thing is . . ." Sarah looked down at her lap. "The thing is, Charlie's dad has invested in this château near Perpignan and there's work for us in the vineyard. Like a mini year abroad before we get proper careers. And he's asked Claire and Emma and Rob and Dan too."

In the short second I spent waiting for my name to be added to the list, I tried to think of a way to reject the offer. But excuses were not going to be necessary.

"And . . . God, this is really awkward," said Sarah. Her hands fluttered and tapped on her glass without the remote control to busy them. "Simon's going to be there too." The girls shot a triangle of secret looks at each other. "With his new girlfriend. I'm really sorry. But he's Charlie's friend, and I haven't really got much say in it. If it really bothers you . . ." They were all watching me now, waiting for my reaction.

"Oh," I said, relieved and insulted at the same time. Then I forced a smile. "I don't mind at all about Simon. Really, I don't. You're welcome to him." I really *didn't* mind about Simon, although I minded that they had known about this girlfriend, probably even while Simon and I were still a couple. The realization stung, and I understood that I still valued their friendship more than I had thought. "What's her name?" I asked, as brightly as I could.

"Isabel," said Claire. A smothering hush followed her name,

during which I wondered where I would live while the others were in France.

"I suppose," said Emma, "that you don't mind about Simon having someone new now that you've got a new secret *lover* of your own." She drew out the last syllable of the word *lover* and rolled the *r.* I appreciated her stab at humor, but couldn't return it. She was near enough to the truth to summon the blood to my cheeks.

"I told you, it isn't a new boyfriend." I twirled my glass, wishing there was more to drink.

"There's another thing," Sarah went on. "You'd be doing me a favor if you stayed here for the summer. I mean, in the autumn when we come back I'm probably going to just move in here with Charlie or something, but you can have the house rent-free over the summer." It was her way of apologizing, I knew. "And I know that Dad would be happy if there was someone keeping an eye on things." One of Sarah's father's fixations was that people don't burgle houses when people are in them, when of course they just do it far more violently.

The surge of happiness that welled up within me felt inappropriate and I tried to conceal it. A whole summer to come and go between here and Highgate, with no one to keep tabs on me and two months' rent burning a hole in my pocket.

"Okay . . ." I agreed. "When are you off?"

"Yes, that's the last thing," said Sarah. "We're off next week."

"Next *week*!" I heard myself squeak. "But that's before you've even got your results!" I said.

"You can open them for us, we'll call you from France," said Sarah.

"Yeah." Emma spoke now. "You can tell us all about your First while we're notching up our Two Twos and resigning ourselves to lives as au pairs or teachers."

"Or we could just get married," said Claire.

"Yes . . ." said Sarah.

They weren't joking.

Emma usually disappeared from the kitchen when her name wasn't on the list, and I knew that tonight's eagerness to help me clean up was partly to cushion the blow of this evening's news and part opportunity to interrogate me about the secret boyfriend she had fantasized into existence.

"Why don't you want us to meet him?" she wheedled. Steam billowed from the dishwasher into her face, making her upturned collar wilt.

"Because he doesn't exist!" I said.

"But you're staying out all night and you've got that look," said Emma. "That glow. You certainly never looked like that when you started going out with Simon."

"Perhaps it's the absence of Simon that's given me the glow."

"That's understandable." Emma laughed. "I have to say, I'm not looking forward to sharing a house with the sound of his voice all summer. You got off lightly there. So, this new guy. Why are you keeping him a secret? Is he married?"

"No."

"A drug addict? A drug *dealer*?" She put down the cloth she was holding. "Oh my *God*, it's not one of your students, is it?"

"Jesus, Emma!"

"A lecturer? Is it Dr. Ali? He's rather lovely, I've always thought." I smiled. Of all of them, it would be Emma I would miss.

"What then? A murderer?" Her remark was throwaway and so was my reply.

"Yes, Emma. He's a serial killer, and the prison service has started to offer overnight stays for new girlfriends. I've told you: There. Is. No. Secret. Boyfriend."

I was spared further interrogation by the shrill of the telephone. Claire handed me the chunky white handset with the aerial already extended.

"It's for you," she said, looking pleased with herself. "It's a *man*. A man who isn't your dad." Even as I was wiping my hands down on the towel I could hear a tinny little voice calling my name.

I took the telephone and went up to my room before holding it to my ear. As I kicked the door closed behind me I could hear Emma's gleeful "I *told* you."

"Hello?" I said.

"Karen." It was Rex, his voice crackly and urgent. I pictured him sitting in the kitchen with the dirty telephone pressed to his face, losing a battle with the unruly curls of the cord. "I don't suppose Biba's with you, is she?"

"She doesn't know my address," I told him. That had been deliberate: I wanted to keep her out of my world almost as much as I wanted to keep myself in hers.

"Fuck!" he said, and I heard a scratch of unshaven chin against the receiver as he cradled it in his neck. "She's not there, Nina." A muffled conversation that I couldn't understand took place in Highgate and went on for longer than was polite.

"Rex!" I shouted into the receiver, after what felt like five minutes. "Rex!" He came back on the line.

"I'm sorry," he said, and there was a catch in his voice. "It's just that Nina's only just told us that she's leaving us to go traveling. B hasn't taken it too well and she . . ." He checked himself and bit back a word or phrase. "Never mind. Listen, if she gets in touch, will you tell her to call me? Literally the second you hear from her." He dictated the number to me and I wrote it on the flyleaf of my Spanish dictionary.

"I think you're overreacting a bit, but yes, I will. Okay, bye Rex."

I dropped the phone in my lap. Rex's hysterical overprotectiveness annoyed as well as puzzled me. Biba was twenty-one, and from what I had seen, more capable of looking after herself than he was.

I sprawled on my bed, finally alone to let the events of the last twenty-four hours sink in. My friendship with Biba was cemented; my home was mine alone for the summer. I could go to the gym as often as I wanted, safe in the knowledge Simon wouldn't be there. I could visit Biba every day: we would explore London together in a way I hadn't before, seeking out the parties and clubs I'd missed out on, spending what would have been my rent money on wine and taxis and drugs. I could take her shopping, buy her some new clothes. I would be intrigued to see what she would buy when she didn't have to forage through thrift stores for other people's cast-offs, and also curious to discover the kind of outfits I would put together for myself shopping under her tutelage. The phone on my lap shrilled out. I pressed the green button to answer.

"Karen, it's okay, she's back," Rex said, as though we had been partners in hysteria. "She's fine, she's here, she came back to me."

"Give me that," I heard in the background. There was a tussle for the telephone. When Biba's voice came on the line it was as cool and reassuring as a glass of water.

"I'm so sorry he did that," she said.

"Are you okay?"

"What? Yes, just really embarrassed. Fucking . . . Rex has called *literally* everyone I know. Nina leaving was a bit of a shock and I got a bit . . . het up. It's fine, though. Listen, we're having a leaving dinner for her on Thursday. Will you come?"

It was the evening before my German literature exam, a three-hour, hand-cramping paper on which 5 percent of my final results rested. I said yes.

After I folded the antenna back into the body of the telephone, I still wanted an excuse not to leave my room, and the digital clock on my bedside table gave me one: the green numbers told me that it was 8:05. If I called my parents now, the conversation would fall neatly into the gap between two soap operas that punctuated their week-day evenings. I pushed the usual numbers and there was the usual fuss as my father took possession of the downstairs telephone in the living room while my mother ran into the kitchen to talk to me on the extension. I sometimes wondered if, apart from when my father was at work, this was the only time they were ever in different rooms.

"I'm going to spend this summer in London," I told them. "I've been asked to do some tutoring in the languages department." It didn't occur to either of them that there would be no students to teach during the summer. It was the first time I had ever exploited their absolute ignorance of the university system and term times, and my guilt at doing so was alleviated by a kind of impatience with them for being such easy dupes. "Tutoring," said my mother. "My daughter, a lecturer! Well done, love. That's amazing." The ping of a kitchen timer summoned her away from the telephone and left me alone with my father.

"Karen, love, I worry about you," he said in the soft voice only my mother and I ever heard.

"I'm fine. I've got loads of work to do."

"That's the problem. You work all the time. You know your mother and I are very proud of you, you don't need to work any harder. If you need money, you can always ask us. You could have taken this summer off to just relax and do something for yourself."

The fact that this was exactly what I intended to do compounded my guilt.

"You'll be out in the world of work soon, and then you'll never have a long holiday like this again," he said. He cleared his throat. "You're only twenty, love. You're an old head on young shoulders, you always have been, but give yourself a break. Every young person should have one summer they look back on for the rest of their lives. Fall in love. Go and see some live music, have a proper holiday." I flopped forward onto my bed and steeled myself for another of my dad's homilies about the summer of '75, his last of freedom before my mother's pregnancy changed his life forever. He heard my sigh and changed his mind. "I'm just saying. There's no rush to work. Even me and your mum had a long hot summer."

I tried to imagine my parents being young, crazy in love, dancing in dirty houses, swallowing strange tablets from strange men, sick and dizzy with excitement with one foot on either side of the threshold of a new world. But I couldn't imagine their feelings or experiences having the depth or color of mine. They were just my parents; a young couple, the same age I was then, but with a baby on the way, and a mortgage and a lifetime of work and soap operas stretching out ahead of them. Mr. and Mrs. Everyman. People who come from nowhere.

The white car is outside the house for the third time this week. I had never seen it before Rex came home and I am not imagining it now. It is conspicuous by its cleanliness and its size. A white Nissan Micra, especially one so clean, is not the kind of car that people drive around here, where you can go for miles without encountering a single traffic light and the hazards are hairpin turns and mud and floods and slow-moving trucks that disgorge loose onions onto unsuspecting windshields. This is a boxy little car belonging to someone who drives in town, who prioritizes parking and fuel economy over horsepower and tire grip. I think that the figure in the driver's seat is a woman, although I cannot be sure. I do know that the silhouette is writing something down. The head is bent in concentration and occasionally I see a clipboard or file rest on the steering wheel while notes are made. If that's not proof it's a journalist, what is? He or she parks in a slightly different place every time, but that won't fool anyone. In the country, a new car is as reliable an indicator of an outsider as the stranger who walks into the village pub and hushes every table. The conclusion is inescapable that Rex is being watched, that we are being watched. What was that quote that Biba once used to tease Guy with when he had had too much to smoke and was convinced the drug squad had cameras in the woods? "Just because you're paranoid doesn't mean they're not out to get you."

It sounds stupid, but entire days go by when I forget that Rex is a convicted murderer. Men like him will almost always leave in their wake someone who wants to avenge a death, and Rex has two against his name. The circle of devastation fans out further than we can see. I can conjure only the known bereaved. I think for a moment of the children and try to calculate their ages now. What have they been told? Do they know everything or are they like

Alice, drip-fed details until they are judged old enough to know it all? They will not yet be independent enough to seek any real revenge, and neither are they old enough to drive. But there must be others touched by the deaths, others whose identities we could not begin to guess at. Or perhaps our persecutor is someone he met in prison? I can't see Rex deliberately offending anyone, but I know from TV and film that everyone has to side with someone on the inside and that it's often the weakest, most passive inmates who inadvertently choose the wrong protector. I have always kept Alice away from any films that depict life in jail and wonder if perhaps I should have avoided them myself.

Maybe someone followed us back from the prison. Perhaps there are people who do just that, who lurk outside the gates and follow people on to their new lives, waiting until the time is right to blackmail them. Who would blackmail us? We have nothing to give. This house is still heavily mortgaged, and unlike neighboring towns closer to the sea, this part of Suffolk is not so fashionable that I am sitting on a great deal of equity. If not blackmail, then we might be threatened with violence. That I know I could not bear. While it is not true to say that I have seen a lifetime of violence, it is true to say that I have seen enough violence to last me a lifetime. I had been protected from brutality, I had never seen blood that wasn't my own until that night.

Asking Rex if there is anyone with a grudge against him is not something I want to do, but I am far from relieved when Alice beats me to it.

"Will we be seeing any of your friends from prison?" she says over dinner one evening. She has made her mashed potatoes into a little cake and is feathering the surface with her fork. It's an attempt to look casual and disinterested but I know that she only loses her appetite and plays with her food when something is really worrying her.

"Friends?" says Rex, as though pronouncing a new word in a foreign language for the first time.

"Yes. Did you make any friends? Like in *The Shawshank Redemption*?"

"Where did you see that?" I snap. Even my parents, who bend most of my rules when she is in their care, carefully monitor what she is allowed to watch.

"At Sophie's," replies Alice. "She's got a TV with a built-in DVD player in her room. And she's got her ears pierced."

"I didn't really make any friends, no," says Rex. "Nobody that I'll be seeing again, anyway."

Alice suddenly becomes serious.

"What about enemies?" she asks. "Have you got any enemies who are coming after you?" There is a wobble in her voice and the tip of her nose has turned pink, always a sign that she is damming up tears. She frowns down at her food. She has lined up all her baked beans around the edge of her plate so that they look like a child's plastic necklace swimming in sauce.

"Why do you ask?" I say, trying not to let my tone become as sharp as my panic. "Has someone said something? Have you seen something? Tell me." Alice shakes her head and looks to Rex for reassurance.

"No one's coming after us," he says. "No one's out to get me. I'm home now. It's over."

"Promise?"

"Promise."

Rex's guarantee is good enough for Alice. She clears her plate and then steals a sausage from mine. I have lost my appetite.

Later, I do the dishes while Rex reads Alice a story. Before he came home, we had long abandoned the bedtime routine of turning back the sheets and being tucked into them, of storybooks and night lights, but they both seem to derive real comfort from this babyish ritual. I don't hear him creep up behind me over the rush of the tap, and when an arm encircles my waist, I flinch. The glass of wine that he was carrying in his other hand is flung back in his face, and when I turn around Pinot Grigio is dripping from his eyelashes.

"Hey," he says, wiping himself with a dishtowel, "it's only a glass of wine."

"Sorry." I am rigid with tension.

"What's happened to you, Karen?" he says, his hands unclawing my own. "You used to be so calm and comfortable and now you're all twitching curtains, snapping at Alice, jumping every time the phone rings . . ."

My reply is an inadequate and defensive shrug.

"I blame myself," he says. He pulls me close and I breathe in the wine that has soaked his shirt. "I did this to you. But I can make it all right again now. I'm home, I'm out. Don't you understand? It's over."

For him, for now, perhaps.

"I know how lucky I am," he says, and he pulls me even closer. "I will never, ever take you and Alice for granted. I'm going to get a job, and love you and protect you. Let me take the burden."

Exasperation swells my chest. Does he realize how hard it will be to get any kind of job with his background? He could not protect us even if he was capable, because to do that he would need to be armed with all the facts and I can never tell him everything. I do not mind being the family protector as long as I am left alone to do the job without interference from him. His rib cage expands and I think he's gearing up for another speech. I don't want to hear it. I am not in the mood for his useless words. I just want a drink. I break away from his arms knowing that it hurts him but still I pour another glass and drain it without turning away from the sink. As the wine melts into my veins, it becomes impossible not to voice my worst fears, if only to myself. Rex's conviction is spent and public. My own guilty verdict is a private one and my sentence one only I know about. Or is it? What if, despite all my efforts over the last ten years, someone has found out? Perhaps it is not Rex that they are chasing at all. Perhaps they are after me.

I BEGAN TO REGRET driving to Nina's party at the exact point it became futile to turn back and take the Tube. My rust-speckled, banana-yellow Fiat Panda had been a present from my parents on my seventeenth birthday and was far from new even then. In recent months it had begun to groan and huff like a little old man and the ground it covered had shrunk to a mile-wide radius between my house, Simon's place, and the tennis club. It showed its lack of training for our sudden marathon around the North Circular by short-circuiting the buttons that lowered the electric windows and air-locking me in the car. A traffic jam crawled me to a halt on a section of the road flanked by a kind of favela of boarded-up houses and corrugated iron lean-tos. Wembley Stadium's twin towers loomed large to my left, a row of lock-up garages squatting beneath them at the roadside. A young man with no shirt on began to smear gray, sudsy water over my windshield with a grimy wiper. To avoid making eye contact with him, I turned my head to stare at a handwritten sign advertising cheap vehicle storage. I finally managed to pry the sunroof open as I inched over a scorched overpass near Brent Cross.

The engine cut out a dozen yards from Biba's front door and retorted with a backfire that displaced a tree full of wood pigeons as I pulled up in front of their neighbors' driveway. The curtain that twitched as I struggled with the ignition was an elegantly draped white voile, not a grubby gray net, but the watcher behind it was as fixated on the street as any suburban housewife. I had only seen the top of Mr. Wheeler's head so I had to imagine him and his pregnant wife crouched over a notebook, actively waiting for something to happen that could be recorded in their noise diary. Probably he didn't recognize me, or if he did, he didn't associate me with the house. If he had, my role in events would have become public knowledge. Sometimes there are advantages to being unremarkable.

I let myself in through the gap in the fence. The garden was crawling with children. Little bodies, some shorter than the unmown grass, outnumbered the adults. This promised to be a different kind of party from the last one, one with hippies and guitars and nursery rhymes rather than DJ sets and chemical excess. These were Nina's people, not Biba's: the adults were older and fatter. Smoke rose from a barbecue that I'd last seen lying on its side on the terrace, its grate covered in bird droppings. I resolved not to eat anything cooked on it. Searching for a face I recognized I saw only Inigo, eyes just peeping over a lavender bush. He met my stare with his usual grave expression.

"Hello, Karen," he said formally.

"Hello, Inigo," I replied. "How are you?"

"Tris and Jo have gone to Devon," he told me. "And tonight we're going to stay on Arouna's boat, and then we're going traveling."

"That sounds exciting," I said. "Who's Arouna?"

"He's Gaia's dad, stupid. Do you want to see?" I let the little boy lead me by the hand to the bedroom that had been his, the room they called the Kitchen Bedroom. Clothes bulged from suitcases and spilled out of black trash bags. A man in a muumuu, nearly as tall as me even sitting down, sat cross-legged in the middle of the bed with a sleeping Gaia on his lap.

"Say hello to Arouna," ordered Inigo. I flexed my hand in a wave at the man, whose black skin was highlighted all over with

Nina's jewelry. Silver hoops with turquoise insets hung at his ears and his neck and wrists were wound with thick ropes of the same white metal. I looked down at blond Gaia, with her button nose, green eyes, and light gold skin, far paler than Nina's. Arouna's skin was deep onyx and his nose thick and fleshy. If this guy was Gaia's biological father, I was Biba's sister.

"Hello," he said to me in a thick accent that I recognized as West African French.

"*Ça va?* Karen," I said. "*Il fait beau ce soir, non?*" His features puckered at my unintended insult.

"Out of respect for my hosts, we speak English," he said gravely.

"So sorry. Of course. So . . . I expect you'll miss Nina when she goes?"

The sigh he gave seemed to bow the walls of the room. He launched into a highly charged history of his love affair with Nina in such stilted, hesitant English that I bit my tongue to stop myself speaking to him in French. He told me that he had served her a chicken tagine in Camden Lock and fallen madly in love with her on the spot. The gap between locking up his stall, having a drink, and consummating the relationship was apparently a short one. "That's the night we made my baby girl. When she told me about Gaia, I took her into my home," he said. "She and her boy come and live on my boat. We were so happy. When she leave me for Rex, she break my heart *overnight*," he said, as though the swiftness was more callous than the act of leaving itself.

Arouna was the most masculine man I'd ever shared space with, but perhaps the least sexualized. Everything about him, from his limbs to his accent, was broad and strong; but in conversation he came across as a big, stupid child. I wondered if he was what my mother would have called "special needs."

"One minute, my boat is full of babies, the next, she meets that man—that *thin* man—and he take her away. We were going to move into a flat together. She was writing the letters for me. You know? She was my *woman*."

"Do stop bleating, Arouna," said the voice I'd been waiting for. "Karen doesn't want to hear about your broken heart." Tonight, Biba appeared to be auditioning for the part of an East End housewife in a feature film about the Blitz. She wore a loose-fitting dun pinafore over a T-shirt and her hair was wrapped in a frayed green scrap of silk. I wondered if the cigarette that dangled from her lip and completed the look was deliberate. "Nina wants you next door," she said. Arouna stuck out his lower lip, balanced Gaia on his chest, and took the sleeping child into the other bedroom.

"Is he *really* her dad?" I asked.

"God knows with Nina," said Biba. "I wouldn't put it past her."

"He seems a little bit . . . slow," I ventured, not wanting to insult a close relation of the household. I needn't have worried.

"Christ, he's thick as shit," said Biba, holding her cigarette between her teeth and talking as she lit it with a match. She sank down on the bed and I sat next to her. "But he's a sweetie. He's been really good to Nina. He's a gentle giant. I like gentle giants."

"But I luff her," I said, mimicking his gruff voice. Biba clapped her hands together in delight, dropping her matchbox.

"That's brilliant!" she said. I was so pleased I'd made her laugh that I couldn't help returning her smile. "You should be a dialect coach. Seriously—there's heaps of money in it. You should look at it. And then we can work together! You can come and be my personal coach when I'm in my trailer in Hollywood. You'd love it."

"Maybe," I said. "Let me get my degree first and a secure job placement and then we can take it from there."

"Oh, Karen," said Biba. "You don't want to get into all that politics and diplomacy stuff. It's so not *you*."

Her faith in my creative ability was flattering but insulting. How did she know what was and wasn't me? Our conversations had so far been a one-way street: I'd listened to her hopes and ambitions but shared nothing of my own plans, as vague and provisional as they were. I felt that while I was studying her, desperate to unlock all her mysteries and moods, she had decided already what I was like. The inertia that had carried me to Queen Charlotte's prevailed again, and this time it was my personality, not my academic career, I allowed to be molded in someone else's vision. After all, I hadn't really known who I was or what I wanted before I met her. I might as well become who she thought I was as anyone else.

Like a dying queen, Nina held court in the Garden Room as friends came to bid her good-bye. One by one they drifted away, making vague but confident promises to meet up somewhere on the Continent. Biba drifted off to refill our glasses while Rex hovered in the corridor between the two rooms like a stick insect in a glass box. I realized that without the distraction of Nina and the children, I'd be seeing even more of Biba's brother.

"Can I please use your car to drop them off at the barge?" he asked.

"All of them?" I asked. I wasn't sure that my vehicle could take two kids, Nina and Arouna's combined bulk, and their luggage. "I suppose . . ."

"It's okay, we can always get Arouna to get out and push. I don't know why she wants to stay with him for her last few days," said Rex challengingly, as though the whole thing had been my idea. "We've got so much more space here. Inigo's asthma won't be helped with all that damp. Even a couple of nights could trigger an attack."

He had to squeeze into the room to allow Arouna to pass in the narrow corridor, a suitcase half his size hoisted effortlessly up onto his shoulder.

"Nina wants to see you," he said to me.

She sat in the lotus position on a plain bedspread. It was the only time I had seen her without a chaotic tangle of things— food, metal, books, children—around her. She looked smaller and younger without her cloud of clutter.

"I'm so glad I get to say good-bye to you," she said, patting an indentation next to her. "Listen, I want you to have this." She unhooked one of the chains around her neck. A thick silver cord held an intricate turquoise flower with a tiny orange stone in the center. She hung it around my own neck. "It looks beautiful on you," she said. "As soon as I saw you I thought, Karen will like this. It really brings out your eyes."

"Thank you." I was touched by the gesture, flattered that she thought of me when I wasn't there. "I really didn't expect anything. That's so sweet. How are you? Are you all ready to go? Is there anything I can do to help?"

"You already have. The loan of the car is a godsend," she said, telling me that she had been behind Rex's request. "I'm going to call you all when I'm settled, you know. Check everything's okay." Why shouldn't it be?

"I kind of hope you never do settle. When I'm a boring old fart working for the Foreign Office, promise me that you'll be off traveling having lots of adventures on my behalf."

Nina laughed.

"When you're a boring old fart working for the Foreign Office, promise you won't set Interpol on me if I still haven't put the kids through school." Her embrace was soft and warm. "Look after them for me."

"Nina!" Arouna stood in the doorway, a sleepyhead Gaia clinging to his leg. "Come on. We go. Bedtime."

Nina scooped Inigo into her arms and heaved her bulk up from the bed. Rex reached under the pillow and found Inigo's inhaler, which he pressed into Nina's skirt pocket.

"Thanks, babe," she said absently. Rex blocked the kitchen stairs, holding a trash bag that was stuffed with tiny clothes. A single sock wiggled like a stripy worm through a hole in the stretched black plastic. He looked at it forlornly and I realized it wasn't Nina he was mourning but the loss of but the children he'd helped raise for the past two years.

Nina tucked the sock into the top of the trash bag and kissed Rex softly on the cheek, to Arouna's evident and bitter resentment.

As Rex stood aside to let the family pass, Biba spoke to her brother with a tenderness I had never heard before in her voice.

"You're doing really well," she said. "We'll be waiting for you when you get back. Go on. Go. It'll be fine."

We watched them leave from the window of the Velvet Room. The car stalled a couple of times as Rex tried to get used to the ancient, bouncy clutch. With a gentler and more patient touch than I had ever managed, he cajoled it into gear. It groaned its way along, making a noise like a firework as they rounded the corner of Muswell Hill Road, a bang loud enough to wake the neighbors, and probably earn an entry in Tom Wheeler's noise diary.

The house echoed with the sudden absence of people.

"It's never been just me and Rex," she said. "Never, not since . . ." Biba trailed off. "I don't want to be alone with him. He won't leave me alone now he's got no one else to fuss over. You haven't seen what he gets like. I'll never have a moment's peace."

"You could always ask someone else to move in with you," I said.

"I could," she conceded.

"Not a stranger, or a lodger, but someone you already know and like. Someone who's here all the time anyway. Someone who has no one else to live with and nothing better to do."

"If only we knew someone who fit the bill!" she said, throwing up her hands in actressy hopelessness. I kicked her under the table and she grinned mischievously.

"I've had an idea!" she said. "Karen, would you like to come and live here with me and Rex?"

"Funny you should say that," I said. "There's actually nothing I'd like more, but I've got to ask you something first. Are you sure you don't just want someone nice and stable to replace Nina?"

"Who told you you were nice?" she said, then grew serious. "Absolutely not," she said, looking me in the eye. "I want you here because you're you."

"Good. Because I'm not doing all the cooking," I said.

"I wouldn't expect you to," she replied.

"In that case, I'm in," I said.

"Fucking fabulous," replied Biba, drumming a celebratory fanfare on the kitchen table with her palms. "Now then. I happen to know that Rex has hidden a good bottle of champagne in the cupboard under the stairs. He's saving it for a special occasion. I think we should drink it now, don't you?"

Alice is currently reading a book about a boy who cuts holes into parallel worlds with a knife. With one slash of his blade he can slice open and peel back the fabric of this universe to reveal another, fantastical world that was there all along. That's how I felt that summer with Biba, as though a curtain had been drawn back and a door opened just in time for me to run through and embrace everything I found. I grew younger with every hour I spent with her. My adolescence had been spent in Europe, assimilating adult culture and habits along with new languages. I had learned about food, wine, and art at various universities. While these experiences, encouraged by a conformity that must be innate, had given me a kind of precocious maturity, in none of these places had I been to a party thrown by my peers, or to a nightclub. But in those early weeks Biba introduced me to the blithe rebellion of youth. Most girls my age had exhausted this phase and were moving on to the next one. But I was immature enough still to be divested of my innocence: at twenty, just old enough to know, and to appreciate it as it happened.

Innocence is an unusual quality in that it has two opposites. One is experience. The other is guilt.

I never saw my Brentford housemates again. Once they'd packed, a week early, Claire and Emma decamped to their boyfriends' houses. We said good-bye in a series of scribbled notes and letters shoved under bedroom doors and pinned to the fridge with magnets. They wished me luck with my one remaining exam and promised to call with a contact number as soon as they had one. Sarah was only sporadically at home, prepaying bills and writing list after list of instructions on how to look after the house I'd been living in for three years.

I tidied my things with the diligence of someone about to commit suicide, getting my house in order as though I expected never to return. Not that there was anything distressing, incriminating, or even interesting to throw away: only the ordered, tidy paperwork of a life lived in translation. I packed the rucksack that had taken me all over Europe with all the summer clothes I could carry and the few cosmetics I wore. My CD player and most of my books remained in my room. Why would I need books when I had conversation?

I moved in on the day of my last exam. I didn't end up living in Nina's room but was shown to the attic room where Tris and Jo had slept. I was the ninth person to live there in five years and the faded lemon walls documented the previous tenants. Only Tris and Jo, true to their zero trace principles, had left no mark on the room. After carrying my bag up the forty-two stairs, Rex pointed out the bracket on the wall where someone called Hugh had ripped out a cupboard that had offended him: a ragged square inch of William Morris pattern was just visible behind the bad paint job with which a girl named Val had tried to cover up the mess. The soot marks on the underside of the bookshelf were made by someone called Phil, whose conviction that candlelight was the best way to seduce girls had nearly burned the house down one New Year's Eve.

I hung my clothes inside the leaning canvas wardrobe and wrapped a string of fairy lights around the headboard of the bed, winding the rubbery green wire around a nail that jutted out of the picture rail so that the lights hung overhead like an awning of stars. This, the third floor, was set in the thick of the leaf canopy. There was a tiny round window, like a porthole into the sea of green, and a skylight at the foot of my bed. I lay with my head underneath it, counting not my lucky stars but my lucky leaves, when Biba came in with tumblers of red wine for the pair of us.

The drink and the fairy lights and the conversation softened the comedown into darkness.

"It feels like you've lived here forever," she said after an hour or so. She pointed to the tiny blisters my indoor constellation had already made in the paint. "You're already leaving your fingerprint here. One day, I'll look at this and trace the pattern your lights made. I'll be able to picture how the room was when you were here." She smiled and squeezed my arm, and despite the heat of the June night I shivered because Biba had implied that there might come a day when I didn't live here anymore. The thought of being reduced to a throwaway anecdote like Hugh, Phil, or Val made my heart turn to ice and the walls close in around me. The house had been my home for only a couple of hours, but I already knew that my time there would not be a phase in my life but would *be* my life, would be the defining time of it. It was, of course, but for reasons I could never have guessed at that evening. Then, it seemed impossible that the summer could ever come to an end. I was already looking forward to the next summer, and the one after that, too. My father had told me that everyone has one summer and I felt desperately sorry for him. I was convinced then that this was just the first of many amazing summers, interspersed with wonderful winters and autumns and springs too. I was blind to all the signs that this summer would be the last as well as the first of its kind for me.

THEY TOOK MY CAR while I was asleep. The long, deep sleeps of that summer were a revelation to me. After a few days of rising at eight and waiting for hours at a kitchen table still scattered with the debris of last night's dinner, I realized that daily lie-ins were customary when there was nothing to do—and that first week there was never anything to do. We converged for dinner, but breakfast and lunch were foraged from the fridge during the day or simply overlooked. At first the fluid timetable of the house left me in freefall. It took a few days to learn to sleep where I fell, skip meals if I felt like it, and drink red wine with brunch—a fluid term applied to any meal involving eggs and eaten before dusk—if that was what Biba was doing.

So when I woke to find the note under the door telling me that they had taken my car, it didn't occur to me to be cross: quite the opposite. I was gratified that they thought me so relaxed and laid-back that my permission was a given. It was the first time I'd seen Biba's handwriting other than as a graffito.

"Morning, Sleeping Beauty. We didn't want to wake you. We're giving Nina and the kids a lift to the airport. Took the car, hope that's OK. Back around 8ish, 9ish. See you for dinner then. B and R." She had drawn smiley faces in the loops of their initials.

It was eleven o'clock. I had ten hours in which to occupy myself in this house and no key to secure it if I left. Letting myself out wouldn't be a problem: the faulty latch had failed again and a chink of morning sunlight shone through the inch-wide gap between the front door and its jamb. At least this time it wasn't swinging wide open, inviting every burglar in North London to help themselves to . . . was there anything in this house worth stealing? I looked around the black and white hall, which was empty save for a white-painted, glass-topped bamboo telephone table fifteen years too young to have any kitsch value. I listened for the click of the Yale lock and leaned a pile of telephone directories against the door to buttress the seal.

There was no milk so I drank my coffee black. The caffeine rush brought the mess of the kitchen into focus. I found an unused pair of rubber gloves and an industrial-sized bottle of bleach in the cupboard under the sink, its cap carpeted with a fuzz of gray dust. I began with the fridge. I took everything out, threw away all the food that was past its sell-by date and a couple of cheeses with green fur growing on them, then scrubbed its interior until it gleamed. I wiped crumbs and scum from the counters and then swept them from the floor, arranged toppling piles of cookbooks in height order and did four sink-loads of dishes.

The washing machine was ancient, a top-loading contraption as big and ugly as the industrial ones that line the walls of launderettes. In went the bedclothes from mine and Biba's beds, the food-encrusted Indian bedspreads that covered springy sofas and any clothes that were littering the house. I threw the lot into the drum, hit the largest button and hoped for the best. The rattling thrum that issued from it shook the glasses on the draining board.

Gathering pace, I worked my way up, forcing open landing windows that had been painted shut for years. The stuffy house seemed to sigh with relief. I retrieved enough plates and glasses to fill the huge sink for a fifth time. In the bathrooms I chucked out all moldering toiletries. In the main bath, the one where I'd found the unconscious boy on the night of the party, I scrubbed until the only marks left were the milky-blue crackles that spiderwebbed its gleaming surface.

Lunch was a dry baguette dipped in cream cheese, eaten before I laid the quilts and cushion covers out on the terrace. It was another equatorially hot and parched day and I knew that everything would be dry within the hour.

The vacuum cleaner was a large, unwieldy piece of apparatus with a dust bag that I had to empty into the garbage and a nozzle that was too big for its metal tube and kept falling off. Progress was slow, but I drove it over each individual stair, using my fingers to pick at strands of Biba's hair that seemed to have woven themselves into the woolen knots of the carpet. There was no question of vacuuming Biba's bedroom floor—I'd have had to find it first—but I went in and sat on her bed for a while, breathing in the light musk that hung in her room and permeated all her clothes.

On the landing outside Rex's bedroom I hesitated. It was the only room in the house I hadn't yet entered. Was it ruder to neglect to clean it or to trespass into it? I used my toe to prod the edge of his door and it swung open obligingly. His room was as neat as hers was cluttered. It was the brightest and barest in the house. A pale cream color covered the walls and met the brilliant white of the ceiling in an imperfect and patchy line that betrayed the unsteady hands of an inexperienced DIYer. Magazines about interior decoration filled a pine bookcase, and on the windowsill, a row of tester pots of paint in various shades of wheat and pastel were lined up like whey-faced toy soldiers. A plain beige carpet curled at one corner to reveal not floorboards or underlay but another, older carpet in hellfire reds and oranges. I understood at once that this well-ordered, hygienic haven must have been the only thing enabling him to live among the mess and chaos created by his sister and their tenants.

The nozzle fell off again and rolled underneath Rex's bed. I crouched on all fours and peered beneath the valance, expecting the usual underlay of dust balls and fluff, but it was as spotless as the rest of the room. Under the middle of his sagging mattress, so perfectly central that it must have been put there deliberately, was a low, oblong box, rather like the one my mother kept her wedding dress in.

The box was intriguing because it was hidden, rather than because it belonged to Rex. Had it been Biba's room, I'm sure I would have had a sense of trepidation and guilt, but as I flattened my body and stretched out my arms to retrieve the box, I felt only the mildest curiosity. When the thing was sitting in my lap, I could see that it was actually a shoebox, and a very old one at that. The lid bore a pen-and-ink printed picture of a pair of knee-high boots that took up one side. They had cost ten pounds, a long time ago. As I lifted the lid, it occurred to me that the contents might be pornographic, and my hands hesitated, from distaste rather than guilt or respect.

It was not pornography but something that made my heart beat much faster than that. The first thing I saw was an unsorted selection of photographs of Biba, apparently in character for plays performed before I met her. Her monochrome image stared up at me from a shiny sheet of photographic paper. She was heavy-fringed and kohl-eyed, her hair ironed and sliced into the swinging geometry of the perfect sixties girl. She couldn't have been more than about fourteen when it was taken. The second photograph showed her wearing a bikini and biting into an ice pop. A third, blown up to the size of a magazine, struck me as familiar: perhaps I'd seen Biba wearing that white dress. She stood in a buttercup meadow and smiled over her shoulder at the camera while strong sunlight lifted her dark hair into a golden aureole. A fourth showed her looking somehow older than she was now and unhappy, her dark shrug of hair bleeding into the mink of a coat that enveloped her shoulders.

A card-backed envelope, its edges frayed with age, contained sheet after sheet of glossy paper checkered with monochrome images the size of passport photographs. They were miniature storyboards chronicling the successes and failures of professional photo shoots: models poised to perfection in one tiny picture, then captured mid-blink in the next. A grungy band betrayed by the hand of a makeup artist creeping into the shot. Some sheets had been scrawled on in a china clay pencil, with images either ringed or struck through. I ran my fingers over the markings, which were raised and still tacky to the touch. I picked out a page filled with almost identical images of a man playing the piano with his back to the camera, and turned it over; on the reverse of the sheet was written, "James, 1978," alongside a tiny sticker saying, "Roger Capel Portraits" and the address of a Soho studio. I gasped as I realized that I held in my hands their father's work—possibly all that remained of it.

Next came a loose stack of flimsier papers, a seemingly random selection torn from old magazines. Some were advertisements featuring slick-limbed models, while others were interviews with actors, writers, musicians, Roger Capel's photo credit their only common theme. Satisfaction at solving the mystery was immediately replaced by puzzlement. If their father was long dead, who had taken those very recent pictures of Biba?

I found my answer at the bottom of the box; more loose photographs, snapshots this time. The first curling photograph was blurred but there was no mistaking the two children who splashed in a wading pool surrounded by trees, or the woman who crouched at the edge of the water in her bikini. Rex and Biba's mother shared their features as well as their laughter. I flipped back to the top photographs: now that I looked again, they weren't of Biba at all, but of the woman who had bequeathed her her face. The likeness was uncanny.

There were a few more from the same film, mostly of Rex and Biba frolicking in the wading pool, their parents out of the shot. Finally the photographer appeared before the camera; the man I presumed to be Roger Capel sat on the edge of the pool, jeans rolled up to his knees, feet in the water. I was only guessing that he was their father from the indulgent expression on his face: he was short and stocky, with full lips and a round, feminine face, far removed from the etiolated beauty of his wife and children. I wondered if it had bothered him, fathering two children to whom he had had no evident genetic input. Another more formal and much earlier portrait, posed in a studio on a sheepskin rug with pampas grass motionless before the dappled backdrop, showed the infant Biba asleep in her mother's arms while Rex sat on his father's lap, his serious little face regarding the camera with something like suspicion. I wondered again what double tragedy had robbed these happy children of both their parents.

I would have overlooked the sliver of newsprint if I hadn't been so diligently trying to replace everything exactly as I had found it, to remember which photographs had been where. The slim, yellowing column had been folded three times, the creases as sharp as razors through years of being pressed in Rex's box.

The photograph was a reproduction of the sunny meadow picture. It was impossible to tell which newspaper the cutting had originally come from, whether it had been national or local press, and there was no date. The language was the unambiguous and unembellished terminology of a court reporter.

A coroner today recorded a verdict of suicide in the death of the model Sheila Capel, who is remembered chiefly for the Natura Shampoo television advertisements in the mid-1970s.

It was reported that Mrs. Capel had been suffering from depression after the stalling of her career and the breakdown of her marriage to the photographer Roger Capel, and had attempted to take her life on two previous occasions.

She is survived by her two children, Rex, 16, and Bathsheba, 12. It is understood that they are in the care of their father. Members of Mrs. Capel's family were not available for comment at the time of going to press.

Rex watches any retrospective television programs with the concentration of someone cramming for an exam. He doesn't discriminate between the lowbrow and the heavyweight as long as the time documented is the time he spent inside; he pays the same attention to clip shows featuring celebrity scandals as he does to serious political debates. Today it's the latter; a discussion program about Tony Blair's legacy is showing on a worthy channel somewhere in the high numbers. The studio debate is preceded by a montage of news footage from Blair's career. It's the same old footage they always show. It begins with clips that Rex would have seen for the first time by my side in Highgate, the fresh-faced PM eulogizing the People's Princess, and soon leads to footage that he will have seen, if at all, on the television in the common room in prison. The baby on the doorstep of number ten. The Millennium Dome. The airplanes crashing into the towers. The aerial shot of the lonely car, its owner's body hidden beneath a tree. Crowds jumping in the fountains at Trafalgar Square as the Olympic bid is won. The London bus, its top deck opened out like orange peel. The flag-draped coffins carried onto the runway. The final wave good-bye. The images are soundtracked with the song that will always be associated with Blair: "Things Can Only Get Better." It was still being played on the radio well into the summer of 1997. Things did not get better for us. We were not supposed to end up here.

The conversation is dominated by Iraq, but a woman in a blue tweed suit is keen to move the discussion away from the war and toward home policy; prison reform, to be precise. She wants to build more prisons so that judges will be able to hand down appropriately lengthy sentences for serious crimes. She cites a couple of examples of men who served only half or even a third of their sentences. Rex's name is not mentioned, but it could be in this context. My hand is poised over the remote but Alice zoned out as soon as she heard the word *politics* and is absorbed in her magazine.

"I'd say New Labour did us a favor, then," says Rex. "If there were more prison spaces perhaps I'd still be inside."

I'm sure that, while overcrowding and lax sentencing are to

some extent responsible for Rex's early release, other factors played their part.

Alice decides that now is the time to vocalize her boredom.

"This program is completely *retarded*," she says. *Retarded* is a banned word.

"Fifty pence," I say automatically. That's the amount docked from her weekly pocket money whenever she says anything that doesn't fit in with my idea of what's appropriate or, I suppose, politically correct. Rex looks bemused but doesn't question me. I suppose I will have to commit to paper the list of proscribed words and phrases that, until now, it has been enough to carry around in my head.

Alice shrugs and doesn't argue, revealing that that was no slip of the tongue but a deliberate test. She has done this a couple of times in the last few days: purposefully pushed her boundaries to see if I will relax now that Daddy, the soft touch, is home. I need her to learn that this only means I will play bad cop to his good cop. I have seen what happens when children grow up without boundaries and without love, tough or otherwise. I will not spoil Alice.

She stomps the few paces to the dark kitchen and opens the fridge with an ostentatious sigh. She is spotlit in its glow. When she shouts out it is with unnecessary volume that makes both of us jump.

"Mum, *se nos ha acabado el zumo de naranja, ¿No queda mas?*" My reply is automatic.

"*Sí, en el armario al lado de la nevera, donde siempre.*"

Alice and I realize our faux pas at the same time and for a second we are conspirators. She is waiting for permission to giggle but Rex's voice denies it.

"Alice, can you give Mummy and me a moment?" he says firmly. No *sweetheart*, no *please*. It is the first time Alice has heard Rex speak with decision and authority and only the fourth or fifth time I have. It's rather thrilling.

"Why don't you give Jade a call?" I say to Alice. "You can use the phone in my room."

Her delight at unsupervised telephone time quenches Alice's thirst and her curiosity.

"What the hell was that?" he demands.

"Spanish."

"Since when does Alice speak Spanish?"

"It was her first language when she was little," I admit.

"And when were you going to tell me? Or were you going to keep it a secret between the two of you? To push me out of the only family I've got left?"

"She was only asking where the orange juice was," I say.

He closes his eyes, runs his hands through his hair, and takes six or seven deep breaths. When he looks up again he has regained control. Is this something he learned in prison? Ten years ago this flight of fancy would have escalated into full-blown paranoia, but now he is able to put the brakes on it. If the last decade has nurtured in me an instinct to protect at all costs, then Rex has mastered the art of suppression. "I just can't believe you didn't tell me, that's all. I could have learned too. I've had ten years."

"I can teach you," I say feebly, my heart sinking at the idea of the patience I will need to teach Rex, one of nature's monoglots, a foreign language. Perhaps now is the time to tell him about the darkness I experienced when Alice was a baby. How the scope of the world, so recently made available to me in widescreen, dwindled to a pinhole. The loneliness and frustration of living back in Bletchley with my hurt, confused parents and a dumb but vocal baby. Speaking to Alice almost exclusively in Spanish for the first few years of her life was the only thing that kept me sane. It preserved somehow the identity I had had before Biba and was a threadlike connection, a flimsy lifeline to the future I could have had if I had never met her. Instead I give him the acceptable answer, the one I gave to my mother and father at the time. "I thought it would be nice to pass a skill on to her."

Our discussion is curtailed by Alice hovering at the top of the stairs. The staircase lines the left-hand side of the living room and she is sitting on the top step, peering through the banisters with a mixture of apprehension and curiosity. She has changed into the beloved and vile pink pajamas my mother bought her during an unsupervised visit to Lakeside. The words I'M A LITTLE PRINCESS are emblazoned across her chest in purple glitter, as if she needed the encouragement.

"New rule," I tell her. "One I should have told you before. Daddy doesn't understand Spanish, so when he's around, we only talk in English, just like we do with Grandma and Grandpa."

"Of course," she says seriously, either because she doesn't want to cause another argument or because she is mulling over the divide-and-conquer potential of what she's just learned. I wouldn't put it past her. Children are naturally Machiavellian and Alice is no exception. "I wish I'd never been born" is the insult hurled from the child to the parent, but in my darkest times, especially when she was little and I was so alone, I often thought its reverse: "I wish you'd never been born." It is a poisonous thought to carry around. Like Alice, I have a list of proscribed words and phrases. I can never casually say, "I'll kill you," "I could kill her," or "I could kill him." That empty cliché was a favorite of Rex's.

"Who wants fish and chips?" I say, more to break this chain of thought and get out of the house than to fulfill a craving for battered cod. Alice, unused to such spontaneity, claps her hands and races upstairs, returning seconds later wearing the cheap zirconia tiara she saves for exciting occasions, and which never fails to enchant. She *is* a manipulative child with her preciously stage-managed outfits. Her clothes are never just thrown together but chosen with delight and calculation, just like Biba's always were. But she has something else in common with Biba; when Alice's mood exults, it is contagious. Rex and I need that dynamic, that third person brimming with possibility and irresponsibility to draw us out of the diffidence to which we are both naturally inclined and into a world of potential and fun. Rex helps her tuck her pajama legs into her green rain boots, which have frog's eyes and a red mouth on the front of each toe. With any luck she will ruin the trousers on the beach.

The coast is only twenty minutes away but we have left it late and are the last people in line for the fish bar. Alice can barely see over the counter, so is hoisted onto Rex's hip and insists on reading the whole menu aloud before making her choice. The girl behind the counter, sheened in grease, is visibly cheered and charmed by her enthusiasm. By the time Alice's wrapped-up food is handed over, she is so overexcited I worry she'll make herself sick before the first chip is eaten.

We eat our fish suppers with our fingers in a pool of lamplight on the edge of the dark beach. There is no moon tonight and the sea is invisible behind a ridge of shingle, the only evidence of it the boom, shatter, and drag as every seventh wave advances and retreats. Above our heads, seagulls circle in a starless sky, biding their time. When we have finished we shake the hard little chips and flakes of fish from the bottom of their wrappers and the white birds swoop.

Our house seems smaller than ever after the expanse of the beach. The cottage seems to have been resized since Rex came home. His height has shrunk the place and turned a pretty and feminine home into something quaint.

Before we go to sleep, I press 1471 to see if anyone has telephoned while we were out. The automated voice informs me in mechanically flawless Received Pronunciation that I was called today at 20:49 hours. The caller withheld their number.

12

A LOUD CREAK AND a pulling on the bedclothes around my feet broke into my sleep. Biba had used my bed as a launchpad to propel the top half of her body through the skylight. Her legs dangled through the frame like the severed bottom half of a shop mannequin.

"Weather report," her voice fell through the hatch. "It's a beautiful day. Let's go out. Let's have a Sunday, like normal people do."

"Speak for yourself," I said. "I'm perfectly normal." I turned my pillow over to the cool side and closed my eyes again.

"Employed people, then. We can go and have a nice pub lunch and read some papers and then, at around seven o'clock, we can start to grumble about having to go back to work tomorrow." Her enthusiasm infused the most mundane activities with magic and it was contagious: with Biba, everything felt like you were doing it for the first time, no matter how often you'd done it with other people.

I sat up in bed, my face catching the angled sunbeam. I was reminded that I had serious work to do in clearing the backlog of fun I had accumulated during my studious past.

Biba dropped beside me with a thud that was followed seconds later by a loud crack from the foot of the wooden bed frame.

"Have you asked Rex?" I said, half-hoping she would say that he was busy.

"I've *told* him, yes." She laughed, a shrill descending arpeggio, amused by the idea that Rex's time was his own to spend. "Now, hurry up and have your shower. I want to get going while the sun's shining."

I don't know why she was in such a hurry to catch the midday sun. Her skin and Rex's were protected by an almost constant canopy of leaves, and they treated a walk on the open heath like some kind of desert mission, smothering each other with gloops of high-factor sunblock. With his sleeves rolled up, I saw that Rex was less puny than I'd imagined; biceps bobbed like Adam's apples in his arms. He slipped the straps of Biba's dress down and covered her shoulders, using his thumb to rub the white cream into the notch in her collarbone. She stood on tiptoe to smooth it into his cheeks. In reflected profile their likeness was more uncanny than ever. Rex's eyes returned her smile: something about the proximity of his face to hers animated him, like electricity that arcs from one cable to another. I turned my eyes away from this rather unsettling mutual massage to wipe the smears from my sunglasses. By the time they'd finished, the cream had left a pearlized sheen on their bodies, making them look paler than ever.

Leaving the house was an adventure in itself, a scrabble for loose change and lost purses. Rex checked the front door three times to see if the latch had closed properly before we could set off and would have checked it a fourth if Biba hadn't stood on the bottom step, arms folded, forbidding him to go back.

If she had instigated our day out, he was our tour guide, striding ahead with his hands in his pockets. Traffic fumes formed tiny black beads that clung to the fine hairs on his forearms, already clotted with zinc from the sunblock. A sweat patch appeared between his shoulder blades and I could taste the salt on my own upper lip.

We walked up North Hill, a new route for me into the heart of Highgate village. The hill looked steeper than it was because of the tall, tilting buildings that lined it: elevated by slanting, cracked walls, the houses and apartment blocks seemed to lean inward and gave the wide street a dizzying and claustrophobic feel. Scaffolding at regular intervals confirmed this sensation of sinking and subsidence. I could imagine millions of pounds' worth of bricks suddenly sliding down the hill like lava.

The pubs were already beginning to throng with people enjoying prelunch drinks. We passed a dozen thirsty dogs collapsed around the ankles of their owners, pink tongues skimming the pavements, the lucky ones drinking water from plastic containers and a border collie tentatively licking a puddle of spilled beer.

Had I been on my own with Biba, I would have suggested that we take our place among them, staking out a corner table from which to pass conjecture on the other people in companionable silence. Our great expedition to the heath would have turned, like so many of our other truncated excursions, into an afternoon's dedicated people watching, well lubricated by a bottle of good red. But Rex's presence stopped me making such a suggestion. While I was confident that he had the patience needed to watch people come and go, I doubted very much that he had the requisite imagination.

By the time we reached the heath my own thirst had swelled my tongue. After a sharp left onto a gravel drive, Kenwood House loomed up so suddenly that it felt as though the house had rounded the corner on us, not the other way around. Sunshine bounced off its white walls. Rex relaxed his pace to a stroll as we walked around the perimeter of the house: an acre of sloping ground led down to the ponds that separated the manicured lawns of Kenwood from the scrubland of the heath. Groups of people like clusters of daisies gemmed the green grass.

"I never knew that London could be so beautiful," I said to no one in particular. I detoured from Rex's route when I saw a sign for a bathroom and dashed into it, jumping the line and glugging greedily from the drinking fountain, closing my eyes against the straw-haired, red-cheeked woman reflected in its shiny steel. Outside, Biba was giggling manically while Rex stood a few meters apart, arms folded and brow knitted. What's happened? I thought. Surely they can't have had a row in the time it took for me to drink and run my wrists under the cold water? But I wasn't imagining the change in atmosphere. As soon as Rex saw me, he stalked off quickly, shooting anxious glances over his shoulder. Biba sauntered behind, a snigger on her lips.

Rex led us along a dizzying zigzag of paths and slipped through a low door in a mossy brick wall into a walled garden carpeted with green and silver leaves. The change in air was as sudden as the difference between indoors and outside: thick and heavy to the point of cloying with the smell of lavender and rosemary. Rex gave one final backward glance and then sank onto a patch of lawn, his back to the wall, scowling at his sister. The reason for our scurried departure suddenly became evident as Biba tipped the contents of her bag out. Two croissants, a slice of cheesecake, a packaged salad, and bottles of water and fizzy drinks fell onto the grass. She looked at me in triumph, then gave her bag another shake: a Mini Milk ice pop slid out. A string of liquefied ice cream oozed through a hole in the wrapper and pooled around it.

"When did you get all that?" I said to her.

"She stole it," said Rex. "While you were in the restroom. She went into the canteen and she stole the lot."

"I had to," said Biba. "We're local. We shouldn't pay these tourist prices for this." She held up a bottle of organic cola, beaded with condensation, like it was an exhibit in an old-fashioned murder trial. "Two pounds fifty! Fucking outrageous," she said, although I knew she happily spent twice that much a day on cigarettes.

"If they'd caught you . . ." Rex put his head in his hands.

"But they didn't . . ." she replied.

"But if they had . . ." he pressed on. I twisted open the bottle of cola. Sticky brown bubbles showered everywhere.

"This place is like a maze," I said. "I feel like Alice when she went through the looking glass and whichever path she took, she ended up farther away from where she was going."

"I loved the Alice books," said Biba dreamily. "When I was little I tried to climb through a mirror in my mum's room and fell off the mantelpiece. Look." She showed me a lightning bolt of white scar on her inner elbow and shoved a croissant into her mouth.

"Me too," I said. "My thing was rabbit holes. I was convinced that it was just a question of finding the right one and falling down it."

Rex was trying, and failing, to flick away a marching line of ants that had decided to colonize the ice cream.

"She actually tried to get us to call her Alice when she was about seven," he said. "She spent a whole summer wearing this filthy black headband and asking for a pet white rabbit." His words brought a temporary truce and for a while we munched in silence.

"How come you know this place is here?" I asked him.

"I had to learn my way around here when I was younger," said Rex, his face darkening. The ants had begun to crawl up his legs and he stood up to wash them off with water. "Come on," he said. "Let's get going."

We flitted in and out of light and shade as we crossed the heath. In the wooded areas my friends looked more silver than ever, literally sylvan as their skin glowed in the filtered sunlight. The ground was worn flat with footprints. Unlike in Queen's Wood, where the trails were arbitrary and inconsistent, there were wide dirt tracks here, dozens of them crisscrossing the space like a huge cat's cradle. I suddenly felt the urge to take to my heels and run in a way that I hadn't for weeks, to test my lung capacity and work the muscles of my thighs until they shook. But I knew I'd never be able to orient myself alone. The infrequent maps and signposts we passed left me more, not less, confused about our whereabouts. We walked in single file, me following Rex, Biba trailing behind us, muttering dialogue from the play she was learning under her breath, occasionally stopping to repeat a line that she'd stumbled over.

When she was lagging almost out of sight, Rex and I waited for her to catch up to us next to a tree that had lost a limb. The fallen branch had hundreds of rings, too many to count, border-ing a darker circle in the middle like the yolk of an egg. I explored the rotten wood with my toe, then turned my attention to the tree itself. Its leaves were fat glossy spikes and I plucked a few and held them to my nose. Before I could detect any aroma, Rex had slapped my hand away.

"Don't eat it!" he yelped, an adolescent hiccup in his voice.

"Rex! What was that for?"

"It's toxic! Don't eat it!"

"Why would I want to eat it? I just wanted to know what it smelled like. Christ, Rex." I looked for backup but Biba was still out of earshot, eyes on the path, lips mouthing her lines.

"I'm sorry," he said, panic turned to contrition. "I didn't mean to hurt you."

He reached out to touch my hand where he had slapped it but I drew it away.

"You didn't hurt me, you just shocked me," I said. "Is it really poisonous? What is it, anyway? I've seen trees like this before, they're everywhere. There's one in the wood at home, near the fence." It was the first time I had called his home my own, but this landmark utterance was lost on him.

"It's a yew. They can be deadly. One mouthful can be enough to kill. Biba ate some leaves—off that tree by the fence, actually—when she was six. We thought she was going to die. She was sick for days."

"Didn't anyone warn her?"

"Oh, she knew exactly what it was, Mum had warned us both off it the day before," said Rex. "She called it a poison tree."

"So why did she do it?"

"Dad had just come back from a long shoot somewhere. I think it was her way of welcoming him home. She had a well-developed sense of drama even then."

"Jesus," I whistled, but Biba was on our heels now and I scanned the foliage for a change of subject. To Rex's left grew a thick tree with indecipherable initials carved into its trunk a foot or two above our heads.

"Look at that," I pointed.

"Ah, the mighty oak," he said. "Can't you tell from the leaves? Something you'll find interesting about the oak, if you don't know already . . ."

"Who are you, David Attenborough?" interrupted Biba. "Shut up, Rex. Karen's only being polite, she doesn't want to hear your nature ramble."

His features assumed their version of repose: an expression of glum submission to his sister.

"Test me, Karen," said Biba, as we emerged from the trees and began a steep climb up a sun-bleached hill. She began to sing her German song, loudly enough for passersby to stop and stare. I no longer had any need to correct her: she was word-perfect, if not quite pitch-perfect. She had dropped her voice an octave to achieve the Marlene Dietrich sound that she felt the song deserved. I wondered how her lungs, which I always pictured as child-sized, could project such a noise.

We stopped at the top of the hill, staring out to where the hills of Crystal Palace hid behind the river's haze. Below us, the city huddled in a giant natural bowl. Now the London Eye must dominate that view of the city, but it wasn't there in 1997. The Canary Wharf towers loomed at the left periphery, but Centrepoint and the Post Office Tower ruled the cityscape then.

"Look," said Biba, pointing to a low-rise block that tugged at the skirt of the tallest tower. I pressed my cheek next to hers while I followed the direction of her finger and identified the unlovely buildings of Queen Charlotte's College. She grabbed my hand. "That's where we met."

The narrow streets were clogged and claustrophobic after the air and space of the heath, and the crisp, cleansing sunshine I'd basked in on top of the hill now hung in a low pall and mingled with the other pollutants, turning the air to glue. The smell of freshly baked bread and sizzled garlic wafted from the delis and bakeries that jostled with the boutiques of Hampstead, but I could taste gasoline and diesel in the air, too. A pair of women pushing baby buggies walked abreast along the narrow pavement, forcing the three of us to walk single-file in the gutter. Their husbands, following five paces behind, gave us an apologetic cringe. The shabby pub Biba stopped at was a disappointing destination after our hike.

"Here we are!" she said with a flourish and a bow. The glaze had come off the ceramic tiles that covered the bottom half of the building. Although no sign swung from its upper story, the words THE MAGDALA were emblazoned across its threshold in tall black capitals. Dozens of drinkers crammed into the tiny beer garden, while a couple of rebellious types had taken pint glasses across the road to laze under the trees opposite.

"Oh God, not this one," said Rex, but followed her in. The pub was as dark and empty inside as it was bright and crowded on the outside. Two rooms shared the same central bar, empty apart from an old man in a hat and a coat, sipping a murky brown pint. Enormous checkered, leaded windows with the occasional flourish of colored glass filtered the daylight and cast an eerie gloom at odds with the blazing sunshine we'd just stepped out of. Biba collapsed onto a pew. I sank into a chair beside her. The relief of taking the weight off my feet was instantly eclipsed by thirst.

"Rex, get me a drink," ordered Biba, before he had time to sit down.

"Yes. Sorry," he said, scuttling off to the bar like a butler nearing retirement age. He was back in under a minute with a jug of iced water in one hand, a pitcher of gin and tonic in the other, and three stacked glasses nestling precariously under his arm. "I've ordered three roast dinners as well." I couldn't think of a less appetizing or appropriate meal on such a hot and sticky day, but Biba clapped her hands enthusiastically and I didn't have the heart to raise my objections.

"What do you think of this pub?" said Biba. Her earnest tone made the question feel like a test.

"It's nice," I said feebly. "It's . . . atmospheric."

"You don't know the half of it," she said. She put her hand into the water jug, fished one ice cube out of the glass, and dropped it down her back, wiping another one across her brow. Her brother slid a beer mat across the table to absorb the resulting puddle.

"Easter Sunday, 1955," she said, slipping the cube into her mouth and crunching loudly. I made my face into a question mark and Biba sighed. "Ruth Ellis?" I shook my head again. She tucked her feet under her and rolled a cigarette, a sure sign that she was settling in to tell a good story. Rex tutted and threw up his eyes to the ceiling to show that he had already heard this one before, a daring act of insurgence by his standards, and one immediately followed by a diplomatic retreat.

"I'm off to get the Sunday papers," he announced, and shuffled out of the bar without touching his drink.

"Who's Ruth Ellis?" I asked when he had gone.

"Ruth Ellis?" echoed Biba, her light voice heavy with the fanatic's contempt for the uninitiated. "Only the last woman in England to be hanged. Shot her lover *here*. She was a nightclub hostess, he was a racing car driver. Isn't that glamorous? The bullet holes are still on the wall outside." Rex later told me that Biba knew full well that the holes outside were from a plaque that had been removed and never filled in, but that she continued to stick to her more fantastical version of events. "Have you seen the film of it, *Dance with a Stranger*? It's one of the things that made me want to act. It was all so romantic."

"It's a bit gruesome," I said.

"Bloody hell, Karen, you're as bad as he is." She tilted her head toward Rex's glass, apparently his representative in absentia. "That's the difference between you and me, I suppose. Where you see unpleasantness, I see drama and passion. I don't know what's wrong with you both."

I could not decide what was worse: Biba's dismissal of my capacity for passion or the fact that it gave me something in common with her brother. To bring her back on my side I nudged her, pointing with my gaze to the tall bartender and raising my eyebrows.

"Australian?" I mouthed.

"Gay," she said decisively, and I curled up in the amniotic safety of our game.

Rex returned from the newsstand, arms stacked with layers of newsprint and cellophane. He let the papers fall to the table with a thud, and his sister began to sort through and divide them up.

"Sports and travel for you," she said, handing me folded sections casually and unapologetically. "Real estate for Rex, and downmarket trash and tabloid prurience for me," she continued, gathering the newspapers and their gaudy supplements into a loose pile and encircling them with her arms like a child shielding her exam paper from a classmate.

I wasn't really interested in sports unless I was playing them, and travel at the remove of a journalist's account held no real appeal for me either, so I couldn't get excited about the supplements that Biba had allotted to me. I watched them reading instead, Biba flipping from story to picture with a manic lack of concentration, sometimes opening magazines at the back page or in the middle and working back and forth as her fancy took her. Rex was more methodical. He read every page in turn, bypassing articles about music and gadgets but frowning over stories about interior decoration, property development, or gardening. Now and again he would fold back a page and score it with the back of his thumbnail before tearing it out, folding it up and putting it to one side, presumably to be saved and pasted into one of his scrapbooks when we got back to the house. His fingertips were dabbed with newsprint and there was a streak in the middle of his forehead where he kept running his hands through his hair or rubbing his brow.

Every now and then they would pick out something to read

aloud. It was a charming Victorian throwback, a legacy perhaps of a childhood without television.

"Listen to this, you'll like this," they would say. Rex would read the odd paragraph or quote but Biba would begin with the headline and deliver a two-page story from start to finish, never stumbling over the words. Apart from the one time I saw her on stage, I think it was the longest I ever saw her go without drinking or smoking.

"Your turn, Karen," said Biba, when she'd finished. I had the *Observer* magazine open at a page about tea shops in Granada but I hadn't read a word. "Find something to amuse us."

"Oh, I couldn't," I said, and I wasn't being modest. Then, as now, I could control my accent when I was arguing, when I was excited, even when drunk, but when I read aloud my vowels flattened and distorted.

I was too hot to judge the quality of the roast dinner that arrived to save me. Rex ate all of his, and half of Biba's, and some of mine, using a Yorkshire pudding I couldn't eat to mop up the gravy on her plate. He gave me a pale smile and returned to his pile of magazines. A male model advertising a chunky diving watch stared up from his page and out into the pub, looking less than impressed with us. Rex picked up this magazine and turned it over before clutching it to his chest so suddenly and with such an agonized expression that I thought he was having some kind of heart attack.

"What's that?" I asked. "What's wrong?" Rex shook his head, rousing Biba's curiosity as well as mine. He could have saved the situation even then by pretending to have heartburn—it would have been a credible excuse after what he'd just eaten—or a wasp sting, or a headache, or any other minor acute ailment. But subtlety, secrecy, and subterfuge weren't in his vocabulary, and instead his eyes traveled in a triangle of panic between the magazine, Biba, and me.

"C'mon, Rex, what's the scandal?" Unlike his sister, Rex was no actor.

"Nothing, it's just, it's just a thingy about conservatories."

"Is it fuck," said Biba, grinning. "Come on, share it with the group." He shook his head. "Let me see." There was an edge to her voice now, no longer wheedling but demanding.

"You don't want to," said Rex. He doubled the magazine over, sat on it, and folded his arms, but you had to do better than that if you wanted to keep something away from Biba. She wrestled it from underneath his buttocks. Rex brought his head down to his hands. Biba opened the magazine and uncreased it. All three of us stared down at the cover and into the face of a ghost.

I had seen only a couple of pictures of him, and none this recent, but it was definitely him: several years older, a few pounds heavier, and very much more alive than I had believed him to be, Roger Capel. He was dressed in black; a familiar-looking young woman with long blond hair, not much older than Rex, was wrapped around him like a python. Their eyes were the same blue as the background. The cover line confirmed it in bold yellow type. "OUT OF THE DARKROOM" it announced, and in a smaller font, "The Second Coming of Roger Capel." Biba let out the kind of snivel a frightened dog makes. She scrabbled noisily through the pages until she came to the cover story. She smoothed the pages over and over, her hands working on the paper as though by ironing it flat she could make sense of it. My eyes shuttled between her moving fingers, trying to piece together the puzzle. Columns of pictures flanked the print.

In one he was a round-faced, polo-necked youth in a self-conscious self-portrait, cigarette in one hand, cabled shutter release in the other. Another, taken much later, showed him standing outside an exhibition at the National Portrait Gallery that bore his name. The most recent photograph portrayed him shoulder-to-shoulder with a grinning Tony Blair and cradling a flute of champagne. Black caterpillar eyebrows identified the out-of-focus figure behind them as Noel Gallagher.

If the first page had been a professional album, the next was spread with personal portraits. Roger Capel and the blond woman, surrounded by a brood of fair-haired children, posed in a leafy garden somewhere with a private swimming pool. The tableau was a heartbreakingly glossy upgrade from the photograph I'd found in Biba's room, the one with his first family playing in the wading pool.

"What the *fuck*?" she repeated. Rex, unseen, had joined us on the pew and the three of us scanned the pages in silence. I clung to the solid teak of the table. I couldn't begin to guess what they were feeling. I could only taste a diluted version of their cocktail of snatched grief and hope and confusion. Beside me, Biba shook in silence. I wanted to hug them, to congratulate them on the amazing news that their father was alive, but knew I should take my cue from their own reactions. Until they spoke, all I could do was read on.

The interviewer had made much of the fact that Roger Capel's personal life, as well as his career, was sailing on a second wind. A caption identified the blond woman as his second wife and muse, Jules Millar. Putting a name to the face made the penny drop; she was a model who'd been in a huge ad campaign for makeup when I was a teenager. Now, Jules had evidently turned professional mother, writing books about child nutrition and creative play. Reading between the lines, I guessed that Roger Capel had granted this interview to promote her new career as much as his established one. The children in the picture seemed to be thriving: they were golden and glowing, idealized versions of middle-class childhood. They looked nothing like their half-siblings. His first family was dismissed in a couple of lines in the middle of the article. It was implied that the late seventies and early eighties had been something of a personal as well as professional wilderness, the journalist referring only to a "lost weekend that lasted two decades." Sheila Capel was summarized as his late wife, "the troubled model with whom he had two children." The use of the past tense pricked like a wasp sting, as did the quotation highlighted in bold type along the top of the page.

"I've been given a second chance at work and family," it said. "This is my new Year Zero. Nothing matters but now." Biba turned back a page and shook her head. The dam finally broke and tears flash-flooded her face. The paper grew opaque and the image on the other side, the photograph of her mother, shone through like a ghost. Rex wrapped a protective arm around his sister and tried to blot the paper with a pub napkin.

"Let it go, B," he said. "He's an arsehole."

"Fucking . . . I'm not having this. He can't do this. We were there first." Her voice was rising to a shrill crescendo. She shoved the table to one side, banging it against my rib cage, and looked wildly around the pub as if to gauge which of the exits was the quickest route to fresh air. "He can't do this," she hissed.

"Biba, no!" shouted Rex so loudly that even the little old man looked up from his stout. Finally I found my own voice.

"He's alive," I managed. "Your dad. He's alive!"

Rex has never been impatient but he came close to it then.

"Of course he's alive," he said. "Why wouldn't he be?" A gust of humid air sucked my attention toward the swinging door just in time to see Biba disappear through it. Rex covered the same distance in three loping strides. I picked up the magazine and sprinted into the street after them.

13

BIBA OUTRAN BOTH OF us, to my surprise and mild chagrin. I was the one who'd put in the hours on the treadmill while she spent her life smoking and starving, yet I had to draw on my deepest reserves to keep up with her. What she lacked in lung capacity and muscle power she made up for in lightness and grace. She also had the invaluable advantage of knowing where she was going: she never once turned her head to consult a street sign or check her bearings, and when she turned corners she made the swift, autopilot turns of someone who had trodden this route before. The street names here were black tiles with white lettering but I didn't have time to read the individual names. My lungs swelled and my stomach squeezed around the mash of food and drink in my belly but I kept going. I didn't know where she was going or what I would be preventing when I caught up with her. I had vague visions of rugby-tackling her to the ground, but I didn't really want to stop her: my hammering heart was due to excitement as much as exercise. After weeks chipping away at Biba's secret history, the family storybook was now opening its pages.

I was closing the gap now, and ragged gulps in my ear told me that Rex was keeping pace with me. All three of us were running in the middle of the road now. People saunter through those little private lanes and secret groves, they don't run unless they are joggers or robbers. We weren't dressed for running and we looked like an improbable trio of purse snatchers, but we still drew attention as we flew through the streets. We were going too fast to care about the Sunday strollers who stopped and stared.

My peripheral vision speed-read a sign for Keats House and my mind took an out-of-focus photograph of a big white mansion hidden behind a row of magnolias. As a student, I'd visited Keats's apartment in Rome and my thoughts, so focused just seconds before, began a sharp detour toward that ocher palazzo flanking the Spanish Steps. The weirdest details reared from packed-away corners of my memory, scenes from another life: I remembered a plate of soggy spaghetti I'd shared with Simon on the edge of the piazza. It was an unremarkable reverie that came to an abrupt end when a big black SUV reversed out of a hidden driveway and the chrome of its bumper connected with my thigh.

It wasn't much of an impact—I had been traveling faster than the car—but it was enough to send me to the ground. There was the crunch and whistle of foot pedal and hand brake being engaged simultaneously, and the driver was out of his seat in seconds, his stricken face looming over me. Rex skidded to a halt so quickly that his shoes made an indentation on the sun-melted surface of the road. I could feel a dull thrum in my leg where the car had hit me and in my hip where I had landed, and knew that in the morning twin bruises would color the outside of each thigh. I would deal with that then.

"I'm fine," I told Rex, the driver, and the growing crowd. "Really, I'm fine." I pulled myself up by the bumper and transferred my weight first onto my left leg and then onto my right. Nothing broken. I looked to the spot I had last seen Biba. She was gone.

"We've lost her!" I said. "Rex, we've lost her."

"I know exactly where she's gone," he said with a sigh, and he gestured toward a tiny square at the end of the lane. I jogged away from the driver, his concern turning to anger as I vanished from his sight, rounding a corner to where Biba had stopped.

The house she stood outside was half-obscured by a weft of clematis threaded through wrought-iron railings, but they couldn't disguise its size or gloss or beauty. It looked like a photograph from one of Rex's beloved property pages. It was built of that same London stone as the house in Queenswood Lane, but this building was low and wide, not long and lean. Wooden shutters in the windows, a mature garden, and a graveled drive whispered money. The only vulgarity was a red sports car parked at an angle.

Biba's finger was pressed to a buzzer on the gatepost. No voice crackled over the live intercom and when the gates swung slowly open she looked surprised and unnerved for a few seconds, as though she hadn't really expected them to admit her.

"What's she doing?" I said to Rex as she turned sideways and slid her frame through the bars. "Whose house is this?"

"My dad lives here," he said.

"Your dad lives here?" I echoed, as we crunched across the drive in Biba's wake. Now that the shock of Roger Capel's existence had had time to sink in, I was beginning to take this personally. I felt that I was being played with. Why had she lied to me? Why had she let me feel sorry for her, and pretended to be poor when they came from this kind of money?

"Colin!" a voice came through a garden gate and a latch was fiddled with. "You're early." There was a rustle and some footsteps from a side gate and through an archway that evidently led onto a back garden, Roger Capel emerged, the smile sliding slowly off his face. I heard the gates click shut behind us.

"Hello, Daddy," said Biba in the little-girl voice she used when she wanted Rex to do something for her.

"What are you two doing here?" he asked, poor mathematics or disinterest not allowing him to count me as one of his visitors. His voice was broad East End, a surprise that compounded the others; I'd always assumed Biba's flawless vowels came from years of careful breeding.

"We were just passing," said Rex, his panted breath giving the lie to this feeble improvisation.

"It's not a great time," said their father, looking over his shoulder.

"It never is," said Rex bitterly.

"If we'd called first, would you have seen us?" asked Biba.

"Of course I would."

"Bollocks," she shrilled, and the word was a glass bauble on her lips. "We haven't seen you for over a year. You ignored the invitations to all my plays. You forgot my twenty-first."

Roger Capel drew himself up in defense.

"I didn't forget your birthday, I bought you a present." Then, after dredging his memory: "A bag."

"What color was it?" she said.

"What?"

"The bag. Your thoughtful gift. That you personally chose and in no way got Jules to buy. What color was it?" Roger Capel didn't answer.

"Listen, darling, I've had a lot on my plate," he said.

"So I see." She unfolded the magazine. "Not too busy to tell the world about your amazing new life though, are you?"

He shrugged. "I can't help what journalists put."

"So you didn't say all that stuff about year zero and wiping out the past? Christ, Dad, you can't airbrush us from history. We're here. We exist." She threw the magazine onto the gravel. "You just wait until I'm a famous actress. Then you won't ignore us. Then you'll be proud to call me your daughter."

I bent down to pick up the magazine. Roger Capel suddenly noticed me. It was as though I had to touch something to become visible to him.

"Who is this person?" he said to Rex.

"Dad, this is Karen. Karen, this is obviously my father. Roger Capel."

"What happened to the fat one?" said Roger.

"Right, that's it, we're going," said Rex, anger lending him temporary authority. His fingers found the exit buzzer on the garden wall under a tangle of clematis and the gates began slowly to part. "I'm sorry you're not pleased to see us. But we do need to talk soon. About the house."

"There's nothing to talk about," said Roger wearily.

"It's our home," said Rex. "We haven't got anything else." Roger folded his arms. "*Please*," said Rex. There was a catch in his voice.

"I'm sorry, Rex. We've been over this. It's just not something we can afford."

Every conversation today was raising more questions than it answered. I was confused, but Biba clearly knew exactly what this was all about.

"Can't afford it?" she shrilled. "How much did this house cost? How much did this *car* cost?" She picked up a garden rake that leaned against the wall. I stood rooted, useless with fear and the bright, shameful need to know what would happen next. I didn't have long to wait. With surprising force, Biba raised the rake over her head and brought it down onto the windshield of the red sports car. It bounced off the glass and the alarm began its penetrating, high-pitched pulse.

The noise brought Jules Millar into the front garden. She looked just as though she had stepped out of one of her advertisements. Everything about her looked freshly washed, from her swinging blond hair to the white dress she wore. Roger Capel stepped protectively in front of her as Biba swung the rake down onto the car again, this time making a dent in the windshield that sent a frosted crackle across its whole surface. A baby's wail drifted from an upstairs window, a horrible discordant accompaniment to the shriek of the alarm. Jules looked from the house to the car and then at her husband.

"I'm going to call the police, darling," she said.

"No need," he said. "They're going."

Rex closed in on Biba from behind. I was close enough to hear his whispered words.

"You're not helping," he said. "Come on. I'll sort it out. I promise. Just let it go." Finger by finger, he unclawed her hands and replaced the rake against the wall. She clenched her fists and released them again before allowing him to shepherd her back through the gates. Outside, she barged past a well-dressed man in his forties, cradling a bottle of champagne in the crook of his elbow. This, I guessed, was the Colin that Roger Capel had been expecting, the reason he had dropped his guard and opened his gates to us. On the other side of the gate, Roger had managed to silence the alarm and Colin's words echoed down the lane.

"Bloody hell, Rog! Did those kids do that to your Audi? Who were they?"

The long walk home was silent. I had prepared for tears and histrionics, was even hoping for the clarity and explanations they might provide, but Biba was quieter than I'd ever known her. The smoke from her cigarettes cast a force field around her I didn't dare attempt to penetrate. I let her march ahead and fell into step with Rex. I began with the less urgent question.

"What was that about the house?" I asked. "What did you mean, sort it out?"

"It's not actually our house," said Rex. "We're just his tenants. Actually, that's not strictly true, because we don't pay him rent. But it's all in his name. He was Mum's next-of-kin, so it's his. We don't legally have a right to it."

"But he can obviously afford it. He doesn't need that house."

"He sees it as a future for his family."

"But *you're* his family."

"Not according to that interview," he said.

When we walked back past Kenwood, the families had been replaced by knots of friends and lovers in their teens and twenties, cans of beer and bottles of wine now added to the picnics.

"She told me he was dead, you know," I said, looking at my feet. "Why would she do that?"

Rex sighed. "I'm sorry about that," he said. "She probably wishes he was. I know I often do. I've thought about killing him, I've had dreams where I've actually done it. Not that there's any point in killing him unless he signs over the house. We'd definitely be homeless then." He smiled to show me he was joking and rolled up a shirtsleeve that had come undone, meticulously folding back the flapping cuff before turning it over and over on itself. "The thing is, we need to persuade him by being reasonable and trying to rebuild a relationship with him. That's not going to happen if she goes around attacking his cars and yelling at him. I'm so angry with her, I could kill her, too."

I clamped my lips together with my teeth. The notion of phlegmatic, mousy Rex in a murderous frenzy was too ridiculous to contemplate with a straight face, and I knew that if I started to laugh all the tension of the day would come spilling out in a giggling fit I wouldn't be able to control.

By the time we turned back onto Hampstead Lane, the light was fading and the roads were clearer. Cars whizzed past, covering in minutes the circuit it had taken us most of the day to complete, and when we turned home into Queenswood Lane, it was nighttime proper and the street was the color of green ink.

In the Velvet Room, Biba perched on the end of the sofa while Rex slumped into the red armchair.

"Want to talk about it?" was the best I could do. She shrugged. "Why did you say that he was dead?"

"I didn't!"

"You did, Biba. You told me both your parents were dead. You actually used the word *orphan*. That time in the bar. The day we met."

"Oh." A brief break in eye contact and a small shrug was the nearest I would get to an apology. "Well, I was drunk. He might as well be. He seems to be wishing us out of existence, so I'm trying to do the same to him."

"And your mum . . ."

"Yes, well. That one is true. I wouldn't make something like that up. It's the worst thing that's ever happened to us."

"I'm sorry you had to find out from a newspaper," said Rex. I froze. How long had he known that I'd been through the box under his bed? Then I realized he was referring to the magazine I still clutched in my hand. "I assumed you knew."

"It can't be easy to talk about," I said. "And I'm sorry. I really am. I'm so sorry."

"Stop saying sorry, for fuck's sake," said Biba. "It wasn't your fault. We all know whose fault it was." She glared at Rex, who looked at the floor.

I voiced the thought I'd been playing with for the last hour. "I'm sure you could get a lawyer to get him to sign the house over to you," I said. "I'm sure there must be precedents for it. It's your childhood home, after all. You must have some rights. He isn't poor."

I expected their admiration for my brain wave. Instead, twin expressions of horror dismayed me.

"But he's our *dad*," said Biba. "We can't take him to court. What kind of person sues their own parent?" Rex nodded in agreement.

"But you might get the house," I pressed. "You'd have security for the rest of your lives if he gave you the house."

"Yes," said Biba. "But then he definitely wouldn't love us any-more."

That night in bed, I lay awake on my right-hand side. Bruises, like sunburn, are nocturnal, and the one on my left thigh was waking up as I tried to sleep, a soft dark badge to commemorate the day's chases and revelations. I had always thought of uncondi-tional love describing a parent's devotion to a child, not the other way around. You hear about mothers who can't stop loving their rapist sons, and fathers who stick by daughters who steal and kill. It had never occurred to me that children, even grown-up children, could persevere with a futile devotion to a father who had replaced his first children with new babies with the detachment of someone choosing to upgrade his car or his home.

14

REX'S PAROLE OFFICER IS named Ben Weaver. He is oozing with the youth, eagerness, sincerity, and incompetence of a recent graduate. He sits nervously on the edge of our sofa. I can't tell if the shirt, tie, and cardigan ensemble he is wearing is wildly stylish or the result of absolute sartorial disinterest; those clothes could mark him out as one of the beautiful, fashionable people or a lonely nerd. He can only be seven or eight years younger than I but the generation gap is a chasm.

The purpose of the interview is to set Rex on a career path. Ben keeps using the word *rehabilitation* in reference to his time away. Rex doesn't take exception to this but I do. He is not a real criminal, not in the way that other men are. It is a bitter irony that to explain this to people would jeopardize everything we have achieved since the night he was arrested.

"Most of the people I work with aren't lucky enough to have Rex's setup," says Ben, steam from his cup of tea misting his horn-rimmed glasses. "I mean, they don't all have this kind of family unit waiting for them. I'll be honest with you, I'm used to putting them straight back into the benefit system because I know they'll be reoffending within the hour."

"But not Rex," I say as calmly as I can.

"Absolutely! Not Rex," says Ben brightly. He studies the paperwork in front of him again. "Anyway, he doesn't qualify for unemployment benefits because he's got you to support him. So . . . during your rehabilitation you completed a diploma in systems analysis," he says. "What does that mean, exactly?"

"It's an ITC qualification," says Rex. "Computers. I'd have a degree by now if they hadn't gone and let me out early, the bastards." He breaks the deadpan with a smile, giving Ben permission to neigh a nervous laugh.

"Haha! Very good. Well done, anyway. Now, this sounds pessimistic, but the easiest way to proceed is to rule out the things you can't do with this before talking about the ones you can. CRB checks are becoming standard across most industries, so you won't get security clearance for any big companies. Council work will be dodgy, too. Obviously anything that involves working with children or the vulnerable is out . . ."

"So what *are* my options?" says Rex. "I want to work, you know."

"That's what I like to hear. We want you to work, too. Hmm. Can't you set yourself up as one of those people who takes in computers and repairs them?" suggests Ben. "When my hard drive collapsed I'd have given anything for a local bloke to come around and put things right. Had to take it all the way back to Dixons in the end. You could work from home."

The thought of Rex sharing my desk space, of him always being here, triggers a surge of claustrophobia that swells my lungs and closes my throat. I focus on keeping my breathing slow and controlled, so absorbed in this task that I miss the rest of the conversation and am aware of Ben's presence only when he stands up to leave. He is on the doorstep before I find the courage to ask my final question.

"Ben?" I say. "How easy is it for people to find Rex? I mean, for someone from prison to trace him here, or for someone local to find out about his record?"

"Well, you can find anyone if you really want to," he says. "But it's much easier to disappear than it ought to be. I lose loads of cases." He pulls a sheet from his frilled wad of papers and blinks up and down it. "He was known as Capel in prison, so the name change should go some way to, ah, keeping the wolf from the door." Embarrassed by his own gauche turn of phrase, he shuffles out to his car without a proper good-bye.

We stand in the window and watch Ben go. Even his driving is nervous and hesitant; he checks all his mirrors three or four times before signaling and pulling slowly away.

"It doesn't look good, does it?" Rex murmurs into the fold of my neck, in a voice I haven't heard him use for years. He sounds vulnerable. He has worn optimism lightly since his release, and it hasn't taken much to strip him of it. "What am I going to do, Karen? What am I going to do with the rest of my life? Who's going to give me a job?" His hot sigh condenses on my skin. "I want to provide for you both. Big house, all that . . ."

"There's no rush. This house is big enough for now. Three can live as cheaply as two. I make enough."

"And have you resent me with every day I don't work and you do? No thanks." He has voiced my own fear, and in doing so diminishes it. "I'm sorry, I don't want to sound ungrateful. It's just that I kind of saw leaving prison as the end of a process and actually, it's just the start of a whole new struggle. I don't know if I'm up to it."

"Of course you are," I tell him. "We've been through worse than this."

"You can say that again." He detaches himself from me. "Let's talk about something else. Will that tea still be hot, do you think?"

While Rex fetches his mug I go to draw the curtains, checking the street before I close the house up for the night. I am almost resigned when I see the white car. The driver is still in the seat, face turned toward our terrace but features once again hooded and indistinguishable. I have noticed, although I wonder if it is just a coincidence, that when the white car is parked outside, the anonymous, silent phone calls never come.

In spite of the boasts Biba made to her father, she never did become a famous actress and make him proud. In the end, Roger

Capel's eldest children drew attention to him in a way that he could never have predicted. I wonder if, like me, he often replays that scene in his front garden. I hope he wishes he had played it differently.

I often daydream about the career she could have had. I think she would have been suited to the life of a London actress, still living in Highgate and disappearing to the West End every night to work on her craft and delight her public. She would pick up the odd role in a costume drama or commercial so that when we were walking down the street together, people would nudge each other and whisper that that was the girl from the television. She would be successful and fulfilled, but not so starry that her calling would have taken her away from me. Occasionally I wonder what her life would have been like if she had achieved a Hollywood career, having her face in the press for all the right reasons, on the covers of magazines, and the name Biba Capel emblazoned across the sides of buses. This reverie is less comfortable and one I indulge in less often: there is no place for me in that alternate reality except through Rex.

I had my first taste of what life with Biba as a working actress would be like in the week leading up to her graduate performance. The preparations for her role in *As You Desire Me* were a drama in themselves: pacing, reciting, slammed doors, and agonized, bitchy telephone conversations with Rachael about the director and other cast members that lasted long into the night. I longed to be Biba's confidante, but when I tried to ask her how it was going she told me I wouldn't understand—she needed to talk to another actor.

I had expected the theater to be a sumptuous West End hall, all footlights and gilt, opera glasses tucked into the back of red velvet seats. A closer look at the address should have put paid to those ideas. It was on the wrong side of Marylebone Road, just off Lisson Grove. The theater was a low square building fronted by a pair of unsightly fire doors, watched over by the scowling windows of a housing project block. Inside, it was deceptively spacious but that was about all you could say for it. The walls were exposed cinder block, peeling with layers of wretched flyers for long-forgotten past productions. The artwork, if you could call it that, was weird glazed clay shapes attached to burlap backing. Here and there the strings had broken like old tennis rackets. I wondered if this ugly space would remain unrefurbished for long enough to come back into fashion. I couldn't understand why anyone would build a theater like this when the traditional kind was so much more exciting, so much more appropriate. Biba, I'm sure, would have argued that the language of Shakespeare or Ibsen or whoever should be so powerful that the venue didn't matter.

In the bar, a crowd of parents milled about, their formal clothes at odds with the hot weather. Fathers sweated in heavyweight suits while mothers fanned wilting hairstyles out of their eyes with their programs. Most of the chatter was supplied by people my own age, drama students or their friends. I knew no one and was suddenly desperate to have someone to talk to. Even Rex would have done. But he had taken my car and was running late, probably trying to find somewhere to park.

The warm white wine they served gave me an instant headache. I felt physically sick at the thought of seeing Biba perform. I was about to be let into her other world, the one that took her away during the days when she rehearsed and would take her away from me during the nights when she was successful. Like Rex, I recognized Biba's work as an unassailable rival, something almost umbilically connected to her that I could never compete with. Another doubt tickled the back of my consciousness like a cough I couldn't swallow. What if she was awful? What if the respect and admiration that our friendship was based on fell flat when I saw a bad performance? I hoped I would still be able to admire, or at least tolerate, her artistic temperament even if there was no great talent to justify it.

The klaxon that heralded the opening of the auditorium sounded more like a four-minute warning than an invitation to a performance. I jumped and knocked my elbow against the man behind me, and turned to apologize. Rex stood there silently.

"How long have you been here?"

"Literally just got here," he said. "Don't worry, I haven't been hovering behind you for five minutes or anything," he said, convincing me that that was exactly what he had been doing. He had gotten his hair cut, the cowlick that tufted out the back of his neck replaced by a short back and sides that left the quiff at the front standing up in a proud pompadour. He wore an old suit with a one-button jacket that flattered rather than ridiculed his skinny frame with a faded Rolling Stones T-shirt underneath. It was a look that would have seemed studied to the point of pretentiousness on anyone else, but I knew that it was the only suit Rex owned, and he'd been wearing the T-shirt that morning and it wouldn't have occurred to him to change. The result was a genuine artlessness that was surprisingly attractive.

"This is our little girl's big night, huh?" he said, squeezing my arm. As the crowd filed into the auditorium he cast his eyes desperately around and I noticed that he held four tickets in his hand. "He's not coming, is he? Let's go in."

Like a proud parent, I had made up my mind that she was going to be great before she took to the stage. And like a proud parent I lacked any kind of objectivity. To me, the fact that my friend was on stage was mesmerizing before she even began to perform. I knew nothing of theater apart from the foreign plays I had studied, and I had struggled to care for or understand them. How could I tell good from bad? I could see that she had presence on the stage, that she looked the part, and that she had finally mastered the umlaut, but apart from that I was struggling to form an opinion. The play was such a self-conscious piece of theater—with such absurd dialogue and such a disjointed plot—that it was impossible to tell the wooden actors from the naturals.

"What do you think?" said Rex at intermission.

"I think she's brilliant."

"Really?" he said. "Between you and me, I can't really tell. I don't know what anyone's on about up there. It's all ideas and no proper story, isn't it? Those characters all exist to make a point rather than to develop or go anywhere. It's not what I'd call a plot."

"I actually studied this play," I said.

"Oh God, I'm sorry," said Rex, fumbling for forgiveness as though I'd written it myself.

"Don't be. I don't really get it either."

During the second act, which involved a lot of dramatic posturing on a white staircase in front of a painted sea view, I rehearsed my congratulatory speech, wondering how best to praise her without giving myself away.

"What happens now?" I asked, after it had ended.

"Well. There are a lot of agents here, and they'll all be trying to snap up the students. We hope. If she doesn't get approached tonight, then it's a question of waiting for a phone call. Not a situation I particularly want to live with. So I guess everyone's backstage. Still. You can bear my company for an hour or so while we wait, can't you?"

The hour turned into two, during which time the bar gradually emptied. Performers, some looking crestfallen, others elated, left in twos, with parents or partners. Rachael was there, her peroxide hair shorter and brighter than ever. She looked like a lightbulb in the dingy black bar.

"Rex," she said. "What did you think?" She kissed the air on either side of his ears.

"Well done, I thought," he said. "Really, really well done." Rachael looked expectantly at me.

"Yes, well done," I said. "I didn't recognize you."

"I'll take that as a compliment," she said, and then to Rex, "Are you guys having any kind of after-party?"

Rex blinked. "Not that I know of," he said. "Is that what Biba's saying backstage? I mean, we could, but we haven't got anything in, and . . ."

"No, I was just hoping. Biba hasn't said anything," said Rachael with a wink. "Where is she, anyway?"

"Is she not backstage?" asked Rex.

"Hard to tell, darling," said Rachael, beginning to lose interest in us. "It's a bit of a scrum. Listen, I've got to go. Let's get together soon, yeah?"

"Who did she play?" I asked Rex when she was out of earshot.

"No idea," he said.

We were a pair of nervous parents desperately restraining the urge to seek out their child in order not to embarrass her in front of her friends. We waited until the foyer was empty and echoing, our small talk bouncing half-heartedly off the concrete and glass walls. A bronze plaque told me that the theater had been unveiled by an actress, a dame no less, in 1969. She was no one I had heard of. I caught myself and Rex reflected in the surface of a convex mirror hanging from a square pillar and tried to see us as others would. We looked like a couple, but not, as I would have expected, the awful kind who go out to dinner and eat in silence, but an established pair, comfortable in each other's silence. I hadn't noticed, until I saw his arm slung over the back of my seat, that he had been sitting so close to me.

"When B's a working actress," he said, "we're going to use the money she gets and we'll redo the rooms so we can rent them out to other actors as digs when they're in London," he said.

"Does that mean I'll have to train as an actress if I want to stay living with you?" I asked.

"Please don't. I'll need your normality as an antidote to the insanity of a house full of mad theater people. I want to get the walls properly plastered, a couple more bathrooms, and you can get this laminate flooring stuff that looks just like the real thing. Not to mention sorting out the wiring."

"It wouldn't be the same if it conformed to health and safety standards. Come on. How many houses in London are left like that?"

"Believe me, the novelty wears off, especially in the winter," he said. "What I'd really like is to install underfloor heating through-out, but Biba will have to get a major role before we can afford that kind of upgrade."

Or perhaps you could get a job, I thought, but what I said was, "Don't take this the wrong way, Rex, but why don't you work?"

"As what?" he said. "I haven't got any skills. I haven't got any qualifications."

"None at all?"

"I dropped out of school when I was fifteen to look after Biba," he said.

"Don't you ever resent that?" I said. It helped to explain why Biba's career was so important to Rex. If she did not make it as an actress, the failure would be his as well as hers. The value of formal education had been so impressed upon me that I could not imag-ine giving mine up for anyone, no matter how much I loved them.

"Resent what? No. I hated school," he said. "Well, my mum kind of put it in my head that exams weren't important because I wouldn't have to work if I didn't want to—that my dad would always look after us. Actually I didn't mind the academic stuff, I quite liked lessons, but there was so much emphasis on sports, and the other boys . . . I didn't exactly have lots of friends." Had Rex *ever* had any friends of his own? Everyone I had met so far, even Nina, his lover, had been drawn to the house through Biba. Perhaps he too was ponder-ing the bleakness of his social situation because after a short pause he returned to his default topic of conversation, home improve-ment. "Of course, we're lucky in that there isn't really that much major structural work to do. Knocking the ground floor through to make it a kitchen-diner is the biggest job, and the supporting wall is already reinforced. The only real challenge is how we're going to fit a bathroom in that attic level where your room is. Actually, I'd like your opinion on that. Do you think an en suite—"

"Okay, that's it," I said, to snuff out this soliloquy. "We're going to find her."

The backstage area was behind a black door with a steel handle in a corridor near the lobby, between the men's and women's restrooms. It smelled like a school gymnasium changing room and gave directly onto the stage. I looked out into the dim auditorium, trying to work out what it was about that sea of faces that actors craved so much. Even with it empty I felt on show, exposed, as though I was about to be found out for a crime I couldn't name but knew I was guilty of. I once heard someone say that everyone lives in fear of being "found out," that all you have to do is tell them that you know their secret often enough and paranoia will make them confess. I didn't believe that to be true—not everyone, I thought, harbors a secret so terrible that they can be made to confess in that way. I reasoned that it was just a quirk of human nature, an abstract and innate paranoia, like fear of the dark or hating the sound of nails on a blackboard. That was before I had a past worth covering. Now, I read accusation and knowledge into the most innocuous everyday encounters.

Directly behind the stage was another corridor, with a few tiny, open dressing rooms misted with perfume and hairspray and cigarette smoke but empty of people. We had a look in the other corridor, navigated the concrete angles, and by the time we came right back out into the bar it was midnight and the last of the glasses were being loaded into the dishwasher.

"The bar's closed," said the pockmarked teenager behind the Formica counter.

"Are you sure there's no one left in the theater? Anywhere in the building?" I said to him.

"They're doing the final check now," he replied, sliding the shutter down to end our discussion. The lights were extinguished with a finalizing click and the dark squeezed us out of the theater and into the street.

Rex was starting to twitch, his brow bisected by a deep vertical groove.

"It can't be good news," he said in the voice I'd heard on the

telephone the evening he overreacted to Biba's two-hour disap-
pearance. He put both hands up to smooth down his hair. He
had forgotten he'd had it cut that day, and looked at his hands as
if he expected his fingers to be laced with clumps of it. "Right,
let's think about this logically. If she hasn't got an agent, then she
needs to be at home in case one calls. There's still a chance, isn't
there? Or maybe she's gone off somewhere. What shall we do?"
He looked at me expectantly.

"I don't know, Rex," I said. "She's your sister. She's also twenty-
one."

Impatience at Rex's panic was eclipsing my own dismay that,
on one of the most important nights of her life, Biba had not come
immediately to me, to seek my opinion or to share her news.

"I'm going back to the car," I said.

"I'm not leaving without her!" he almost sobbed.

"I meant, to look for her."

The car was outside some apartments a block away from the
theater, and Biba sat on the hood. She was still fully made up but
wearing an oversized man's shirt as a dress, belted at the middle
with a scarf, her legs crossed underneath her. She was babbling
away to three men who stood around the vehicle, stopping Rex
and me in our tracks. Light from the streetlamps above distorted
their features and gave their faces an eerie, menacing cast. One
of them, the tallest of the three, with scruffy blond hair, looked
familiar. He was the only one actually listening to Biba. The other
two I had never seen before. One was stocky and swarthy with
buzz-cut hair, while the other had a ponytail and a ring through
his eyebrow. A leather lead was wrapped around his wrist; on the
other end was a white pit bull terrier, a solid, violent-looking little brute, unmuzzled and straining in our direction. They exuded
the kind of danger that I could tell Biba found thrilling but that I
found simply unpleasant and uncomfortable. I had the feeling that
they might actually get into my car and drive off and, worse, that
if they did so, I would probably let them.

Biba saw us and called our names excitedly. As if by prior arrangement, her companions receded into the shadows and began a muttered discussion.

"Where were you?" cried Rex, no anger but only relief in his voice. "I was worried sick!"

"Well done," I said, when I was close enough for her to hear me and then, "How did it go? Are you okay?"

"I got one!" she said, clapping her hands and sliding off the hood. The name and the agency she gave meant nothing to me, but the other actors the man represented were familiar, their names recognizable from regional detective shows and hospital dramas.

"When did you find out?" Rex and I asked simultaneously.

"Literally as soon as the curtain fell. He just came straight up and said he'd like to represent me. Fucking . . . it's the best-case scenario. No waiting, no tension, nothing."

Not for her, but for me and Rex, three hours in the bar, the wait had been interminable.

"And I couldn't have done it without you," she said to me. "Thank you so, so much." She left a port wine kiss on my cheek. "I'm sorry I didn't come and find you," she said. "I got chatting to Guy and lost track of time. But I've been waiting for you here. You've been ages."

"Guy?" I said. The name was familiar but I couldn't conjure a face.

"You remember Guy. Can I bum a cigarette, darling?"

The blond man muttered to his companions and grazed knuckles with them in a careless handshake before they shuffled into the night, the dog alone giving a backward glance.

Up close, I knew exactly who he was; the mysterious benefactor who had given me the free E on Biba's birthday. Guy reached into one of the many pockets of his voluminous khaki jacket—it was far too heavy for such a hot night, and I wondered what he kept in those various compartments—and pulled out a packet of Marlboro Lights.

"Thank you, darling," she said as he lit it for her. "I was *dying* without my cigarettes." Biba was always dying. Dying of thirst, dying of boredom, dying for a cigarette. It is a turn of phrase I shudder to recall.

Guy grunted an acknowledgment of our presence. I wondered if he ever spoke, or appeared in daylight.

"Guy came to see the show," said Biba, "and he's going to come back to the house for a smoke, aren't you?"

I waited for Rex's protest but instead he held out his hands to me.

"I haven't had much to drink at all," he said to me. I tossed him the keys. When he unlocked the car door, even in the relative cool air of the night, it was like standing next to an opened oven.

"You'll have to go in the front, mate," said Rex to Guy. I winced: Rex saying "mate" was like hearing your dad pretend to like dance music in front of your friends. Biba and I pressed together in the backseat while Guy and Rex extended the front seats as far back as they could go. Neither man spoke throughout the drive. Rex tapped impatiently on the steering wheel at the Swiss Cottage traffic lights and then climbed up Frognal in too high a gear before cutting through the heath. There, a breeze finally found its way through our open windows. Biba threaded her fingers through mine and spoke in a whisper.

"I'm getting lucky tonight and no mistake," she said. She let go of my hand and began to stroke the back of Guy's neck with her left hand. "I'm glad I've got you to distract Rex. He can be a bit funny about things like this. You can stay for a bit of a smoke with us, but you don't mind making yourself scarce afterwards, do you?"

Rex parked the car on the pavement directly outside the house, right tires perched on the double yellow lines.

"Remind me to move that first thing in the morning," he said, before thundering ahead to the house. He left the front door open for me but let it swing back as Biba and Guy staggered up the steps behind. It would have slammed shut in their faces if the faulty lock had not caused the door to bounce open against its jamb. They had already established themselves as a single physical unit. Their bodies were as entwined as they could be and still walk, as though they were entering some kind of three-legged race.

In the Velvet Room Rex lit the candles while Guy lay with Biba on a balding corduroy beanbag that had once been orange. I could see that he might hold attractions for her that went beyond the lure of free drugs. He was extraordinarily good-looking in an obvious, immediate, almost intimidating way. Unlike the Capels' beauty, Guy's did not steal up on you slowly: it hit you in the face with all the subtlety of a cola commercial. Muscles rippled beneath evenly burnished skin, blue eyes and full lips dominated a face that was saved from femininity by a strong brow and solid jawline. A feathering of blond hair curled around his face like daisy petals closing for the evening. He had finally taken off his jacket. Underneath he wore a kind of undershirt with the number 66 printed on the front. His upper arm and shoulder were covered with overlapping tattoos. They were pancultural designs: an anchor, the word *Mum* etched in a scroll beneath a heart, Chinese letters, Maori symbols, and Celtic knots, needlework representing hours of pain. Biba's dark little features tilted toward his face like a sunflower to the rays, and every time she shifted closer to him, tiny polystyrene beans bled through a tear in the sack and rolled around on the floor. Her dark eyes wore an expression I'd never seen before. Not love, not humor, there was none of the intimacy that she reserved for Rex, and for me. They sparkled with something less substantial but more compelling.

Rex was flipping noisily through a selection of uncased CDs that had fanned on the floor beneath the stereo until I selected one at random and thrust it into his hands. Obediently, he placed it in the tray and the speakers broadcast the synthesized strains of something slow and unsyncopated. Guy began to roll a joint without taking his hand off Biba's thigh. A voice inside my head that wasn't mine screamed, *Get your fucking hands off her.* Across the room I saw Rex's obvious discomfort and wondered if he'd heard it too.

"So . . ." exhaled Rex. "Here we all are." The silence hadn't been awkward until he said that but it was then. Even stilted conversation, I reasoned, must be better than this.

"Herbs or chemicals?" Guy said to Biba, holding up two tiny plastic bags with Ziploc seals, one containing what looked like dried basil, the other a white powder. Whatever it was there was an abundant supply, a whole party's worth, but it was clear that the offer didn't extend to Rex and me. He was talking about the provenance of his drugs the way some people enthuse about the vineyard their wine is grown in, telling Biba that the marijuana had come all the way from Thailand. I wondered what Guy's background was. The glottal stops and dropped *h*'s that flecked his speech sounded like an affectation to me. Round and expensive vowels slipped through the wide net of his London drawl.

"Going for a piss," he said suddenly and slunk out, taking his jacket with him.

"What do you think?" she said. "Isn't he gorgeous? I think I might have found a new partner in crime here."

I thought that was my role.

"What does he actually do, apart from take drugs, sell drugs, and talk about drugs?" said Rex. "Has he got a proper job?"

"You can talk, dole boy," retorted Biba. "Anyway, when did we start demanding to see people's pay stubs before we let them cross your precious threshold?"

"I don't want a dealer hanging around the house," said Rex as he swept up beanbag stuffing with his hands and piled the little balls in a ceramic ashtray. "I didn't like the look of his friends, either."

"It's just little bits, here and there, for friends. He's hardly Carlos the Jackal. Don't roll your eyes at me." She passed me the joint and I balanced it between my first and middle fingers before taking a drag. I was learning that the trick of achieving pleasant befuddlement without nausea was to hold the smoke in my lungs for no more than a second. This was not a problem when faced with the bitter, acrid taste of Guy's cannabis.

"It's just that I really don't think it's a good idea to get involved with him, sweetheart," said Rex. "He's always off his head. Is he someone you want around you right now? This is the crucial time we've been gearing up to for years. You got an agent, what, four hours ago? You should be putting all your energy into your work."

Biba stuck her chin in the air. Her stage makeup was starting to cake at the corners of her nose and mouth, and her heavy black eye shadow was starting to flake and settle in the feathery creases around her eyes.

"Actually, someone like Guy could really help me develop as an actress. I can't only mix with nice middle-class drama students. I mean, it's not like every audition will be for a costume drama. There's a whole other side of society they don't teach you about in drama school that I haven't got any experience of. Guy has access to these people, real people. Even Tris and Jo are only playing at slumming it . . ."

I have often wondered whether Guy, who came back to lie down beside her then, overheard that remark. It wouldn't have made much difference in the moment, nothing she could have said would have dampened his desire for her. But he could have heard, and if he wasn't bright enough to grasp the concept of method acting or the implications that accompanied it he would certainly have understood what she meant by the phrase "slumming it," even if, as I suspected, he was little more than a class tourist him-self. Would it have had any bearing on what he did later, the stupid thing he did that changed everything? Probably not. Even now, years later, I am still trying to look for clues that might shift the blame somewhere else.

Their lust locked us out. His hands were on her body, and she had her legs wrapped around his waist. I felt a stab of something more than the usual jealousy of anyone who got closer to Biba than I could: a pang of nostalgia for something I had never experienced. Their kiss grew louder, making a noise like someone glugging olive oil into a bowl of pasta. The sound was as repellent as the sight was entrancing.

Rex had refilled his wineglass and was already halfway up the staircase. I couldn't resist one look back into the Velvet Room before I closed the door behind me. They had managed to pry their bodies apart and Guy was crouching in front of the coffee table. He had tipped a pile of fine white powder from a folded square of paper onto the surface of a CD, using a credit card to chop it into skinny lines while Biba poured more wine.

"Don't worry about Guy," I said to the lonely figure silhouetted in his bedroom doorway. "He's just a good-looking thug. She only likes him for novelty value. We'll probably never see him after tonight."

"In my experience the girls go for the good-looking thug over the nice guy every time. Still, you might be right." He pressed the heels of his hands deep into the sockets of his eyes. "I don't think I'll wait up for her tonight. I think I'll try to get some sleep for once."

The following hours were fitful. The wine I had drunk had made me sleepy but the joint made my heart beat loudly and irregularly in my ears. I didn't sleep deeply but struggled to wake up from uncomfortable dreams. The Velvet Room had turned into a stage, with Biba's alter ego singing her German song as her real self and the rest of us stretched out on the floor. Our clothes tangled around us and floated off us like seaweed and our bodies came together. There were no words. Biba was in the center of the orgy: sometimes she was kissing Guy while Rex stroked my skin, sometimes it was her brother's face she held on to while she searched his mouth with her tongue and sometimes it was my body she threaded herself through like a vine. Guy and I were on the verge of congress in my dream when his voice, his real voice, broke into it. I could hear him, three floors below me, rattling the French windows and shouting at Biba.

"Come on," he said. "Help me with the door, you dozy bitch." Then his tone changed. "Oh, fucking hell. Wake up! Wake up! Shit . . ." In the silence that followed, I think he was trying to remember Rex's and my names, because when his call for help came it was an impersonal but urgent "Oi!"

Rex was already on the landing by the time I made it down, his cheek pillow-printed and his eyes pink and blinking. He still wore, or had just changed back into, the clothes he'd been wearing earlier that night. I rushed behind him into the Velvet Room. Guy was outlined through the windowpane, struggling to turn the rusty handle and support Biba at the same time. Her body dangled limply from her left arm, which was slung over Guy's shoulder. A yellow light suddenly illuminated them from the left: a switch had been thrown somewhere in Tom Wheeler's house, another black mark against us.

Biba was barely conscious. Her makeup now looked like a death mask, the corners of her mouth were encrusted with vomit and her eyes rolled back in her head. Rex scooped her into his arms and carried her as far as the landing, where he dropped to his knees and held her in a pietà embrace, her head lolling back and her legs outstretched. Her feet were bare.

"What happened?" I asked. "What did you give her?"

"Only a bit of charlie." Guy was defensive. "She said she'd done it before. I didn't know she was going to flip out. She fell over while we were in the woods."

Guy's fly had been undone and he fastened it and checked his belt buckle.

"You bastard!" spat Rex. I sank down next to him and tried to pull Biba's dress farther down over her hips and her underwear farther up. "If anything happens to her, I'll bloody kill you. I mean it. I'll kill you!"

"Hey," I said, stroking Biba's hair and gripping Rex's forearm. "It's okay. I've got you both. Don't worry. We'll get her to the emergency room or something. She's going to be fine. We're all going to be fine." I spoke calmly even as a hot geyser of panic rose inside me and scalded my throat. "I think you'd better go," I said to Guy.

"Glad to," he drawled, walking backward down the stairs away from our panicked little tableau. "It's not my fault she can't handle herself, man."

His words were defiant but he stumbled on his way to the door and his hands were trembling so much he could hardly undo the chain.

15

I SEE ALL OF them all the time, impossible sightings in the most unpredictable places. Even the bit players in the tragedy, people whom I met only once or twice, loom in and out of my consciousness, their half-remembered faces reconstructed in my imagination. They lurk everywhere, ready to manifest themselves whenever a certain paranoid mood moves in.

A couple of years ago, I thought I saw Nina and her children in a shopping center. The woman dripped with silver jewelry and jangled when she walked. She had a little girl balanced on her hip while a boy pulled at his mother's layered skirts and circled her like a maypole dancer. Of course I knew it couldn't have been them: Inigo and Gaia must be young teenagers now and these children were little more than toddlers. And Nina, with her love of markets and craft fairs and her hatred of mass-produced goods and the chain stores that sell them, would never have patronized that shiny, out-of-town mall. But this didn't stop me crying out and stumbling toward her, ready to duck into the arms of the only person who might have understood, the only other person who knew them like I did. The child in her arms heard the thud and rustle as my shopping bags hit the floor and turned to stare. I looked away before he had a chance to alert his mother.

Guy I see less frequently, only when I see his likeness I shrink from it. He too is an archetype: the youth tribe to which he belonged has evolved little in the last decade, even to my out-of-touch eye. You still see them everywhere, these rich boys who dress like they are poor in faded denim and designer tracksuit tops, wearing sneakers that will never know the speed or impact for which they were designed. Pub trainers, Simon used to call them. As with Nina and her children, it never occurs to me that he would have evolved, had a haircut, or bought some new clothes.

Biba of course is everywhere. I will transpose her image onto pretty much any white woman between the ages of eighteen and thirty. I look for her less now than I used to.

Some of the sightings have not been phantom. I did see Rachael, Biba's actress friend, four years ago when I was taking Alice to the theater in Covent Garden. Her peroxide crop had been cultivated into a shining wheat-blond drape, but her face remained exactly the same. It was as though having fought against her good looks for so long she had finally decided to accept them with the kind of resignation most of us reserve for weight gain or gray hair. She was arm in arm with an older man who wore a white silk scarf and black leather gloves. A miniature dog tucked under her other arm sniffed the air, and Alice cried out that the lady had a rat in her handbag. Rachael looked at Alice but apparently saw no trace of her former friends in my little girl's face.

Tris and Jo I have also seen, at the remove of television and along with most of the rest of the country. The documentary series about their attempts to build a carbon-neutral, off-grid, self-sufficient life in the Scottish Highlands has been the hit television show of the season. The natural warmth that made them impossible to dislike translates onto the screen, and they have retained their ability to educate without preaching. They have a brood of four or five free-range children who are as blond and bronzed and scruffy as their parents. I bought the book that accompanied the television series: it is hidden spine-backward on a high bookshelf, ready to bring out and present to Rex when he is ready, or when I am. The discovery that they once lived at the Highgate house would be a journalist's dream, but I don't worry too much about that. Tris and Jo never left any kind of footprint, carbon or otherwise, anywhere they lived, and their zero trace approach extended to money and forms and documents. They had no more been official residents in Queenswood Lane than I had. I sometimes even wonder if they know what happened two months after they left. I picture them living without TV or newspapers. They famously spent a year touring the UK in a gypsy caravan while Jo was pregnant with their first child, who looks about the same age as Alice. Perhaps they were already on the road when Rex first made the news and they remained there until after he was sentenced. Or perhaps they do know, and are as keen as anyone not to publicize the connection. Perhaps they talk about Rex and Biba and speculate on what happened, what led to it all. I bet they never wonder what happened to me. In a haunted life like mine it's ironic that I am the faintest, most hazy ghost of them all. My face and personality will have been forgotten by now if they were ever remembered in the first place. Zero trace.

I should not have been at the wheel as we sped down the hill to the Whittington Hospital, but Rex was not sober either and he held his sister in his arms. She was half-conscious now, her head on his shoulder, and her feet, dirty from the wood, rested in my lap. She smelled of vomit and something else I didn't want to identify. I ran a red light at the deserted Archway traffic circle and parked the car untidily and illegally in a residents' space directly opposite the hospital. Rex was out of the car almost before I had time to put the hand brake on.

"Are you responsible for her?" asked the paramedic who interrupted his cigarette break to help Rex arrange Biba on a stretcher and carry her through into the emergency room.

"Yes," said Rex. "I mean, I didn't give her the drugs but I think I know what she's taken. She's my sister. Is she going to be okay?"

A nurse took him to reception where he leaned on the counter with his head in his hands. Biba was swallowed up by a cubicle, sectioned off from the corridor by a swish of curtain violently patterned with green and pink swirls. If you didn't feel sick before you came in here, you would after a few moments staring at that print.

I sat on the floor in the long rubber corridor outside the cubicle with my legs crossed. It was the first time I had been in a hospital since my birth and I was not impressed. Instead of the whitewashed Cubist paradise I had always imagined, the walls were mint green. There were no baseboards in the corridor where I sat; the floors curved upward to join the walls in what was probably an innovation designed to make cleaning easier, but dust balls and human hair blew along on the convex curve. A thick peachcolored ridge ran along the corridor like a chair rail. It looked like it was going to be made of a soft padded material, but when I touched it it was hard plastic, and I wondered what its purpose was. The rattle of carts, the clatter of metal implements, the yowling of patients, and the low rumble of conversation in the waiting room and among the staff made it impossible for me to hear what was being said on the other side of the curtain where Biba was. Somewhere behind another curtain, a man screamed.

Rex dropped to a squatting position beside me and stayed there, apparently unable to commit to sitting on the floor.

"They won't let me go in, but they're going to come out in a minute," he said. "If anything happens to her, I'm going to have that Guy charged with everything . . . murder . . . assault . . . dealing . . . I should never have let her bring him home."

The white-coated medic who emerged from Biba's cubicle looked like he had been up for days: black half-moons cupped heavy eyes and I wondered how long he had been at work.

"She hasn't taken an overdose of anything," he said. "Not in the way you think, although she says she had a line or two of cocaine that would have made her throw up if she's not used to it. She's simply extremely drunk, and possibly concussed, and there's a gash on her thigh that looks as though it might be contaminated with rust. We're going to put her on a drip to rehydrate her and keep her in to check that the bang on the head isn't going to give us any problems. She also needs to have stitches on her leg and a tetanus shot."

"We'll stay here," said Rex immediately.

I hadn't cried for weeks but the thought of spending the night here under the flickering strip lights caused tears to sting the inside corners of my eyes. They were tears of self-pity and exhaustion as well as of anxiety. But I blinked them back, and sat with Rex in half-silence for the second time that night, drifting between the cafeteria and the corridor, watching the light change every time we refueled on coffee. At ten o'clock in the morning, a different doctor told us that we could take her home now. Her face, when they finally let us see her, was a bad actress's approximation of repentance.

"I'm exhausted," she said. "I just wanted to go to sleep but they kept waking me up to check I wasn't concussed. I'm going to sleep forever when I get in."

And how did she think we'd felt, forcing ourselves to stay awake, not knowing whether she would pull through?

When I saw how badly the car had been parked I was surprised that we had not been clamped or towed away. There was only a parking ticket inserted under the windshield wiper. Rex put it in his pocket and told me that he would take care of it, that it was the least he could do. If I had not been in a fit state to drive to the hospital, I was worse on the way home. I had sobered up but I was buckling under the weight of a tiredness I never knew existed, and the rush-hour traffic was clogging our route home. I drove through Highgate village, reasoning that although it was a less direct route, I wouldn't get up enough speed to do any damage. Still, Rex twice had to point out pedestrians on the main street who would have ended up in the Whittington themselves if he hadn't alerted me.

Biba stank of stale disinfectant, and I wondered if the hospital smell had permeated my hair and clothes too. She felt my tiny recoil when I helped her out of the car.

"I know . . . I know. I'm disgusting. I'm going to wash it off now. I think I've got sick in my hair."

I heard her wince in the shower as the soap stung the stitches in her leg, stitches that she had been told not to get wet. While she washed, I stripped her bed. She had been smoking in it: tips of ash had been smeared into little gray comets on the sheets. I dressed the bed with fresh sheets and waited for her.

"Darling," she said when she dripped back in, "that's the sweetest thing anyone's ever done for me. You're the best friend I could wish for. I don't deserve you."

"Indeed you don't," I said. "Come here." She laid her head on my lap and I combed her damp tendrils through with my fingers. The pad of wet hair cooled my thighs.

"They weren't very nice to me in there," she mumbled. "They knew it was an accident, that I was just another pisshead. They treat you completely differently when they think you mean it. They were lovely to me the last time."

The evening had been a horrible inversion of the first, endless night I had spent at the house. Then, on the evening of Biba's party, the more I tried to prolong the hours the more they turned into minutes and rushed by me. Again, the sleep I slipped into in the morning was fully clothed and grateful. I didn't wake until three in the afternoon, when a threatened implosion in my abdomen reminded me that it had been twenty-four hours since I had last eaten. There was nothing in the kitchen apart from a bunch of browning bananas. I ate three and took the other two back up to bed with a pitcher of water.

There was a light snoring from Biba's room but in Rex's a noise that I thought was laughter told me that he was awake. My tiptoeing wasn't subtle enough: he called my name in a hoarse whisper. He sat cross-legged in the middle of his immaculately made bed in his Rolling Stones T-shirt and a pair of boxer shorts, a cup of tea resting in the diamond-shaped space between his legs. His upper and lower teeth were exposed in a weird grin and he rocked back and forth. It took a few seconds to realize that it wasn't laughter but tears. I had never seen a man cry before. It was fascinating and repulsive and pitiful in equal measure and I knew that I would say or do anything I could to stop him doing it.

"Would you like a banana?" I said. He batted away the proffered fruit.

"I thought I'd lost her," he said through a sob. "I thought she was going to die."

"Oh, Rex." I sat down next to him. "Have you been to sleep at all?" He shook his head.

"I'm so tired," he said, and I got the impression he wasn't just talking about the last few hours. I didn't have the words to soothe him so I held out my arms and he fell into them like a little boy. I inhaled his hair as I stroked it. Rex's smell was like Biba's but also his own, like a subtly different blend of the same fragrance. His scent carried a top-note of soap rather than cigarettes. I waited until I was sure he'd stopped crying and tried to pull away.

Inching in, he held his forehead against mine for a long time and then softly, slowly, pressed his lips on mine. When I returned his kiss, he tasted of salt and sugary tea. The sensation of absolute yielding was sudden and unfamiliar yet instantly recognizable. I felt liquid, like warm milk, and was astonished by the rapid rise of instincts I never knew I possessed and a confidence that was a revelation to me. The qualities that made Rex a frustrating housemate made him a wonderful lover; the reticence and consideration, the attention to detail were exactly what I had never known I needed. The climax that he coaxed out of me was my first.

"I've wanted to do that for so long," he said when it was over. "Since the first time I saw you. You're the most beautiful girl I've ever made love to."

He was asleep seconds later. I kissed the small of his back before creeping back up to my attic. When I awoke I took a few seconds to figure out that the dusty gray light in my bedroom was not dawn but dusk.

The two of them were at the kitchen table. Biba, apologetically dressed in a demure pale yellow smock, had evidently enjoyed a restorative sleep. The red graze on her forehead was the only evidence of her ordeal. Rex had a hollowness about his eyes that was worse than a reprimand and made me feel as though I'd kicked a puppy in the face. The wrench of guilt was so acute it was physical. Biba had a selection of magazines and newspapers spread out in front of her—*The Stage*, I think, an Equity magazine, and a thick doorstop of a book called *The Actor's Yearbook*. She and Rex were circling with pink and blue highlighters courses, auditions, and theater companies that might be of interest. She was engrossed in their task, but his focus was only on me.

"I've been telling Rex how sorry I am," she told me, without looking up from the page in front of her. "But things are going to change. I know I gave you both a scare, and I scared myself, too. Fucking . . . I'm never drinking again."

"And never seeing Guy again," said Rex, still holding me in his gaze.

"And never seeing Guy again," confirmed Biba, tipping her Golden Virginia packet upside down to confirm its emptiness. "Although I do seem to remember that he left a pack of cigarettes somewhere around that beanbag. I don't have to boycott them, do I? I mean, waste not, want not. I do hate having to resort to rollies." She swung her legs off the bench and headed up to the Velvet Room, leaving Rex and me alone.

"Was it so bad that you had to leave?" was all he said.

"No! Not at all, I just didn't want Biba to find me there." He reached across the table for my hand and traced circles on my palm with his thumb. His body began to exert a centrifugal pull on mine. "Rex. It was amazing. No one has ever made me come before." I had never said anything so explicit. I think it was the first genuine smile I'd ever seen him give: it took up his whole face and endowed him with beauty that was a match for Biba's. Her footsteps on the stairs and a preceding plume of smoke told us she'd found the cigarettes.

"Tonight?" he asked in a whisper. I wasn't sure when we had conspired that she wasn't to know, but the agreement was as solid as if we'd signed a contract. He dropped my hand with seconds to spare. Biba was unreceptive to the tension.

"I'm really enjoying this new sobriety," she announced, although her blood alcohol content was probably still at the level that costs people their driver's license. "I feel really energized and positive."

"Do you want me and Karen to stop drinking too? We don't mind."

Didn't we? Anger diminished my newfound desire. I wasn't sure I was ready to abandon this lovely disorientation that I'd come to bathe my nights in.

What we denied ourselves in wine that evening we consumed in hot drinks. Mismatched mugs replaced empty bottles on the terrace where we lay. Rex retrieved a tin of herbal tea that Nina had left in the kitchen and made pot after pot of it. It smelled more like something you'd pour into your bathwater than drink. Laced with honey it was palatable, but it was no Shiraz. The transition from day to night felt incomplete without alcohol, and I was almost surprised when the sun set without wine.

Biba began to drool onto the splayed pages of the magazine she was reading, and when Rex suggested she head to bed she did so with uncharacteristic meekness. Rex slithered across the blankets and quilts like a snake until he was stretched out with his head on my belly. I glanced up at Biba's bedroom window, directly above where we lay.

"She'll sleep for hours," he said, teeth nipping at my waistband.

"She might not," I said. "She was in bed all day."

"She will," he argued. "She's had five milligrams of Valium."

"Why would the hospital give her Valium?"

"They didn't. I put it in her tea." I sat up and he fell out of my lap.

"You did *what*?"

"Don't worry, I know what I'm doing," he said, as though the dosage and not the act itself was the problem. "Nina was a bad sleeper. Too much coffee. She left a handful of downers behind when she went."

"Jesus, Rex! Is this so important that you have to drug your own sister to get to me?" I asked.

He put his hands on my shoulders and gently pushed.

"Yes," he said, arranging his body over mine.

Something else I learned about sex that night; you can despise someone's actions and it won't lessen your attraction to them in the least. I sank back onto my blanket and dissolved into his kiss.

"You promise she won't wake up?" I whispered.

"She's dead to the world," he said.

Biba kept her resolve for a week; she didn't drink, and her focus was entirely on her career. Although she had just spent three years studying drama, she promptly enrolled in a course at a private West End drama center—paid for with Rex's dole money— to equip her for the realities of life as an auditioning actress. "It's awful, really," she said cheerfully, heading out of the front door at eight o'clock in the morning. "You spend three years immersing yourself in Chekhov and Ibsen and Shaw and preparing monologues and then you come out and it's all about standing in front of a bloody camera. But I'm meeting with actors who've been working for years and they still study. That's the thing about the craft: you never, never stop learning."

I was on a steep learning curve of my own. Those tangled, sultry days were passed in Rex's bedroom or mine, bodies locked together and always listening out for the door. Every day I was newly surprised and delighted by the way I could reciprocate his tender brand of passion. I remembered what Nina had said about needing something "a bit more Latin" and thought her mad.

Nothing about his personality changed: the confidence he showed in the bedroom did not extend beyond it. He was still simultaneously deferential to and controlling of his sister, neurotic about the house, and uptight, even boring, but my feelings for him were undergoing a subtle evolution. Perhaps Rex was filling the void left by Biba's absence, or perhaps that's just what sex does to you, but the focus of my attention and affection was slowly transferring from sister to brother. Nina had been right that Rex was someone's idea of the perfect lover; he was mine. I wondered how I could have ever doubted his loveliness. His face was no longer a simulacrum of Biba's but beautiful in its own right.

16

THE COMPUTER I WORK on is in the space under the stairs, my chair facing away from the living room and its distractions. When I come back from the village, the papers that I left piled on its keyboard have been dumped on the coffee table. Alice is sitting up at the screen on her own, her tongue rolled into a little pipe of concentration as she scrolls through a Web page I don't recognize.

The machine should be accessible only to me, not because I have anything to hide but because I want to control exactly what Alice views. It is protected by a password that she could never begin to guess but Rex evidently has, or knew how to bypass or disable. It's a long word and an unusual name, one with four consonants in the middle. If it was a laptop I'd slam the lid down on her fingers but instead I pull the plug out of the wall.

"Mum!" says Alice as the machine accepts its blackout with a compliant sigh. "I was looking at that?" There appears to be nothing her teachers or I can do to turn her sentences from questions into statements. Rex comes in from the kitchen, knife in one hand, onion in the other, which is why, I suppose, he looks as though he's been crying.

"She's not allowed unsupervised Internet access," I say.

"I was literally ten feet away," he says. Of course he was. It's physically impossible to create more distance between two people in this tiny house.

"She thinks I'm going to be abducted by a pedophile," says Alice, rolling her eyes. She stomps across the room and falls onto the sofa cushions in a flounce. She did not pick up this flair for the dramatic from me. "Like I'm dumb enough to let myself be *groomed*. We had a talk at school. I know what I'm doing."

Actually, pedophiles are the least of my worries.

"I was only out of the room for a minute," says Rex apologetically. But that is all it would take. I know that I can't protect her forever. But she is still so young. For now, I can keep her within my sight. I can hold her—not back, exactly, but where she is, for a little while longer.

Alice has so far been content with the scraps of the story I have fed her, but she will soon want to put flesh on its bones. She doesn't know that Rex's surname used to be Capel but I have let slip the name Biba and that clue is all it would take. I discovered the Capels' history slowly and by stealth: not for Alice. She won't have to scavenge scraps of newsprint and listen at doors like I had to. The stories it took me months to learn and years to cover up she can probably unearth with a few clicks of the mouse. The names Rex and Biba are unusual enough to come up with a hit for that kind of thing, newspaper archives. The perceived glamour of what happened— the youth, the money, the bohemian family background—means that Rex's crime tends to be anthologized on grisly Web sites run by people who fetishize these things. I searched for it myself once a month or so before Rex came home. It's all there.

There is one thing at least that she can't find out on the Internet, and that is the nature of my own undetected crime. That is not to say that my secret is safe. Far from it. There are things that could happen, potential emergencies that could force the facts blinking and unwilling into the light. Time does not lessen the odds in my favor. If anything, it becomes more likely every day as she grows up. What will happen if I am found out? I don't even know what law I have broken, but I must have, it must be illegal. And how would they punish me? What punishment could be worse than the knowledge I live with every single day?

"You've got until the end of the day to give me your list."

"Excuse me?"

"The guest list for your party. We've only got two weeks, we should have started inviting people ages ago, really."

My own twenty-first birthday fell a couple of months after Biba's, at the end of July, and she approached it with the same enthusiasm with which she had done her own. My heart sank as she described the party she was planning: the music we would play, the ball gowns we would wear, the kitchen table brought up to the dining room and laid with a whole roast hog for us all to tuck into "and then lots of amazing drugs for pudding. Everyone will be fucked." The party sounded like one I would have loved to attend with someone else as the guest of honor, but with me as its hostess it was pure fantasy. Who was there to invite? My tiny social circle, the three people I counted as friends in London, were somewhere in France with my ex-boyfriend. Nina was similarly unreachable. Even the friendly and nomadic Tris and Jo were unlikely to come all the way back from Devon to celebrate the birthday of someone they had met only twice. Rachael was nearby, but to have Biba's other close friend and the former occupant of Attic One as the only guest I knew at my birthday party smacked of desperation. I'd rather have either twenty other people or just the three of us.

"I don't want any fuss," I said, and on seeing Biba's crestfallen face, "Perhaps we could just scale it down a bit. I have the best evenings when it's just us three. We can still have the music and the hog roast and the excellent drugs."

"Yeees . . ." she said doubtfully.

By the time my birthday came around, no plans had been made, no provisions had been bought, and the only acknowledgment of the occasion was a birthday card signed by the two of them. It was a beautiful card, a local artist's watercolor of the woods that captured perfectly the way I saw them: shimmering, ethereal, and almost unpeopled. It sat on the mantelpiece in my attic for the rest of the summer. It was one of the few possessions I salvaged from the house when I ran away, but I don't have it now. I burned it on the patio of the house in Brentford when I was finally alone. But that was all I had: no presents, and certainly no party, not even a secret visit from Rex. I lay on my bed for two hours in the middle of the afternoon, ostensibly reading but really waiting for Rex to seek me out, but he did not come.

At five, he turned up on the terrace where I was sunbathing and Biba was reading, a smile dancing shyly at the corners of his mouth. I wore a bikini and Biba the T-shirt she'd slept in.

"You can't go out dressed like that," he said to us. He looked at his watch. "You've got two hours to get ready for Karen's birthday banquet." From the pocket of his cut-off jeans he produced a roll of twenty-pound notes. "I'm taking my two favorite girls out for the evening." He clapped his hands twice. "Come on! The earlier you start, the prettier you'll be."

Biba had opened a window in her bedroom, perhaps in honor of my birthday, and the usual stifling smell of hair and skin and bedclothes was absent. There was a knock on the door followed by the sound of Rex's sandaled feet flapping away down the corridor. Outside the door, a bottle of supermarket cava stood in a flower pot filled with ice on a tatty old black tray with a gaudy seventies print of concentric circles on it. The two champagne saucers that flanked the bottle already sparkled with gold bubbles.

"What will I wear?" I said to Biba as the first glass disappeared in two gulps. "I haven't got anything dressy here."

"You have now," she replied. From somewhere in the bowels of her wardrobe she produced a flat, tissue-wrapped package. "Happy birthday, Cinderella. You *shall* go to the ball!" The scarlet dress that I shook out was old but immaculate: it was a full-skirted halterneck dress, the kind girls wore to go jitterbugging with GIs in the forties. It fit me better than anything new I had ever worn.

"Thank you," I said. "I love it."

"Perfect!" Biba clapped her hands with delight. She picked a red lacquered chopstick from a pewter mug on her crowded dressing table and fixed my hair on top of my head in a loose chignon, exposing the brown roots that looked black against the blond of my hair. Finally she handed me a lipstick the same color as my dress and turned her attention to her own outfit. She chose a pale pink petticoat and wrapped a black ribbon around her neck. With her hair in a low bun, she looked like a Degas painting. She locked eyes with me in the tarnished glass.

"You realize that he's in love with you, of course," she said to my reflection, pulling a loose strand of hair away from my face and winding the end of it around the chopstick. "Is there anything you want to tell me?" she asked with a sly smile. The blush that spread across my neck and chest, a brighter, hotter red than my dress, was all the answer she needed.

"How long have you known?" I said to my flounced lap. "I wanted to tell you, but . . ." When I looked up, she was smiling. "You don't mind?"

"Mind? I was *willing* it to happen. If you're with Rex, you've got two reasons to stay here. So now you *have* to stay with us."

"Why would I ever leave you?" I said. I wanted more champagne but the bottle was already empty. I had only had two glasses.

"Everyone does." She shrugged. "Eventually."

"Ladies!" The summer air was so thick that Rex's voice was muffled, as though he were in the house next door and not on the landing outside. "Your carriage awaits!"

A taxi—the black kind, not a minicab—waited with its motor running in the street. Biba slid down the banisters and whirled Rex around in a little polka at the foot of the stairs.

"As you might be able to deduce, she knows about us," I said to Rex.

"I couldn't be happier for you both," she said. Then she smacked Rex lightly across the cheek. "That's for not telling me," she said.

Her slap had been playful, but it left a four-fingered handprint that didn't fade until we were nearly at our destination.

The restaurant we went to was somewhere in Bow or White-chapel or Shoreditch. I didn't know the fashionable part of the East End then, and I still don't know it now. Perhaps if I had stayed lon-ger, Biba and I would have explored this hinterland on the other side of the Old Street traffic circle, but I didn't stay and who else would I have gone with on my return? I was not too old, I am still the same age as many of the people who will throng the bars and clubs of Hoxton tonight. But circumstances limited my opportu-nities in every conceivable way. I doubt those places have baby-changing facilities or a children's menu, even today.

I had read in one of Biba's magazines that this area was the new Soho, but that you had to know where you were going if you didn't want to spend your evening wandering around abandoned ware-houses in the hope of stumbling across the week's must-visit bar or restaurant. Every building we passed looked derelict and foreboding to me; even those modernized few where entire walls had been replaced by glass intimidated me, showcasing as they did sprawling groups of confident, fashionable people who would surely recog-nize and despise me as an outsider. Fortunately, and rather aston-ishingly, Rex appeared to be among the cognoscenti: the sooty four-story building that he instructed the taxi to pull up along-side was one I would never have given a second glance were it not for the flaming torches that blazed on either side of the doorway. I don't remember the name of the restaurant and wouldn't know how to find my way back there, but I can recall every detail of its astonishing interior to this day. It was a high-concept, high-fashion place a world away from the pizzerias and gastropubs of my experience. Stuffed animals lurked under glass jars and hung from the ceiling. A bulldog with butterfly wings, suspended by wires, swooped perilously close to the two giant crystal chande-liers that dominated the room and cast sequined highlights on our skin. Oil paintings in rococo frames crowded the walls, and huge candelabras flickered on every table. The wait staff were works of art in themselves, beautiful people dangerously dressed. I noticed that the sober, suited city workers who made up around half the diners were seated in the darker corners of the restaurant, and I was gratified when our waitress, a mixed-race beauty with dreadlocks that swung to her hips, led us to a table in the middle of the room.

"Well done, Rex," whispered Biba as she took the most prominent seat. "You've finally found your fabulous gene. Proof at last that we're related." As if anyone who saw them together could ever doubt that.

The menu was the size of an unfolded broadsheet newspaper and written in complex, florid French with English footnotes that did little to enlighten. I translated as best I could, and when the waitress came, ordered for all three of us. It was the first time Rex had heard me speak a foreign language and only the second time Biba had. I lapped up their admiration.

"How can you afford this?" said Biba as her first course arrived, a stack of interwoven green vegetables drizzled in a white sauce. "I mean, I'm not complaining, I love it here, but I thought we were broke?"

"I sold a contact sheet," said Rex. Biba halted, an asparagus spear on her fork hovering an inch away from her mouth. I remembered again just in time that I wasn't supposed to know about the boxed memorabilia beneath his bed. "They're, like, these sheets of paper with little prints of all the photos from one session so you can choose the one you want to use. My dad left some behind when he went. They can be quite valuable if they're of someone famous, or they're signed. We flogged all the real collectors' items years ago, but I got a couple of hundred quid for one of the leftovers."

"Did it mean an awful lot to you?" I asked.

Rex shrugged. "This means more."

We could have caught the Tube home but Rex insisted on another taxi, which used up the last of his twenty-pound notes.

The three of us sat on the backseat together, and they each put their head on my shoulder without realizing the other had done so. In that moment, I experienced happiness on an almost transcendental level and didn't want the journey to end. I no longer felt like an outsider but something they had in common.

The house stood in darkness. My nose twitched as I waited at the foot of the stairs while Rex and Biba bickered about the faulty lock. When you don't smoke, I've noticed, your sense of smell is sharper and you can smell things that smokers can't (woe betide Alice when she's a teenager if she thinks she can get away with secret cigarettes). Someone nearby was, or had recently been, smoking marijuana. It was a heavy, dizzying smell quite unlike the light, almost floral hash that Rex kept. This was dark and spicy, like the pungent skunk weed that Guy had brought to the house. I followed my nose with my eyes. Guy was quick, but not quick enough to disappear into the wood completely before I saw him withdraw, as though afraid of a confrontation. He needn't have worried that I would tell the others he was there; I would not have let him intrude on my perfect birthday. The orange tip of his joint was the last thing to disappear between the trees. With a crackle of footsteps that could have been anything, he was gone, leaving only a trail of smoke imperceptible to anyone but me.

The days that followed my birthday seemed to span an entire season. I think that the contentment I knew in them is what my father was talking about when he gave me his "one summer" speech. I had accepted soon after moving into Queenswood Lane that the messy hedonism of Biba's birthday party and the boisterous company of Tris and Jo would not be a daily or even weekly occurrence, but I could not have predicted the comfort I took in the loose routine that supplanted those things. I can't tell you what we did: we drank, we ate, we talked for hours and hours, Rex and I went to bed and Biba read plays and papers, waited for her agent to call, and every few days went into the West End for auditions, classes, or mysterious informal meetings with casting directors or nebulous people she referred to only as "contacts." Her acting friends she saw mainly in town: most of them lived centrally and apparently saw Highgate as an unconquerable backwoods, a visit to be attempted only if a fabulous party was being thrown.

So there were no visitors during those weeks. We didn't need any. Everything we wanted and needed was almost literally within arm's reach at all times. If we couldn't find each other in the house we sought each other in the clearing at the edge of the wood and usually found each other there. Every now and then we would see more people in the woods than usual, and idly deduce that it must be a weekend or a bank holiday.

I walked alone in the wood daily, as if by treading their childhood paths I would somehow insinuate myself into the Capels' pasts as well as their present and future. I loved the wood best after one of the tropical showers that characterized that summer, when the space between the topmost leaves and the ground underfoot was as sultry as any rain forest. For half an hour after the rainfall had ended, I would have the place more or less to myself and the drops would continue to fall from the trees and the shower felt like it was not happening in real time. I began to pick up litter when I saw it, to notice and mind if a bench or tree had a new graffito etched into its wood, and gradually to inherit the sense of ownership that Biba and Rex talked about. I could not conceive a time when I lived anywhere else, or with anyone else. My anger toward Roger Capel grew: he, who had so much and had done his first family so much damage, owed them the legacy of their home. *My* home.

I had intended to return to Brentford at least once a week, but didn't bother. So what if the mail piled up and the houseplants withered without me? I could sort the mail out once a month and by the time Sarah found the dead plants I wouldn't care what she said about them. I was never going to live with her again. I had a vague notion that I should fetch the rest of my things, bring my books and my CD player and the rest of my clothes, but I saw no rush.

Rex was happy in servitude to his sister and me. When he wasn't ensuring our comfort or indulging our whims, he would daydream out loud about what he would do with the house when his father finally signed it over to him. He had nowhere else to go and nothing else to do.

17

REX HAS GONE FOR another of his evening walks, cap on and collar up, flashlight at his hip like a gun in a holster. There is an area of woodland half a mile away, a forest really, a managed and replanted working forest unlike the nature reserve that was Queen's Wood. The pine trees are different, for a start, and it's ten times the size. But Rex seems to be making it his own. He never sees anyone, he says. It will be different in the summertime when the local kids congregate there, but for now they are content to hang around outside the kebab shop and the trees are all Rex's. Sometimes he goes as far as the coast, other times he stops to explore the building site that will soon be a development of luxury homes between our village and the sea. It is important that he begins to feel a sense of ownership and knowledge of this new corner of England, the one that we hope will be his home for the rest of his life. I remember how I didn't really truly belong in Highgate until I had explored and mapped Queen's Wood for myself.

Before he leaves I make him tell me the exact time he will come home again. He has complained that I am treating him like a child but he humors me: so far, he has always returned on or before schedule. And although I worry about him when he is out, I too need this time. It does me good to have an hour or so alone every night, to catch up on the work I can't concentrate on when he's tiptoeing around the house, or just to be, in silence, with no one to talk to. I pour my first glass of wine as soon as he is out of the door and it is always empty by the time I hear his key in the lock.

I turn on the computer. For a few seconds it sulks after yesterday's abrupt shutdown. The screen remains black for a few seconds and the word ANALOG flashes on and off in a sort of primitive, robotic-looking font before the reproach ends and the familiar desktop setup resumes. I look up Alison Larch, wondering if journalists begin their investigations with Google or if they go straight into the mysterious half-official sources and databases they have access to. I don't need secret records or hidden catalogs but strike lucky on my first hit. Alison Larch has her own Web site, listing all the documentaries she has researched, edited, written, directed, and produced (the differences between all these jobs must mean something to people in her industry). I recognize one or two of the titles, one about plastic surgery in teenagers and another about a co-faith school in Northern Ireland. It's an interesting career she has, combining hard-hitting news with mass-audience titillation. A click on a button marked "Current Projects" opens a new window. The text tells me that Alison Larch is currently working on a freelance job for Channel Four. That could mean anything. I close the window more unsettled than if I had found out one way or the other. I enter my own telephone number into the search engine but it doesn't come up. That doesn't mean much either. Anyone who knew my line of work could track my details down via my agency. I must call them tomorrow and tell them not to give out my numbers or my e-mail. I will tell them I have been receiving nuisance phone calls. It is not really a lie. I check my e-mail, the same one I have had since I was a student. Along with the usual advertisements for penis enlargers and bingo Web sites, there is a reminder about the harvest festival at Alice's school and a forwarded joke from my dad.

I turn detective on my own family and investigate what Alice and Rex were researching yesterday. A glance at the search history shows they were looking up nothing more sinister than the release dates for the new Harry Potter film. I think about booking tickets, but am loath to sit through any more teenage wizardry. Rex seems to have enjoyed the DVDs Alice has made him watch so far, as I did the first three or four times. Perhaps he'd like to take her to see the next installment on his own.

By the time I hear him scraping his boots outside the front door, I'm on to my second glass. I shut down the computer, properly this time, and pour a large one for him. White, of course.

It was the cool part of the night when the city seemed to exhale, but Rex's bedroom was still oppressively hot. Even the fingernail-sized flame of the single candle he had lit seemed to send out a furnace of heat. I kicked the covers off, making my body into a starfish in an attempt to cool down, but the air was as warm and sticky as my skin. I looked at his watch on the bedside table: it wasn't the first time I'd woken up to find him gone, but this time half an hour passed before he came back. By the time he returned the first sunshine had begun to percolate through the windows and bleach out the tiny flame. He carried a jug of cloudy water and two greasy, fingerprinted glasses. You might be able to forget you were in London when you looked out of the window, but you remembered when you saw the chalky, dusty recycled water. We waited for the dregs to settle before we drank.

"Where do you go when you vanish at night?" I asked.

"I watch Biba sleep," he said.

"Why?"

"I don't know. To check that she's alive? To check if she's still there?" His constant checking in the night was not the voyeur's furtive gaze but the anxious father obsessively checking the baby in the crib. Still I grew impatient with it.

"Why are you so worried about her? She's not your responsibility, Rex," I said.

"Oh, but she is. Whatever I do, it's never going to be enough for her."

Rex ran a damp hand over my breasts and belly and let his palm rest above my navel. I felt a fresh thrill at the unguessed alchemy of his flesh on mine.

"It's my fault," he said, the water clouding as he poured it from jug to glass. "She's like this because of what happened with our mother, and that's my fault."

"What do you mean? Your mum killed *herself*."

"But I caused it."

"No one caused it," I said, in what I hoped were soothing tones. "It was no one's fault."

"Yeah, but if you know someone's not well, and you know that they're going to do mad things, and you know how to stop them doing those things and you don't stop them, even worse, if you actually provoke them, then you're as guilty, because you knew what you were doing. Do you know what I mean?" Rex sat up, and his voice rose and grew shrill like his sister's.

"I don't understand," I said. He glanced around the room as if hoping a third party would come and take over the storytelling.

"Okay. Shit. Shall I tell you?" He addressed this question not to me but to the door, on the other side of which Biba slept. "I think you ought to know, and I think you'll be okay, and I don't think it will wreck things for us." I took his hands in mine and undid the fingers that had balled into tight fists, smoothed his fingers one by one, massaging the flesh between them while he talked. He took a deep breath.

"I was sixteen when she died," he said. "By then, Mum was too ill to leave the house—I don't mean physically infirm, she was too depressed, too mad, whatever you want to call it. Biba was twelve, and she wasn't allowed out in the woods or the heath or anything on her own, or after dark. But Mum didn't mind sending me running forward and backward to Hampstead, to Dad's new flat. The fuck-flat, she called it. There was about four years between leaving

Mum and meeting Jules and I think he fit a lot of women into them. There isn't a bus between Hampstead and this part of High-gate, and if you want to get the Tube you've got to go all the way to Camden Town so it was quicker to walk. I used to have to go three or four times a week. I reckon I know the heath at least as well as I know this wood. Well, as you know, it's a good few miles, and it's hilly. It was a proper hike, hard work. That's probably why I'm so skinny," he said, extending a thin, white arm that resembled a knotted sheet. I kissed the inside of his elbow.

"She used to write to him," he continued. "She spent hours writ-ing letters on that bureau in Nina's old room. She scented them and sometimes she used to seal them with wax, too. Sealing wax, for fuck's sake . . . I think she thought it was romantic, like some-thing out of a Victorian novel. It broke my heart, seeing her pour so much hope into those letters, but it made me feel a bit sick as well, if I'm honest. Is that an awful thing to say about your own mother? Especially when I knew I'd have to take it to Dad and more often than not he wouldn't even be there. I'd get home and she'd be wait-ing up, asking what he'd said, what his reply was. I used to make stuff up to comfort her. I'd say that he'd said thanks, and that he'd be over to see her soon. That probably did more harm than good."

"You did the wrong thing for the right reasons," I interjected.

"I'm glad you see it like that. I wish I could. Anyway, this one day I'd just had enough. It was cold, I'd been playing rugby all day, which I hated, and all I wanted was to come home and curl up in the warm. She was in one of the worst states ever. She was really pissed, and she hadn't cooked anything, and she had a letter she wanted me to take to Dad. I knew it would be more of the same: how she'd borne his children, and given up her youth, and why he should take her back, and how good it would be if he came back to his family, all that. But I read it anyway, and I wish I hadn't. It was all about sex. She made all these offers of things she'd do for him if only he came home . . . she told him she'd . . . I can't even say it. But you can imagine. Just the last things you want to think about your mum doing."

"Poor baby." I tugged his hair into little peaks.

"If you can believe it, you're actually the first person I've told since Nina," he said. "And that was when things started to go wrong between us, so you can understand why I might want to delay it."

"It won't change anything," I said, kissing him to show him that I meant it. When he spoke again, he looked into my eyes.

"She said I was the man of the house now and I had to look after her, and that the best way to do that was to take the letter to Hampstead. I thought, if she wants me to act like a man I bloody well will: I'll stand up to her. I told her I wasn't taking her letter anywhere. In fact, I think I told her to shove it up her arse. She went mental, screaming around the house, her husband had left her and now her only son was going to do the same thing. I said I wasn't leaving her, but I was cold, and I was hungry, and I wasn't going to go out and take her letter, that he'd never read any of them and that I'd been lying to her. I can still see her face now. I couldn't have said anything to hurt her more. She said she didn't believe me but we both knew I was telling the truth. I thought I was being cruel to be kind, that I was forcing her to get dressed and go to Hampstead herself and then she'd see the truth, that he didn't want her, and that he'd tell her to fuck off, and she'd have to get over it. I thought I'd been too soft on her and made her lazy. The next morning before school, she seemed okay. It was a nice day, freezing cold but really crisp and sunny."

I tried to imagine this house ever being cold. The idea of it existing in another season blew like a chilly breeze down the back of my spine.

"I thought, the weather's nice, she'll wrap up warm, and she'll go. I was so happy, I thought I'd done the right thing."

"And did she go?" I asked.

Rex closed his eyes. "When I came home from school, I saw her feet at the top of the stairs, and I knew. She'd hung herself from the banister on the first-floor landing. She'd wet herself. I could smell my own mum's piss and her feet were all mottled and swollen. I'd have had to go upstairs to see her face, and I didn't." He paused and I froze, terrified that tears would come, but I guessed that he had cried himself out when it came to this. He pinched the skin between his eyebrows with his thumb and forefinger and when he took his hand away white fingerprints stayed.

"I rang my dad but there was no one there so I went next door to Mrs. Howard—she used to live in the house before the Wheelers moved in. She called the ambulance and she made me a cup of cocoa and a biscuit that I couldn't eat so I put it between the sofa cushions. She wouldn't let me go back in on my own. That's the worst part—that I didn't go back in, and I always think that as bad as things had got by then, I should have gone back, and I can't bear to think of how much worse it got because I didn't go back."

"I don't understand," I said. "Do you mean your mum was still alive?"

"No, she was dead. She'd been dead for hours, I couldn't have done anything about that. While I was next door with Mrs. Howard, Biba came home. She was supposed to be at drama club, she wasn't supposed to be home until seven, but her teacher was ill. The door wasn't shut properly and she came in. She was only twelve, Karen. When the ambulance came, they found her standing on the stairs trying to hold my mum up. It took two of them to pry Biba off her . . . off the body." He turned on his side and met my gaze with a mixture of defiance and fear. "So that's it. That's the story. It was my fault that Mum killed herself in the first place, and it was my fault that Biba saw it."

"Oh, Rex," I said, "oh, no. You're wrong to blame yourself for either of those things. You can't be responsible for your parents' behavior, you were a child, you were sixteen! You weren't to know."

"I *was* to know. I lived with it every day," he said. "So this is to answer your question. She might as well not have a dad, and the one parent she did have, I as good as killed. I stood up to my mum and look what happened! If I do the same and I lose Biba, that's it, it's over."

"She's done it before, hasn't she?" I said. "Biba. She's tried to kill herself."

He nodded.

"When she was about sixteen, she got it into her head that she was going to go to some acting school in New York. Dad said no and I agreed with him, although for different reasons. He didn't want to pay, I didn't want to lose her. But I sided with Dad against her, that's how she saw it."

"What did she do?"

"She washed down a bottle of Tylenol with a bottle of Jack Daniel's," he said. "I don't think she really meant it as anything more than a cry for help; she called the ambulance the second she'd done it. But that's why I fuss over her. I daren't risk hurting her like that again. I know what it's like to lose someone that way and I love her too much to let that happen. She's all I've got left, or she was until you came."

He curled up into a ball, wrapped his arms around my waist and laid his head on my breast, more child than lover. I suddenly felt hot and suffocated for reasons that had nothing to do with the closed windows. The first real shaft of sun brought a new heat that filtered through the ivy that grew against the window. The leaves pressed against the pane, poison-bottle green, the size and shape of human hearts.

18

THE HOUSE IN BRENTFORD looked familiar but strange, as homes do when you've been on holiday. The only outward signs of neglect were the odd weed or blade of grass pushing up between the chessboard tiles of the garden path. The porch was shielded from the street by a large laurel and I had deliberately left the door on the latch to avoid a telltale buildup of free newspapers wedged in the mailbox. There were one or two such papers, plus the usual scatter of manila and white envelopes. Splashes of color were provided by takeout menus. On top of this mille-feuille of junk mail sat a huge spray of stargazer lilies, the water from their cellophane wrapping long evaporated. The flowers were curling and browning now, but they had been pink and white when fresh. Their stale and cloying scent filled the porch. My heart plunged as I read the handwritten note on the back of the birthday card nestled between two blooms.

> Dear Karen, we came to give you a surprise birthday tea but it looks like you were already out celebrating! Haven't been able to call you lately, so get in touch. We're a bit worried. Lots of love from Mum and Dad.

I had been calling home regularly from Highgate, but a flip through my mental calendar alerted me to the fact that I hadn't been in contact with them since the day before my birthday. During that conversation they must have been planning their drive down to London. Perhaps they had even booked a restaurant for the three of us. I had been so absorbed in the new family I had chosen that I had not given a thought to the one I came from. I pictured them in the car, Dad braving the heat in his favorite leather jacket, Mum reapplying her lipstick when they left the M25 as though all London was judging her. I imagined too their nightly appointment by the telephone, becoming more disappointed and concerned every night that I didn't answer. People say that you don't understand what anxiety is until you have children, but I had done enough worrying and listening and sympathizing over the past few weeks to gain a new sensitivity to the distress I must have caused. I gathered the disintegrating lilies in my arms, dried pollen falling like yellow ash over my clothes, and crouched to retrieve the rest of the mail.

The house looked as though it had been cleaned up for an inspection. Each cushion was perfectly plumped and arranged in a diamond on the sofa, and the empty fridge buzzed like a bee in the spotless kitchen. The first thing I did was pick up the telephone— so clean, so convenient, I thought, as I extended the antenna and walked around the house—and call my parents. It was one o'clock: Dad would be home for his lunch. They weren't the kind of parents to haul me over the coals for something like this—for anything, really—but still I preempted a telling-off with an apology and then disarmed them with the news that I had a new boyfriend.

"Is that where you were, then? When we came over?" said Mum, while Dad told me that he hoped I'd found a proper boyfriend this time and not another "rugger-bugger idiot" like Simon. All comparisons between Rex and Simon made me smile.

"He's as far from a rugby boy as you can imagine, Dad."

"Glad to hear it," he replied, and I heard him exhale as he sank into his chair.

My parents' house appeared in my mind's eye: the net curtains and the three-piece suite and the television that was always on and

my old room, pastel blue and cream with clean sheets that smelled
of fabric softener. All these things I had learned to scorn suddenly
seemed desperately comforting, and I craved just one evening in my
childhood home. I had a full tank of gas and no pressing engage-
ments; if I left now I could be there in time for a home-cooked dinner. I wanted to listen to my mother moan about the new housing
development in the meadow behind our house and to gossip about
people I had known all my life. I wanted to hear my Dad shouting
at the television in his embarrassing accent. I wanted to be somewhere I didn't have to try to understand the people I lived with. I
wanted, I realized, a day off from surprises and dark passions and
dramatic revelations and dead mothers and cruel fathers. I wanted
it so much and so suddenly that a lump rose in my throat.

"Can I come home, Mum?" I said. "Just for a bit?" She clicked
her teeth impatiently.

"We're going to Madeira, aren't we?" she said, as though I
should have known, and in fact I *should* have; my parents had spent
the first two weeks of August at the same hotel every year since I
was ten. It was in that resort that my aptitude for languages had
first surfaced, when I had found myself translating an entire Portuguese menu for a table of amazed adults after only a few days in
the country.

"When are you back?" I asked. She named the date my degree
results were published. They would be flying into Heathrow and
leaving the car in the long-term parking lot, as they always did.

"Come back and see me on the way from the airport," I said.
"You virtually go past the front door. You can help me open my
results. And you can cook for me."

It took ten minutes to sort through the mail. I separated the
others' letters into three neat piles before going to work on my
own. Apart from a few bank statements that I left unopened—
my checking and savings accounts had barely been touched in the
last few weeks—my mail consisted mostly of prospectuses and letters from modern language departments. There was literature

from all over the UK, one university in Philadelphia, another in Missouri, and one from Uppsala in Sweden. Just two months ago, I would have been flattered and excited by these foreign prospectuses. Now my first thought on seeing them was whether they would allow me to defer for a year. I wasn't ready to leave London yet. Would I ever be, now? I called my tutor, Caroline Alba, and made an appointment to see her the following day.

The final piece of mail I nearly threw away with the junk. The postcard of a flowerbed in Perpignan airport was printed in the same gaudy colors as a takeout pizza menu. I would have rejected it as another of the same if its stiff texture hadn't made me give it a second glance. The writing was Emma's.

"Having a lovely time working on the vineyard and drinking lots of yummy red wine. Will you be in on results day? We'll call you at 9 p.m. UK time. See you soon, love and hugs, E, S and C." I put it on the mantelpiece alongside framed pictures that had been taken a lifetime ago. The parking ticket that Rex had promised to take care of had reappeared on my doormat in the form of a letter from Haringey council: the fine would double if I did not pay it within the next three days. I looked at the date. Had it really only been two weeks since that night?

The woman behind the desk at the tennis club was pleased to see me.

"I haven't seen you and your friends for ages," she said. "We wondered where you'd all gone. I said you were probably off being au pairs or something." I was confused for a second, wondering why she would be expecting the Capels to visit a gym on the other side of London. Then I understood; she was used to seeing me with the girls, or Simon.

"Not me," I said. "I'm staying in London for once." She handed me a clean white robe and a matching fluffy towel. Like the club itself, they smelled of cleanliness and health and the twin luxuries of money and spare time.

With no tennis partner available, I hit the gym. I began on the bike and worked my way around every weight machine I knew how to operate. I knew I'd pay for it in aches and pains the next day, but I didn't care. You'd think that so long without exercise would have made a workout grueling, but I felt that I had all those weeks' worth of energy stored in my muscles begging for release. I finished with fifty minutes on the treadmill, a personal best. The joints I'd smoked with Biba had diminished the capacity of my lungs but to me the shortness of breath was just a challenge, a come-on. I thought of nothing but the mindless dance music that blared through the gym as I pounded the conveyor belt with my feet until my muscles sang out for mercy. In the shower afterward I savored the post-gym fatigue that bordered on euphoria. I examined my body as I soaped it; there was no denying I had put on weight. My arms and legs were looking less toned than before, and the softness and swell of my belly was new and unwelcome and all my fault. I told myself I would find a gym in Highgate, I would begin running in the woods, I wouldn't let myself go like this again.

That evening, I trawled my bedroom for the flimsy green piece of paper that would allow me to collect another three months' worth of contraceptive pills without having to make an appointment with my doctor. I eventually located the prescription pressed between two books on my shelf and folded it into a neat little square in my purse. Taking the pill every day had been easy to remember in my old, regimented life. In Highgate, the habit was becoming as erratic as my meals and my sleeping patterns.

Midnight was too early for me to sleep so I watched television in bed. A French film, part of the Three Colors trilogy, was on Channel Four. I couldn't concentrate on it. I desperately missed the Capels. My ears were empty without Biba's conversation, and my body missed Rex's touch. It reminded me of the displaced feeling you get when you come back home after living in another country: you're homesick for British food and television and company while you're away, but the minute you come home you begin to pine for the place you've just left.

My last thought as I went to sleep was that I couldn't remember the last time I had had to speak a foreign language. I had been abroad every summer for six or seven years. This was the first summer I had been content to live life in my mother tongue.

The staff at Queen Charlotte's referred to their stuffy little studies as their "rooms," a throwback to—and possibly a yearning for—older colleges that equipped their staff with suites of living and teaching rooms rather than six-foot-square boxes in a reclaimed office block. Caroline Alba's "rooms" were smaller than most, affording a view of a standpipe on an opposing wall, but she had plastered the interior with pictures and postcards that her students sent her every summer. To the left of the plate glass window was a flyer advertising a student play I'd seen in a natural amphitheater somewhere just outside Rome and brought back for her.

She was impossible not to like: clever without being formidable and warm without being sentimental, she was the only person who understood my aptitude for language without my needing to explain. In my more narcissistic moments I wondered if I reminded her of her younger self. She had graying hair and good enough bone structure to wear it cropped. She dressed soberly but I never saw her in the same earrings twice. The day I met her in her study two ropes of amethysts strung on silver pulled on her lobes and grazed her collarbone. The file with my name on it was already on her lap when I entered.

"I wouldn't usually say this, but your first is a foregone conclusion," she said, smiling, flicking through papers and pamphlets.

"Do you know something I don't?"

"No. But your existing marks are the strongest I've ever seen. You're a very bright young woman. It's lovely to be able to say this to a student, Karen: you can pursue whichever career path appeals most. What do you want to do?" Her eager face searched for similar enthusiasm in mine, but there was no point in lying.

"This sounds incredibly feeble," I said. "But I don't know what I want to do with my life. I haven't got a vocation or anything. I love what I've done here, but I have no real ambition beyond that."

"I don't think I could phrase better the exact mind-set you need to remain in academia," she said. Her earrings swung back and forth as she nodded her way down a list in front of her. They looked like Nina's designs and I wondered whether Caroline had ever been shopping in Camden market. "It's obvious that a master's is the natural step for you and a doctorate after that. Then perhaps you can think about a position at one of the great universities. You do know that you'll never be wealthy that way—that you could probably earn more as a freelance translator?"

I nodded.

"Well, you can do that on the side—I still do."

"Do I have to decide now?"

"I think you ought to apply for these," she said, pulling out five or six forms. I recognized the Uppsala insignia on the uppermost sheet. "In your case I feel we can begin the process before results are published."

"What about staying here?" I asked. "Would the department be able to accommodate me as a master's student?"

Caroline Alba blinked at me. "I do think you ought to look closely at the caliber of institutions that have expressed an interest in you, Karen. QCC is of course well respected, but the resources and sway on offer at some of these departments far outstrip anything we can give you."

"Is that a no, then?" I asked.

"No, it's not a no . . . I suppose we should be flattered that you'd like to stay. Okay. There are some private companies that might support someone with your talents at this level and I'd encourage you to pursue these scholarships." From a file on her desk she pulled out another selection of papers and added them to the pile on her lap. "A living wage, especially in London, is virtually impossible without sponsorship. Naturally, publishing's the holy grail but . . ." She gestured toward her own doctoral thesis, hardbound in leather by the University of London's in-house bindery but yet to be picked up by a publishing company. I thanked

Caroline for her time, promising to return the forms before the week was out.

"We haven't discussed areas you might specialize in for your MA," she said as I stood up to leave. "Perhaps you could think of three or four aspects of linguistics you'd like to explore and we can examine them next week."

I had decided against the foreign universities before I got to the elevator. I think I had already made up my mind that I would try to stay at Queen Charlotte's. The silent summer corridors full of lecturers and professors in hushed, unhurried study appealed to me much as the same passageways intimidated me when filled with the clatter and chatter of students. If I could get the funding— and think of a field that would sustain my interest for the next few years—then there would be nothing to disrupt the life I wanted to live. But the disruption had already taken place during my two-day absence.

I drove home brimming with hope and lust, looking forward to dinner with Biba and bed with Rex, but the forlorn figure on the doorstep told me that both those things would have to wait. Rex crouched on the middle step, a glass of red in his hand and a nearly empty bottle by his side. Although we drank together every night, this was the first time I had seen him drunk. His mouth bore the unmistakable kiss of red wine and his face was contorted with angst.

"Where were you?" he asked. He didn't put his arms out to me and I remained at the foot of the steps.

"What's happened?" I said.

"It's all gone wrong," he said. "Why did you have to go? I couldn't stop them."

I pushed past him into the house and followed the dance music that blared from the Velvet Room. The furniture had been rearranged so that for a disorienting moment it felt like I was approaching the room from the wrong angle. The coffee table was up against the wall, the beanbag was in its place, and someone had pushed the green sofa over to the terrace. Biba lazed on it, her feet in the evening sunshine but the rest of her body in shadow. She was wearing my red string bikini, the straps tied too tight and the triangles puckered and gaping on her small frame. When she saw me she greeted me with a slurred, "Darling!"

The leather Chesterfield had also been pushed toward the French windows. Facedown on it lay a tanned man wearing a pair of gray tracksuit pants rolled up into shorts. The soles of his bare feet were black with dirt. When he heard Biba's greeting, his blond head turned in my direction. Bloodshot eyes held mine for a couple of disinterested seconds.

"All right?" said Guy.

19

"APPARENTLY SHE'S BEEN SEEING him behind my back for *weeks*," said Rex. "She says they bumped into each other on the Tube and he apologized and she forgave him—just like that! She thinks it was a coincidence that they met."

"Maybe it was," I said.

"Bullshit. I wouldn't put it past him to follow her around until he saw his opportunity." I remembered the figure lurking in the woods but it was too late to say I'd seen him now. "What can I do? What can I do about it?" He ran his fingers from his temples to the back of his head in an obsessive and repetitive gesture.

"Personally, I think we should just let it run its course," I said to him. "You know what she's like. The more you tell her Guy's a bad influence, the more attractive he'll become to her. That's why she didn't tell you she was seeing him. The novelty will probably wear off now that it's not a big exciting secret anymore." It sounded like bogus psychology to me even as I said it, and it didn't wash with Rex.

"She lied so convincingly," he said. "Telling me she was off having coffee with Rachael and all the time she was meeting up with him." He poured the remainder of the bottle into his glass. His lips and tongue were mottled with red wine and his teeth had a dark blue tinge to them. I wondered if this bottle was even his first of the evening. I took the glass from his hand and drained it.

"We can't very well get after her for having a secret relationship," I said.

"That was completely different. For a start, I didn't fill you full of drugs, rape you, and leave you for dead the first time I got off with you."

"He didn't leave her in the woods," I said. "And I think *rape*'s a bit strong . . ." Remembering the car journey from the theater to the house when Biba had told me in a whisper that she couldn't wait to sleep with Guy, I was sure there had been no coercion.

"That doesn't change the fact that he just took off," he said. "And it's still completely different from you and me. He's only screwing her. He's not in love with her."

Rex's panic stemmed from a sense of impotence. He was powerless to get rid of the man he saw as a threat to his sister and even to his home. But he had challenged her in the strongest terms he dared. Knowing this, it was easy to predict his next question.

"Will you talk to her?" he asked. "She'll listen to you."

It would be a while before I would have the chance. The house now had four residents, not three, and the dynamic shifted from that night on. I had moved in with a bang and a fanfare, a big decision and announcement that made the real event—a bagful of possessions tossed casually into the car—an anticlimax. Guy's residency was achieved in the opposite way. It was never announced or discussed, either because Biba was too smart for that or because it really was a genuinely spontaneous and organic process. He had told us that he came from Ladbroke Grove, and we knew he disappeared for a few hours every couple of days. On the rare occasions he mentioned his West London apartment, he implied that it was little more than a squat, a crack house peopled with gangsters and drug dealers. Details were beneath Guy: he never let on exactly which complex the apartment was in, or who else lived there. He remained as vague and noncommittal as on the first evening he'd spent with us.

The silence was the first thing to go. The peace that Rex and I so treasured was usurped by the constant thud of trance and techno. He moved the speakers from the stereo so that they were out on the terrace, and produced and installed a MIDI system for Biba's room so that he had access to amplified beats wherever he was. Guy's music followed Rex and me down into the basement kitchen and up into my attic bedroom. For someone who spent almost all his time in Biba's bedroom, Guy managed to fill every room in the house with his possessions: you'd find a pair of sneakers in the bathroom, a music magazine in the living room, a record bag in the hallway, a jacket slung over the back of a chair, and always a flat black cell phone in the last room he had occupied. Cell phones were becoming commonplace then for the people I still regarded as "the grown-ups," employed people with deals to broker and money to make, but among students and the very young they were still a rarity. Guy was the first person I ever knew to have one. He carried it with him at all times. It was laughably crude compared with the ones we use today, a prototype really, but still a piece of space-age technology as far as Rex and I were concerned. Guy never used it to dial out—that he did from the house telephone—but on the rare occasions he received an incoming call, he made a big show of extending the antenna, thumbing a button, and then leaving the room to "conduct his business" away from prying ears. The garden was his favorite makeshift office. From the drawing room terrace I often watched him pacing back and forth through the waist-high grass, his hand clamped to his ear. He would have had more privacy on the other side of the fence, but as far as I know his first unfortunate excursion into the trees was the only time he went into our part of the wood.

We came back from Highgate village one day to find the white pit bull terrier tethered to the front gatepost, its domain extending from doorstep to curb. A family crossed the road to avoid it, and we were too afraid to try to run past it and had to enter the house the back way, through the woods.

"This is the last straw," said Rex as I splintered a finger squeezing through the back fence. My fingertip glowed red and blood oozed from the tiny cut. "I'm going to go upstairs and have it out with him." But by the time he had teased the splinter from my flesh, only Biba was left in the house.

"It was only for today," said Biba importantly. "He needed the dog for protection."

"If he brings anyone or anything dodgy to my house, I'm calling the police," said Rex. "I mean it, I will." Later that evening I found him on his hands and knees, scrubbing dog shit off the doorstep. When he was finished, he tipped his bucket out. Soapy water cascaded down the steps, and the pavement smelled of floral disinfectant for days afterward.

When he wasn't brokering nebulous business deals or babysitting animals that contravened the Dangerous Dogs Act, Guy's favorite pastime was to get very stoned and leaf through a picture book, an album of aerial photography of Great Britain that he had found somewhere in the house. Every now and then he would turn a page, stare at the photograph in silent contemplation for a few minutes before nodding and saying something like "Mad," or "Headfuck." The pictures were able to hold his attention for so long that he was making his way through the book at the rate of three or four pages a day. The photograph currently mesmerizing him depicted Beachy Head in Sussex, a white slice of grass-topped cliff overlooking a red-and-white-striped lighthouse. He mumbled aloud the caption that explained that as well as being a beauty spot it was also one of the country's prime locations for suicide attempts. This immediately piqued Biba's interest, and she scrambled from her position at his feet to sit at his side.

"Well, if you were going to kill yourself, you'd do it somewhere like that, wouldn't you?" she said. "I'd wear my best dress and float elegantly to my death. It's by far the most glamorous way to go."

I knew that Rex was out but quickly scanned the room to confirm his absence. My face must have been bunched in consternation because Biba laughed and said, "Oh, come on, Karen. We've all secretly planned our own suicides, haven't we?"

"No!" I said, meaning it, although months later her words would echo off the mountains in Switzerland when I would find myself on a high bridge above a tempting icy snake of river. I heard the front door open. "Rex is coming back," I said. "Please stop talking like that."

"God, okay," she said, rolling her eyes. She flipped the page over to reveal a photograph of Stonehenge in the summertime.

"Crazy," said Guy, staring at the standing stones. "Fucked up."

We stood on either side of the clothesline.

"I knocked on the door earlier to get her bedsheets and she wouldn't let me in. He told me to fuck off and she just *let* him," said Rex, efficiently unpegging a giant paisley duvet cover. Folding the sheet between us, we took two steps toward each other then two back, dancing the steps of an Elizabethan pavane. "Three weeks she hasn't changed them," he said with a wooden peg in his mouth. "Three weeks he's been here."

"He's lasted longer than I thought he would," I admitted. Rex was at least able now to talk about Guy and remain calm.

"I'll never trust him," he said. "But there's more to it than just disliking him. I miss her. I miss *us*. The three of us being together."

"Me too," I said.

"He's got to go," said Rex. "I don't care how, he's just got to."

The fug of smoke emanating from Biba's room covered the whole landing. It hung there like a featureless ghost, haunting the landing between her room and Rex's. We threw all the windows open as wide as they would go but no breeze came to disperse it.

Even with both doors closed, their voices were still audible. Rex and I stopped making love in his bedroom across the hallway and began to sleep at the top of the house in mine.

"I won't be back tonight, so don't wait up," said Biba. She had on a long brown dress with some kind of tribal markings on it and a pair of earrings made of wooden beads and feathers. The clothes were made for someone dark and voluptuous like Nina. They made Biba look like a totem pole, but as usual she gave the impression that the trend was about to catch on wildly.

"Where are you going?" said Rex.

"To a party with Guy," she said. It was the first I had heard of it. "We've got a ride waiting outside. It's a shame there isn't enough room in the car for you two, but I'm sure you want to be left on your own anyway." Actually, there was nothing I would have liked more than to go to a party with Biba. I minded desperately that I wasn't invited, but I was too proud to beg her.

Hiding behind one of the saris that still hung from the front window, I watched the street as Biba clambered inelegantly into the backseat of a beat-up black sports car. It would have been a squash, but there would have been room for me alongside her. The driver's face was obscured by a baseball cap and Guy was rolling a joint in the passenger seat. He looked up at the house and I hid behind the pink and purple silk like a shy bride behind her veil.

It was the first time we had had the house to ourselves for days, and disappointment at being left behind was soon surpassed by thrill and anticipation. Rex and I were free to wander naked throughout the house, making spontaneous love in every room of it. But he immediately began to fill the hours with housework. If he couldn't physically evict Guy from the house, then he could at least purge the shared rooms of his detritus, and he set about doing so with a grim and focused determination that allowed no room for seduction. Guy's things painted a perfectly accurate portrait of his personality and priorities. Jeans, sneakers, and T-shirts flopped over the backs of chairs as though hung out to dry, but they all stank of stale tobacco. You could tell which CDs were Guy's: they were the only ones still housed in their plastic jewel cases, and they joined the pile. A packet that had contained twelve ribbed condoms now held only one. Ragged copies of the *NME* were intact, but the glossier music magazine *Mixmag* had had the bottom left-hand corner of the back cover torn out to make roaches for joints. The inside pages he had cut up, scoring neatly around pictures of album covers, to make wraps for speed or cocaine or whatever it was that he had his hands on that week. A glass bong, the kind they sell in head shops in Camden market, had apparently never been used; the makeshift one that he actually used, fashioned from a pen and an old Coke bottle with dirty water pooled in the bottom, went straight in the bin. Everything else was piled in Rex's arms. He gathered Guy's possessions from throughout the house and laid them on the kitchen table in a kind of memory game; appropriate, really, because I still remember those identifying, incriminating items with absolute clarity. We bundled all of them into a black Nike sports bag—also Guy's—and dumped it in the corner of Biba's room. He never bothered to unpack it. As far as I know he no more noticed the bag was there than he registered the absence of his belongings from the rest of the house.

That night, we went to sleep without making love for the first time. I lay next to Rex and saw the whites of his eyes glitter in the dark, but when I reached out to touch him he rolled over and feigned sleep. Nor was he there the next morning when I awoke. It was a rare overcast day and my mood matched the weather. Three empty coffee cups on the Velvet Room table told me that he had been up long before me. He was pacing on the terrace. His footfalls made no noise on the green and bronze devoré curtain that was topmost on the layers of bedding spread on the terrace, but there was a scuffing sound when his heels made contact with the uncovered stone at either end of the makeshift rug. I had never seen anyone actually pace before, walk up and down over the same patch of ground again and again and again. It is as though the mind contains too much activity and some of it must leak into the muscles and move the body around in this pointless way. Perhaps that's why it is so horrible to witness. The exasperation that roared up in me was almost violent, a hugely magnified version of the irritation you feel when someone else is tapping his fingers on a dashboard or clicking a ballpoint pen. I found that I was mirroring Rex's own rising hysteria.

"Fucking . . . just . . . *stop* that!" I said, in a voice that belonged to Biba. It worked, up to a point. He stopped pacing and began instead to frantically work his fingers through his hair. His eyes were reddening and his teeth were exposed in a kind of snarl. A string of saliva linked his top and bottom lips. I had once thought his face neutral and unremarkable. Now I realized that if he could be beautiful, he also had a capacity for ugliness I could never have guessed at.

"I can't help but think the worst. I picture her dead, Karen, she looks so like my mum that I can't help but picture her dead, hanging there or from a tree in the woods. I'm losing her to him, I can feel it. It's making me ill. I'm going to have a heart attack."

His breath came in short, serrated wheezes and I recognized the beginnings of an anxiety attack. I had seen one once before, when trapped in a Spanish elevator with a woman who had chosen the wrong day to try to overcome her claustrophobia; there had been a brief power outage and I had spent three frightening minutes trapped in a tiny metal box with a woman who convinced me that she was going to die in front of me. I hadn't known how to cope with her then, and I didn't know what to do with Rex now. I knew that paper bags were supposed to help, but only in the same vague way that most of us know that women in labor need towels and hot water. I resorted to that other folk remedy we all know but hope we will never have to use, the slap to the cheek, but my hand was frozen in midair by the ringing of the telephone inside the house. Rex sprang forward like an animal.

"That'll be her," he said. He sounded like someone was strangling him.

"Let me get it, then," I said. "You're in no fit state. Stay here and . . . take deep breaths, or something."

The two flights of stairs between the Velvet Room and the kitchen were now so familiar beneath my feet that I was able to descend them all in seconds, hardly feeling the individual treads beneath my bare feet.

When I picked up the handset, the voice that said, "Darling?" was not the expected one; it was warm, low, and musical. It took me a split second to place it.

"Nina, is that you?" I said.

"That's Karen, isn't it? How lovely to speak to you. Have they moved you in yet?"

"Yes," I said. I didn't like her assumption. It made me think that Nina had discussed my installation in the house with Biba and that the two had agreed that I should be her replacement. "How are you? Where are you?"

"In Tunis," she said. "It's gorgeous. I'm as brown as a berry and the kids have gone to sleep. We're in this five-star hotel room. Can you believe it?" I wondered who was paying for it. "We met this guy on the train who said we could stay with him for a bit. I think he's on some kind of conference or something, I don't know. I'm not going to turn it down: this is the lap of luxury after some of the places we've been staying. I'll have to be quick, actually: he's just nipped out and I'm not sure his generosity extends to phone calls to London. How are things, anyway? You all okay?"

"Yes," I said. Then, realizing I was talking to the one person who might understand: "Actually no. Biba is a bit late back from a night out and Rex has got himself into a bit of a state."

Nina accurately interpreted my euphemism. "Is he all out of breath and hysterical and talking about her dying?"

He came toward me then, his face set and his hand extended.

"Let me talk to her," he said. Nina must have heard him.

"Do you want me to handle this?" she said. I left the room but waited on the stairs behind him.

"I know, I know, I can't help it." Nina's voice fizzed down the line but I couldn't make out her words. "With a bloke called Guy." There was a much longer silence this time, and when Rex spoke again his voice had returned to normal.

"I know you're right," he said. "It just hasn't been easy lately. I've been trying to talk to my dad, and there was a bit of a setback." Another pause. "Karen? Yes, very much so. No, it's brilliant. She's about all that is good at the moment," and then her next question brought a smile to his voice. "Yes, we are, actually. Thanks, Nina. How are the kids? Can I talk to them? Oh, fair enough. Will you give them a cuddle from me when they wake up?"

I closed the door behind me and left Nina to finish talking Rex down from his ledge. I wondered if I, too, would learn coping strategies for his outbursts over time, or if they were something he would grow out of. I remembered with a pang my first few visits to Highgate when Nina and Rex had quietly assumed the roles of mother and father while Biba and I ran wild like children through the trees.

"You weren't talking for long," I said when Rex replaced the handset with a bang and a clatter. "I thought you'd have loads to catch up on. Did that man come back into the room?"

"No. I wanted to leave the line free for Biba." He took another deep breath, controlled but shaky. "The irony is that when she gets in, I will be so happy she's alive and then a split second after that I will be so angry that she's put me through this that I'll feel I could kill her. Why does she do it? How can she be so cruel?"

Rex didn't kill Biba when she came home at five o'clock that afternoon, minus Guy and one of her shoes. Instead, he gave her a wounded look before tossing his head and marching out of the house in a dramatic flounce that would have been worthy of the actress herself.

"What's wrong with him?" said Biba as he slammed the door, which bounced back open again. I decided to spare her the details of last night's hysteria.

"I don't know," I said. "How was the party?"

"It was wonderful," she said, her eyes saucering at the memory. "It was in a place called . . . oh, where was it again? Somewhere east. Bromley-by-Bow," she said, with the wonder that most people save for describing exotic, paradisiacal locations. "It was in a squat on the top floor of a housing project. It was just like something out of a cop show. They actually had a bloke with a huge dog at the door. The police came so we broke onto the roof and hid from them while they raided the place." I realized with a sickening and absolute clarity that Biba had fallen out of love with her world just as my place in it was secured. "We watched the sun come up and then we went to sleep on the sofa with the dog. It was one of those big black and brown illegal ones that eats children. It could have savaged me at any time but it didn't. You'd have loved it." I wasn't sure I would have. "Such a *shame* you couldn't come." She had genuinely forgotten that it was she who had denied me an invitation.

"Where's Guy?"

"Taking care of business," she said. "How lovely to have you to myself for a while without any horrible boys getting in the way. Shall we have cocktails? It's not too decadent to start now, is it? The sun's over the yardarm and all that."

"What is a yardarm, anyway?"

"No idea, darling. Come on. I fancy a martini." She retrieved some vodka from the freezer and found an ancient bottle of vermouth with a peeling label and a crystallized neck under the sink next to the bleach. She sloshed them into mismatched tumblers.

"Is it supposed to taste like gasoline?" I asked.

"Um." She found a couple of shriveled olives in a container in the fridge and dropped them into our glasses. They sank immediately to the bottom. She fished one out and bit into it. "Oh. Now the olive tastes of gasoline, too."

We took the drinks not onto the terrace but into the garden where the trees towered over us, living but silent witnesses to everything that happened. The outer leaves had begun to yellow where the sun had bleached them. Their mustard-colored tips created an illusion of autumn. I turned away, never wanting the season to change.

20

"I'M JUST SAYING THAT I don't like it," she says. "Don't start on at me again, Karen. I only want what's best for my grandchild." My mother and I are trying to negotiate how my parents will pick up Alice when they visit tomorrow. I want her to come in and see Rex, have a cup of tea, get the awkward first visit out of the way. My mother wants to toot the horn and have Alice run down the path, like a Sunday father who can't bear to see his ex-wife.

"Right, so what are you going to do? Never come into my house again? He's not going anywhere, Mum. He lives here now. He's her father. You've got to accept it." Silence. "Mum, trust me."

"It's not *you* I don't trust," she says. My guilt is always at its strongest when she says things like this.

If my mother's phone call puts me in a bad mood, then Rex's late return from his walk exacerbates it. It is unheard of for him to miss our evening meal. I am convinced that someone has found him, someone intent on revenge or exposure or both. Alice eats her dinner while I push mine around the plate and Rex's portion of lasagna shrivels in the oven. Seven, eight, nine o'clock come and go, and still no sign of him and no phone call. The struggle to get Alice to go to bed and stay there without his good night kiss takes nearly an hour, during which I at least stop watching the clock. When I finally return to the empty living room it is twenty past ten. Mentally I map the radius he can cover on foot: the forest, the beach, the construction site, miles of winding high-sided lanes and alleyways, all places he might easily be beaten up and lie undiscovered all night. A muscle in my eyelid starts to jump and flicker. When his key clicks in the front door at eleven, anger immediately subsumes relief.

"Where've you been?" I demand.

"Out," he says. He won't meet my eyes, and instead of offering me a kiss he goes straight to the kitchen, mud and leaf mold coming away from his boots in wet black flakes.

"Where?" I repeat.

"Just out," he says, truculent as a teenager. "Doesn't matter." His eyes are unfocused and his speech is thick. As he retrieves his dinner from the oven and staggers to the kitchen table, I realize that he's drunk: drunker, I expect, than he has been in ten years. He is an unlovely sight as he stabs clumsily at his food with the wrong end of a fork and when he finally figures out how to turn it around it is no better. He eats sloppily, sauce dribbling over his chin.

"I was worried about you," I press. "Rex, what happened?"

"Nothing happened. Leave me alone."

"Since when do we have secrets from each other?" What I mean, of course, is that while I am allowed to have secrets from him, he may not keep any from me. "You could have told me where you were going."

He stands up and slams his fist down on the table.

"I spent ten *fucking* years in prison with every second of my day accounted for," he hisses, spittle flying across the table and landing on my cheek. He has never seemed so much taller than I am. "I didn't realize that I was coming home to another fucking warden." He launches his plate across the room like a Frisbee. I brace myself for the smash of china on tile but it hits the trash can and lands softly in a basket of laundry that rests by the back door. The kitchen appliances, my clothes, and his face are all covered in food, as though someone had operated a blender with the lid off.

I have been afraid for Rex before, but never afraid *of* him until now.

"If you must know, I walked to the pub," he says. "I sat there with loads of drifters staring at me, I got drunk, I thought about how I'm shit and I can't get a job to provide for you both, and I thought about how much I was looking forward to coming home to you," he says. "I wish I hadn't bothered. When did you become such a control freak?"

"Fuck you." I run up to the bathroom and lock the door, sit on the closed toilet, and wait for him to come up and apologize. When he doesn't, I linger over the nightly routine of taking off my makeup, flossing and brushing my teeth until I judge we have both had time to calm down. Still, nothing can justify his behavior. I go downstairs to tell him that I want him to sleep downstairs tonight, but he is already out cold, feet hanging over the arm of the sofa, mouth lolling open. I go to bed without covering him up. When he slides into bed at five o'clock in the morning his skin is cold and goosefleshed.

"I'm sorry," he says. "I've cleaned the kitchen."

"You frightened me."

"I'm so sorry. I'm still getting used to freedom. It all went to my head a bit. I won't do it again."

I can't bring myself to offer my own apology even though I know he's right. I *am* a control freak. I have had to be. When I was the one left holding the reins of this family, is it any wonder I grip them so tightly?

※

When Guy returned to the house, he kept his sunglasses on indoors and carried a laptop computer underneath his arm. It was as unlike the slim notebooks we use today as his cell phone was unlike the sleek clamshell currently in my handbag. I was familiar with computers then, but this was very different from the substantial, anchored desktop kind I worked on in the computer lab on campus. Guy's laptop looked like a baby that had been born with all its organs outside its body. Wires sprung from sockets all over its chunky little surface. One thick black cord led to a disc drive, another to a transformer and in turn to a main plug, and the giant one that looked like the foot pump for an inflatable bed was a modem. Guy explained all this as he set it up on the bureau in the Velvet Room that had a red leather surface and was angled like an architect's drawing board. We all looked at it expectantly.

"It's a present for me, apparently," said Biba.

"You're probably receiving stolen goods," said Rex pointedly. Guy didn't deny this but rather smiled into the nest of wires he was untangling.

"Right," he said eventually. "Where's your phone extension?"

"I'm sorry?" said Rex.

"Your extension, the other phone jack. You're not telling me that in a house this size you've only got that one crappy little phone down in the kitchen."

"I'm afraid so," said Rex.

"No," said Guy. "This house is *riddled* with cables. I've seen them. There's got to be another outlet somewhere." He began his search at the kitchen telephone and, with blunt fingertips, began to trace the cables that snaked all over the walls. I stood in the doorway of the Velvet Room, watching him. Sometimes the wires were tacked over surfaces where the wall met the ceiling and some-times they were buried deep under layers of wallpaper and paint. They led him along baseboards, up over doorways, and under-neath picture rails. Rex joined me in the doorway and slid his arm around my waist. His body carried none of the tension that he had been holding the day before, and when I tentatively leaned back into his chest, I felt his whole body welcome mine. The wild goose chase Guy was on couldn't have been better designed for our amusement. Occasionally we would hear a mumbled "Fuck it" as the cable disappeared through a hole in a cornice or abruptly doubled back on itself. Like everything else in the house, this was due to neglect and bad design, but I felt a small thrill of victory, as though the very layout of our home was conspiring to frustrate and reject Guy. Eventually Guy crawled in on all fours, kneading a ridge in the rug in the middle of the room. The gap between his jeans and T-shirt revealed a tanned, muscular lower back and an inch of crisp white waistband. His underpants said CALVIN KLIEN, the misspelling marking them out as street-market fakes. I wondered if this was an affectation.

"I don't know what he thinks I'm going to do with a computer," said Biba, as though Guy wasn't kneeling directly at her feet. He didn't look up. He had a habit of ignoring any remark about him unless it was addressed directly to him and prefaced with his name. It gave the impression that he didn't hear anything we said and the temptation was to talk about him, in front of him. We found out later that he had taken in far more than we gave him credit for, but by then it was too late to take back some of the things we had said.

"He's trying to impress you," said Rex.

Guy interrupted not with an objection but with a grunt of triumph. He had located whatever it was he'd been searching for behind a wicker bookcase that leaned against the far wall of the Velvet Room. It groaned with dusty books and magazines. With one hand Guy picked it up and deposited it ten inches to the left. A telephone jack, gray with years of disuse, protruded from the wall just above the baseboard. He traced a line in the grime with his thumb, to reveal the yellowing plastic below.

"I told you, didn't I?" he said to us.

"Well done," said Biba dispassionately. "Aren't you clever?"

Rex was staring at the wall as though he'd never seen it before.

"I've just had the most vivid memory," he said. "Of Mum on the green sofa talking on that phone. So there must have been one here once. Isn't it funny how you can completely forget something and then you can remember it like it was yesterday?"

"When was this, Rex?" said Biba.

"God, I dunno . . . years ago. Dad was still here, I think. She was laughing, so . . ."

I stayed silent out of a tender respect for this memory and because I did not know how much family background Guy knew. What he and Biba talked about in her bedroom was anyone's guess, but I could not imagine him listening with the sensitivity and attention the subject of their mother demanded. I found that I liked the idea that I knew more than he did.

"Your wiring's all to shit," said an apparently unmoved Guy, flinching only slightly as a blue spark shot out of the first plug he tried. Sweat began to patch his T-shirt underneath his arms and between his shoulder blades. Eventually he found a secure jack, did something that made a green light on the modem flicker on and off. A few minutes later, a bouncing buzz told us the computer was dialing a connection to the Internet. Rex, fascinated and impressed despite himself, looked over Guy's shoulder at the little gray icon that flickered in the middle of the tiny screen. I sat on the sofa next to Biba.

"There you go. You're online," said Guy in triumph. Biba finished the cigarette she was rolling and sparked it before speaking.

"Now what does it do?"

"It doesn't *do* anything unless you tell it to," said Guy. Biba looked blank. "You don't seem very pleased with it. I went to a lot of trouble to get this for you."

"Yes, where exactly did you get it, Guy?" interjected Rex. "I can't see a receipt or any packaging."

"It's lovely of you," she said. "I just don't see why I need a computer. I mean, that's what I've got an agent for, CVs and stuff like that. Did Sarah Bernhardt need the Internet? Did Katharine Hepburn?"

For a moment I almost felt sorry for Guy. I understood the cold darkness you felt when the lighthouse beam of Biba's affection swung suddenly in another direction.

"Why don't I set you up with an e-mail address?" I said, carefully removing the computer from the bureau and placing it on my lap. The tiny keys were clustered together in the middle of the board, making my fingers seem oversized and clumsy, and my attempts at using the sensor mouse were inept. "Type your name in there," I said, maneuvering the cursor to the appropriate box. She wrote her full name out. Watching her type was painful: each letter seemed to take her a minute to locate, index finger circling over the keyboard like a buzzard. I deduced that the theater studies department at Queen Charlotte's had been one of the few that still allowed its students to submit essays in longhand. Her new address was displayed on the screen: bathshebaelizabethcapel@ hotmail.com.

"Now put a password in," I said. "It has to be something close to your heart, something that makes it easy to remember, but not too obvious. Something I can't guess." I looked away while she typed her secret word. "There you go. You've got your very own e-mail address. Aren't you modern?"

She remained unimpressed.

"I'll bet you anything I never use it," she said.

21

THE GREEN VELVET SOFA was the one remaining item of furniture from the suite that had given the Velvet Room its name. Nobody ever thought to bring it in from its new location at the edge of the room, one arm overhanging the flagstones of the terrace. It meant that the French windows could not be properly closed, which left the house vulnerable to burglars. But as the front door gave way with the tiniest kick, and there was nothing inside worth stealing, nobody bothered to change things. The sofa had been dewed with splashbacks of rain during a rare downpour but I liked the sheen that the spray had made on the velvet and even the slight dampness the upholstery retained. It brought the outdoors inside. I liked to imagine that it was a huge stone, shaped to accommodate my body and covered with a spongy layer of moss.

Rex and I lay end to end on it, my left hand holding my book, my right his ankle. It was a German novel that I had studied in my first year and one of the few things I'd retrieved from the house in Brentford. I had not liked studying the book but was enjoying rereading it for pleasure. Rex drifted in and out of sleep, a thriller facedown on his lap. The *thud-thud-thud* of Guy's music came from above, spilling out of Biba's bedroom window and seeping through the floorboards, but we had both learned to tune it out, unlike poor Tom Wheeler who complained in vain on an almost daily basis. The

music, once so oppressive, had now become part of the white noise
of the city and the wood. It had gotten to the stage where I could
hear the birdsong and rustle of the leaves again. So when his cell
phone rang, it felt like the silence that it pierced was true.

It was unlike Guy to leave his phone unattended but on this
occasion, in the haze of lust or in a stoned stupor, he had lumbered
upstairs without it. I picked up the handset. A London number but
not a local one and the word HOME flashed up on the tiny screen. I
looked up at the ceiling as though it would help me gauge whether
he would come running down to grab it from my hands, but he
would never hear it. I extended the antenna as I had seen Guy do
himself and stabbed a few random keys with my fingertips before
hitting the one that made the connection to a tinny voice shouting a staccato of repeated hellos. Rex was awake now and watching
me with interest.

"Guy's phone."

"Who are you?" said the voice. It wasn't the low male rumble
I'd been expecting, but a female whine. The accent was moneyed,
educated, middle-aged London, the sound my mother was aspir-
ing to when she adopted what my father called her "posh telephone
voice." I didn't give her my name.

"Are you Guy's roommate?" I asked.

"Roommate? *Roommate?* Certainly not. I'm his mother." Guy
having a mother did not sit well with the myth he had sold us about
himself, a lone ranger in the gritty urban environment. "If it's not
too much to ask, could I possibly speak to my son?"

"Guy," I said when Rex and I were outside the bedroom door.
"Phone for you." I wondered if his mother could hear the giveaway
sigh and creak of the bed as it pitched beneath their bodies.

"Tell them to ring back, I'm balls-deep," said the ever-
gallant Guy.

"It's your mum," I said. An abrupt stillness was followed by the
music being extinguished and an under-the-breath "Fuck," audible to us if not to his mother on the telephone. Then there was a

fumble and a crash as, presumably, Guy extricated himself and his balls from Biba. He opened the bedroom door and grabbed the phone from my hand. He was clutching a bedsheet around his groin. Biba sat up in bed, wrapped in the rest of the sheet, apparently unconcerned by the interruption. She had picked up on the crackle of tension that foretold a drama about to play out. Uninvited but unopposed, Rex and I crossed the threshold of the room and sat on either side of her. Guy turned his naked back to us and mumbled, but his mother's voice was strident enough to be heard through the receiver.

"What has happened to your father's computer?" she was saying. "It's missing from his study. Have you taken it out of the house?"

"No." He spoke in an unconvincing, unsteady warble.

"It's not even his personal computer, you know. It belongs to his office."

"I just borrowed it."

"Guy, I'm very disappointed in you. I have no idea where you are, but you will come home tonight and you will bring the computer with you."

"Aw, *Mum* . . ." I wondered how old Guy actually was. His height and bulk had always led me to assume that he was well into his twenties, Rex's age at least, but this was the first time I wondered if he might be younger than the rest of us, years younger, a teenager still.

"Oh Mum, nothing. Supper is at eight. I expect you and the computer to be here. Is that understood?"

"I s'pose." Rex, Biba, and I exchanged a three-way glance and I knew that laughter would ensue if we didn't break eye contact immediately. I fixed my attention on a pint glass filled with cigarette butts and roaches in the middle of the floor. My lungs ballooned with the effort of staying silent.

"Do you want shepherd's pie or lasagna?"

"Shepherd's pie."

THE POISON TREE   213

Beside me I felt Biba begin to convulse and heard a bubble of laughter burst from Rex's lips, and it was too late.

"Thank you very much. I don't suppose you're going to tell me who answered the phone. No, don't tell me. I don't want to know. We really do need to have a conversation about your future, Guy."

Guy retracted the telephone's rubbery antenna and silenced his mother with a curt beep. He rounded his shoulders and our laughter bounced off his broad back.

"Guy," teased Rex, "do you still live with your mum?"

"I don't live there *as such*," he said to the wall.

"But this apartment in Ladbroke Grove that's full of your 'people.' Is that actually where your mum and your dad live?"

"Yeah, well," he said in futile and belated self-defense. "It's the life you live on the streets that makes you who you are. B's met my entourage, she knows." He looked to her for support but Biba was laughing with us, at him. The moment marked a triumph for Rex. Guy may have laid a temporary claim on his sister, but Rex, who knew her better than anyone, could see that this was the beginning of the end. He knew that Biba could forgive—even glamorize and admire—low-level criminality, idiocy, bad taste in music and drugs; but inauthenticity was the one thing she would not tolerate. Now it was just a matter of time. Like the hairline crack in the plaster that appears above the doorframe, all Rex had to do was keep slamming the door hard enough, often enough, for the whole wall to come apart.

"Don't laugh at me," said Guy, turning to face us now. "You don't know shit, holed up here in your house in your little bubble, and the three of you pissing about in the woods like Hansel and fucking Gretel." I had never heard Guy speak so emotively before. Just as my mother's posh telephone voice slipped to expose her true class when she was drunk, or angry, Guy's accent slid up the social scale as he lost control of his temper. *T*'s and *h*'s suddenly found their way back into his alphabet, making him sound more public schoolboy than inner-city gangster.

"Whereas you're keeping it real by stealing your father's computer and eating your mum's shepherd's pie," said Rex. Glee at finally having one up on the man he hated was making him confident and even witty. "Guy, can you sort me out with some spliff? A shooter? A *lasagna*?"

Guy was pathetic in his scrap of bedsheet.

"Yeah, well, don't think I couldn't get a gun because I could!" he said. His lower lip was actually protruding in a toddler's pout and I half expected him to end his sentence with "So *there*." "I know people who can get anything. Whatever. I *could*."

He bent at the knee to pick up a pair of jeans he had discarded at the foot of Biba's bed, dropped his sheet, and marched out of the room. Seconds later he returned, wearing the jeans, to retrieve his phone. "Fuck all three of you," he said, before storming out again. "Just fuck right off."

"He'll be back," said Biba.

And he was, a day later, having been fed by his mother and returned the laptop to his father. He and Biba spent the afternoon having noisy reconciliation sex, but all four of us shared the evening and it was apparent that a subtle shift had occurred. Guy was chastened, and his silent demeanor, once heavy with potential menace, was now exposed as an embarrassed sulk. Physically he and Biba seemed as close as ever, but her face no longer wore the rapturous expression it once had, and her attention and conversation were turned back to Rex and me.

We had a pink and gray quilt covered in dubious stains laid out in the near-side corner of the gardens. The sun, which had been chasing across the garden all day, had painted us into a corner of warmth away from the woods and next to the fence that divided our garden from Tom Wheeler's. We were close but—crucially—out of sight. Wheeler's neighborhood-watch campaign had gone from reactive to proactive and he had begun to actively seek out evidence of our antisocial behavior, real or imagined. More than once we'd seen him craning out of the oriel window at the top of his house to look at what was happening in the garden or on the terrace, and Rex had a theory that it was only a matter of time before he began to take photographs. We joked that he had a whole room in his house devoted to noise-measuring apparatus, with flip charts that plotted graphs of our delinquency.

"He'll have one of those line graphs with a jagged red line that shoots down," said Biba, "showing how the tone of the area has been lowered because of us. It'll be called *There Goes the Neighborhood*."

"Even though you've been here for years longer than he has," I said.

"Too right," said Biba. She shouted through a knothole in the fence. "Did you hear that, Wheeler? We were here first!"

Wheeler didn't take any photographs and he did not have a room full of visual aids but we had not underestimated his attention to detail. It all went into his book, blue ink on white paper, bound with moleskin, the pages and Rex's fate sealed with a little leather strap; when he was arrested, the book was immediately produced from next door. That night, Wheeler made a note that the smell of marijuana was clearly detectable between the hours of 10 p.m. and 1 a.m. and that conversation directly outside his children's bedrooms had kept them awake. He wrote that he heard two male voices and one female one. He didn't refer to me, although I'm sure I spoke just as much as any of the others that night.

❧

When the knock on the door comes I am upstairs in my underwear doing my hair. I curse Rex for forgetting his keys, retrieve the spare set from my bedside table, and go to toss them down with a reprimand. But what I see when I lean out makes me ricochet violently from the window. A police car, a Suffolk police car, sits outside the house. Two uniformed officers, arms folded and sturdy legs parted, stand back from the front door and look up at the eaves where the windows are, their eyes traveling up and down the terrace as though trying to establish which of the cottages contains me. I crouch on the floor as though hiding from a marksman, inelegant in mismatched underwear with a large round barrel brush rolled up in a lock of hair at the front of my head. Even in my fear I am grateful that Rex and Alice are still at the swimming pool and that whatever happens, they won't find out like this.

After a minute or so, squatting like a frog becomes uncomfortable, and I stand up. Before I dare look out of the window again I reach for the oversized T-shirt that lies on the back of my dressing table and pull it awkwardly over my head. The hairbrush becomes tangled and its bristles scratch my forehead. By the time I unknot the snarl of hair, there has been a development in the street outside. I open the window, letting the words ride in on a sled of cool air, and slowly realize that the house the policemen were shouting up to was not mine, the hammering is not on my door but two houses to the left. Noises carry like that in these cottages, and I've often opened the door only to find one of my neighbors welcoming someone over their own threshold. I look out of my bedroom window so that I won't have to put on a dressing gown and disrupt my day.

"Come on, Dave," says one of the policemen. "You know what this is about."

I hear the click of the catch and feel the reverberation of the swinging front door as, two houses to my left, Dave lets himself out. He walks toward the policemen, dressed lightly for the weather in an Ipswich Town football shirt and gray sweatpants. One of the policemen says something to him, and Dave disappears back into his house, only to emerge a minute or so later wearing a big brown fleece. His neck sinks into the cowl of its collar.

Not until Dave is being driven away in the police car do I register the presence of the white Micra. Its driver is perched on its hood, the scarf that had been draped over her head like a hood now loose around her neck. It is a middle-aged woman with a little wizened face and thin hair escaping from a loose topknot, clutching a file to her chest. I can just about decipher the letters *SCC*— Suffolk County Council—on the chunky plastic ID badge that swings from her neck on a thick ribbon. Not a journalist after all, but a local government employee. She has a look about her that reminds me of Rex's parole officer. A small smile of satisfaction thins her lips as she finishes filling in her form.

Neighbors gather in the front gardens to analyze recent events. It's benefit fraud according to one neighbor, an elderly woman I don't know very well. Apparently Dave has been claiming disability benefits, pleading a bad back, but working as a casual laborer on the new housing development. How she knows all these details within minutes of the police driving him away she does not say, but she seems confident of her sources.

"It just goes to show," she says as her audience disperses. "You could be living next door to anyone."

The degree results were published on the last Wednesday of August. Although they were sent out by mail the same day, it was expected that students would go to campus to pick them up. Biba didn't bother to collect her results, claiming that her degree had only ever been a means to the end of getting herself an agent. Fairly confident that my first was in the bag, I stayed away too: I didn't want to risk running into Caroline Alba. She would want to know why I had not looked at the application forms she had given me or drafted a proposal for my MA, and I could not give her a good reason. I had picked up Rex's head-in-the-sand attitude, every day relinquishing a little more responsibility for my own future. I was not yet too deep in denial to realize that this was a problem, and resolved to go alone to Brentford to read my delivered results and to use the space and silence I knew I would find there to make my decision. I gave myself a deadline of midnight that night either to commit to a university and a master's subject or reject the idea altogether.

I had another reason for returning to my old house: a scheduled telephone call from the Continent, my former housemates crowded around a single telephone somewhere in France while

I tore open their envelopes. None of the three would get first-class degrees, but they might scrape by with upper seconds, or in Emma's case a lower second. Their futures were not in any case dependent on the outcome of their degrees.

The car keys were already in my hand when I told Rex not to expect me back that evening.

"Can I come with you?" he said, rounding his eyes. It was a trick he shared with Biba, a parting of upper and lower eyelid without exposing any white: instead, the pupil and iris seemed to expand and blend to fill the whole socket so that you felt you were drowning in hot chocolate. Both of them knew that this expression could be fortified by a semi-ironic projection of the lower lip that I was powerless to resist. Alice too has inherited this ability; it must be innate because neither Rex nor Biba was there to show her how to do it. "I want to know everything about you. I'd like to see how you lived before you lived here."

"I still do live there, officially," I said, but he had already gone to fetch his toothbrush.

I had forgotten about my parents until I turned the corner of my street and saw my father's Ford Focus parked a few doors away from my house. Its two-week holiday in the long-stay parking lot at Terminal 4 had done nothing to take the gleam off its pale blue paint job. I did an emergency stop and threw Rex forward in his seat.

"What was that for?" he said, rubbing the back of his neck where it had rebounded against the headrest.

"Nothing," I said. I looked in the rearview mirror to check the state of the road behind me. I was actually considering turning back, reversing all the way up the street. I tried to articulate the reason for my reluctance to introduce everybody. Had it been Biba in the passenger seat beside me I would have understood myself; I still wanted her to believe that I was the kindred bohemian spirit she had at first taken me to be, but five minutes in the company of my parents would have shattered any illusions I had managed to create about my background. But I was not with Biba. I was with Rex; undramatic, unassuming Rex, whose devotion I was sure of. Perhaps, I realized in the seconds it took to stall the engine, fire it up again, and wonder which gear to put the car into, my misgivings lay not with them but with him. Rex didn't have Biba's ability to flirt with and charm everyone he met. He did not have a job, or any history of employment, skills or trade or income or any of the other assets that my parents and their friends used to measure a person's worth. He did not even have the education that they had learned to recognize as a substitute for all these things.

A car pulled up behind me and a loud blast from its horn forced me into action. I pulled into the only parking space available, directly opposite the one my parents occupied. We looked at each other through the windshield, Dad recognizing me and my car before he spotted the man sitting in the passenger seat. Rex's face was obscured by the sunshade.

"Your neighbors seem very pleased to see you," he said, unfastening his seatbelt. "Can you imagine Tom Wheeler waving and smiling at us like that?"

"They're not my neighbors," I said. "They're my parents." He goggled at me incredulously. "I'd *completely* forgotten they were going to be here."

We all faced each other on the pavement, Rex hovering a few paces behind me like a queen's consort. My mother clutched a bottle of Portuguese wine and a Marks & Spencer freezer bag.

"Mum, Dad, this is Rex. Rex, this is my mum, Linda, and my dad, John."

I tried to see each through the others' eyes. Mum looked good: tans age most women but my mother, whose skin is like mine, looks young and refreshed after a fortnight slathering herself in olive oil on a beach. Only her clothes let her down; her eye shadow, dress, and shoes were in an aging and overly formal coordinating shade of pale blue. Dad stood proud in his holiday wardrobe, safari shorts and a yellow polo shirt that contrasted unfortunately with lower arms baked to the color and texture of a chorizo sausage. Rex's skin shone white and his hair and clothes were in their usual state of happy negligence.

"This is a surprise," said Mum.

"So pleased to meet you, Mrs. Clarke," Rex said, shaking Mum's hand. "I've heard so much about you. Mr. Clarke." He took my dad's hand, too.

I saw from the flicker of eye contact that passed between my parents that Rex's accent and manners had had the predictable effect of eclipsing his other shortcomings.

"Let's get inside." Rex and I trampled on the mail that littered the porch but Dad stopped to pick it up before handing it all to me. I took the bundle of envelopes that contained four people's futures and put them to one side. Mum had brought milk with her and it was just as well. Otherwise, I wouldn't have been able to make tea and coffee for everyone and we would have had to stand awkwardly in the kitchen without cups to stare into.

"How's that car running, Karen?" said Dad into a silence punctuated by sips and slurps.

"Fine, fine."

"You taken her out for a good long-distance run lately?" he asked. I shook my head and Dad mirrored the action, embellishing his gesture with a tsk of disapproval.

"You noticed anything, Rex?"

"There's a bit of a funny sound when she changes gears," said Rex. I wasn't used to Rex engaging in blokeish banter and wasn't sure if the "she" he was referring to was the car or its driver. "Sounds like the exhaust dragging on the ground, but I've checked that out and it's not that." Had he? Wasn't it? If Rex was an expert on cars, this was the first I had heard of it.

"I'd better get under her hood, see what's going on," said Dad, placing his cup decisively on the counter.

"I'll come with you," said Rex.

So my father and my boyfriend went to look at a car while my mother and I stayed in the kitchen. I helped her unpack the groceries she had picked up on the way over from the airport.

"He seems nice," she said. "Where did you meet him?"

"His sister was at my college," I said. Mum nodded, pleased enough with this association not to follow it up with an interrogation about Rex's own qualifications. "She's an actress," I added.

"He's quite artistic-looking, isn't he? And he's got a lovely speaking voice. You can tell he's been well brought up." The thought of Rex as artistic was as amusing as the idea of him being raised by a happy family was heartbreaking. She held a long string of my hair up to the light and then looked down at my clothes, a pair of cut-off denims and a red gypsy top with a hole in one puffed sleeve. "Your roots need doing, though. He'll know that you're not a natural blonde if you let it grow out. And I don't know what you think you've got on. I suppose he likes you like that, though." I did not point out that Rex already knew that I was not a natural blonde and that even weekly appointments at the hairdresser could not have convinced him otherwise.

Before dinner I opened my results, my hand steady as I sliced into the envelope with a steak knife. It was the predicted First, announced without any kind of congratulations. Most important letters are very short and this was no exception: just a printout of my name, my course, and then, in the middle of the page, the news that I had gained a first-class degree. I took it back to the table and set it before my mother.

"My baby, with a First," said my mother, radiant with pride, and then just to check, "That's like an A, isn't it?"

"Well done, love," said Dad, raising a glass of wine in my direction. Rex and Mum joined in his silent toast. "We always knew she'd do well," he told Rex. "We're very proud of our Karen."

"So am I," said Rex, his foot firm against my calf beneath the table.

I can't remember what we ate that night—some kind of lamb, I think, with a good Vinho Verde—but I do remember that we ate it from clean, matching dishes and silverware. I remember that Rex praised the preprepared food she had brought for us as though she had been cooking from scratch for hours. I remember, too, the way his obvious gratitude warmed her face and thinking how pretty she still was when she smiled. The three of them discussed interiors, house prices, and holiday destinations as though they had known each other for years. By the end of the meal, I felt like the newcomer.

The telephone rang in the gap between the main course and whatever frozen pudding my mother had brought with her. My old friends' results lay sealed on the top of the pile of mail and I picked them up and carried them to the kitchen table. I had expected to hear three voices and to speak to each of them in turn, but only Sarah was on the other end of the line, her voice crisp and echoing, as though she were calling from a giant underground cellar. Perhaps she was.

"Are the others with you?" I asked her.

"Hm? No, they're all drinking in the château. I think they're a bit nervous." She was speaking in the chirpy, distracted tone she used when she was nervous herself. I cradled the receiver between my neck and shoulder as I tore at the envelopes: 2:1s across the board.

"Above average—well, that's respectable," she said. "And you?"

"A First," I said.

"Well done you." She was brisk and businesslike. "How's the house?"

"Oh, you know. Ticking over. When are you coming back?"

Her answer would be the new deadline I gave myself for making a choice about what to do with the rest of my life.

"It's looking more like early October than late September now. Charlie's got a job to get back to then, so we might as well wait and all come back together. Apart from that, there's no rush. I mean, it's not as if we'll have a summer like this again, is it?" We exchanged lies about how much we were looking forward to seeing each other again before putting the phone down. It was the last time I ever spoke to her.

I lingered awhile in the doorway before returning. Mellow evening sunshine gilded the dining room and its contents that night. Rex sat with his back to the window, and seeing the light pick out strands of copper and fawn I wondered how anyone could call hair that shade mousy or colorless. He was lit from within, too, by a simple happiness I think he'd been chasing his whole life and finally found in the banal setting of a suburban dining room. He had never looked more beautiful to me than he did that night. In the months immediately after we parted, that was how I chose to remember him, illuminated and animated, not as I last saw him, white and clenched and already becoming a ghost of his own potential.

At ten o'clock my parents, who had traveled from a country only one hour ahead of British Summer Time, claimed to be jet-lagged. They went to sleep in the master bedroom with bathroom that had been Sarah's and the house finally became mine and Rex's.

"Did they like me?" he asked, perched on the edge of the sofa.

"They *loved* you. I think they liked you more than they like me."

"It explains a lot, meeting them," he said. I tensed. "Where you get your strength and integrity from. That must be what comes of having parents like yours, who are still together and who love you and are proud of you."

He lit the fat white candles that stood on waist-high, wrought-iron sticks on either side of the mantelpiece and in the corners of the room. Those candles had stood in place from the day we had moved into the house and no one had ever taken a flame to their wicks before. I made a mental note to gather a few of them up and take them back to Highgate where they would burn every night. The flames were reflected in a glass frame on the mantelpiece. It contained a photograph of Sarah, Claire, Emma, and me with our erstwhile boyfriends and portrayed a version of myself I no longer recognized: wholesomely drunk, hair freshly highlighted and neatly bobbed, a pink pashmina scarf slung over my shoulders and diamond studs in my ears. Simon's arm was tossed around my neck in a chummy headlock. The smile on my face had been genuine enough at the time but the whole tableau now looked like a dress rehearsal for real life. Rex traced the outline of my face in the thin dust that had gathered on the frame.

"Is this him?" he asked. I nodded.

"That's my old life in that picture," I said.

"Did you love him more than me?" The jealousy he showed toward his sister was directed my way for the first time.

"Rex! I didn't love him at all. I'm not sure I ever even liked him. He was just something I did, like tennis."

His hands were on my cheeks. I let them stay there, one or all of my senses telling me that if I tried to move, he would not allow it.

"You do love me, don't you?'" There is only one acceptable answer to that question and I did not give it then. He told me he loved me, he said it every day, but I had yet to make my own reciprocal declaration. Was what I felt for Rex love? Doubts about the pedantic and neurotic aspects of his character still surfaced whenever there was a long enough gap between our lovemaking. There was attraction and affection, but love—that obsessive, all-encompassing feeling that all the songs are written about—was still a word that described how I felt about Biba. On a good day I convinced myself that it was him I had first recognized in her, but most of the time it was the other way around.

"Let me show you." I reached for the buckle of his belt. In the bed I had once shared with Simon we didn't speak and barely moved, rocking our way to a silent climax. Sex with Rex was a doubt-canceling panacea whose effectiveness increased the less he spoke. He fell asleep on my breast, his breath slowing and deepening to a rhythmic growl that I found comforting in the aftermath. At the other end of the corridor, separated from us by two closed doors, my mother was listening to my father snore, too. My last thought before I went to sleep was to wonder what Biba's results had been, and what she was doing now.

What Biba had in fact been doing during our twenty-four-hour absence was getting her first acting job. The role was small but the production was a lavish BBC drama about the life of Charles II. It was ironic that she had spent the last few weeks pursuing grimy modern reality with Guy to contemporize her craft only to land a role in a costume drama about the Restoration that would draw on her classical training.

"The whole thing begins with a montage before the narrative kicks in where he's basically fucking his way through the court," she said. "It's meant to illustrate what a randy old goat he was. So they have five-second clips of the king shagging the queen, and then all his mistresses, from Nell Gwyn to servant girls to ladies-in-waiting. And me. Get this. I play a *nun*."

Rex scowled. "Do you have to take your clothes off?" he asked.

"Nope. I just flip up my habit so you see my legs but that's it," she said. "I mean, it's only a tiny part. But the point is, it's BBC and it's a big-name director who seems to like me, and my agent's really pleased." A sudden frown pulled her features down. "I hope that it's not too blink-and-you-miss-it, though. And I hope they don't cover my face with one of those winged hat things."

"You mean a wimple? Why?" I asked.

"I want my dad to know it's me when he sees it."

The job took ten days. Biba was right about having a rapport with the director. As well as the sex scene, which took just a morning to film, she was given a handful of lines throughout the series and was also required to appear in the background in several scenes, a significant face among dozens of nameless extras. Filming took place in the studios at Elstree and once on location at Hampton Court. A car came to pick her up every morning before the rush hour and dropped her home again after the shoot. Rex and I would always be waiting for her when she came home, eager to hear all about her day. Guy would eat with us, offering around a joint that nobody seemed to want anymore. He had sensed that Biba was drawing away from him and made repeated, wretched attempts to draw her back into his world.

"I took a call from Chris this afternoon," he said over dinner. He had brought a curry from one of the Indian takeouts on Archway Road. Most of it remained untouched in foil containers. He alone seemed to be enjoying it, the marijuana giving him an appetite for gristly chunks of lamb bobbing like turds in a septic tank of fluorescent orange oil. An unidentifiable herb nestled between his front teeth and yellow grease infused with turmeric jaundiced the corners of his mouth. "He's working the door at Bagley's tonight. He can get us all on the guest list." It was a mark of his desperation that he included me and Rex in this invitation. We turned to Biba for our cues.

"I don't think so," she said. "I'm shooting tomorrow. I need an early night."

"You never want to come out anymore."

"Darling, I can't keep up that party lifestyle forever," said Biba with a wave of her hand. She had adopted a rather camp, jaded, and world-weary persona in the last few days and I wondered which veteran actress she had picked it up from. "You go, you have fun." Guy didn't extend the invitation to Rex and me again but went out alone.

When the shoot was over Biba slumped into a kind of depression.

"It's heartbreaking," she said. "You're thrown together with other actors and crew and you form this bond so quickly, you become like family, and I know I'll never see them again. It's such a cruel industry." She was too ecstatic at being employed by the industry to experience real heartbreak. Actually, the actor's

itinerant lifestyle would have been perfect for Biba, with her ability to dip in and out of intimacy.

"Don't they have a big blowout when the shooting's finished?"
I said, dredging this knowledge from somewhere. "Wrap parties?"

She brightened. "You're right! So I'll see everyone again then."
But she didn't.

22

I T WAS APPARENT TO everyone but Guy that his days at the house were numbered. He was no longer a threat or a menace to Rex and me, because Biba barely registered his presence. Occasionally she would notice him sitting at the table or on a sofa and blink, as though surprised to find him still there. There was no evidence of the fierce physical attraction that had made me so uncomfortable just a month or so before, although he still slept in her bed every night. She was in no hurry to get rid of him but she would not have begged him to stay. So why did he?

I understood one Saturday afternoon. Biba had spent the afternoon watching television, weeping and wailing along to the coverage of the funeral of Diana, Princess of Wales. I had thought at first that she had been grieving her own mother too, but half of London seemed to be overwhelmed by disproportionate sorrow. She had cried herself out and fallen asleep on the green sofa. The sun had traveled through the open doors and made a trapezium of white light on her bare belly. Guy stood over her, a bottle of maximum-strength sun lotion in his hand, and rubbed it into her exposed skin with a tenderness that did not wake her. I knew then that Guy loved Biba, perhaps as much as Rex and I did. He was hanging around the house not out of inertia but out of hope. His task completed, he sat at her feet and surveyed her with a kind of adoring misery that almost made me feel sorry for him. We had not taken his feelings seriously, and it was our fatal mistake. If only he had taken the hint and left then. We would all still be living in that house in the woods. Me, Biba, Rex—and Alice.

Rex's campaign to take possession of the house accelerated in the last weeks of August. He was buoyed by Biba's budding career and by the aggressively held belief that, in getting his sister to the age of twenty-one in one piece, he deserved the reward of his own home.

"Don't tell her what I'm up to," he said. "I want to protect her until I know where we stand." He began to take the first tentative steps in finding out what his rights were, a route that would inevitably lead to confrontation rather than reconciliation. Whether he was successful or not, the close relationship both children craved with their father was not the likely outcome. No wonder he had deferred the task for so long. Rex could not afford to hire a lawyer so he did his own research. He took himself to Highgate Library on Shepherd's Hill and taught himself to use the Internet. What he uncovered was not encouraging. He came home every day with printouts not from law firms but from housing agencies, and one afternoon I overheard him make a telephone call to the Citizens Advice Bureau asking about squatters' rights. Squatters! He and his sister were not even tenants in their father's house. At the stationers in Muswell Hill he bought a spiral notepad to set out his case and a foolscap file for the loose documents. In the evenings, while I found excuses not to look at letters offering me academic opportunities on the other side of the world, Rex studied his papers. He gazed at them as though the answer were there, encoded in ink and paper, not in a big house across the heath behind an impenetrable gate.

Sitting at the old red bureau where his mother had written so much of her wretched and futile correspondence, Rex began to draft letters to his father. His pen pressed through the paper onto the desk and made indentations on its leather surface, Rex's elegant and spiky letters upon the palimpsest of his mother's desperate scrawls. If I had been a superstitious person I would have said that this was a bad omen. Biba, had she known what her brother was doing, would certainly have interpreted it this way. But I was not superstitious or dramatic, and I did not point out the parallel. Instead, I stood close behind him and watched him write. Some of the letters were formal, with Rex's address and Roger Capel's laid out at the top as though for business correspondence. Some did not even bother with the formality of "Dear Dad." Many didn't get further than a sentence or two, tentative lines like "I am writing because . . ." or "I just felt the need to say that . . ." fading into the white nothing of the page. Some drafts were conciliatory to the point of apology; some were formal and procedural; others were emotional and rambling, memoirs rather than persuasive prose. Some letters begged. Others threatened.

"I'm trying to work out whether to win him with honey or vinegar," said Rex, laying his ballpoint crosswise against a blank page. I picked one at random from the pile. It began formally enough but soon degenerated into rambling invective. It called its addressee a selfish cunt and threatened legal action if he didn't sign over the property to Rex immediately. One line stood out, the letters controlled, deliberate, separate. "You owe us this much. Your leaving helped to kill Mum."

"Well, this one's certainly vinegar," I said. Rex took the page from me, scanned it, and winced before folding it in half.

"Oh God, I never intended to send that one, I was just letting off a bit of steam. I meant to just make a list of the legal stuff but I got a bit carried away. It's a bit strong, isn't it? Can you imagine if I sent it? Although I felt better after I'd written it. Maybe getting all that pent-up anger down on paper means I won't blurt it all out if I see him face-to-face. But I don't seem to be getting any nearer to the one I *should* send." My arms were around his neck now, enjoying the scratch of his unshaven cheek against my smooth one. He gave my cheek an absentminded prod with his tongue.

"Is a letter really the answer?" I asked. "Why don't you call

him? Have you got his number?" Rex recited the seven-digit London number in a flat voice, and then said, "He'll be busy, though."

"He might not," I said. "Call him now, while Biba's out and
Guy's asleep. Quickly, before you have time to think about it."

Rex trundled out of the room, hands in pockets, and made his
way slowly down the stairs. I shuffled the remaining letters into a
neat pile and settled down to read them. He was back before I had
had time to skim the first.

"He was out?" I presumed.

Rex's face was scrunched in bemusement. He ran his hand
through his quiff and down to the nape of his neck where it stayed.
"No, he was in."

"Oh, darling. He didn't hang up on you?"

"No." He rubbed the stubble on his chin. "Something rather
odd. He wants to meet me for a drink."

"But that's brilliant!" I said. "When?"

"Now. Well, in a couple of hours. As soon as I can get to Hampstead." His smile was diffident. "I've never been for a drink with
my dad before. Actually, I haven't been on my own with him since
I was about ten. He wants me to come without Biba." I replayed the
image of her lowering the rake down onto the car.

"That could be for the best," I said. He opened the folder and
pulled out a few highlighted pages of legal precedent, then threw
them back on the bureau.

"What am I even doing, thinking of taking this with me? I
know it all by heart anyway. He's asked to see me, I'd be mad to
confront him. He might be ready to come around. This could be
it, Karen. Maybe it's actually going to be all right. I'm going to
this empty-handed and with only an open mind."

I could taste the expectation in his kiss good-bye.

"I'm doing this for you as much as me and Biba," he said.

"I know, darling," I said. "I appreciate it. Good luck."

I watched him go. He looked taller than usual and as
though something was missing. In his shirtsleeves he looked *too*

empty-handed, as though he had decided to jettison his burden of responsibility in favor of the light and untrustworthy onus of hope.

Guy surfaced, shirtless and yawning, in the early afternoon, when I was cooking myself a bacon sandwich in the kitchen. Unshowered and with unbrushed teeth, he wore a pair of soccer shorts and sleep cobwebbed the corners of his eyes. He had given up all pretense of hope and swagger and had begun to look rather miserable.

"All right?" he said. It was not the kind of greeting that invited a reply but I gave one anyway.

"I'm not bad, Guy," I said. "How are you?"

"I feel like shit," he said, peering into the pan. "Did you know that burning human flesh and cooking bacon smell exactly the same? A fireman told me that. That's why firemen hardly ever eat bacon sandwiches."

"Thanks for that." I put the meat between two slices of thick white bread and pressed the bread knife diagonally along the sandwich, watching ketchup bleed from the crusts. I held it to my lips for a few seconds, unable to get Guy's unlovely nugget of trivia out of my head. Eventually I put it back on the plate.

"I'll have that if you don't want it," he said, and gobbled up half of it in one bite. The sight of the food churning in his open mouth was the nail in the coffin of my relationship with bacon sandwiches. I made an excuse and went upstairs to get away from the sight, sound, and smell of him.

Sandwich demolished, Guy followed me up to the Velvet Room. I folded Rex's dossier closed as he crumpled onto the sofa next to me and began to work on the business of his day, deftly rolling cigarette papers into a long, thin cone. His work surface was the aerial picture book, open at the page showing Biba's clifftop. The crease between its pages was already dusted with flecks of tobacco and as I watched, more tiny brown leaves floated from his hands. He took his Zippo from the pocket of his shorts and held it underneath the rough cube of hash, crumbling it into the paper: none of this, I noticed, was wasted. He clamped the long white joint between his lips and sparked his lighter. A burst of flame, and a cloud of smoke immediately surrounded his head. He took two or three drags before easing it from his lips. I watched the smoke curl out of his nostrils before turning my attention back to Rex's papers.

The sound of Guy's bovine mouth breathing was an unwelcome distraction and I was relieved when he used his big toe to press the stereo into life. The CD that was in there may not have been to my taste, but the music at least masked aural evidence of his presence.

"I need a grand gesture," said Guy after half an hour or so, apropos of nothing.

"What?" I looked up from the Land Registry document that I had been trying to decipher, wondering what "adverse possession" of a property was.

"I'm not stupid," he said. He had gone from comatose to animated and intense, and he used the joint as a baton to underline his point, jabbing the air in front of him. "She's going off me, and I need to win her back. So I need to make some romantic . . . statement or something to show her what she means to me. Something a bit dramatic. I don't know with girls like Biba. I've never met anyone like her before. You know her better than anyone else. What can I do?" This time when he held out the joint I took it. If I had to converse with Guy it might be more bearable if I was somewhere in the orbit of whatever planet he was on. "I'm miserable like this, man," he said. In the stoned silence that followed I watched the lights of the graphic equalizer dance up and down in time to the beats, the electric blue bars and orange neon numbers bleached almost to invisibility by the sunbeam that harpooned the room.

"What if I put the speakers out in the garden? Do you think she'd like that?"

It was such a feeble idea that I laughed. "I think it'll take more than a new sound system, Guy. I'm sorry, I don't know what you can do." He wanted reassurance but he would get no encouragement of any kind from me. It was not just that I wanted him gone, but also because I knew it would be cruel to give him false hope. His eyes slowly hooded themselves and he opened them again with apparent effort. His fingers were the only fast thing about him. They worked their swift origami to conjure up another joint in under a minute. The lighter blazed again.

"Can I help out with this thing about her dad and the house that Rex is doing?"

"How do you know about that?"

"You talk as if I wasn't in the room, you and him," he said. "I'm not as stupid as you think I am."

The accusation smarted because it was true. In the course of our short conversation my feelings toward Guy had swung violently from irritation to pity to guilt.

"I wouldn't get involved in that." I tapped the blue folder and tidied the loose papers away inside it. "It's all in here. Rex is working on it now. If Roger Capel's own son can't persuade him to sign over the house, then I don't think your rhetoric will win him over."

"My whatoric?" If, as I suspected, Guy had been expensively educated, then it had been a waste of his parents' money.

"Doesn't matter."

I didn't think Guy would be in the house long enough for it to matter whose name the property was in, but I bit my tongue. I took another drag of the joint, this time holding the sharp smoke deep in my lungs for a few seconds, savoring the sour taste for as long as I could bear to. When I exhaled I was dismayed to find that he was still talking.

"But let me get this straight. The thing that would make her happier than anything else would be to get this house?"

I tried to say that for Biba the house only represented the love and acknowledgment she craved from her father, but the perfectly formed statement remained trapped inside my head. Coldness in my limbs and tilting in my head told me that I had only seconds to go before losing consciousness. With what dignity I could salvage, I crawled to the orange beanbag, curled up on it, and let Guy's music and his voice wisp away into silence.

When I woke up again, Rex, not Guy, was reclining on the green sofa, lit by candles rather than daylight. He was watching me indulgently and must have been in the room for a while. Guy's belongings had been arranged into a tidy pile on the table, and the blue folder was not on the floor where I had let it drop but stacked on its side on top of the bureau.

"Oh God," I said, stretching out, trying to stand up and finding that I still had sea legs. My mouth was stale. "What time is it? I had a smoke with Guy."

"So he's trying to poison my girlfriend as well as my sister, is he?" said Rex, but he looked in good humor.

"How did it go?"

"Well, I think. I mean, I didn't get any clear promises from him and whenever I tried to get him onto the house he changed the subject. But he's definitely softening. He said he wants us to get to know his kids—I mean, his little kids."

"But that's amazing!" I said. I sat up straight. Rex treated me to one of his rare smiles, all glittering eyes and teeth.

"I think Jules has been working on him, to be honest. But I don't really care why, if it means we can build some kind of relationship."

"Biba's going to be so happy." I crawled over to his feet and rested my head in his lap. He began to stroke my hair.

"And this is the best part," he said. "I told him about you. He wants you to come, too." His grin faded like the flame on a spent candle and the crease between his eyebrows returned. "I don't trust all this luck in my life all of a sudden. My dad coming back. The way things are going with you. Biba's career starting to take off. I don't think I've been this happy since before my mum got ill. I didn't really think I ever would be again and I don't quite trust it. I never thought I'd say this but I'm actually *pleased* that Guy's here now, getting under our feet and annoying us. He sort of puts the brakes on things, like a reality check. He stops it all from being too good to be true."

23

THAT SUNDAY MORNING THE neighborhood looked like an urban Eden. I walked up Queenswood Lane, past Highgate station, and across Archway Road at eight o'clock and there was an unpeopled, unspoiled quality to the tree-surrounded streets.

All the shops apart from the convenience store were shuttered, and the street, usually clogged with three lanes of traffic, was deserted apart from the odd car or bus waiting patiently and alone by the traffic lights. Above me, Southwood Lane was a thin gray ribbon leading up to Highgate village. Below me, Muswell Hill Road rose and fell and rose again, cutting its way through the woods. If you squinted and forgot about the cars it was easy to freeze the vista into a sepia photograph, wide-hatted Edwardians walking to church in groups of four or five. Rex would have made a good Edwardian gentleman, I thought, imagining him in a starched collar, twirling his mustache. Biba would have been an actress and suffragette, bringing disgrace and exhilaration on the family in equal measure. I would probably have been a governess.

I bought milk, newspapers, and a liter of overpriced orange juice. Before returning home I took myself into the woods where I lay on my front on the cool and crunchy forest floor, spreading the papers out in a pool of sunlight and drinking the orange juice from its carton. I thought it again: an urban Eden. Before midnight I would be expelled from my private paradise.

There was a positive charge to the house that day. The air fizzed with our happy secret: we exchanged surreptitious smiles whenever our eyes met and sex had become a twice-daily ritual again, a new playfulness present between us. Since Rex's meeting with his father, the blue folder had lain untouched on the bureau. We had not yet said anything to Biba, preferring to wait until the invitation to dinner in Hampstead was confirmed.

Guy, too, was in an odd mood. His characteristic moroseness had been replaced by high spirits. His cell phone was busier than ever, ringing and bleeping six or seven times a day. He kept his conversations hushed, but nobody cared to listen anymore. The last couple of days had seen a spell of manic activity as, contrary to my advice, he undertook to install a pair of speakers in the back garden. He had been doing something complex with a length of wire and strips of copper filament, shinning up and down the terrace steps with pliers between his teeth, connecting the battered, ten-year-old CD player to a pair of amplifiers better suited to an outdoor rave than a London back garden.

Whatever the reason behind Guy's gear change, it wasn't the hoped-for reunion with Biba. She was absorbed in a new script she would be reading at an audition next week. It was another television production but a contemporary part this time, the role of the next-door neighbor in a comedy about a man who won the lottery and kept it a secret from his wife. This screenplay was not the usual stapled few sheets but an inches-thick wedge of pages bound with a plastic spiral. She carried it with her everywhere and grew distressed if parted from it, like a child with a favorite toy. That afternoon she even eschewed her beloved Sunday tabloids in its favor. The script was balanced on her knees, and she mouthed the words to herself under her breath, occasionally sipping from a glass of red wine.

"How does that go in when you're drinking?"

"It focuses me, darling," she said. "Things tend not to come to life until you're slightly drunk, don't you find?"

It was too dark to read in the garden, but she took her script and her drink down there when, at nine o'clock, Guy summoned us to the garden to eat the meal that he had provided and to admire his handiwork. Dinner was a stack of boxed pizzas but the wine he had supplied was good and the glasses were clean. The two amplifiers stood like monoliths in the garden. Guy flipped a switch and they came to life with a soft boom. He pointed the remote control at the stereo, balanced precariously on the ledge of the terrace, and the music swelled to the sky. He alone nodded in time to the drums. Rex looked over his shoulder to the house next door. "He's not going to like this," he said.

Only seconds later came a violent hammering on the front door that shook the whole house. Biba rolled her eyes.

"My turn to deal with him, I think," she said, peeling herself away from the mat she was lying on. Her script was discarded facedown on the ground. A blade of grass sprang up through a crack in its spine.

Rex turned to Guy. "Turn it down, will you?" With a sulky shrug, Guy decreased the volume so that we could hear Biba's footsteps filter through the open windows. There was the usual creak and thud as the front door swung open and hit the wall. Instead of the patient but sarcastic exchange with Wheeler that we were expecting, we heard Biba's yelp of surprise and a high-pitched, astonished "Daddy!" Her childlike greeting was followed by an adult, animalistic roar of rage. It was only a few strides and one staircase up to the Black and White Hall but Rex and I covered the distance so quickly that it left us both slightly breathless. Guy followed us at his own leisurely pace and slouched in shadow behind us. In the middle of the hall, a red-faced Roger Capel stood opposite his daughter, knuckles on hips, a scrolled document in his left fist. He stood directly underneath a glass lampshade, its base filled with the bodies of moths and flies. The shadows of the dead insects dappled his skin and the rolled-up paper.

"What the hell is this?" he was shouting over and over again. "What the *bloody hell* is this?" Rex recognized the document in his father's hand seconds before I did and he made a whimpering sound inaudible to anyone but me. "I've never been so insulted in my life. I had to come over to check it was actually true. What did you expect to achieve by this?"

The five of us stood as still as chess pieces on the checkered floor, as though waiting for a giant hand to come and direct our next move. Rex and I had not planned for this ambush.

Capel had not been in his former family home for over ten years, I realized. In the silence that followed his tirade I tried to see the place through his eyes. A tide of old newspapers lapped at the edges of the room and the pile of empties that had never been taken to the bottle bank was waist-high. A cigarette had been ground out on the ceramic floor as though it were a bus stop pavement. Clothes that had been thrown at hooks and hat stands lay where they had fallen. He looked at Guy and me as though we were just more debris. He ran one hand over his bald head and rested it on the nape of his neck, a gesture I had seen Rex perform dozens of times. I watched the flesh of his face darken to the color of the Merlot we had been drinking all night and I realized that Roger Capel was silent not because he was growing calmer but because he was paralyzed with mounting anger.

"What the hell's been going *on* here?" He addressed the question to his children.

"Daddy, please," said Biba. "I don't understand. Why are you shouting? What's happened?"

"I've just come back from a weekend in the country with my family to find *this* on my doorstep." He handed her the letter and folded his arms. While she read, Capel's eyes darted from Rex to me to Guy and back to Rex again, never allowing us a few seconds' respite to make vital eye contact with one another.

"Rex, this is your writing," said Biba.

"I didn't send it," he said. I had a flashback to the evening ear-lier in the week when I had passed out in the Velvet Room. I saw myself tapping the blue folder, telling Guy that everything to do with the house was in there. When I had woken up it had been moved . . . but not by Rex.

"You bloody wrote it, though," said Capel. "I was willing to make peace with you, I took you to the pub, and two days later I get this, this abusive letter calling me a cunt and listing all the ways you'll get the law on me. The bloody *law*. I'm your *father*. You don't know how good I've been to you. Do you know what this house is worth? Do you know what I could charge if I rented it out?"

"You weren't supposed to see it," said Rex.

"I bet I fucking wasn't, but I'm glad I have. I know what your true colors are now. You nearly had me going as well. I was this close to signing it over." Capel made a pincer of a meaty thumb and forefinger.

"Dad, please. Let me explain." Rex rocked back and forth on his heels, his hands clasped to his head. I had seen him in this state before but then Nina had calmed him down. I wished with a fervor that was close to prayer that I had asked her to tell me the words that would bring him back to me.

"Look at the pair of you. Look at this place. You can't look after a house. You aren't up to the responsibility." He looked at me and then craned to see Guy. "You've turned it into some kind of . . . hippie commune." He spat out the phrase.

"Dad, no! I love this house, I've got so many plans for it . . ."

"I don't want to hear it." The idea that occurred to him mani-fested itself as a cold, thin smile. "In fact, I want the lot of you out."

"But where will we go?"

"You're twenty-six years old," said Capel dispassionately. "Get a job. Rent an apartment."

"He's twenty-*four*!" shouted Biba, but her words bounced off her father's back. Capel did not slam the door but closed it quietly behind him, leaving his children homeless with the softest of clicks. The engine of his expensive car purred softly into the distance.

Rex leaned back against the wall. I don't think he would have been able to support himself without it. He closed his eyes. So this is what someone looks like, I thought, when their world is destroyed. Biba looked from the letter to the door and then back again. If there had been any good glass in the house, her shriek would have shattered it.

"Is anybody going to tell me what the fucking hell is going on?" She stood like a little girl, arms and legs stiff and splayed.

"It was never supposed to be sent," said Rex weakly. "I was just letting off steam."

"Then how the bloody hell did Dad end up with it? Karen?" I shook my head. "*Guy.*" His name was a statement, a conclusion, not a question. Even then he could have lied, he could have denied sending it. But while Guy might be able to spin an alter ego for himself at leisure and lie by omission, when put on the spot he did not have the resources to defend himself with stories. He stepped out of his dark doorway making an open-handed gesture.

"I did it for you," he said to Biba, showing her his dirty palms. "I was trying to force his hand. I did it for you so that he'd give you the house."

"How did you even find out about it?" asked Rex. He had recovered from the blow of his father's words and was shaking with a white, wild anger. Guy looked to me for support and explanation. I could have taken my share of the blame then, but I did not see why I should board his sinking ship. I shrugged and poked a loose tile with the toe of my shoe.

"How could you do that to us?" snarled Rex. A little fleck of spittle from his mouth landed on my cheek. "Your stupid idea has ruined three lives. We've lost everything, and it's all your fault."

"I was only doing it for you," Guy repeated, turning to Biba. "I love you."

"Love? You couldn't have thought of a better way to make me hate you!" Guy drew breath to speak again but she cut him short. "Shut up! Shut up! I'm sick of the sound of your voice! I'm sick of the sound of your music! I'm sick of the sound of you eating and *breathing*, and your *fucking* cell phone."

As if Biba had summoned that particular nemesis, she was interrupted by a thin melody, the inescapable peep of Guy's cell. The little green screen glowed through the pocket of a hooded jacket that hung on the end of the banister.

"I'm going to turn that bloody phone off once and for all," said Rex as though by extinguishing the phone he could eradicate Guy himself and all he had done. Guy acted as if electrocuted and ran to pull it away from Rex, tugging so violently that the hood, which was fastened to the body by snaps, came away in his hand. The pocket containing the phone was heavily weighted down and Guy stretched trembling arms out toward it.

"Give me my jacket." His voice quavered. "Give it to me."

"Fuck off." Rex held the jacket by the scruff of the neck and slowly reached into the pocket. It continued to ring as Rex fumbled and then froze. His expression changed from one of anger to one of terrified recognition. Now his hands, too, were unsteady as he pulled out not a ringing telephone but a small black pistol.

We had mocked Guy's background and teased him about his ability to get his hands on a weapon. Desperate to prove us wrong, desperate to impress Biba, he had risen to our careless challenge.

It is extraordinary the things you think of in extremis. So much had happened in the space of a few minutes and so much was threatening to happen in the moments that followed. But I was not wondering where we were going to live, or whether we were going to die, or where Guy had gotten the gun, or anything related to my immediate and terrible circumstances. The uppermost thought in my mind was, why is that dark, dull shade of gray called gunmetal? The gun that Rex gripped was not gray at all. It was a stocky little L-shape and its casing was the same satin-sheened black as a cockroach's shell.

Rex flexed his fingers and rearranged them around the weapon in an approximation of the correct grip. He held it up to the light and then slowly lowered it until the barrel was level with Guy's brow. His hand was steady. The only tic that betrayed emotion was the rapid rise and fall of his Adam's apple as he swallowed hard, twice.

"Why shouldn't I?" he said, raising one eyebrow.

Guy and Biba both looked like they were going to cry. They were the self-proclaimed risk-takers while Rex had always played safe to the point of tedium. Now that real menace was at his fingertips, the hedonists were losing control while he remained calm. I told myself not to panic, that Rex did not know how to use a gun, but I did not convince myself. I was ignorant of firearms and how they worked. I did not know whether it was necessary to be taught how to operate a gun at all or if training was only necessary if you wanted to learn to fire it accurately. I did not know if Guy knew how to shoot, either. He was certainly not acting like someone comfortable or familiar with weapons. He had brought it into the house but he was as afraid as the rest of us. Rex moved his thumb a fraction and a click reverberated through the hall. Was he releasing the safety catch or pulling it back on? Did he know, himself?

I did not know what I was going to say until after I began to speak.

"It's okay," I said. I found myself between Rex and his weeping target without quite knowing how I had gotten there. I began to gabble, feeling no control over my cascade of words. "It's only a fake, isn't it, Guy? Just something you got hold of to freak us out. Well done. It's worked. Joke's over." I was confident only that Rex would not hurt me. I stood before him, opening my hands like a book, and his amnesty was marked by a tiny sigh of resignation. The gun that he placed in my hands did not feel fake. It felt heavy and powerful and clammy and horrible. In my right hand I held it lightly by the handle, letting the barrel dangle down toward the floor, terrified of touching a trigger or a catch that would fire the gun. Removing myself from the gap between Rex and Guy, I extended my arm behind my back so that neither of them could reach it. All that mattered was keeping it away from both of them.

When I had taken four or five steps back, Guy sprang across the room like an animal released from its trap. He seemed twice, three times Rex's size as he stood over the smaller man and drove his fist into his stomach. Rex's body folded toward his knees like a pair of scissors closing. When he looked up, it was to see Guy's fist coming on course for his jaw. The opening of the flesh was almost audible as the lips that I had spent the summer kissing were split. Blood spilled from Rex's mouth and onto his shirt, splashed on the tiles below him. I screamed stop it, stop it, stop it, over and over but my words were wasted. I could not break up the fight with words alone and I did not dare to put the gun down in case Guy took possession of it. On my right, Biba was clutching her own stomach as though she, too, had been struck.

"Biba!" I said. "Do something!" I gestured to Rex and Guy and then to the gun in my hand, showing her that I could not intervene myself. My grip was so loose that she took it from me without effort. My hand made a series of vain clutches in the air but by then she had it in a two-handed grip. The click of the catch was loud enough to catch Guy's attention. He threw Rex to the floor and scrambled for the stairs. When she said his name again it was not a scream but a hiss.

"Guy."

He turned to face her as she pulled the trigger. The impact caught him on the shoulder and sent his body flying backward: it was the first time I had ever seen him move quickly. His head made contact with the bottom stair. There was a sickening crack that I think was the sound of his neck breaking. He came to rest with his head propped up by the stair at an unnatural ninety-degree angle to his body and his eyes looking out into the hallway, wearing an expression not of accusation but of absolute surprise.

The bang had felt like a punch to both sides of my head. I had my hands over my ringing ears as I turned my attention from Guy's body to Biba. She had stumbled backward after firing the gun. Her grip on it had loosened only slightly and she stared at it as if it had found its way into her hands and fired itself. Rex's mouth looked as though it had been smeared across his face and his teeth and gums were outlined in red. He drew himself up to all fours and then to a standing position and stood with his back to where Guy lay. Biba and I followed his eyes to the spot where Tom Wheeler stood.

His body was convulsed by a silent, dry retching and his hands were clasped over his mouth. His eyes blinked rapidly behind frameless glasses. He must have let himself in to complain about the noise but not even our arch-critic could have predicted the scene he surveyed now. He shook his head once, twice, and then turned on his heel. He could not have run quickly enough. The first bullet spun into the mountain of wine bottles, sending emerald shards into the air, but the second shot hit Wheeler in the collar, penetrating his body at the point where his neck became his spine. He fell forward, landing facedown on the rough and dirty weave of the welcome mat, the weight of his body jamming the door shut. With alarming swiftness the blood flowed from the wound, staining his pink polo shirt a deep rose that darkened to burgundy as it spread. It was like watching a flower bloom on a time-lapse photograph. The gun dropped from Biba's hand and clattered to the floor. In the street outside, a woman's voice began wailing. The ringing in my ears distorted the sound of her voice, bringing it in and out of my hearing. Biba sank to the floor and arranged herself in a crosslegged sitting position where she stared at her hands. My insides felt sluiced with icy water and for a sickening moment I thought I would lose control of my bowels. Hands flat on my stomach, I fixed my gaze on the wall behind her, afraid to look up, afraid to look down, afraid to turn around. I wanted to throw myself on the floor with the other bodies, to lie facedown with my eyes closed until something happened to make the whole horrible scene go away.

Rex dripped tiny beads of blood across the black and white floor as he crossed the room to where the gun lay, halfway between Guy's slouched body and Wheeler's prone one. He bent down and picked it up, holding it gingerly this time and making sure it pointed toward the floor. He wiped it clean against the fabric of his trousers and then polished it with the hem of his shirt. His lower lip was clamped underneath his top one, and when he released it to speak he winced.

"I'll handle it." He managed to sound confident even through a thick lisp. For a moment an upward-lurching euphoria gripped me. He's got a plan, I thought. Rex is going to clean our fingerprints from the gun and put it in Guy's hand. We can blame Guy for killing Wheeler and say that he went on to shoot himself. Nobody will ever have to know the truth apart from the three of us. Rex will think of a version of events that we can all agree on and by the time they—I could not yet bring myself even to think the word *police*—arrive, the three of us will know it verbatim and we will be impenetrable. The notion was dismissed almost as soon as it was thought. They will know, I thought with a sinking heart. They have people who specialize in this sort of thing. They can tell the difference between murder and suicide from the angle of the bullet and the way the body falls. Rex has got a plan, but they will know. I reached out to touch his cheek but he held his hand out to stop me.

"I'll handle this," he said again. "Get your things and take Biba and go out through the back."

"They won't believe he did it." I nodded toward Guy but didn't look at him.

"I'm not going to say he did," said Rex. He finished polishing the gun and closed his own palm around it. I understood at once what he was doing.

"Please don't do this," I begged.

"Just take Biba and go."

My handbag had been hooked over the edge of the banister, underneath Guy's jacket. In it was everything I needed.

"Come with us," I said. *"Please.* I can't leave you."

He shook his head. Biba was the first to move. She sprang up from her position on the floor and extended her hand, dragging me toward the stairs that led down to the kitchen. I made a weak, whimpering protest but she was silent, lips drawn into a pout the way they did when she was concentrating hard. Her movements were swift but controlled, as though she were rushing to catch a train rather than running for her life. She stopped in the garden to pick up her script before helping me to pull the loose plank to one side. I followed her through the gap and into the woods.

24

DAWN HAS MADE GOOD on her threat to welcome Rex to Suffolk. I didn't want to go, and I wasn't going to, but Sophie told Alice that a parallel party was being arranged upstairs for them and some other girls from their class, and the whole thing was presented to me as a fait accompli.

"What shall I wear?" says Rex, standing in front of the wardrobe that he is still unfamiliar with. When I knew that he was being released, I went into Ipswich and bought him all the clothes I thought he would ever need. I felt like a pregnant woman shopping for her soon-to-be-born child, imagining the activities that would go with each outfit, from the Barbour jacket I bought him for walks along the beach to the tracksuit for wearing after swimming. When I bought the suit I'm holding up for him now, I was thinking more about job interviews than dinner parties, but it will be appropriate.

"It feels a bit formal," he says, opening the jacket to inspect the silver silk lining. I remember another suit that he wore, a slim-fitting secondhand two-piece that he teamed with a T-shirt, and try to suppress the memory of the night he wore it.

"Isn't this a bit much for just going over to someone's house?"

"You don't know Dawn Saunders," I reply. I tease open the top button of his gray shirt before selecting my own clothes, pulling on sheer black tights and slipping a simple black shift over the top.

I wonder if he, too, is comparing the clothes I am wearing now with the ones I wore that summer. What would we have said then if we were to see the selves we have now become? Rex would probably have said that we looked great. I would probably have asked where Biba was.

"What?" I say. There is something about the intensity of his gaze that is making me feel shy.

"You look beautiful," he says. "In a really grown-up way."

"I look old, you mean?" I tease him. He holds out his hand in a parody of a gentleman asking a lady to dance. I take it and he pulls me in for a kiss.

"You'll always be twenty-one to me," he says.

Dawn opens the door in a red dress. Her makeup creates a mask from her hairline to her cleavage: some kind of glitter nestles in the crepe between her breasts. She looks at the spikes of my heels and, from a console table just behind the front door, produces two little plastic moldings that she drops into my hands.

"They're covers for your heels," she says. "I hope you don't mind wearing them, only marble floors are so terribly expensive." I bend down, click the little coverlets into place, and test out the click-clack of my feet on the smooth floor. "I'm so glad you've come," she says, air-kissing us both, and then to Alice, "My goodness, don't you look like your daddy?"

"Yeah," says Alice rudely, and then she is up the stairs and into Sophie's bedroom without a kiss or even a glance good-bye. The house is large enough and the doors solid enough that the girls' music and squealing is inaudible from downstairs.

"Come through, come through," says Dawn. I can see that Rex is intrigued by the house despite himself: even if the interior, with its ruffled silk Venetian blinds, marble floors, and leather furniture is not to everyone's taste, it is hard not to be impressed by the dimensions of the rooms and the money spent in each one. I hope that he doesn't look down. The tiles on the floor are of the same design as the black and white hall in his old house in Highgate, although naturally here they are smooth and polished and not a single tessellation is out of place.

Dawn herself is serving canapés on a silver platter. In the room she calls the drawing room, two other couples I recognize from the school gates, also crackling in formal clothes, are holding glasses of wine and balancing little towers of blini and sausage rolls in their hands. It is almost impossible to find somewhere to put the tiny doilies and napkins Dawn has provided. The room is scattered with occasional and coffee tables in matching green cut-glass, but their surfaces are forbiddingly covered in art books, arranged in little pyramids. Perhaps that is deliberate, as Dawn's husband Andrew is keen that we should keep refilling our glasses. He declares himself sommelier, pronouncing it to rhyme with *camellia*, asking us whether we'd like to drink red or white. He even has a white napkin draped over his arm.

We all make small talk while Dawn disappears into the kitchen. Minutes later, she reemerges in an apron that is suspiciously clean apart from a single, rather ostentatious, berry-colored handprint. It looks like blood.

"Andrew," she says, and her husband jumps to his feet at the one-word command.

"Dinner is served," he says, opening a set of double doors that lead into the dining room. "Please take your seats."

The long table is broken up by three fresh flower arrangements, and place cards dictate where we sit. Rex is opposite and one across from me. He sits underneath a huge reproduction Jack Vettriano painting, the kind where the print has been painted over with a sealant, brushstrokes giving it an air of authenticity. I study the painting again. Actually, knowing Dawn, it could well be an original. Tall flames lick the fireplace behind Rex, even though the central heating is on and it is not a cold night. His cheeks remain pale, but the poor women sitting on either side of him are sweltering in their satin and nylon, their faces already a mess of melting makeup and flushed cheeks.

Rex is the best-looking man here by far. He is only two or three years younger than most of Alice's school friends' fathers, but while they are starting to skate into middle age, he is only just beginning to grow into his beaky, awkward features.

Dawn brings course after rich course to the table, and Andrew bobs up to refill our glasses every time she totters in with another dish. Rex and I will have to walk home tonight. Once we would have driven drunk but the idea would horrify both of us now.

"My compliments to the chef," says Rex, raising a glass to Dawn.

"Well, I like to make an effort, seeing as I don't work," she says, bestowing a pitying glance on the other women around the table, workers all of us. "And I do think it's nice for people to go to a dinner party and not be served yet more Nigella or Jamie, don't you?"

Later, I excuse myself to go to the bathroom just as Rex is on his way back from it and pass him in the hall.

"Are you all right in there?" I ask him.

"She's nice."

"She's a complete nouveau," I say, as though I came from old money myself.

"Actually, she reminds me of someone," says Rex. I know exactly who he means and stuff my fist into my mouth. He may have only met my mother once, but he understood her immediately.

"Don't say it," I tell him, but he has evoked her presence and I know that, given the budget, she would have created an almost identical temple of tastelessness for her own family. It actually makes me glad that I grew up without wealth.

The lapel of Rex's suit is beginning to curl upward and I smooth it down with a flat hand.

"She's had the party catered," he says.

"What do you mean?"

"I opened the wrong door when I was looking for the bathroom and ended up in a utility room," he says. "There are loads of restaurant bags and foil containers and a list of when everything needs to go into the oven. Or the microwave. She hasn't made any of this herself."

"Sad cow," I say, borrowing one of Alice's phrases, but the exposure of Dawn's tiny fraud makes me feel more secure about our own, more dreadful secret. And I need that extra confidence because when I return from the bathroom, my hands slimy with the expensive lotion Dawn keeps next to the liquid soap, the conversation has veered away from food and toward work. Rex, it appears, has reinvented himself as some kind of journeyman computer expert during my short absence.

"And what is it you were doing abroad, Rex?" Andrew is saying as I slide into my seat. Rex looks wildly at me and for an awful moment I think he has forgotten he was ever supposed to be abroad, that he's going to tell the truth, and as he lets his mouth fall open I scramble for a subtle way to prompt him. The woman on my right breaks the top of her crème brûlée with the back of her spoon. In the silence the crack resonates like a twig snapping underfoot, and seems to help Rex recover his composure.

"Systems," he says, cupping the bowl of his wineglass in his hand. "Nothing at all exciting, I'm afraid."

"What would that be, contract work?" says Andrew.

"Mainly," says Rex.

"Anything lined up at the moment?"

"I'm just reacclimatizing right now," he says. "Just taking time to be with Karen and Alice again."

"I might have something for you," says Andrew thoughtfully. He jumps up from the table and returns carrying not another bottle but a business card. "E-mail your CV to me during the week and we'll see what we can do, eh?" I don't doubt Andrew's sincerity, but there is a note of patronage in his voice that Dawn uses when she is talking to me. He is enjoying playing liege to Rex's lief.

"Thanks, Andrew," says Rex. "I'll do that."

He won't, of course. His CV is a one-line summary of the diploma in computing he achieved during his time in prison.

There is nobody to give him a reference, he has never been in a modern office, let alone worked in one, and besides, there is the lurking specter of a Criminal Records Bureau check that would accompany certain job offers.

To change the subject I tell the story of Dave's arrest, naturally leaving out the part where I crouched on all fours in my bedroom fearing for my own liberty.

"You know why, don't you?" says Andrew. "They're running weeks behind schedule. They're using any old unskilled labor just to make their deadline. The Poles *must* be desperate to start hiring the English." He laughs at his own joke.

"They've started working on it at night," I say. "The floodlights shine right into Alice's bedroom. They keep her awake."

"That building site's a disgrace," says Dawn. "We drove past it the other day, didn't we, Andrew? There were kids climbing all over it. There's no security, nothing. They've got these gaping holes in the ground, twenty feet deep, full of wet concrete, nothing to stop children falling in. Makes you shudder to think." And she gives a theatrical shiver.

"That's what you get with foreign labor," says Andrew authoritatively, and as the conversation turns to the perceived scourge of immigration on the Suffolk coast, the heat in the dining room becomes unbearable. I am glad when the coffee is served, in gold-rimmed china.

Alice begs to stay with Sophie for the night, so at least Rex and I can walk home unburdened by a tired nine-year-old. I open the car door, not to drive but to retrieve my walking boots from the floor of the passenger seat. Ever since I was a student, I have always had at least one spare pair of shoes in the car. It is a habit I began when I would regularly go out straight after tennis, and after everything happened it became a kind of superstition, as though I had to be ready to take to my heels at a moment's notice. The boots look ridiculous, brown clumpy boxes at the ends of my nyloned legs, but I don't mind.

The cold snap of night air is a relief after that fire, and our flashlight cuts a swath through the navy blue night. Rex upturns the beam to make a searchlight in the sky before focusing on the road in front of us again.

"It's funny, before I came out here, I thought that you didn't need a flashlight in the country," he says. His voice is thick with wine. "I thought everything would be lit by moonlight." He extinguishes the light for a second or two. "But this is absolute darkness, isn't it? It never got this dark in the woods, never."

"That's not quite true. You do learn to see in the dark after a while." To prove my point, I turn the flashlight off when we come to the hamlet between Dawn's house and ours, where a trio of streetlights illuminate the crossroads. By the time we are out of range of their orange glow, our eyes have adapted to the dark. The tall banks of gorse and bramble that line the lane are just distinguishable from the grays of the road and the sky.

I ask Rex to walk behind me, joking that if a car swoops out of nowhere I want him to take the hit first. That's not the real reason, though. The euphoria I felt when the police disappeared with Dave has vanished and the familiar fear has returned. I imagine that the telephone has been ringing into the void of our house all evening. Its electric trill echoes in my ear as I walk. Would tonight have been the night that the caller identified him or herself to me? I am becoming more anxious with every day that passes. Even on a deserted country road in the middle of nowhere, at one o'clock in the morning, I cannot shake that eerie sense that I am being pursued. By asking Rex to walk behind me, at least I will know that I really am being followed, and I will know by whom.

❧

The vale of trees had never seemed more alive with swift darting presences and strange faces. Finally I knew the way as well as she did, but still I stumbled and clutched at branches and in the end she had to lead me by the hand along the paths that she and

Rex had taught me. The trees disgorged us at the edge of Onslow Gardens. Her breath was uneven and I was struggling, too: I was unnaturally aware of the push and pull of my lungs.

There was only one house overlooking my parked car, and nobody at its windows. Biba fumbled in my bag and found the keys for me. Once we were inside, she clicked my safety belt and then hers into place. "Come *on*, Karen," she said, with a click of impatience. I thought that I would be too distressed to drive, but once I had one hand on the steering wheel and the other on the gearshift I felt oddly grateful for the focus it gave me. I drove us to the only place we could go.

There was a clammy silence in the car as I drove through East Finchley and made our way onto the westbound North Circular. Somewhere near Neasden the road fanned out into four lanes and as we cruised downhill into the underpass, I astonished myself by making a noise I did not know a human being was capable of, a long howl that distorted the muscles of my throat. I stopped only when Biba grabbed the steering wheel to pull the car back within the road markings. The shock left me panting, and when I tried to swallow, it was with a rasp and a wince. The silence fell again in the aftermath of my scream. It was broken somewhere near Ealing.

"I can't get through this without a cigarette," said Biba. "There must be a convenience store or gas station somewhere. Stop when you see one, will you? Can you stop?" I pulled up on a double yellow line outside the gas station and told her to be quick. From her pockets she could gather only a scattering of dirty silver and copper. I nodded toward my handbag and she delved in and retrieved my wallet.

I watched her silhouette against the cashier's window. The phrase "two men are dead" repeated itself like tribal drums in my head. Already I had a sense that this journey occupied a kind of non-time; that it was a last suspension between the events of my immediate past and a bleak and uncertain future.

Biba came back with two packs of twenty and a purple Bic

lighter. I couldn't find the words for the big questions so began with a smaller one. "Where did you learn to shoot a gun?" I asked. It hurt to talk.

"Fencing, archery, and firearms skills," she said. She looked and sounded very young. "It was an optional module in the second year. We went to a shooting range."

"Jesus *Christ*!" I banged the steering wheel with my fist. The horn gave a quick sharp blast. We turned onto my old street.

Biba looked as uncomfortable in this house as Rex had looked at ease. Now was not the time to enforce the household's no-smoking rule as she sat on the oatmeal chenille sofa, the tar-black soles of her feet imperiling the pale pile.

"Have you got anything to drink?" she asked, but there was nothing alcoholic apart from a few frozen cubes of wine. There was juice, and we drank it from tumblers like children.

"Biba, what the hell have we done?" I heard myself say, and wondered why I was emphasizing my own complicity.

"Fucking . . . I panicked," she said, as though explaining away a rash decision behind the wheel.

"He can't seriously intend to take the blame for it," I said. She considered the possibility with her head on one side.

"I think he does."

"You're not going to let him?"

"I don't know," she said. "It might actually work."

I didn't know which of them I hated more at that second: her for what she'd done, or him for letting her get away with it. "You should be relieved," she said. "This way, you get a clean slate."

"I don't want a fucking clean slate! I don't want to not see you and Rex anymore!" She didn't reply but used the lit end of the cigarette she was smoking to light another. I began to cry properly now, blinding tears and hoarse sobs. "I want to go back and get him."

"Don't be ridiculous. Look, could you please stop crying?"

"It's a bit late for that now! Two men are *dead*!"

Her eyes, when they met mine, registered only irritation. I knew then that no tears or words would penetrate, and something in me surrendered. "I'm going to bed," I said, with the last of my voice. "Don't come near me."

Of course I did not sleep. It was an alien concept, like eating, or happiness. The pillow still smelled of Rex and I half suffocated myself in an attempt to breathe in the traces of him that lingered in the cotton. Where would he be sleeping tonight? Not in his room or mine, that much was for certain. Would they even let him sleep? If he went through with his plan to confess to the murders his sister had committed, would the police still question him, or would they leave him alone, glad that he had made their job so easy? I could not silence the cynical voice in my head suggesting that, on one level, Rex would be relishing this once-in-a-lifetime chance to martyr himself for his sister. As the sun began to rise, tears gave way to the aftershock shudders that follow extensive, exhaustive crying and, sometime between six and seven, I fell into a light, fretful sleep.

I had not locked us into the house deliberately, but had double-locked the front door through force of habit. If I had not, she would have gone without waking me. I was shaken out of sporadic sleep by the sound of her rattling the back door handle. I called her name from the landing. Like me, Biba still wore the clothes we had fled in the night before, but she had taken a shower and washed her hair before dressing again. From my perspective on the stairs, her eyes in that little face looked bigger than ever.

"Where are you going?" I asked.

"To my dad's," she said.

"To your *dad's*? Do you think he'll take you in after what's happened?" I had not meant for my words to crush her but they did.

"Home, then."

"I'll come with you."

"No, Karen. Rex was right. This is our mess. You don't need to get involved," she said.

"Don't get involved? I was there. I *saw* it. You'll need me as a witness, or an alibi or something." I could not believe that I was using these words in the context of my own life. "You need me." I wasn't sure if I was still talking about the same thing.

"Look, it's all over, Karen. We've lost the house. We've lost each other already. What else is there? Me and Rex will keep you out of this."

"But my stuff is all over your house!"

"I'll say it's all mine."

"My fingerprints are on everything."

"So are lots of people's. We'll say it was the party." She was growing impatient. I heard myself beg her to incriminate me just so that I wouldn't lose my friends, and recognized this as madness. They had both decided they did not want me. Something inside me buckled under the weight of my own sudden resignation.

"I really should go," she said, when I made no move to let her out.

"You don't even know where you are. Let me drive you to your train at least."

I dropped her off outside Brentford station. She checked her hair in the mirror, tucking a strand behind her ear and smoothing down her fringe, using her forefinger to wipe an imagined smudge from below her eye.

"Can you lend me five pounds to get me home, please?" The new formality of her good manners marked an unhappy shift in our relationship. I fished in my purse for the note. Finding only a crisp new twenty, I handed her that.

"What are you going to say when you get there?" I asked.

"I don't know yet."

"When will I see you again?" I asked. Her face was set and she shook her head decisively, but there was a catch in her voice when she said, "I'm sorry." She did not lean in for the expected kiss good-bye but shut the door gently in my face. I adjusted the rear-view mirror so that I could watch her enter the station. The street was busy and I could not linger. Alone, I returned to the place I would have to force myself to think of once more as home.

The first newspaper to run the story was Monday's edition of the *Evening Standard*. I forced myself to walk three streets to the corner shop and bought the early afternoon edition. My old home, my real home, loosely wrapped in tape, was pictured on the front page underneath the frowning headline MILLIONAIRES' ROW MURDERS—2 SHOT. I folded the paper inward so that only the sports section was visible to others, sure that anyone who saw me reading the story would be able to deduce my associative guilt.

I locked the front door behind me and dropped to my knees in the front hall, spreading the paper out in front of me. Pages three and four of the paper portrayed a grainy photograph of Guy and a crisp portrait of Tom Wheeler. I still don't know how journalists get photographs so quickly. They must literally sprint to the victims' families' homes and ask for access to the family album almost before they offer their condolences. The words took up less than half the space occupied by the photographs and gave little away, although the journalist did reveal Guy's age.

"Nineteen," I whispered into my lap. "He was only nineteen." The text stated only that a twenty-four-year-old man was helping police with their inquiries. The euphemism comforted me. It allowed me to imagine Rex fetching cups of tea for friendly detectives, rather than shivering in a cell. There was no mention of a twenty-one-year-old woman being held or questioned.

The final edition of the newspaper two hours later ran the same story but this time the picture of Wheeler was a family portrait, a formal studio shot showing him with Jenny and their four children. Jenny Wheeler, widow. Hers must have been the screams we heard as we ran through the woods. I looked at that page for as long as it took to glean the printed facts—there was no new information—and then stuffed the whole paper into the kitchen wastebasket. I remained aware of its presence for the rest of the evening and that portrait of the Wheelers, though glimpsed only once, impressed itself onto my retina so vividly that I can still see it today with almost no effort if I close my eyes.

At half past six I turned on the London news, so nervous that I left a sweaty palm print on the remote control. There was a one-minute item, a young male reporter standing in Queenswood Lane summarizing the report in the *Standard* and promising more developments on this case as they arose. The case did not make the national bulletins, which were still dominated by Diana's death and its aftermath. Without that distraction perhaps the murders would have received greater publicity. As it was, our story was buried like the layers of flowers being crushed under the weight of their own cellophane outside Kensington Palace. I went out again only to buy a bottle of wine to help me sleep; my hand hovered over a dusty Shiraz, but it was the color of the stain on Tom Wheeler's shirt and instead I chose a Chardonnay. It was sharp and bitter, but it was all gone before dark, and sleep was as elusive as it had been the night before. I wondered if Rex had had any rest yet.

The press had obviously been as diligent and industrious as I had been frustrated and idle. On Tuesday morning, every newspaper carried the story. The *Daily Mail*, the paper my parents took, had devoted three pages to it. They, along with the other tabloids, had gone with the headline HIGHGATE HOUSE OF HORRORS. Rex had been named and pictured: the photograph had been taken the night I met him. I recognized the frayed shirt collar. He was freshly shaven and looked terribly young and vulnerable. A slim female arm wrapped around his neck and in the edge of the frame a flare of peroxide blond hair was just visible. Rachael had wasted no time. In the twenty-four hours between the story breaking and now, the journalists had discovered everything, from the fact that Guy was a small-time drug dealer to Tom Wheeler's employer and even his salary. They knew that Biba had filmed a sex scene in a forthcoming drama, although they did not say where she was. They had made the connection from Rex to Roger Capel and thence to Jules Millar. A boxed-off column headlined

TRAGIC BEAUTY gave a sensationalized précis of the life and death of Sheila Capel. All that was missing was me. I closed the *Mail* and smoothed the front page. Diana looked up at me from underneath heavy black lashes as the telephone started to ring.

It was neither the dreaded call from the police nor the longed-for one from Biba but the expected one from my parents. My parents, usually so careful on the telephone, spoke at once, their words tumbling over each other like leaping salmon.

"It's the same Rex, isn't it?" said my mother, at the same time as my dad said, "Karen, are you all right? What's happened?"

The first words I had spoken to another human being for three days were the first lie I told in connection with the case.

"I don't know any more about it than you do."

"But you must know something . . ." said my father.

"It says here it was drugs," said my mother. "You wouldn't have any part in that, would you?" When I said no, I was being truthful. I knew that I had taken my last illegal drug.

"I've had a bad feeling since we met him," said Mum, contradicting her words of only two weeks before.

"We're coming down to get you," said Dad. "We haven't been able to get hold of you at all since you took up with him. I want to know where you are."

I pressed my head against the window, my throat swollen with the effort not to tell them everything and surrender myself to their care.

"I'll drive myself home," I said. "Tomorrow. But I've got to go into college first." My one-size-fits-all excuse worked on them even now. The guilt twisted my empty stomach into a tight little knot. To ease it, I made my lie come true.

I took a shower and changed my clothes for the first time since leaving Highgate, watching as the water ran gray. I turned my bedside radio on while I dressed. Elton John was still singing goodbye to England's rose, and my hand hovered above the off switch, but I decided to hear him out and wait for the next news bulletin.

At nine o'clock, the newsreader announced in even tones that Rex Capel had been charged with the murders of Guy Grainger and Tom Wheeler and that he had been remanded in custody. The police, she said, were not looking for anyone else in connection with their inquiries. I waited all morning for Biba to call and tell me what had happened and what she had said, but the phone remained silent.

Technically I was no longer a student at Queen Charlotte's, but neither had I severed all links with the department. I was still in the care of their Graduate Service and would remain so for the twelve months following my results. Even if this had not been the case, I felt confident that Caroline Alba would help me with my master's application if there was still time. At this late stage, I would go anywhere that would take me.

The elevator doors sighed open on the fourth floor and discharged me on the landing, where I found myself standing opposite the notice board where it had all started. With the new intake of students due in less than a week, someone had stripped the patchwork of flyers and notices from the board. The pinpricked cork was bare save for a poster welcoming the new intake to the languages department and showing photographs of all the staff, and a few smaller notices underneath. It was a large poster but could not quite hide the request for a native German speaker scrawled on the wall at the beginning of June. In faded red pen the letters poked out from the bottom right-hand corner of the poster. BIBA XXX. I stepped forward to touch it, traced the letters of her name and the X's with my fingertip, astonished to find that I did not wish I had never met her.

My old mailbox no longer bore my name. All of the empty recesses contained the same badly photocopied leaflet advertising for graduates to work as English teachers in Switzerland. Force of habit made me remove the leaflet from the box that had been mine.

The double doors that sealed off the department corridor were not propped open with a fire extinguisher as they would be during term time, but were closed. Through the slit window I could see Caroline Alba halfway down the passage in animated conversation with another member of the staff. I leaned my hand on the steel panel and prepared to push. Then I looked down again at the leaflet in my hand. The words "immediate start" had caught my eye. I took my hand off the door, turned my back on the department, and summoned the elevator.

The woman who answered the telephone, Sylvia, was an English expat living in Bern with her family and trying, not very successfully, to establish a School of English in the city.

"The teacher I had lined up let me down," she said. "That does happen in this line of work, I'm afraid. I am rather frantic. Term starts next week, and all the teachers here in Bern are booked up."

"I'm not TEFL-qualified," I told her, but reeled off a list of my qualifications, the languages I could speak well, and my experience as a classroom assistant at various schools and colleges all over the Continent.

Sylvia gave a nervous laugh. "Don't take this the wrong way," she said, "but aren't you a little overqualified to take this post? Why do you want to come here?" I expressed the desire to escape, the feeling that I would begin to tear off my own flesh if I had to stay in London and not see them anymore, in the mildest terms I could muster.

"I fancy a change of scenery," I said.

Sylvia would pay my airfare and my first month's housing if I could get to her by the beginning of the term. This was, if not the deciding factor, important. My savings, substantial at the beginning of the summer, had dwindled into the low hundreds, and with Sarah due to return from France in a couple of weeks, I would soon find myself without a home.

Thirty hours after my conversation with Sylvia, I had packed my room into the trunk of my car and driven to a parking garage in Wembley, the one I had spotted from the traffic jam on the way to Nina's going-away party. It was more of a shack than a garage, but the owner did not ask me my name or any questions when I paid him for a year in advance and left holding only my keys and my Travelcard. Too cowardly to have the uncomfortable conversation, I wrote to my parents and to Sarah telling them where I was going. Then, stuffing a rucksack with clothes I had not worn since the previous winter, I took the train to Heathrow Airport. In the check-in line for my flight to Zurich I noticed a few fallen leaves ground into the base of my bag, the first outward sign that summer was over.

From a call box in the departure lounge I dialed the number of the old house. I let it ring for five minutes, but there was no answer.

Bern is an ancient city laced with wires. The old Gothic and medieval buildings are linked with electricity and telephone wires that crisscross above the heads of the people who walk the paved and cobbled streets below, and the cables that power the trams string the streets like fat lines of licorice. After a few days, you cease to notice this web in the sky, but in the beginning its incongruity is distracting.

I had three days to settle into the studio apartment that Sylvia had arranged for me, and I spent all of them wandering the streets, looking up at the tangle of wires that wound around and avoided each other as effortlessly and elegantly as the languages of French, Italian, German, and Romansh coexisted in the city. I avoided coffee shops and bars on my own in case I reverted to my old, cherished habit of turning to my right and pointing out an interesting passerby to Biba.

Teaching English abroad is the ideal way to surround yourself with people without the risk of intimacy or connection. There is a concatenation of students, all young and eager to talk and drink and simply to be with others. My pupils came from all over the world, either attracted to the banking industry or employed by those who were already part of that machine. They came and went.

Some of them stayed for long enough to perfect their English, others took just enough classes to enable them to travel to London and wait on tables there. Many students dropped out without explanation, but there was always someone new, and every week brought a new birthday, or a departure, and there was always a reason to head into the bars when the lesson was over. During these extracurricular drinking sessions, I did unpaid overtime, listening to my students' stories and deflecting their questions by correcting their grammar and making them repeat their anecdotes until I was satisfied. I told no anecdotes of my own. I had only one story to tell and it was not one I could share with anyone.

I dreaded the weekly call to my parents in which I assured them I was fine and they pretended not to know that I was lying. I let my hair revert to its natural dark blond. I took refuge not in exercise but in food, growing fat on chocolate and the pastries that students brought to class and the huge plates of creamy pasta that were all I could be bothered to cook in my studio apartment. And I drank, too, liters of frothy beer, not caring about the consequences. I grew unrecognizable from the girl I had been in the summer. I hid my body in ever more shapeless clothes. The afternoons drew in and I wrapped the winter around me like a scarf, grateful for the early darkness and the extra anonymity it afforded me.

I was ignorant of the British criminal justice system but presumed that Rex must soon stand trial. Occasionally I went to the Central Library and flicked through their copy of *The Times*, but the case was never mentioned. While I was there I always checked my e-mails. It was the only way that Biba could have reached me, but no message ever came. I wished I had looked over her shoulder when she was typing in her password. That way, I could have accessed her inbox and established whether she was ignoring me, or whether the mailbox was untouched and she was simply making good on her promise never to use the address I had set up for her. Emma and Caroline Alba had both written to me expressing concern. Simon had dropped me a line telling me that he was getting married to Isabel and hoping that there were no hard feelings. I sent the same curt message to all three of them saying that I was taking a year off and that I would be in touch on my return. I could not have cut the lines of communication more effectively: I have never heard from any of them again.

In November yet more wires appeared above the city streets, these studded with lanterns that outlined windows and dressed bare trees in tiny orbs of light. There was an onion festival during which several of my students dressed as onions and danced in the streets. For a few hours I genuinely forgot my troubles, until it occurred to me how much Biba would have loved it.

Christmas brought with it markets and bustle. Christmas Eve, not the day itself, is a day of national celebration in Switzerland, and I spent it with some students who had not been able to travel home. Christmas Day I was invited to spend with Sylvia and her family in their marbled apartment in the heart of the Old Town. We ate a traditional English roast and pulled crackers that they had ordered from Harrods. I think they were relieved when I went home. I know that I was. The streets leading from their apartment to my studio were almost empty of people, and the fountains in the Bundesplatz had been turned off.

The Capels were still my default thought. Nights when I did not dream about them were rare. I had thought that ignorance would be bliss but it was hell, and one day an unseen presence decided for me that knowledge, however terrible, must be preferable to the spiraling stress that was my existence. This force steered me into the Central Library, and there, instead of logging on to my e-mail page, I typed in the URL for the Lycos search engine and left me sitting in front of that blank page of possibility. I took over then, silently thanking whatever impulse it was that had guided me here. I searched for Bathsheba Capel. I found her on the Internet Movie Database Web site. Her bit part in the Charles II program was mentioned and she had another television credit to her name underneath it. The broadcast date given was spring 1998. I scrolled up and down the page, unable to make sense of this, until I read the production notes and realized with a jolt that it was the comedy about the lottery winner. While her brother was being questioned by the police, Biba had successfully auditioned for the part she had been preparing for all the previous week. I had thought that nothing about her could shock me anymore, but this did.

Rex's name yielded very different results. I found the details I was dreading in an article on an online legal journal, cited as a model of savvy plea bargaining. The text, written by a lawyer, was muddy with legal jargon. There had been no trial. Rex had immediately pleaded guilty to the manslaughter of Guy Grainger and the murder of Tom Wheeler, and it was the swiftness of those guilty pleas that meant his sentencing was exceptionally lenient for a double killer. He had been sentenced to five years for Guy's manslaughter and twenty for Wheeler's murder, the two sentences to run concurrently. Twenty years did not sound lenient to me: my lifetime, lived out again in incarceration.

They might not want me but they could no longer argue that I was jeopardizing my liberty or theirs. It was time to go home. I gave Sylvia two weeks' notice and booked my flight back to London.

25

THE TRAIN HURTLED THROUGH Essex and into London's eastern outskirts, the satellite towns and then the suburbs a blur of illegible platform signs. The landscape seemed flat and drab compared to the dramatic Swiss contours I had become accustomed to. I imagined that the black raincloud that kept pace with the train was a lurking mountain range. Liverpool Street station came before I had even begun to acclimatize, and I walked the few blocks to Moorgate feeling like an alien in the city that I had once thought to possess. It had been raining and the puddles were black oil slicks. The city smelled and tasted of dirt and fuel, and the fanned aromas of the coffee shops and bakeries were overpowered by the heavy air. There were so many cars. There were so many *people*.

I broke into a fifty, the only sterling I had, and bought a coffee at a Pret A Manger next to Moorgate station. The unsmiling girl behind the counter handed me a crumpled pile of tired five-pound notes and some strangely familiar coins. The money looked as if it had been handled by each and every person in London. Glancing once more at the sky, I bought an umbrella in Boots. My last act before descending the steps to the Underground was to enter a phone booth and dial Biba's old number. Even when punching unfamiliar metal keys I could do it by touch alone. The unobtainable tone came as the expected surprise.

Little black mice scurried in the void where the train belonged, camouflaged in the soot of the gutter but occasionally revealing themselves when they ran over the live steel rails. The Northern Line forks in two at Camden Town and it's easy to take the wrong one. More than once I had absentmindedly found myself sitting on a train to Edgware, which runs through Golders Green, instead of the correct High Barnet train that would have taken me home to Highgate. On this occasion, however, I let two High Barnet trains go by and when I boarded the Edgware branch it was deliberate. The carriage was not full but it was fogged with rainwater that had evaporated from the passengers' clothes, bags, and umbrellas and was condensing on the windows. I sank into a seat and placed my rucksack on my lap so that I wouldn't be able to see my own reflection in the window opposite me. Next to me, a teenage boy was tracing the word BOLLOCKS in the mist with his fingertip, breathing onto the glass the better to display his artwork.

It was the first time I had been to Hampstead station. It was deep-sunk, tiled, and almost empty, rather like Regent's Park. Outside, it took me a while to get my bearings. The last time I had been here it had been blazing mid-July and lush; plucky little shoots of greenery had sprung from every crack and crevice in the pavement. Today, the rain fell at a perfect forty-five-degree angle and washed all color from the high street. There was no green anymore, only gray. I followed a sign guiding motorists toward the Royal Free Hospital and began an unpleasant trudge down the hill, wrestling with my new umbrella, which had a complicated catch mechanism. The shops' windows were brightly lit and the sky was darkening, so catching a glimpse of myself in the reflective glass was unavoidable. I looked like a middle-aged woman, plump in the face, shapeless body, lank hair plastered to her head, outwitted by an umbrella. At South End Green, an old West Indian lady in a sheepskin coat and with shopping bags for shoes sat on a bench under the cenotaph, shrieking the names and dates of England's monarchs.

I had spotted the landmark I had been trying to locate—the Magdala was just where we had left it. I turned my back to it, trying to recall the route our mad dash had taken. I grew confident when I took a right turn and found Keats House. I touched my thigh, remembering the bruise that had lingered there for weeks and the way Rex had soothed the faded yellow skin with his lips and hands. I wondered why I had thought the route such a warren at the time. My destination was only two streets removed from Heath Street.

The railings were free of their tangle of summer clothes, only a snake of clematis remaining. The red sports car was not parked on the driveway but a large SUV was, and light shone through opaque blinds at the front windows. I pressed the buzzer, grateful that they did not have closed-circuit television installed at the gate.

"I've got a courier delivery for Juliet Millar," I said to the soft female voice that answered.

"Come in," she replied. I was so surprised by the ease with which I had gained entry that I almost missed my opportunity, letting the gates part and then begin to close again before I slipped through them. I reached the front door at the exact moment that Jules opened it, her face lit with expectancy. Her expression changed when she saw me, not because she recognized me but because she realized she had been lied to.

"Jules! Please don't shut the door. I need to talk to you," I said. She attached the chain and left the door a few inches ajar. "We've met before. I'm Karen. I'm a friend of Biba's." I looked so different from the last time she had seen me, but her eyes narrowed with the effort of identification. "I'm—I was—Rex's girlfriend."

The door was shut in my face before it was reopened without the chain.

"Come in," she said.

She looked even lovelier than I remembered her. Few women give meaning to the ridiculous epithet "fragrant," but Jules did. Even in casual clothes, she looked better than most women do after hours in front of the mirror. Her blond hair hung in a smooth pane and she was swathed in an expensive garment of cashmere or mohair that had no identifiable beginning or end. I was acutely and uncomfortably aware of the contrast between us. Jules opened a door to a utility room and spread my dripping coat, rucksack, and boots over a radiator to dry. The layers of clothes I wore underneath were mostly dry and although I was hot, I did not remove them. I was not sure yet how long I would want to stay here, or how long this tentative welcome would last.

The only sound in the house was that of a radio coming from the kitchen. The children, although not of school age, were evidently elsewhere. Perhaps their father had taken them for a day out, either for a walk or to lunch. The thought of him lavishing attention on his second family while his first were God knows where made me rigid with anger.

I followed Jules through to a vast airy kitchen that occupied half the ground floor. Only the children's paintings stopped it from looking like an operating room. The white counter ran the entire length of the room, white appliances dotted at one-meter intervals. The only color relief was a copy of Jules's own book on a stand to the right of the empty sink.

She made coffee in a percolator; glad, I think, of the ritual and the opportunity to turn her back to me while she fussed with beans and milk and sugar. I was reminded of my first meeting with Nina: another kitchen, another pot of coffee, another young mother, another lifetime.

"So," she said, far too brightly when the drink was in my hands. "How've you been?" I could not bear the agony of small talk. I had come here only because I knew of no other way to trace my friends.

"Where's Rex?" I asked. "I mean, I know he's in prison, but where exactly?"

"Brixton," she said. Naming Rex's prison made his situation grimly real.

"And Biba. Where's she?"

"She was here for a while," said Jules. Her hands gripped her large shallow mug for comfort and reassurance as well as warmth. Three rings circled her ring finger: one plain band, one fat solitaire, and one encrusted with tiny stones. "We thought it best that we take her in after . . . what happened."

"You thought it best, or Roger did?"

"Well, it was my idea. But I'm afraid it didn't work out."

"Why not?" The coffee was fierce. Just a couple of sips had given me a jittery, confrontational confidence.

"Biba can be very unpredictable," Jules said with a sigh. "We had the children to think of. She took them out for a drive in the car."

"That sounds quite nice," I said.

"She was drunk, Karen. She crashed into the back of another car and when the police breathalyzed her she was three times over the limit. We couldn't let her stay after that, no matter how much . . . trouble she was in."

"Do you know where she's living?" I asked. The thought loomed suddenly in my mind. No. She couldn't be. "She's not back at . . . ?"

"Oh! No. No, she didn't go back at all apart from once to pick her things up after the police had . . . well, you know. Did you leave anything there? I'm afraid that most of the things we couldn't identify went to thrift stores, or we just threw them away. I know that Biba has some of Rex's things in storage, but . . . well. You can see why it's hard for us to keep them." A shy, proud smile came over her face and she couldn't resist telling me what had happened to the house. "You wouldn't recognize the old place now, actually. We've turned it into five flats. I was surprised how much I enjoyed property development. It really has been rewarding, I—" The insensitivity of her words became apparent to her and her cheeks flushed. Even her blush was ladylike, a neat petal of high color on each cheekbone.

"Do you know where she's living?' I repeated.

"We know where she went," said Jules, implying that it wasn't the same thing at all. "I've got an address somewhere. It's been a few months since we saw her." She turned her back to me and riffled through kitchen drawers and cabinets. A torn-out page from a notebook was eventually produced. Seeing Biba's handwriting was as much of a shock as seeing her face would have been. The scrawled, one-line address had only half a postal code—NW1—and made no sense until I turned the page and saw the map that she had drawn, the long swoop of water and a doodle of a boat on a wave. I smiled to know exactly where she was and who she was with.

"This is very near," I said. "It's Camden Town. It's just down the road, it's a twenty-minute walk."

"Biba and her father, all of us, we didn't part on the best of terms," said Jules. "Tell her that she's welcome to visit whenever she likes."

"Just not to live," I couldn't help snap back.

"No," and she was steely now. "Not to live. I've got to think of my children. When you have your own you'll understand." She glanced down at my stomach, disguised under layers of wool and cotton, as she said this, but, like most people who are loath to offend a fat woman, she was far too polite to ask the obvious question.

My journey continued down Haverstock Hill away from Hampstead. At the top of the hill every pub I passed was advertising food on blackboards outside, and when I reached the bottom, they were all using music to entice drinkers in. The neighborhoods lowered with the gradient as I went from the stuccoed town houses of Belsize Park to the mansion flats of Chalk Farm and finally arrived at the cramped architectural chaos of Camden Town. I had begun to remember how to be a Londoner; effortlessly I sidestepped whispering drug dealers and parted shoals of wide-eyed students carrying Invicta backpacks. When I reached the Lock and descended the narrow steps that led to the canal, I was as low as I could go.

The towpath was hung with a fine mist quite distinct from the drizzle at street level. It was dark now and I followed the mist of my own breath as well as Biba's vague directions. I headed west, away from the picturesque end of the canal where fairy lights dotted the trees and lanterns lit the walkway. I passed London Zoo, wrinkling my nose as the stench from the netted peaks of the aviary reached my nostrils. A leisure barge, crammed with half-drunk tourists on a dinner cruise, chugged in the opposite direction. I went dipping under dripping bridges where the people walked quickly and didn't make eye contact. There were few other pedestrians in any case: just the odd dog walker, a lone cyclist, a duo of committed joggers, and the usual drinkers on benches.

I rounded a corner to find that the canal disappeared into a yawning tunnel, and cursed myself for having missed the boat I was looking for. Then I saw it: the last but one in a row of moored barges that had lined my way. A red boat, perhaps the tattiest I had yet seen, the name *Aminah* painted on the side in a washed-out yellow italic script. Where the other barges had old geranium pots and little hedges on their roofs, this one had a precarious topple of wooden pallets and boxes. The gap between barge and bank was wide. The only way to get on and off would be a kind of *grand jeté*, which I wasn't about to attempt. A light burned in its sunken little window. I stopped, suddenly shy. If this was the last stage of my paper chase, I was nervous after so long apart from her. After a few moments' cold hesitation, I called his name, not hers.

"Arouna?" I shouted into the night. "Arouna! Hello?"

He appeared not from within but from somewhere on the deck, as silent and dark as a shadow who had suddenly discovered the ability to peel away from the darkness and make himself flesh. Only his eyes and earrings shone as he squinted at me.

"Hello, Arouna," I said gently. "Remember me?"

He heaved up his massive bulk and I wondered how such a big man could live on such a tiny boat. He must have to leave home every time he wanted to stand up. He wore a puffer jacket over his muumuu and a pair of tracksuit bottoms peeked out from underneath it.

"Yes!" he said, teeth exposed in triumph after a moment of intense concentration. "I remember you. You're a friend of Biba's, and so a friend of mine, too. Come in, come in." The hands he held out wore fingerless gloves. Gripping his wrists, I felt confident enough to put one foot on the stern of the little boat and make the leap across. The force of the pack on my back tipped me face-first into his chest. He laughed and kissed me on each cheek before turning me around and relieving me of its weight. A few wooden slats, more ladder than staircase, led down into the living quarters, which glowed red and gold and pink with tapestries and throws. A small oil stove intensified the smell of damp. Evidence of Nina filled the tiny space—there were silver, beaded things all over the place, photographs of her and the children—but there was none of the cigarette smoke or sandalwood perfume or even just the clothes that would indicate Biba's presence. This entire boat wasn't big enough to accommodate Biba's wardrobe, let alone house her and Arouna.

"You poor child," he said. "You look tired. Have a drink with me."

He brought out a Moroccan tea set with its tiny glasses and my heart sank. I was already tired and wired with caffeine and even the thought of sipping at strong tea laced with sugar made me shaky and irritable. I could not have disguised my delight when he pulled out not tea leaves but a bottle of brandy. He poured a swig into two tea glasses and offered one to me. Arouna knocked his back in one and laughed at the sour expression my face pulled.

"I need that after a day at my stall," he said, and refilled my glass. I decided to wait awhile to let the effects of the first one take hold. He took both my hands in his. "Now then. I think you're here because you want to see your friend." I nodded. "She's gonna be happy to see you, Karen."

"You remembered my name!" I said.

"Of course. She talks about you all the time."

"Is she here?" My voice cracked as I got the words out and my eyes threatened to water.

"Not anymore." Real tears of disappointment came and I gulped at my brandy. Arouna smoothed them away with a garlicky thumb. "Don't cry, girl. She's not far away."

"Thank you. I really, really appreciate this." I meant the brandy as well as the news.

"She did stay for a while. I looked after her for Nina."

"Have you heard from Nina lately?" Not for the first time, I wished that Nina were there. She was the only person in the world to whom I could tell my story.

"She calls every few weeks. She's still on the move. I'll go out when she settles down for good. She's in India at the moment. Gaia was three last week but Nina said not to send her a present. They'll have moved on by the time it gets there." He said this patiently and without bitterness.

"Is Biba in touch with Nina?"

"They are always in touch, those women. They find each other across the world if they have to. But listen. You need to know where she is, yes? She's staying in an apartment. The council gave it to my friend and she's looking after it while he's traveling. The barge is too damp for her. This isn't a healthy place to live."

"Is she on her own?" I asked.

"Yes. I go to see her on my days off but she lives alone."

"Have you got the address, please?" I said. Pathetic gratitude for Arouna's help and kindness wrestled with an impatience to see her again.

"I will do better than that. I will take you there."

The temperature drop, which is the real division between night and day at that time of year, had turned the air bitterly cold. Arouna's long legs cleared the gap between boat and land easily, and he lifted me down onto the ground. I landed in a puddle and felt the beginnings of an icy dampness that told me the sole of my boot had parted company with its leather upper. He carried my ruck-sack for me; without it, I felt lighter than my bulk would allow.

"Do you think she'll be in?" I asked, as we climbed Haverstock Hill.

"Oh, she's always in," he said. We turned right onto Prince of Wales Road. Every step we took drew us farther and farther away from the kind of place I could imagine Biba living in. We passed a floodlit, youth-infested soccer field and adjoining recreation center and a railway station—Kentish Town West—that I had seen on maps but never at street level. We were, I realized, walking the no-man's-land between the two branches of the Northern Line. Either side of the street was filled with a sprawl of low-rise blocks, all branded by Camden Council. Some of the more attractive brickwork buildings were old enough to bear the Corporation of London logo, but the one that Arouna stopped outside was a gray tower ten stories high, its walls clad in huge concrete slabs.

"She lives here?" I said in disbelief. I only had to look at the graffiti-covered elevator to know what it smelled like. Arouna laughed but not unkindly.

"Sixth floor, number thirty-nine," he said. I looked up, trying to identify which of the lit windows was hers.

"Do you mind if I go alone?" He hooked my rucksack back over my shoulders. Was he going to tell me something? Twice he drew breath to speak and twice he closed his lips again.

"You send my love to that girl."

I took my chances in the elevator, managing not to breathe in while it wheezed its way to the sixth floor, where it belched me out with a shudder. An open walkway linked the apartments and I glanced over the edge of the flaking railings. Streaky wet taillights trailed after the crawling cars in the street below. It was a long way to fall. I looked in through the front window of apartment 39. It gave onto a small, dimly lit kitchen. The stove was electric, the kind with coils for hot plates, and filthy. A wine bottle filled to the brim with cigarette butts stood in the middle of the lonely little table shoved up against one wall. I recognized the blue silk scarf that hung over a lampshade, a pretty fire risk that was pure Biba.

There was no knocker on the door and the letterbox was the kind that takes the skin off your fingers without making the slightest noise. I rapped with my knuckles but there was no answer, so I hammered. I let it all out now, yelling the name that I had carried around for months like a heavy little secret. A voice, small and shrill, emanated from some unseen quarter of the flat.

"Is it you?"

I pressed my face against the tiny panel of frosted glass embedded with a grid of shatterproof wiring. I found myself eyeball-to-eyeball with a pixelated version of the face I knew so well, black eyes peering out from underneath a thick fringe. I pressed my own forehead to hers against the glass and she disappeared; I heard hands undoing the locks, as noisy as looms, that bolted out the world. At first, only her head and shoulders appeared around the side. I opened my arms and she fell into them. And then I recoiled in shock and something like horror as I encountered the swollen balloon of her stomach, such a contrast from the tiny frame I had expected to embrace. I took a step back and allowed my eyes to confirm her pregnancy.

"What took you so long?" she said.

26

S HE FILLED THE NARROW entrance hall. There was no natural light inside. A maroon carpet, balding and stained, covered most of the floor and textured wallpaper had been washed over with a magnolia emulsion that did little to lighten the place up. We passed only two doors before arriving at the end of the corridor, in the living room, which was dominated by a brown, fake leather three-piece suite meant for a room four times the size of this one. A muted but flickering television set and an ashtray on a stand were the only other items of furniture in the room. Biba sat in a shiny armchair with her legs apart. She had put weight on all over, not just on her abdomen. Breasts larger than mine sat heavily on top of her bump. Her arms and legs were plump and her neck thicker, her cheeks puffy, her nose the only pointed feature remaining on what had been a strikingly angular face. I wondered how I could ever have thought her beautiful. I felt some-how betrayed to find that she had the kind of good looks that are dependent mainly on being very, very thin. I sank into the sofa opposite her.

"I don't know where to start," I said. "I had so many questions, and now I've got so many new ones."

"Well, let me answer the obvious one. It's Guy's," she said. "And I'm eight and a half months gone, I think." I tried to do the calculations but I struggled. She must have seen my eyes flickering and failing over a mental abacus. "I'm pretty sure it happened that first time."

"The night you went to the hospital? After your show? You conceived a child that night?"

"Hmm. It's not a very auspicious start to life, is it? A drunken fuck up against a tree. And then this . . ." She gestured around the room. She lit a cigarette. "I know, I know. Give me the lecture now and get it over with."

"You're *huge*."

"You can talk," she said. "What's happened to you?"

"It doesn't help that I'm wearing all my clothes at once," I said defensively, peeling off a couple of layers and dropping two dress sizes. "That's what happens in Switzerland. It's all beer and cheese. It'll go now that I'm back in London."

Biba had been watching a game show. Her next-door neighbor had the television tuned in to the same channel and the dialogue was intelligible through the wall.

"How are you paying for this, anyway?" I said.

"Arouna sorted it out," she said. "It's some kind of scam with the housing benefit. I don't really understand it myself, but basically Arouna's friend pretends to charge me rent, and I get the dole. This wasn't in the plan, was it? Who'd have thought I'd have ended up signing on? I was supposed to be world famous by now."

"I take it you're not acting anymore."

"Well, I'm still with my agent, just about. He wasn't impressed. The intention is to go back to it when the baby's born."

"I'm surprised you decided to keep it," I said.

"I didn't know for ages, I wasn't keeping track of those things, and when I found out, I'd already . . . it had . . . Guy was dead by then, and I thought, well, this is the least I can do."

"What does Rex think about it?" I asked. It was only the second time I had spoken his name for months, and my voice buckled under the weight of it.

She shook her head. "I didn't really look big until a couple of months ago and I haven't seen him since before then." I put my head in my hands, unable to process all this. "My dad doesn't know either. The only people who do are you and Arouna."

I recalled how Nina had convinced Arouna that Gaia was his child and said, "Oh Christ, Arouna doesn't think it's his, does he?"

I had forgotten how much I had missed the chime of her laugh. "Karen, don't be *ridiculous*."

"Why not? Nothing anyone does would surprise me anymore."

The closing credits of the game show blared from the apartment next door and I heard the flick of a switch and the roar of water as a kettle was put on to boil.

"I'm so pleased you're back," she said. "Rex will be, too. We've missed you. I mean, we understand why you kept away."

"You told me we couldn't see each other again!" I said. "I didn't *want* to go away. I wanted to stay and help you both."

"Yes, but it worked out for the best, didn't it? You were the only one who wasn't to blame for anything and you didn't get dragged into it at all, did you?" While you, I thought, got away with murder.

"How is he?" I couldn't say his name this time.

"As well as can be expected considering they sent him to South London. I do think that's rather cruel of them. He's such a North London person." Did it really make any difference which side of the river you were on when you weren't going to see the water for twenty years?

"I mean, how is he in himself?"

"Getting on with things. Being Rex. He rings me. I ring him. We talk about you a lot."

She lit another cigarette. A rebuke nestled at the back of my throat like bile.

"What are you doing now, anyway?" she asked. "Are you back in that house in Richmond?"

"Brentford," I corrected her. "I only got back this morning. I didn't have a plan beyond finding you and now that I have I don't know what else to do."

"Will you stay with me?" Big eyes, small voice. "Until the baby's born?"

"Do you want me to?"

"Yes, please."

There was only one bedroom in the apartment. An unfolded futon was surrounded by Biba's clothes, refugees from the house. They burst from bags, and hung in and around the wardrobe door and from a plastic clothesline strung on a diagonal between two corners of the room.

"You can sleep in this," she said, tossing me a T-shirt that I recognized.

"This is Rex's," I said, passing it under my nose.

"I thought you'd like that," she said. She leaned over to a shopping bag on the floor and handed it to me. "I rescued this for you, too." It was the red dress, crumpled now and too small for me. "I thought that keeping it for you would bring you back, and I was right."

Biba slept on her side, a pillow wedged between her calves. I nestled into her curled C-shape and tucked my legs into the backs of her knees. I pressed my face between her shoulder blades and inhaled the smell that was so like her brother's. Pulling her close, I felt the gentle rise and fall of her rib cage, pressed my palm into her stretched and swollen skin, and gasped to feel the tiny dancing kicks of her unborn child.

With me holding her elbow, Biba felt strong enough to take a daily walk, or waddle, around her neighborhood. She was breathless and had to stop every few hundred yards to lean against a wall and wheeze until she felt strong enough to go on. I was convinced that every gasp and twinge was a sign of imminent labor.

"Where are you having this baby, anyway?" I asked. We were having a greasy breakfast in a café in Kentish Town when it suddenly occurred to me that I had yet to hear her mention a midwife or a hospital. I had a notion that women who were Biba's size ought to be monitored by some kind of medical professional, and to have a bag packed and waiting in the hallway.

"I haven't bothered with all that," she said, dipping a triangle of fried bread into her egg and watching the yolk bleed all over the plate.

"Biba!"

"What? You turn up at the ER or whatever and they'll just take you in. Or you call an ambulance. As long as I feel okay, and I do, what's the problem? Nina had Gaia in a mud hut somewhere in Malaysia, and she's fine."

"Yes, but Nina had already had Inigo, she knew what it was like to have a baby. And that's not even the point at all."

"If you turn up at a hospital they can't exactly turn you away, can they? I'll be fine. I always am." She heaved herself up out of her chair, as clumsy as she had once been graceful. We had to pause twice on the way back to the flat.

"I hate walking everywhere," she said. "I wish we still had your car." The sudden recollection of the key tucked in the inside pocket of my rucksack made me stop in my tracks so abruptly that an old man with a shopping cart walked straight into my back.

"You're in luck," I said.

It took three buses to reach the garage where I had left my car in September. To my astonishment, the man who ran the place recognized me instantly.

"Yellow Fiat," he said before I had opened my mouth. "I never forget a face or a car. What've you got stashed in there, anyway? A dead body?"

"Very funny," I said. "Nothing that interesting. Is it all okay?"

"Well, it hasn't turned into a Mercedes while you were away," he said. Biba joined in the wheezy laughter that followed the joke. He jangled his jailer's key ring ostentatiously before unfastening the padlock and pulled up the rusted garage door to reveal my little yellow car. It was filmed with grime but there was still a quarter of a tank of gas. The registration was paid up until April, and the papers were in the glove compartment where I'd left them: I took my crumpled driver's license out and put it in my purse.

I pulled the passenger seat back so that Biba's bump could be accommodated. She hauled herself into the car and sent it six inches toward the ground. Gas there may have been, but I'd certainly have to put some air in those tires before I attempted to drive back to North London.

"Help," she said. She was wedged solidly in between the seat and the dashboard. I reached between her legs and pulled the lever that sent the seat flying back on its coasters so that she had room to breathe.

"I wish I'd known it was here," she said. "I could have been driving it for *months*. Public transport when you're pregnant is no fun."

"You couldn't drive," I said. "Look at you. You'd never be able to fit behind the steering wheel. You're far too big."

"I bet I could," she said. "Go on, let me try now."

"No. Apart from anything else, you're not insured to drive it."

"You used to let Rex drive it. He wasn't insured."

"Well, I shouldn't have. Have you even got a license?"

"Christ, I'd forgotten how anal you could be about paperwork," said Biba with a grin. "Come on, let's get out of here. Oh, it's *delicious* not to have to take the bus. Let's never get on a bus again."

As we pulled out of the garage, the man waved us off. "Don't forget where I am if you need to store a dead body," he called after us, and crumpled into helpless laughter.

"I mean, I know he doesn't know about what happened," said Biba. "But I do think that's rather insensitive of him."

One of the first things she had ever said to me was, "I haven't any money." Her two acting jobs had been well paid but she had saved nothing from them, and was as poor now as she had been when I met her. I had been happy to subsidize her then, and did so out of necessity now. She had bought no clothes for her baby: it was me who went to Boots and Mothercare to buy diapers, blankets, and starter kits of miniature clothes. What was left of my wages from Bern I shared with her, paying for the food we ate and taking responsibility for topping up the plastic cards that fed the electricity and gas meters. Spending summer evenings by candlelight in a rambling house in Highgate was one thing. Freezing in semi-darkness in a flat in Kentish Town was quite another. Frequently I woke in the morning to find that the power had gone out in the night, and if I wanted a hot shower or a hot drink, I would have to walk the mile to the nearest corner shop offering a top-up service. On one such morning, I left with the key to the flat, the electricity card, and a twenty-pound note in my pocket. Craving caffeine, I bought myself a polystyrene cup of instant coffee from a café and drank it in the window. I returned an hour later, fed the key into the meter, and watched several appliances, including the television and every light in the place, spring to life at once. No wonder we ran out of power so frequently. I turned everything off and made a cup of tea to take to Biba in bed. She had been asleep when I crept out of the flat but her bed was now empty. The flat was not large enough to suppose she was anywhere else, and there was only one reason why she would leave the flat, in a hurry and alone. There was a Yellow Pages discarded in the hallway. With shaking hands I liberated it from its cellophane wrapping and looked up the number of the Royal Free Hospital.

"I'm looking for a Biba Capel, I think she's having her baby now," I said to the nurse in the maternity ward. She told me that they had no one by that name on their books. "What about Bathsheba Capel? She won't be on your books, but she might have come in as an emergency." The nurse transferred me back to the switchboard but nobody in Casualty could help me either. I worked my way through all the hospitals in North London, from the Whittington in Highgate to UCL and St. Thomas's in the South Bank, and as far out as Barnet and Edgware in the suburbs. None had admitted a woman in labor with her name. I began to understand the impetus that had made Rex pace. I ate frosted cornflakes with milk for breakfast, lunch, and dinner. The sugary gloop made a hard paste in my stomach but I was unwilling to leave the apartment even for the five minutes it would take to stock up on provisions at the shop across the road. I went to the toilet with the bathroom door open in case the telephone rang and, at 11 p.m. when exhaustion threatened, I pulled the duvet cover onto the sofa with the telephone by my head. It finally trilled at seven the following morning, pulling me out of a shallow sleep.

"Will you come and get us?" she said. "We're waiting for you outside the Royal Free."

There she was in a shapeless tracksuit, a little bundle in her arms. Plain white shopping bags were piled at her feet; she wedged the baby under one arm before throwing them onto the backseat. A packet split open and mysterious waddings and gauzes escaped. The baby on Biba's lap was asleep but it did not look relaxed. Its face was a red ball, screwed up tight.

"I called them," I said. "They said you weren't there."

"They went through my bag," she said, as though that explained everything. I raised an eyebrow. "I had your purse with me. I needed money for the taxi and your license was in there. I had it in my hand when they wheeled me in. They assumed I was Karen Clarke and I just . . . let it stand."

"You could have got them to call. I would have been there with you."

"Darling, I couldn't even remember my own name while I was in there, let alone my phone number. It *really* fucking hurts. You have no idea."

A tiny grasping fist emerged from the white bundle, opening and closing like an anemone underwater.

"What is it?" I asked.

"A girl," said Biba. I put her deadpan voice down to exhaustion. "It's not drinking out of my boob, though. I'm ravaged enough as it is. Did you know that you hemorrhage for up to six weeks after giving birth? As though I hadn't been through enough indignity.

I suppose it's nature's revenge for not having had a period for nine months."

The white shopping bags contained diapers, clothes, bottles, and cartons of baby formula.

"They gave them to me at the hospital," she said. "The suits are castoffs from other babies and the other stuff they give you if you haven't got any of your own."

The baby had little apart from the meager layette I had bought; no nursery, no toys, not even a push chair. Only a sling made out of hemp to carry her, which had been a present from Arouna, given before the birth.

"How long does it all last? What is it all *for*?" I couldn't figure out if the large cotton wad I held in my hand was a sanitary towel for Biba or a diaper for the baby. Biba shrugged.

"There's a booklet in there somewhere."

While Biba and the baby slept on the futon, I read the booklet. I made up a bottle of baby formula, testing it on the back of my arm like the instructions told me to. I had no idea whether it was the right temperature but a bottle was ready for the baby when she awoke, her tiny body emitting a huge sound that made the next-door neighbor turn up the television in retaliation. Biba sat up in bed with a wince. There was an old stain near her left nipple and a fresh one leaking from her right. At the end of the bed a pair of stained tracksuit trousers were screwed up in a ball and the sheet was smeared with bloodstains where she sat.

"Is this much bleeding normal?" I said. The clothes gave off a musky, metallic smell that provoked painful memories.

"Me and normal parted company a long time ago."

I went to fetch a towel from the bathroom. When I came back, the baby was on Biba's lap, puckering her lips and kicking her arms and legs as though trying to swim toward her mother's breast.

"Isn't she clever?" I asked. "She knows exactly what to do."

"It'd better not get ideas about *that*," said Biba. I handed her the bottle and she tipped it upside down over the infant's mouth. The baby rejected the rubber teat twice and her screams got louder.

"I can't do it," said Biba. She threw the bottle down on the bed and looked as though she might do the same with the baby. "Here," I said. "Give her to me." I cradled the baby in the crook of my left arm and gently placed the bottle a few millimeters from her frantically working mouth. This time she latched on and suckled. "We should think about a name," I said. "We can't just keep calling her 'she' or 'the baby.'" The child opened her eyes briefly; they were not the black-brown eyes of her mother and uncle but fathomless dark blue pools. Her lids lowered and they were two perfect seashells, pink and glossy, and her lashes were thick, black rushes of grass. I felt the little body slacken in my arm and she looked like nothing so much as an old man drifting happily off to sleep in his favorite chair after half a bottle of whiskey.

"She's happy now," I said to Biba, but she, too, was asleep.

Without discussion, I had become the baby's nurse, attending to her feeding, patiently confident that Biba would fall in love with the little girl as soon as she was over the fatigue that had confined her to bed since her return from the hospital. I was the only child of two only children and had never so much as held a baby before. I had no expertise, only a handful of leaflets and a Miriam Stoppard book acquired from a local thrift store to equip me with the bewildering array of new skills necessary to keep the baby dry, warm, fed, alive. I would consult the book in the middle of the night, my spare hand flicking frantically through the index, the letters seeming to exchange places on the page in front of me as sleeplessness and the baby's screaming conspired to rob me of my ability to read. I had thought myself tired before, in the days immediately after the murder, but I was now coping with exhaustion as debilitating as any illness I had ever experienced. The selflessness and drudgery involved did not come easily to me, and certainly not to Biba, who was content to let me feed and change the baby while she recovered. Rex would have been a natural at this, I thought, one freezing night when I was scooping powdered milk into boiled water. We needed Rex.

Ten days in, Biba was still refusing to endow the baby with a gender, referring to her as "it." Whenever I made up a bottle and offered Biba the chance to feed her daughter, she would roll over and tell me that she didn't feel well enough, that she wasn't up to it. She did feel well enough to drink, revealing a stash of boxed wine in a cubbyhole under the stairs that she may or may not have been drinking throughout her pregnancy. We kept a box balanced on one arm of the sofa and were drinking it when I tried to bring up the subject of the baby's name again. Biba deflected my question with a startling non sequitur.

"He had to get legal aid, you know," she said. I had been trying to get her to talk about the night that had forced us into this situation since my return from Switzerland. "It's really good. You get a solicitor and a barrister and they know exactly how to work the system. They were very clever. The police already knew the gun, like it was a person with a criminal record. They traced it to some bloke Guy knew. So they knew that Rex didn't—what's the phrase they used?— oh yes, that Rex didn't *procure* the weapon, so it was manslaughter or self-defense or something. They sentence you to five years but you get out in two and a half. He's served six months already so he'd be out in a couple of years if he hadn't shot Tom Wheeler."

"He *didn't* shoot Tom Wheeler!" I said. "You did!"

"Sorry!" she said with a giggle. "I heard it so often I almost believe it myself now. The thing with lies is to stick as near to the truth as possible. Rex told the truth, which was that Guy was shot in panic, but there's still no excuse, really. That wasn't self-defense, you see, it was murder and he pleaded guilty to that one, too." I pressed my fists into my cheeks. "It's money, really. They don't bother to challenge your story if you plead guilty because it saves them the expense of a trial and stuff."

"Did it never occur to you to tell the police what really happened?"

"Darling, of course it did. I said that to Rex when I was visiting him, but he wouldn't hear of it. He said the one thing that was keeping him going was knowing that you and I were totally safe. He did it to protect us."

"There's more to it than that, though," I said. I had promised myself that I would stay relatively sober for the baby but now I poured myself another glass of wine. "He blames himself for how your mother died, and he blames himself for you finding her. It's his fucked-up idea of atonement for something that wasn't even his fault in the first place."

"Look, it's done now," she said wearily.

"But he *didn't do it*! He's in prison for a murder you committed! Do you know what happens in prison? Men are *raped* in prison. Heroin and gangs and beatings and . . ." My intention had been to shock Biba out of her lethargic state, but I only seemed to be distressing myself with these images. "Are you even listening to me? This is your brother we're talking about!" Furious on Rex's behalf, I grabbed her by the shoulders and went to shake her, but the movement roused the baby, who gave a strangulated wail before settling back to sleep. I let Biba go. She remained silent for a long while, swilling wine around her glass and frowning.

"I was very angry with him at the time," she said eventually.

"Why?"

"He lied to me, Karen. Anything to do with my dad, we swore to each other we would always do together. It was bad enough that he wrote those letters behind my back, but telling Guy about them. Guy, that bloody idiot. Rex betrayed me utterly. Rex, who I trusted more than anyone . . . I wasn't thinking straight. Do you know what I thought when he told us to get out of the house?

I thought, it's the least he can bloody well do after betraying me like that."

I took her hand in mine, guilt deflating me. All I was thinking about when I replied was healing the rift between brother and sister.

"Biba, he didn't," I said.

"What do you mean?"

"Rex didn't tell Guy about the letters. I did." Her hand flinched under mine and she withdrew it.

"You did? *You?*" She lit a cigarette, and I automatically stood to open the window for the baby's sake. Biba jumped up and slammed it shut again, nearly catching my fingertips. "How *could* you?"

The air in the room was dead. A pulse throbbed somewhere between my ears, and my eyes seemed to beat time with the muffled roll of a bass line from somewhere else in the building; above, below, or adjacent, I couldn't tell.

"I didn't know what was going to happen, did I?"

"You were the one person I thought I had left after Rex," she said. "But it just goes to show that you can't fucking trust anyone." She flicked the tip of her cigarette in the baby's direction, deliberately and in anger. I wiped the flake of ash from the baby's cheek and took her next door to the bedroom. When I returned to the living room, the television was on. She never really looked at me properly again.

In the days that followed I found myself echoing Rex's behavior patterns, consumed with guilt and doing anything and everything I could think of to make her happy. I made sure she always had wine and her cigarettes. I became the most overqualified and underpaid nanny in London: when the baby woke in the night it was me who rose to feed or change her. I bought Biba a copy of *The Stage* and encouraged her to read it, told her that I would look after the baby if she got an acting job, but she never opened the magazine. I wrapped the baby up in her mother's sundresses and ball gowns to try to make her laugh, but nothing worked. A smile from Biba, even an acknowledgment of all that I was doing, would have wiped out every wrong thing she had ever done. But none came. She slept on the sofa while I stayed in the bedroom with the baby. It was impossible to believe that we were not strangers, let alone that she had once drawn me into her magical intimacy and made promises of everlasting friendship underneath a full moon. She disappeared into a world of her own, and this time she did not invite anybody to follow her in.

I stayed despite her malevolent sulk, hoping against all the evidence that our friendship was still retrievable. I had nowhere else to go except back to my parents' house. And besides, Biba and the baby needed me. One afternoon, I returned home from the supermarket to find Biba leaning on the rails of the balcony, the little girl half-frozen in only an undershirt and a soiled diaper, balanced rather than held. Biba's embrace was so slack that had the baby moved unexpectedly, or thrown out her arms and legs as she was wont to do when startled, she could easily have fallen to her death. When I reached out my arms for the baby, Biba simply relaxed her grip and let her fall. I only just caught her. She had risked her child's life to scare and unnerve me. With chilling unease I realized that I could not leave them.

⁂

She had left the note tucked into the pouch on the front of the baby's romper suit.

"I've had enough. I can't stay here with you, and I can't look after a baby. I'm so, so sorry. Tell Rex I love him. Biba." No stars or smiley faces brightened the page this time, but there was a postscript in the bottom right-hand corner. "I like the name Alice."

My handbag had been tipped upside down and my purse turned out. She had left my cards and my license, but forty pounds in cash was missing and my car keys were not on the hook by the door where I had hung them. I placed the crying baby on my shoulder and went to look over the balcony. There was a space where my car had been, a pale gray rectangle untouched by the rain that had been falling all night.

27

FIVE DAYS LATER, HALF crazed with exhaustion and with the baby drooling in her sling on my shoulder, I risked tying up the telephone line and called my parents. It had been nearly three weeks since we had last spoken. As far as they were concerned I was still in Switzerland, and even as I heard their telephone ring I was not sure whether I would tell them where I was. The relief in my mother's voice when she answered was disproportionate.

"Thank God, thank God." She sounded close to hysteria. "Karen, thank God! John!" she called, before I could explain myself to her or she herself to me. "It's her!"

"What's up, Mum?" I said. "I'm only a couple of days late." Alice wriggled on my breast, her mouth rooting for her bottle. I had none prepared and cursed myself for this oversight. I crooked my little finger and stuck my knuckle between her gums.

"More like a week! Are you okay?"

No. "Yes."

"How long have you been back?" said my dad, coming on the line. The urgency in his voice disarmed me and my rehearsed lies were forgotten.

"How did you know?"

"We had a call from the police," she said. My limbs felt loose in their sockets.

"What did they want?" I tried to keep my voice neutral.

"They found your car abandoned at Beachy Head. We thought you'd done something stupid."

I recalled a large square book, its spine cracked, lying open at a photograph of white cliffs. The memory of the photograph was as vivid as any other tableau from that summer. The flecks of cannabis and tobacco that scored the point where the pages met. I could picture the curve of the cliff where the grass, smooth as baize, met the chalk. And then I visualized the cluster of cars parked in the curling corner of the page, so tiny that they looked like miniature plastic beads. My car would have been among their number in the last few days. Was it still there? The inappropriate thought came to me that Biba would never have paid to park, and I wondered if the National Trust or whoever owned the parking lot bothered to chase parking fines in suicide cases. Laughter that tasted like vomit caught in my throat and the realization of what she had done, what she must have done, overwhelmed me. I tortured myself with a mental image of my friend standing on the dizzy edge. I remembered her speech about it, floating elegantly to her death, words that I had dismissed as yet more attention-seeking, actressy hyperbole and knew that she would have jumped or stepped or thrown her body down not in petulance but in anger and sadness and a desperation I could not begin to fathom. I felt like I was the one falling.

"Karen?" Dad was saying, over and over. "Karen, love?"

"It must have been stolen," I said. "I've never been to Beachy Head."

"Enough's enough," said my dad. "We know it's been tough for you but you've got to come home. Just come home. Please." His voice cracked.

Alice took in a lungful of air. I said a rushed and inadequate good-bye and hung up the telephone while both my parents were still speaking.

An unbearable sense of responsibility compounded my grief,

and I knew that I must bear this guilty burden as surely as I held the orphan in my arms. A fresh wave of despair came over me as I realized that I would have to inflict a similar level of pain, or something like it, on Rex. I would have to tell him. I could not bear to imagine the look on his face when he realized that his terrible sacrifice, his years of drudgery and adoration, had all come to nothing. It would rob him of any strength he had left. How would he survive without the incentive of protecting his sister? Losing the house, losing his liberty would be nothing to this. Alice parted her lips and began to wail. Throwing my head back onto the sofa, I cried as loudly as she did. The next-door neighbor banged on the wall and told me to keep the noise down. I picked up a tumbler that contained the dregs of the last wine we had shared and threw it at the wall. It broke neatly into three pieces and the wine trickled down the wall. The plum-colored stain it left was translucent, like a watercolor.

Camden Town Hall does not look like much from the outside. Its entrance is in a nondescript side street near St. Pancras station and its facade is the kind of dark gray concrete that always looks as though it's just been rained on even in blazing sunshine. But inside, a marble staircase like something from an Italian palazzo provides an appropriate sense of stateliness and occasion. It divides the main atrium in two and all the function rooms feed off it. Arriving early for my appointment, I walked Alice up and down the staircase, inviting her to guess what was happening on the other side of the doors, not bothered if anyone heard me asking rhetorical questions of a month-old infant. A few days into my role as her mother and I was already losing the self-consciousness that had at first forced me to whisper my baby talk so that no one heard me.

A wedding party burst out from the door nearest to me, hooting and cheering. There were only a handful of guests, their similar ages suggesting friendship rather than kinship. The bride wore a long-sleeved shift dress cut off at the knee and carried a tiny posy of roses in place of an elaborate bouquet. Saddled with a baby and a backpack, I thought that I had never seen a woman look so free and unencumbered. It was a wonder that both her feet were still on the ground. In her position I was sure I would develop the ability to fly. She kissed her groom at the top of the stairs while their friends whooped and cheered and took photographs. Their echoing voices and handclaps woke Alice, and I scurried down the steps before I had a chance to find out what a newborn's cry sounded like somewhere with such sharp acoustics. She flexed her lungs as I was on the very bottom step. The flowers flew past my ear and landed in a heap at my feet. The bride and her friends shrieked with laughter.

I followed the sign on the wall that told me where to commit my necessary crime.

The registrar's name was Comfort Murphy. She wore a navy suit and a cerise corsage in her lapel. Her hair had been relaxed and then teased into a hairstyle rather like the queen's and her voice had been given a similar treatment; her vowels were those of a minor aristocrat but she dropped her *h*'s from the beginning of her words and the *g*'s from the ends.

"I remember what they're like at this age," she said. "You think you're goin' mad for the first three months, but it does get better."

"Do I look that bad?" I managed to laugh, and she joined in. For a second we were conspirators, mothers together. There was a bang on the door behind me and I nearly dropped the baby, expecting the police to swoop, but it was only the wedding party making their way into the street. There was no reason why anyone should come after me. She was not a missing baby and the hospital records I showed the registrar bore my name alongside "Baby Girl Clarke." The registrar shuffled the documents that would bind us together forever and I tried to shrug off the enormity of what I was doing. I tried to make myself think like Nina, who I knew would have done this in a heartbeat, done anything that made life easier for her and gave security to this orphan child. But I was not like Nina. I was not a rule breaker or a free spirit. Alice wriggled and looked at me with eyes that had only learned to focus in the last couple of days. The woman's glance at the naked ring finger on my left hand was so discreet I almost missed it.

"Were you married to the baby's father at the time of the birth, Miss Clarke? Because you only have to put his name down if you were."

I looked at the form in front of me.

"If I give you his name, do I have to give you his address?"

"Yes, please. His address at the time of the birth."

The pen was slippery in my hand as I wrote the name Rex Caspian Capel in one box and HMP, Brixton, London SW2 in the other. If the registrar was surprised or disapproving she did not show it. She filled out the vellum-colored certificate in front of me using an old-fashioned fountain pen and waved it in the air for a minute or two waiting for it to dry. Then she rolled it into a scroll, placed it in a plastic tube, and handed it over. She wrapped my hands in hers for a second or two before letting it go. Her skin was powdery and soft.

"Keep this somewhere safe," she said. "And good luck. With everythin'."

He runs his hand over my hip bones that pregnancy never widened and the stomach that childbirth never stretched or scarred, and cups the breasts that never slackened after breastfeeding. My body remains more or less unchanged and, to our mutual surprise and delight, seems to have grown more responsive to his hands while it was deprived of their touch.

"Let's give Alice a brother or sister," he says, the heel of his hand over the skin just below my navel. "We could be a real family."

Shivers fan out inside me. We make love without contraception and for the first time since he came home, and for once the pleasure I show him is only partly sincere. My body shows itself to be more faithful to him than to me, responding to his touch even while my mind is wildly distracted. How do I even know that I am fertile, or that Rex is? I have never had a serious pregnancy scare in my life, not with Simon, when I took my contraceptive pill every day, and not with Rex, when I took it haphazardly and we made love once, twice, three times a day for months. Rex was with the lush and fecund Nina for nearly two years and nothing happened. Future emergencies suggest themselves, each scenario more gruesome than the last. The most frequently recurring worry is that Alice, or any forthcoming children, will become gravely ill, and tests will show not only that they are an imperfect match but that they are not siblings at all.

While my family sleeps, these thoughts spiral inward in my mind, coiling themselves into a hard little core of anxiety. I regret not telling him now. I wanted to do the right thing for Alice, to give her two living parents who loved her. And I wanted to do the right thing for Rex, to give him something to live for. But perhaps the truth told then would have been enough. Rex loved Nina's children like his own, and would have fallen for Alice even harder. He would have loved her as an extension of Biba, as a beautiful little girl in her own right. Rex lacks the capacity to limit his love; it is indulgent and sacrificial.

He reaches for me in his sleep. Does he ever lie like this, watching me sleep, wondering whether my eyelids flicker with dreams or nightmares? He, too, has plenty to keep him awake, and secrets of his own. I wonder if he will ever tell me what happened to him in prison. I close my fingers around his wrist where the skin is thin and shiny. I do not think that I could bear to know.

28

I N THE SLIMY LAVATORY at the station, I changed Alice's diaper and fed her so that she would be on her best behavior when I took her home. Every now and then, her innocence and vulnerability made me catch my breath; when I laid her across my forearm to burp her, I felt her tiny ribs, soft and flexible as willow, beneath my palm. The flesh of her tiny back was so soft that I was surprised I didn't leave a handprint in her, like putty. When I held her, I felt my own bones fortify and my skin toughen and knew that I would become as hard as I had to for her.

I checked the fare with the taxi driver before I got in. It used up all the money I had in the world. Another pound on the fare and I would have had to walk.

They had changed the doorbell since I had last been home. I pressed it with my forefinger and heard an insincere little rendition of the Big Ben chime ring out somewhere within the house. My mother answered with rubber gloves on, her hands slippery with suds. Her face when she saw us was a child's drawing of astonishment, her mouth a carefully crayoned O. She was dumb with shock as I spread Alice's shawl out underneath her and let her loll on her back and kick her legs in the air. She threw her arms and legs out in a series of startle reflexes. It was a novelty to have a floor that was clean enough for her to lie on. After my father had been summoned home from work, my mother unpacked my rucksack.

The outside pocket contained my purse, my passport, and Alice's birth certificate. Almost everything else was concerned with feeding, clothing, or changing Alice. She pulled out clothes, diapers, and wipes. When she got to the bottles and the travel sterilizer, she finally spoke.

"Aren't you breastfeeding her?" she said. I shook my spinning head. It had not occurred to me that I might have to have conversations about pregnancy and childbirth, that I would have to bluff my way through an experience that my mother believed we now shared. I would have to buy a book and read up on it as soon as possible.

Underneath the bottles were a couple of Rex's dirty T-shirts and the crumpled red dress. She held these items gingerly and examined them in wordless wonderment before setting them aside. I heard Dad's key in the door. Mum had obviously briefed him, but he still flinched with surprise to see me crouching over a newborn baby. There was disappointment in his eyes where I was used to seeing pride. The tears, dammed up for six months, now fell almost hourly.

"I'm so sorry," I said. I gathered the baby to my chest, ashamed of myself for using her to disarm his anger but too tired to face it. "I've let you down. I've fucked it all up. Let me have it. Tell me what a disappointment I am."

They sat next to each other on the sofa, so that my eyes were level with their knees. I felt more like a five-year-old than a recent graduate and new mother.

"We're not going to tell you off," said Mum. "I can't pretend we're not shocked, and circumstances aren't exactly ideal . . . Rex *is* the father, isn't he?"

"Linda!" admonished my father.

"Well, we've got to ask," she said. "I can see you've really been up against it. We would have been there, you know. We would have understood."

"I've fucked it all up," I said. "I've fucked up college, I've fucked up my whole life."

"Life doesn't end just because you have a baby, you know," said Dad. "You're only twenty-one, and you'll always have your education. We can help."

"But aren't you ashamed of me?" I said. I wasn't really talking about Alice at all, but using her to make a kind of vested confession. Mum bent down and scooped Alice from my arms.

"It doesn't work like that. You know, you're still my baby. I still feel about you the way you feel about her now," she said. "Does that help you to understand?"

"Yes," I lied. Alice shifted and fixed her eyes on my dad's in that vague unfocused way she had. He held out a finger and she clutched it.

"Can we stay here?" I asked.

"As if you even have to ask," he said. His brow was still clenched, but what I had taken for anger I suddenly recognized as hurt, hurt I didn't know I had the power to cause. "As if you even have to ask," he repeated, shaking his head. He took the child from my mother and held her on his lap, his large, capable hand supporting her head. He looked from Alice to me to my mother and his face softened. "She looks just like Karen did when she was this age, doesn't she, Linda?" he said, and bent to kiss the baby on her soft, downy forehead.

I saw him before he saw me. His face was not turned to the door in anticipation, but looking down and to the side as if afraid of what he would see. The guard at the door had told me that he knew he had a visitor but not who it was. He looked at the floor with the controlled expectancy of someone who has been disappointed time and again and cannot cling to hope for much longer. His hair had grown to collar length, and while the contours of his face were unchanged, the color and texture of his skin had altered. He looked as though someone had shaded the hollows of his cheeks and his eye sockets with a soft pencil. Alice, who had been shocked into silence by the indignity of having her diaper searched by a gum-chewing guard, was now asleep in her sling. Her hair was beginning to thicken and she looked more like a Capel every day. Like her mother and uncle before her, she bore no trace of her father and appeared not to have been born from a union of two parents, but to have sprung from her mother alone.

I had expected the crackle of menace in the prison interior, and it reminded me of my comprehensive school in this and other ways. The orange stacker chairs that bordered the plain tables were the same ones that had filled the assembly hall and the walls were painted the same unflattering, municipal shade of pale blue. But the closed-circuit television cameras that hung from the ceiling and the dark blue tabards all the prisoners wore told me that this was a very different place indeed. Men folded their arms and stared at me as I walked around the side of the room rather than through the gangway at its center. As I passed, a woman, lobes pulled almost to her shoulders by a row of gold hoops and studs, passed a tiny package to a man underneath their table. The look she gave me ensured my silence. She looked far tougher than he did.

Rex did not look up until I was standing opposite him. When he did, the surprise caused him to leap up and push his chair backward. It made a loud screech on the floor tiles that caused the nearest prison officer to hold the palm of his hand up toward Rex, who sat back down with practiced obedience. He looked at the bundle in my arms and then into my eyes, and back again, several times, his eyes moving up and down ever more rapidly. When they finally fixed on mine, they swam with confusion.

"There's someone I think you should meet." On cue, Alice opened her eyes and blinked up at him. "This is Alice." I extracted her from the sling and held her on the tabletop, facing Rex. "Say hello to your daddy, Alice," I said. Rex's hands were in his hair and his face was split by a nervous smile. The sleeve of his sweater slid an inch or two up his arm, exposing a vicious purple bruise. I tried not to look at it.

"Alice," he said, and his eyes were brimming with all the questions we did not have time to answer then. "Karen, I've missed you so much. But this . . . I can't get my head around this. You've had a baby. I've got a daughter. How old is she?"

"Two months," I said.

"Why didn't you tell me?"

"I didn't know," I said. I had rehearsed this over and over. "I didn't know and then by the time I did, I wasn't allowed to contact you . . . then I didn't know where you were."

"I can't get my head around this at all," he repeated. "How did you . . . what? Shit. I don't know where to start."

"I wasn't sure you still wanted to see me."

"Of course I do! Though God knows I don't deserve it," he replied. "Can I hold her?" His question was not addressed to me but to the guard who had earlier moved to silence him. At his nod, I let Rex pick her up. He handled her expertly, one hand behind her head, the other cupping her rump. She had recently developed a trick of yelling whenever passed from one adult to another but settled into the crook of Rex's left elbow with contentment, not protest. I laid my fingers on his forearm.

"I didn't think I'd be allowed to touch you," I said. "I thought we'd have to talk on one of those glass phone thingies." He buried his face in Alice's head and I let them remain like that for a few minutes. When he looked up, he asked the question I had been dreading.

"Where's Biba?" he said. Despising myself for my cowardice, I let a long pause do the work of the awful words. I had to lower my eyes.

"I'm so sorry, Rex," I said. "She took my car. They found it at Beachy Head." Like me, he recognized instantly the significance. I braced myself for his howl of misery, but his reaction was one of resignation, as though he had been imagining and inventorying all the terrible scenarios that might have befallen his sister and this one featured in his top ten likely outcomes. He closed his eyes for a few seconds and I saw his dark pupils tremble beneath their thin, violet-veined lids. He bit his lip and nodded as if confirming something to himself. I think that broke my heart more than if he had demonstrated shock or disbelief.

"She's done it, then," he said, and I thought I detected an undercurrent of reprieve as well as resignation; or were these my own feelings I was projecting onto him? "I knew something was wrong when she didn't come to see me."

"They didn't find . . . her, but there's no way she could have survived," I said. "I wrote to your dad when she left, before I . . . heard what she'd done. I didn't hear back from him. I don't suppose he told you?"

"I haven't heard from him since he came over that night." I closed my mind's eye to the grisly tableau that the reference summoned.

"Do you see anyone?" I asked, wondering even as I spoke who there would be. Rex's circle had been even tinier than mine. The only other person left alive who would want to visit him would be Nina, and she was somewhere sunny, miles away from all that had happened. She could not know about Biba, I thought, and wondered if I should ever get word to her of her suicide. Rex was slowly shaking his head.

"You're my first visitor," he admitted. New guilt sprang from the memory of all the evenings I had spent in Switzerland. I had been lonely—I had been so lonely—but I had had my freedom and all the company I needed. He had had nobody.

"I'm so, so sorry," wondering which part of my involvement in the whole mess I was apologizing for. I tried to reach out to him but he buried his face in the top of Alice's head and this time it was not to smell her but to weep. His whole body shook with silent sobbing. The man at the next table, a skeletal redhead with the word WALES crudely tattooed on the back of his hand and a dotted line inked across his throat, looked on with disdain. Rex's eyes were pink but his cheeks dry when he drew his head away from Alice. He saw my look of consternation.

"It's okay. They've all seen me cry before," he said drily. "I had quite a reputation for it when I first arrived."

"I can't bear to think of you in here for another nineteen years."

"It won't be anything like that," he said. "It'll be more like twelve with good behavior. I keep my head down. I'll be all right." He looked at Alice. "I've got a reason to make sure I am now."

Even the bell that signaled the end of our visiting session sounded like the one from my school. Rex handed Alice back to me, lowering her into her sling and keeping his hands on her as I secured her. His thumb traced the springy velvet skin just beneath her chin.

"Who were you expecting, anyway?" I said as she settled onto my shoulder. "You knew someone was coming."

He grimaced.

"The Drop-ins," he said. "They're a charity group who visit people who don't have anyone. I assumed you were one of them. After a while you'll do anything just to talk to someone new."

"I'll come back next week," I said. "I'll come back every week for as long as it takes them to let you go."

"What, and deprive me of my hour with the Drop-ins?" His grin was fleeting. "Look, did you just come here to tell me about Biba and the baby, or are you back? I mean, does this mean we're back on?"

"Of course," I said. "We're all that's left, aren't we?"

With Alice on my hip, I leaned over the table to kiss him. The tiny current of electricity infused my whole body. I bit his lower lip. "I love you," I said.

❧

I finally summon the courage to contact Alison Larch. Making sure that I withhold my own number, I call her and pretend to be a commissioning editor from Channel Four looking to hire her for a documentary I'm making about women's prisons. The lie comes easily. They do these days.

"God, sounds fascinating," she says, even though I haven't really outlined the project in any real detail. Her voice is just as I remember it; she still sounds blond and overbearing, with an ability to take control of the conversation even when I am ostensibly the senior person. "I've got some great contacts in the prison service. Just finished doing a really juicy piece for the Beeb about lifers and the parole system. There was this one guy I was tailing . . . what was his name?" I hear the flick as she goes through a load of papers on her desk, imagine documents pertaining to Rex's case, old newspapers, grainy photographs of the three of us. Her voice becomes muffled and her fingers click the keys of a computer as she searches a different kind of filing system for the details. "Big black bloke. You know the one." I can't name an individual from that description but am fairly sure that she is not talking about Rex. Alison Larch sighs and her voice becomes clear again. "But anyway. I'm basically not free until the spring. I'm doing a series on oligarchs' wives, I'm going to be in Russia for months. It's only by luck that you've caught me on my London line at all. What kind of lead time are you looking for with this? Any chance we could pick it up next year? What did you say your name was? Shall we meet for a coffee or something?"

"I'm actually working abroad myself from tomorrow," I say, my heart surfing a wave of euphoria at the knowledge that her current project has nothing to do with us. "I'll call you when I'm back." And I hang up. Within the hour, the euphoria has been replaced with the acceptance that the perpetrator of the phone calls is probably just a random dirty dialer, what we used to call a "heavy breather." I wish I had been able to come to this, the most obvious of all conclusions, weeks ago. The time and energy that I have wasted worrying will be better spent focusing on my future, on my family. I will call the telephone company tomorrow and have our number changed.

Rex picks up on my good mood, not staying up to watch the news tonight but taking me and our bottle of wine to bed as soon as he is satisfied that Alice is asleep. We are both falling asleep when the telephone rings. Rex half-opens his left eye.

"It'll be for me," I say. "I'll get it."

I pad downstairs and pick it up. "Hello?"

There is an oddly familiar silence.

I am tightly wound tonight. I know that you should never react to nuisance callers but I am tired and I am angry and I have had enough.

"Look, who is this?" I say. "How did you get this number? I think you should know that I'm going to inform the police about these calls." I hear the ignition click of a cigarette lighter and a soft sucking sound. Can a sigh have its own identifiable timbre? Can you recognize someone's breath in the way you can a voice?

"Is it you?" I croak. There is a protracted exhalation during which I hold my own breath. "Talk to me," I say. "Please, talk to me." The voice is lower than it used to be and husky, polluted with years of cigarettes; but that beautiful accent, the first thing I loved about her, remains pure.

"*Darling*," she begins.

29

I THINK I MIGHT be sick. My mouth is awash with excess saliva. I thought a cold sweat was just a figure of speech but it is happening to me now, perspiration making my hands slippery and my armpits clammy. Saltwater gathers on my upper lip.

"Biba?"

"Hello, Karen," she says, as though we last spoke yesterday, as though she hasn't just unraveled my life with one swift tug on a loose thread.

"Where are you?" is all I can manage.

"At the station," she says simply. To me, "the station" means the nearest stop on the branch line, ten or eleven miles across open country. I murmur the name of the town, more as a reflex action than because I think she might really be there.

"Yes, where else?" she says impatiently. "I wondered if I could pop in."

"Pop in?" I echo. "*Pop in?*" The pathways that connect my mind, body, and mouth appear to have been rerouted and articulate speech does not come easily.

"I'm having a nightmare trying to get a cab," she says, and I suddenly realize the magnitude of the threat. She could be here in fifteen minutes. I glance toward the stairs, picturing myself shaking Rex awake, telling him that his sister is alive and in the same county and on her way over. I have often missed her and wished her back, daydreaming of a happy reunion, but it was only wishful thinking. This is an eventuality I have not planned for and I must think, think faster and harder than I have had to for years. But now that the fantasized moment is here I feel only panic. I have perhaps a quarter of an hour to find the words to tell Biba that I am the only mother Alice has ever known. Then, with Rex, we have until the morning to figure out how we are going to tell Alice, who longs for an extended family, that Daddy has a long-lost sister we never thought to mention. This is too much, too fast. I need space to think, but Biba is jabbering away in my ear, her words scratched out by the poor connection.

"Hang on, darling," she says. "I'm out of change. I haven't used a phone booth in years and it's *eating* money, twenty fucking pee . . ."

The line goes dead. I stare at the phone, almost expecting her to appear from it, for her physical form to squeeze through the holes in the mouthpiece like some kind of genie.

With clumsy fingers I dial 1471. For once, the number has not been withheld. To my utter astonishment a local code is repeated back to me. I jab at the number 3. She picks up the phone before I hear it ring.

"Hi!" she says brightly.

"Where are you? I mean, where exactly are you?" I say. "I'm going to come and get you." I can think in the car, and tell her on the way home.

"Don't worry, I've got money." It is the first time I have ever heard her say that and my astonishment is an aftershock following the news that she is alive. "There's only a couple more people in front of me in the taxi line. I know where you live . . ."

"*How?*" I ask, but the connection has been broken again and there is only a vacuum of silence where her voice was. I punch the numbers one more time and let the phone ring and ring but this time nobody answers. I have to get to her before she gets to us. In desperation, I gather my things and get into the car.

She is still outside the station. I would know her form anywhere, even if she is swathed in so many layers that she is completely shapeless. A huge red woolen shawl shrouds her from head to toe and there are two large bags at her feet, suggesting that she intends to stay. And she is looking directly at me, as though she knew which car would be mine. I find myself gagging on tears.

Underneath the red shawl is another scarf, violet this time, wound around her neck. As she climbs into the passenger seat I notice that she has grown her fringe out, and wonder when this happened. She is downlit by an unforgiving interior light, and I am shocked that she has aged: my memory had preserved her at twenty-one. Older than I am, older looking even than Rex, whom she now resembles more than ever. Her jawline is tight again, but her hair is dull and her skin weathered. Faded freckles dot her nose and cheeks while folds of white unblemished skin around her nose and mouth, and in the crease between her eyes, suggest that she has been squinting at the sun for years. She is still striking, although she has the face of a character actress now rather than a leading lady. Her beaky nose is pink-tipped and shiny and her fingers, when she takes off her leather gloves and lays them on her lap, are skinny and ringless. When she kisses me on the cheek her eyelashes brush my temple and her lips are cold and dry. "Oh my God" is all I can manage.

"Karen Clarke," she says. "You look exactly the same. Aren't you pleased to see me?" She shrugs off her top layer and spreads it over the car seat. "It's hot in here, isn't it?" We are having two different conversations here. I'm struggling to make myself coherent, wondering how to condense ten years of struggle into a ten-minute drive, and she's making small talk.

"We thought you were dead," I say. "You let us think that you were *dead*."

"I'm sorry," she says, and although she seems to mean it, it is such a tiny and poor little word.

"How did you find us?"

"Well, the prison told me Rex was out," she says. "But they wouldn't tell me where he'd gone. So I called QCC. You forgot to take yourself off the Graduates Association contact list. Look, can we talk about this at home?" Not "at your house" or even "your home" but "home," as though I have extended the welcome she takes for granted. *Mi casa, tu casa*. Does she mean to come and live with us? The four of us in a cottage that is too small even for three? For so long, all I wanted was for the three of us to be together again. Now the thought fills me with dismay and even revulsion.

"Was that you, calling and hanging up?" I ask. "Why didn't you ever say anything?"

"I was trying to get through to Rex," she says. "Don't you let him answer the phone?" Despite everything, I am hurt that she only came to me by default. "Are we nearly there yet?"

"Not far," I say, knowing that we don't have anything like enough time to say all that needs to be said, even if I drive the long way home. The pace this time is much steadier, I actually have time to see the rabbits whose eyes catch my headlights and they have time to get out of my way. Biba coos about how lovely the countryside is, starts telling me something about how you think you can see the stars out here but I should see what they're like in Morocco where there is no light pollution and you can still see shooting stars.

"Is that where you've been?" I say. "Morocco?"

"Among other places," she says. "I stayed with Nina and the kids."

"Does she know?" I was aghast. Nina was not a conventional

parent but she was protective of her children, and I could not imagine that she would harbor a killer.

"Which bit? About losing my temper?" She gives a half-laugh at the inadequacy of the euphemism. "Or leaving Rex in the shit? Or having a baby and leaving it? Or leaving you?"

"All of it. Any of it."

"I told her the official story. She thinks I was running away from all that."

"And she believed you? Nina *knew* Rex, she knew he would never have done something like that."

Biba gives a woolly shrug. "Why would someone make anything like that up?"

"Does she know you're here?" With a small sigh, she buries herself even deeper into her coat.

"Nobody knows." I slow down at the railroad crossing out of force of habit, even though the last trains have all gone. It's my turn to talk now: we can fill in the gap of her ten-year lost weekend later. Right now, we need to find a way to explain her presence without exposing the truth to Rex and Alice.

"It's going to be tricky, but I think we can do this," I say, but Biba's non sequitur is the first sign that we are still talking entirely at cross purposes.

"Nina had another baby. A little girl. Oh, Karen, she was beautiful. You should have seen her. But I couldn't stay with her. She . . . the whole thing . . . it *awoke* things in me. I started thinking, Karen. About what I'd done. It made me realize it wasn't too late."

"What are you trying to say?"

"I've come back for my baby."

Vertigo makes me loosen my grip on the wheel.

"I really don't feel well," I say. I pull over at the first opportunity, the junction where the construction site is. The detour up its access road is a matter of yards. I rest my chin on the wheel and survey the bleak little landscape with its portable toilets and its shut-up burger van. The floodlights are off now and the only light comes from my car and the dull orange gloam of safety lamps that dangle from the cranes and the diggers. Concrete posts wide enough to drive a car through are stacked, waiting to be turned on their sides and sunk into the holes in the ground.

There is fidgeting beside me as Biba produces a battered little green tin and a packet of cigarette papers. "Can you do that outside?" I say. She fiddles incompetently with the door handle and I reach across and release the catch for her.

Outside, a freezing sea breeze blusters. We are nearly a mile from the shore but I can taste the brine. We are on my territory: the thought calms me. Biba uses the open car door to shield herself from the wind. A dirty yellow cement mixer is still giving off heat: we must have missed the workers by minutes. Blue tarpaulins are pegged over piles of cinder blocks as big as houses. They flutter noisily and I have to raise my voice.

"The thing is . . ." I begin. "This is all really complicated. Alice thinks that Rex and I are her parents. She doesn't know anything about you. You can't just turn up and expect to play happy families." Biba doesn't say anything: I remember now that once she has begun to construct a cigarette she won't speak until she has taken a drag. In some ways we are strangers but in others we still know each other so well. "We need to get our story straight," I say. My feet slip and slide on a patch of cement that is still wet, and I smooth it out with the unmarked sole of my boot. "I thought we could introduce you as Alice's long-lost auntie. We can tell her you've been traveling for years, and that we lost touch. I mean, it's kind of true." She lights her cigarette on the third or fourth attempt. The smoke is whipped into her face, away from me.

"No," she says. Her voice has switched from quicksilver to steel.

"We'll have to. She's not stupid, she'll know you're related as soon as she looks at you!"

"No." She sighs, as though explaining something sad to a small child. "You don't understand. I want to come back as her mother."

I taste bile. Why didn't I see this coming?

"Oh, Biba, no," I say. "Not that. I'm the only mother Alice has ever known. I mean, that's what you wanted, wasn't it? When you wrote that note? You told me to look after her. I'm not saying you can't come back, but not like this."

"I can and I will," she says, and I know that she is capable of it. I remember the last time I saw Biba with Alice, the filthy, shivering newborn held in a dangerously loose grip on the sixth-floor balcony. She is just as much a threat now as she was then.

The wind changes direction and the smell of Biba's cigarette jerks me out of my reverie like smelling salts. I have been near smoke since then, of course I have, other people's smoke and packs of cigarettes, but the spicy, woody smell of fresh rolling tobacco is not something I have breathed in since the last time I saw her, and it transports me. Through closed eyelids I do not see the usual images that haunt me, but a montage of scenes from the beginning of that summer, before Guy came. The woods. The Velvet Room. The heath. Dancing, kissing, drinking. Her white dress and my red one. Rex. Biba. Karen. The disparity between the happiness I felt then and the misery of the future she has threatened me with is too much to bear.

"This would *destroy* Alice and Rex," I say. "They've been through so much. I've worked so hard to make them secure. If you care about them at all, you won't tell them the truth."

"I'm sorry," she says.

"Then don't do this. Please. I'm begging you." I look at the ground. It is an unwelcoming patchwork of silver-tipped grass and gravel glittered with builders' sand, but I am ready to fall to my knees if that's what it takes.

"A child's place is with her mother." Her voice is heavy with forced patience.

"Oh, please. What do you know about being a mother? Alice had her tonsils out when she was seven. They didn't have any spare beds so I slept on the hospital floor under my coat. I didn't want her to wake up and not know where she was. Where were you?"

"That was then," says Biba. "She needs me now." That she actually seems to believe what she is saying is the most chilling and dangerous aspect of it all. A strong gust sends a rush of whispers through the trees that flank the construction site. The wooden shutter on the burger van strains against its padlock with a rattle, and the site lanterns are blown about, throwing yellow light erratically so that our faces pass in and out of shadow. Unseen machinery makes strange industrial clanking noises and we both have to shout to make ourselves heard.

"I could turn you in," I say in desperation. "Once they know what you did they won't let you within ten feet of any child."

"Rex won't let you."

"How do you know what Rex will and won't do? You don't know him anymore." She raises one eyebrow.

"Blood's thicker than water, darling. You're not even the mother of his child." She stops and lets out a horrible chuckle. "He hasn't even got a child. What will he think when he finds out his daughter is really his niece? You've lied to him, Karen." Her card trumps mine and she knows it. The woman who gave birth to my daughter turns her back to me. Her violet scarf makes a thick coil around her neck, the two fringed ends animated by the wind, chasing and teasing each other. Her voice carries on the breeze, like salt, like spray.

"I'm grateful to you for looking after them, Karen, but it was never forever."

"It was *my* forever," I say. "I can't just pick my life up where you left it. What else will I do?" She has made me into who I am now. Who else could I possibly be?

"I'm sorry," she says, not bothering to turn and face me. "But they're my *family*." If I thought she had broken my heart years ago, it is nothing to how I feel now. She could not have chosen words to hurt me more.

"They are not your family!" I cry. "They're *mine*!" Blood travels through my body at a wild velocity. I am stunned by the physicality of my anger, as though a leak, dammed up for years, has suddenly swollen and burst into a deluge. As I walk toward her, the land seems to undulate like the sea. My hands catch the fluttering ends of her scarf on the first attempt. She is unaware that her life is literally in my hands until I wind the wool around my wrists and tug. She tries to turn to face me but a reflex action sends her hands to her throat, curling her fingers into useless claws that cannot loosen the shrinking coil around her neck. *"They're mine,"* I sob. I pull and pull until the only breath making steam clouds in the night air is mine.

Underneath her layers of clothing, she is as slim as she ever was. She doesn't weigh that much more than Alice, and I am able to carry rather than drag her body twenty yards toward the circular concrete hollow. I do not want to see her face.

To push her into the hole seems callous, so I spread my arms and let her fall. She belly-flops onto the wet cement with a splat rather than a splash. It is all so very far from the glamorous, plummeting death she once envisaged.

For a horrible moment I think that it has set or frozen, and that I am going to have to clamber down into the cavity and retrieve her body. Then, suddenly, the gray gloop swallows her spread-eagled corpse in one slow greedy gulp. Is it my imagination, or does her hair linger for a few seconds after her body has gone, thick strands reaching as though for life, trying to snatch a few final seconds of air? Her bags are sitting patiently on the backseat of the car. I toss them in after her.

Kneeling at the edge, I peer over at the smooth, sludgy surface. The surge of vomit takes me by surprise. On my hands and knees, my stomach contracts and contracts until the muscles that band my abdomen are on fire and there is nothing left inside me.

Epilogue

"WHAT WAS UP WITH you last night?" says Rex through a mouthful of cornflakes.

Alice is in the living room watching Saturday morning children's television. An episode of *The Simpsons* that she has seen a dozen times is playing at an uncomfortable volume.

"What do you mean?"

"You were tossing and turning. It was like sharing the bed with an eel."

"Insomnia," I say, and it's true. If I managed any sleep at all last night I am not aware of it. Physical comfort was impossible and closing my eyes summoned only the obvious, terrible images. Just before dawn I had the awful apprehension that this was what it was going to be like from now on, that I would never again be able to close my eyes, that I would die of exhaustion. But now that I am up and about, what happened yesterday seems necessary, even reasonable, and I know that I will find a way to live with it. Over the years, I had come to wear my grief comfortably. The events of last night have only restored the status quo and increased my family's security. I need only to remind myself of the threat she posed. She kills, she abandons, she lets others take the blame and pick up the pieces. I know that I too am a murderer now, but by definition my crime was a one-off. I am the opposite of a threat: I did what I did to protect. What's one more secret?

"You know what you need," he says. "A nice walk. Get her away from the television. Blow away those cobwebs. I'm feeling a bit cobwebby myself. Was I drunk last night?" Perhaps he was. I did not help him to empty the wine bottle that waits patiently at the back door to be recycled.

Alice clutches the remote control defiantly to her chest, but Rex simply turns the television off at the set. She opens her mouth to protest but he cuts in first. "Boots, coat, walk," he says, arms folded, and she obeys him without question. I'm impressed.

"This is pretty, Mummy," says Alice. "Can I wear it?" Scarlet flashes as she tugs at something tangled up in the hat stand. Biba's shawl. I must have hung it up with my own coat when I came in last night. I snatch it away from her. It might have pockets, and who knows what those pockets might contain?

"You can wear your usual coat," I say, and wrap the shawl around me, smoothing it down against my clothes. There are no pockets, just a huge swath of wool, enough to wrap around me three times. Outside, I hope the wind will carry her smell away. I have to breathe through my mouth.

"When did you get that?" says Rex. "I haven't seen it before."

"Thrift store," I say.

"It suits you," he says. "You should wear that sort of thing more often. But it's a bit grubby. Oh, Karen, *look*. It's even got someone else's hair on it." And he picks out a long, dark, thick hair that has woven itself into the knit, examines it with forensic distaste before releasing his thumb and forefinger and letting the strand float away.

It is one of those white-skied days peculiar to this part of the world that make it impossible to pinpoint where the sun is or what time of day it is. We walk in single file along the lane, Rex in front of Alice and me behind her. To get anywhere from our house you need to walk past the building site, and I am drawn toward it, to make sure, to remember, to begin to forget. If I believed in fate, this would be tempting it.

"Let's see how the building's going," I say, shepherding my family up the access road. There is no police cordon, no scene of crime officers, just a couple of dozen laborers in high-visibility jackets operating machinery, smoking, cradling steaming tea in polystyrene cups. Their cars are parked where mine was last night. I feel strangely calm as I wonder which of the tire tracks in the dirt are mine. A Christmas song, the first I have heard this year, plays on an unseen radio. Above us, yellow cranes are primed and poised, and before us a cement mixer's splattered orange barrel is rotating on the tilt. I could not have timed my visit better: with my family, I stand at a distance and watch it disgorge ton after ton of cement into the concrete cavity, encasing her body forever. My shoulders loosen and lower with the relief.

The aroma of frying bacon reaches us from the burger van. The fact that I do not cook them at home has elevated bacon sandwiches to the status of an exotic delicacy for Alice, and she is rubbing her hands together with excitement.

"Can I have a bacon sandwich?" she says. "Please? Please please please?"

"Sounds great," says Rex. "Karen?"

"Not for me." I wince. "But I'd love a cup of tea. I'll wait here."

I don't think Alice has ever eaten anything from a burger van before. Rex has to lift her up to read the menu, and the man behind the counter says something that makes them both laugh. She drops to the ground and the man throws her a can of something, which she catches in one hand and holds aloft as she does a celebration dance. There is so much more to celebrate than she knows.

I reach into my handbag to check that it is still there and take comfort when my fingers close around its cool slim plastic. Checking that they are not looking at me, then hiding it under the red shawl just in case, I sneak another look at it. It has been three days now and still the blue cross is there, perpendicular lines that prove that I am pregnant.

I am a mother, and I am a murderer. I would never have done it for myself. I would probably have done it for Rex and Alice. But I had to do it for this child, for my unborn baby who will complete my family. I know that I can live with what I have done and I am not frightened.

I have the strength of a woman who has everything to lose.

I was angry with my friend:
I told my wrath, my wrath did end.
I was angry with my foe:
I told it not, my wrath did grow.
And I water'd it in fears,
Night & morning with my tears;
And I sunnèd it with my smiles,
And with soft deceitful wiles.
And it grew both day and night,
Till it bore an apple bright.
And my foe beheld it shine,
And he knew that it was mine,
And into my garden stole
When the night had veil'd the pole;
In the morning glad I see
My foe outstretch'd beneath the tree.

—William Blake, "A Poison Tree"

Acknowledgments

I am grateful to my agents, Sarah Ballard and Zoe Pagnamenta, to my editor Pamela Dorman and to Julie Miesionczek and Sonya Cheuse. Thanks to Jessica Craig and Lara Hughes Young, Francine Toon and Eleni Fostiropoulos.

Thanks to those readers who were with me from this story's conception: Charlotte Northedge, Wendy Grisham, Hannah Borno, Michelle Patel, Loukia Michael, Cath Pick, Lucie Dona-hue, Sharon Connor, and Claire Coakley.

Particular gratitude is due to my dear friends Hannah Black, godmother to this book, and Helen Treacy, its midwife.

Finally, special thanks to my husband Michael for his blind faith in my writing and to our beautiful daughter Marnie, the nov-el's twin, who had the grace not to be born until the ink on the last page was dry.